ACKNOWLEDGEMENTS

I would like to thank Sally Stote and all the team at Salgad Publishing for their help, patience and encouragement during the publication process. Their input has been invaluable.

For my husband, Phil, with thanks for never complaining when I sit at the computer for hours on end

CHAPTER ONE

"I hope we're going to have enough food."

Connie swept into the large banqueting hall of London's prestigious Royale Hotel, clutching an elaborately decorated cake high above her head. If she held her arms any lower, she would trip over the flounced hem of her long dress.

"What're you talking about?" Lucy gestured towards the table. "We've mountains of food. I think you're forgetting we only have five people on our books; the four of us, who set up the whole thing in the first place plus my elderly aunt and she only joined for a laugh."

"Yes, I know all that," Connie huffed. "But don't you see, this is what the launch is all about – getting more people to join and…" Unfortunately at that point, she trod on the hem of her dress and stumbled forward. The cake wobbled dangerously in her outstretched arms while she fought to regain her balance.

Seeing what was happening, Lucy rushed forward and managed to grab the cake before it crashed to the floor. "For goodness sake, your dress is far too long. Haven't you something else you can wear?"

"No!" Connie replied. She hitched up her dress. "Well – not with me, anyway. Besides, I paid a fortune for this creation and I'm going to wear it if it kills me."

The midnight-blue dress, with its sequined bodice had looked gorgeous draped on the model in the shop window. She knew it would accentuate her blonde hair and sparkling blue eyes perfectly. It was a dress to die for. She simply had to have it, no matter what it cost. But Connie hadn't taken into account that the display model was several inches taller than she was.

Even the sales assistant, mindful of her commission, had felt duty bound to point out there might be a problem when it came to actually walking. Yet Connie waved the advice aside, feeling sure it would be the right length when she wore her brand new, platform shoes. However that wasn't the case: the dress was still so long, she kept treading on it with every step she took.

It wasn't so bad when she could hitch it up a little. But carrying something, which needed both hands, was a real problem. She'd very nearly had a catastrophe on her way up the stairs. There was no doubt she would have toppled over when she stepped on the dress without realising it. That was if a rather attractive man hadn't rushed to her side and taken the cake from her in the nick of time.

"It probably will." Lucy carefully placed the cake in the centre of the table. "If not the dress, then those ridiculous shoes will do the job for you. Just be careful when you go up and down the stairs. And, come to think of it, what on earth were you doing carrying the cake, anyway? Surely a member of the staff should be doing that? We're paying enough money!"

"I was coming up here, so I thought I would save someone a journey." Connie smoothed down her dress. "I simply forgot there were so many stairs."

"Stairs!" Jenny screeched across from the other side of the room. "You mean you carried the cake which, might I add, cost us a small fortune on its own, all the way up the stairs? Why didn't you at least take the lift?"

"Because I couldn't press the button to call the lift! I was holding the cake with both hands – remember?"

Jenny closed her eyes and shook her head. For an intelligent woman, Connie could be unbelievably dim sometimes.

"I don't know why we let you talk us into using the Royale in the first place," Lucy grumbled. She and the others would rather have held the launch for their new dating agency somewhere more modest – more within their tight budget. Yet, somehow, Connie had got her own way. But then, didn't Connie always get her own way? "This whole thing is costing an arm and a leg. I'm sure we could've found somewhere less expensive."

"If you recall, I did get a bargain on the catering." Connie was a little put out by their lack of enthusiasm.

"Only because you allowed the catering manager to gaze down your cleavage while you negotiated the deal." Jenny grinned.

"Anyway," Connie continued, ignoring the last remark, "we want everyone to know our new dating agency, for divorcees only, is a high class organisation – not some seedy, back street knocking-shop set up by a bunch of divorced women on the pull. Everyone recognises the Royale as somewhere special." She gestured around the room. "Even the Queen has visited this hotel."

"That may be," said Lucy. "But, I think it's extremely unlikely Her Majesty will be coming to sign up to our dating agency. I understand she's happily married." She frowned. "I still think we should've shopped around."

"I suppose you'd both have been happy to use the pokey, little nook we call an office for the launch?" Connie shook her head, causing her large, gold earrings to swing vigorously. "I simply felt we should make a big impression."

Lucy sighed. "We'll make a big impression in our bank balance if we don't manage to enrol a number of people tonight. And we're not just talking about the Royale. Don't forget all the ads you put in the papers; they don't come cheap, especially the glossy magazines. Not to mention these expensive evening dresses you insisted we buy."

"Talking of evening gowns, how do I look?" Jenny did a twirl. She hated arguments and tried to lighten the mood a little. Lucy was right, though, they had spent too much on this evening. But it was done now, so as far as she was concerned, they might as well enjoy it. Tomorrow was another day.

"You look great; but then you always do." Lucy looked down at her more ample shape. She felt so dowdy compared to the other two women. She had chosen to wear a black dress with an A-line skirt, which she had been assured would keep her hips in check. At the moment the dress and her hips seemed to be battling it out between them. She had tried so many diets during her life, yet she never lost more than a few pounds and even those sneaked back on when she wasn't looking. However, deep down, she knew her love of all things chocolate didn't help. "You have such a lovely figure and that slim-line dress shows off your trim waist and hips beautifully. I love the shade of green, too."

She sighed. What she wouldn't give to look even a little like Jenny. She was tall, attractive, and had the most beautiful auburn hair, which was always perfectly behaved. Whereas Lucy was short and round-ish. Okay, she was very round, with dull, mousy coloured hair, which always did its own thing, no matter how many times she combed it into place.

Jenny also had a lovely bubbly personality – so full of life. In fact she had it all. Lucy had never been able to understand why Rob had taken other women to his bed when he had Jenny at home. Some men were morons.

"We all look good tonight." Connie interrupted her thoughts.

"I only hope it'll all be worthwhile after the trouble we've gone to," replied Lucy.

"Of course it will. However, if you're going to take that kind of attitude, then we're on a loser from the start." Connie crossed her fingers behind her back. She desperately hoped this evening would be a huge success. Lucy was right: she had been the one who insisted on having this grand launch, evening dresses and all. She had told a little white lie when she mentioned the estimated cost of the evening. If they had known the truth, she would never have got her own way.

The idea of starting up a high-class dating agency for divorced ladies and gentlemen had come late one evening when she and her three friends were having a few drinks at a wine bar. They had been discussing how difficult it was to get a decent man interested in them after going through a divorce.

"I joined a dating agency hoping to meet a nice bloke who was looking for an ordinary girl, with a view to marriage." Jenny had wailed. "Yet, every man I've been introduced to seems to think because I'm divorced, I'll be up for a quick grope on the back seat of his car."

When it appeared the others had faced the same problem, Connie suddenly came up with the suggestion they should start their own dating agency for divorcees only. "Something with a bit of class, and an office in Mayfair," she'd slurred over her umpteenth glass of wine. After further persuasion, not to mention several more drinks, the others agreed and Divorcees.biz was born.

The following morning, lying in bed with a cold towel wrapped around her head, Connie hadn't felt so confident about the whole idea. For a start, it would take a great deal of money to set up. Andrew, her ex-husband, had been very generous in the divorce settlement, but her allowance certainly wouldn't stretch to paying for an elaborate launch or renting an office in Mayfair. Not unless she drastically cut back on her wardrobe, which was something she was very reluctant to do. However, as she had proposed the idea in the first place and had insisted on an extravagant launch, and an office in Park Lane, she'd kept her reservations to herself. It was only after phoning nearly every person in her address book that she managed to find a room slightly larger than a broom cupboard on the top floor of a tall building on Park Lane. At least they were able to add Mayfair to the address on the top of their stationery and that was a very important factor as far as she was concerned.

"It's almost time." Lucy looked at her watch. She was beginning to feel a little nervous. "Are we all ready? Does anyone want to go to the loo? We can't have one of us running off to the ladies room the minute the first person shows up."

"*If* anyone shows up. Some people might be put off by such a grand venue." Jenny gestured towards the room with its Roman style pillars, gold-flocked wallpaper, and crystal chandeliers. "I'm not sure I would've even thought about coming to anywhere like this, simply to join a dating agency."

"Nonsense! Of course you would. You enjoy the finer things in life, don't you?" Connie pursed her lips in disapproval.

"Well…" Jenny began. The finer things in life were all very nice, but they usually came with a large price tag attached.

"Of course you do," Connie interrupted. This was no time for Jenny to put doubts into everyone's minds. "The only people who'll be put off by the venue are the kind of people we don't want anyway. Don't forget, this is going to be a high-class agency. The right people will come and I've lined up a photographer to take some pictures during the evening, as well as photograph every person who joins. He should be here any minute now."

Deep furrows appeared on Lucy's forehead. This was getting out of hand. "A photographer! You mean a real photographer – a photographer that charges lots of money for every click of his camera? Do you know how much those people cost? If you'd mentioned it earlier, I could have asked my brother. He'd have been happy to do it for a couple of drinks."

"If we're going to be an online agency, we need to have really good pictures up there on our site." Connie paused. "I don't mean to be disrespectful to your brother, but we want professional photographs to show our prospective clients that we're an upmarket organisation."

"Still," Lucy pouted, "I think this should have been discussed. You seem to have made all the decisions without even consulting the rest of us."

"It's almost time, Madam." Connie welcomed the waiter's interruption. However, her relief was short lived when he continued. "Do you wish me to pour the champagne now?"

"Champagne!" Lucy hissed. "Are you mad, Connie? We can't afford champagne." She looked across at Jenny. "You see what I mean? I didn't know about the champagne. Did you?"

"No, I didn't." Jenny turned to Connie. "Isn't it rather extravagant? Goodness knows how much they'll charge us for champagne in a place like this!"

"Yes, please pour out a few glasses now," said Connie, smiling graciously at the waiter. She turned back to her friends. "For goodness sake, keep your voices down. He'll hear you and think we can't afford to pay."

"He'll be right then, won't he? We *can't* afford to pay!" Jenny insisted. "You're forgetting, I'm the treasurer of our little venture and I know how much we have in the bank. You should…"

"Well, we certainly can't afford to skimp on the drinks." Connie broke in. "Not now we've spent so much setting up the launch. Calm down, have a glass of champagne and enjoy the evening."

"I'll enjoy the evening a lot more, when I know we can pay for it." Lucy grumbled, taking a glass from the waiter. She looked around. "Where's Sadie? She should be here having some champagne. Come to think of it, I haven't seen her yet."

"Wasn't she downstairs with you, Connie?" asked Jenny.

"No! I thought she was up here with Lucy."

"Oh my God! What's happened to Sadie? Surely someone must have heard from her," Lucy wailed.

A loud thump in the corridor caught their attention. The door swung open and Sadie strode in, towing an extremely large suitcase behind her. She was wearing a long, skin-tight, strapless, white lace dress, which looked in danger of sliding down to the floor any moment, and a pair of ridiculously high-heeled shoes. Dumping the case by the door, she hitched up her dress a little, tripped across to the waiter and took a glass of champagne. "I really need this," she said, swallowing it down in one go. She replaced the glass and took another.

"Where the hell have you been?" yelled Connie. "We've only just realised you were missing."

"You mean I could've been stripped naked, raped and left for dead in some back alley, and all the while you guys hadn't even noticed I was missing?" She looked at the waiter. "Some friends, huh?" Her glasses slid down the bridge of her nose and she pushed them back into place.

"You do exaggerate, Sadie," Lucy laughed.

"Okay, we can take it from here, thank you." Jenny took the tray from the waiter, who was grinning broadly. "I'm sure there's something else you should be doing."

"Not really. I'm part of the staff that's been assigned to help out in here tonight," he replied. "The others will be here to hand out canapés to the guests as they arrive."

"Then please help out later. We don't need you at the moment." Jenny placed the tray on the table and watched the waiter walk out of the door.

"Of course we would've missed you. It's just we all thought you were with another one of us – if you see what I mean. Where're you going, anyway?" Connie pointed towards the suitcase.

"I haven't a clue!" Sadie took a sip of champagne. "Alex arrived at the front door a couple of hours ago and said he wanted the flat back. He had some woman with him. He told me she was his new girlfriend." She pulled a face. "Girlfriend – my arse! She had tart written all over her. Her skirt hardly covered her backside." Sadie's glasses slipped down her nose again and she pushed them back.

"Your vocabulary doesn't get any better," sniffed Connie. Sadie was one of those women who never minced their words. She always said exactly what she thought. It could be so embarrassing at times. "I hope you aren't going to use that sort of language during the evening."

"You're such a snob," said Sadie. She swallowed another mouthful of champagne.

"I'm not a snob!" Connie snapped back at her. "How can I possibly be a snob, and still call someone like you a friend?" She bit her lip. Why had she reacted like that? She hadn't meant to sound so harsh.

Connie had known Sadie for several years, having met when they both worked at the same firm. They were complete opposites. While she enjoyed the finer things in life, Sadie was down-to-earth, matter-of-fact and anything else that described someone who just got on with life, whatever it brought. Yet, despite Sadie's outrageous dress sense, her more colourful language, and her quirky outlook on life, they became really firm friends. Even when they had both moved to other jobs, they'd remained very close.

"I see. So…" Sadie began.

"I don't get it, Sadie. Why didn't you just tell him to get lost?" Lucy asked. She knew Connie would never have reacted like that under normal circumstances. But she feared the impending launch was taking its toll on everyone at the moment.

"Because I was foolish enough to agree to something really stupid. I was to live in the flat for the foreseeable future. However, the first one to get a regular partner could claim it for good. Never in a million years did I think he would find anyone to fall for him; he's such a rat." Sadie hesitated. That sounded ridiculous: after all, she'd married him, hadn't she? "Still," she continued, "thinking back to the woman dripping from his arm, I reckon he's got what he deserves." Sadie swallowed down the rest of her drink and took another glass. "This is good stuff!"

"Hey! Steady on. The champagne isn't on the house. Connie ordered it for this evening and it has to go a long way." Jenny sighed. "So where're you planning to spend the night? You were joking when you said you hadn't a clue, weren't you? You must have somewhere fixed up."

"Yes, of course I have." Sadie tried to avoid looking at her friends, but she could feel their eyes boring into her, waiting for her to tell them her plans. "Well, sort of…" She took another sip of her champagne and gulped it down. "Okay. No! I suppose I haven't. I kind of hoped one of you would offer to put me up." She looked at her three friends in turn, but they all remained silent. "Come on, guys. I certainly can't afford to stay here at the Royale and I haven't had time to look for anything else. I had to pack a few things, get dressed and come here. Then I forgot my wallet. All I had was loose change, not even enough for a taxi. I had to take the bus. I looked an idiot dressed like this." She pointed down at her dress. "I could hardly lift my foot up onto the platform and just when I thought I'd cracked it, I trod on my dress. So of course when I heaved myself up onto the bus, my dress slid down and I flashed my boobs at the driver. That happened twice! In the end, he took pity on me and came out of his little cab thingy and lifted me on. He even waved aside the fare. Everyone on the bus cheered! Nice of him really – don't you think?" She swallowed some more champagne.

The others looked at each other. They were trying to suppress their laughter, while picturing the scene.

"You mean Alex didn't even give you a few days notice?" Jenny said, at last. "He expected you to just walk out of the flat and leave everything?"

"Yep! That's about it."

"Knowing you, I'm surprised you didn't shut the door in his face," uttered Lucy.

"I did, but he just opened it again – he still has a key." She giggled. "I did trip him up, though. I stuck my foot out as he strode in. He was trying to look the big man in front of his tart, but fell over my foot, crashed into the hall table and ended up in a crumpled heap on the floor." She sighed. "I guess that's when the shit hit the fan. He got to his feet and booted me out straight away. I suppose he was trying to salvage some dignity."

"You can stay in my spare room," said Connie, heaving a sigh. It was the least she could do after her outburst earlier. "But only for a few days. I remember the last time you stayed at my house; it looked like a rubbish dump. This time, I'll set out a few ground rules."

Sadie screwed up her eyes, causing her rather large, ornate glasses to slide down the bridge of her nose again. "Rules? What kind of rules?" she demanded, pushing her glasses back into place.

"Are they new?" Jenny broke in. She pointed at the glasses. "They look way over the top, even for you!"

"No, I borrowed them from a friend especially for tonight." Sadie removed the glasses and held them out for the others to see. "Cool, aren't they? I can see through them okay – well almost. If I squint a little I get a better view of what's going on." She giggled. "I flagged down the wrong bus twice. Trouble is, they're a bit large for me and keep sliding down my nose. My friend has a fatter face. However, I thought the large white frames with the sparkly bits running around the top went with my white dress." Putting the glasses back on, she peered at Connie. "What rules?"

"And what about that?" Jenny pointed to a large ring on Sadie's finger. "I don't think I've seen it before."

"No, I've only just bought it." She grinned as she held up her hand so they could all see the ring. There was a large, dark coloured stone in the centre. "It's called a Mood ring because it changes colour with my mood."

"How does the ring know when your mood has changed?" asked Connie.

Sadie looked at her blankly and shrugged. "Didn't I just say? It changes colour."

"Yes, I heard that bit. But how does it... Never mind." Connie rolled her eyes. Sadie could take you round and round in circles forever.

"Shush, I can hear voices in the corridor. They might be our first arrivals." Lucy put down her glass. "Sadie, I'll help you to move your case under the table. The tablecloth should hide it." She pointed to the table laden with food. "Otherwise one of our prospective clients might think you've come prepared to move in with him right away."

"If he looks anything like George Clooney I'd be happy to do just that." Sadie giggled and then hiccupped. "Oops, sorry!" She placed her hand over her mouth.

Lucy frowned. First, Connie and Sadie had almost come to blows and now Sadie had drunk too much champagne and was likely to giggle her way through the whole event. She hoped this wasn't an omen for the rest of the evening.

Connie reached the door first and held out her hand to greet a rather distinguished looking gentleman. Behind him trailed another gentleman. The other ladies followed a little way behind Connie. "Good evening, nice to see you," she said, looking the first fellow up and down. He was wearing an evening suit and bow tie. This was a man of class, just the kind of clientele she had in mind for the agency. Very impressed, she gave him a warm smile.

"Is this the Divorcees.biz Dating Agency launch?" he enquired. Taking her hand, he leaned forward and kissed it.

"That's a bit over the top," Sadie whispered to Lucy.

"Yes, that's right, and you're most welcome." Connie gushed, trying to cover Sadie's remark. "I'm Connie Somerfield and these are my partners, Jenny Matthews, Lucy Anderson, and Sadie Grant. You are the first to arrive."

"My name is Quentin Brooke and this is Alan Peterson, a colleague." They all shook hands

"Would you care for a glass of champagne?" Connie pointed towards the tray on a side table. "We have a waiter assigned to us for the evening, but he seems to have disappeared at the moment." Making discreet signals to Sadie to find the waiter, she led the two men across the room and handed them each a glass of champagne. "Please help yourselves to some food." She gestured towards the table. "I do hope you both have an enjoyable evening."

"Yes, I'm sure we will," replied Quentin. "However, I see you have more guests arriving, so we won't keep you. No doubt we shall speak again later this evening."

Connie turned to see about a dozen people spilling through the door. She smiled at Quentin before hurrying across to greet them. By now the waiter had reappeared and was striding towards the champagne. Sadie was tripping along some way behind him, hitching up her dress as she went.

"Looks as though word has got around," Jenny whispered to Connie out of the side of her mouth, before greeting another new arrival. "We're so pleased to see you here," she said to a tall, rather elegant woman, who appeared to be alone. "I'll introduce you to my friends in a few minutes, but meanwhile, please have a glass of champagne."

After about an hour, the room was full of people and still more were piling through the door. Most came alone, though there were a few, like Quentin, who arrived with a friend. Connie was delighted to see they were all wearing formal attire. "Just what I'd hoped for," she said, clasping her hands together. "It shows good taste; exactly the sort of clientele we need in our agency."

Sadie looked around the room and smiled. "I reckon we should get commission from the hire shops. They'll have made a great deal of money from our launch."

"What makes you think they've hired the suits?" Connie gestured towards everyone. "These people might attend formal functions all the time."

"Come off it!" Sadie retorted. "Surely you, with your eye for detail, must have noticed that some of the jackets are way too big or small for the men wearing them." She paused. "Now if they did a swap…"

"All right!" Connie said. She glanced around at the men who were nearest to her. "They might have hired the outfits, so what? At least they've taken the trouble to dress correctly for the event,"

"Okay! Okay!" Sadie held up her hands. "Don't come out in a rash! All I'm saying is, they might not turn out to be the sort of people you think they are – if you get my drift?"

"I'm going for another drink," mumbled Connie. Sadie could be so irritating sometimes. The trouble was, she was so very often right.

"I'll join you." Sadie followed Connie across to the waiter.

"Don't you think you've had enough already?"

"No way!" Sadie uttered, picking up a glass. "For goodness sake, if I'm paying for it, then I want my share!"

During the evening, the four friends were left breathless, as they tried to spend some time with everyone. "It's going well," said Jenny, when they all finally managed to get together for a few minutes, "and there are some rather attractive men here. I rather like Alan, the guy who arrived with Quentin. He has such come-to-bed eyes."

"More like x-ray eyes, if you ask me!" Sadie sniffed. "I could feel him undressing me every time he looked my way."

"That wouldn't take much doing," Jenny said with a raised eyebrow, "your dress doesn't leave much to the imagination, especially when he accidentally trod on it. I thought you were going to flash your boobs again."

"Nevertheless, I think we should keep an eye on him." Sadie heaved up her dress again. "I bet he did that on purpose." She looked across the room. "I prefer the guy over there." She pointed to a young man helping himself to some food. "Now he's what I call attractive. He could rattle my chain any time." She quickly turned away. "Oh my goodness, don't look now, he's looking this way."

"Yes, he is rather handsome," Jenny agreed.

"What're you doing? I thought I told you not to look!" Sadie paused. "What's he doing now?"

"I don't know. You just said not to look."

"Well he's probably seen you watching him by now, so it doesn't matter. Is he still looking over here?"

"Yes, he's still looking," said Connie, joining in the conversation. "No, wait a minute. He's looking at someone else now." She laughed. "I don't think you stand much chance there, Sadie. He looks about ten years younger than you – unless, of course, he likes older women. However, I wouldn't get your hopes up too much, he seems to be devouring a tall, elegant woman right now."

Sadie scowled when she turned back to see him handing a glass of champagne to the attractive woman, who had arrived on her own. "Jenny rather likes Alan," she continued, "but I'm not sure about him."

"Why?" Connie asked. "What's wrong with him?"

"For one thing, he tried to pull my dress down. And for another he reminds me of Raffles."

Connie raised her eyebrows. "Who?"

"Raffles! You know? Raffles. The guy in all those old movies, who used to go to parties and rob the other guests. All he lacks is a shiny top hat and a swirling cloak."

"Sadie! You're unbelievable! You've had too much to drink," uttered Connie.

"No, I haven't. I'm just saying watch your jewellery." Sadie covered the rings on her fingers.

"You've got a vivid imagination." Connie laughed. "Besides, I don't think you've got anything to worry about. I doubt he's here to rip the mood ring off your finger."

Sadie opened her mouth, but before she could say anything more, Lucy joined them. "Everyone seems to be mixing, which is good. I had a horrible notion they might all stand around not saying a word."

"They're mixing too well," grumbled Sadie, glancing around the room. "If we aren't careful, they'll all pair off and leave without joining our agency. I think we'd better start asking people to sign-up or else we won't get a penny."

"Sadie has a point," Jenny added. "It would be just our luck for that to happen."

"My God, you're right. I hadn't thought of that." Hurrying across to one side of the room, Connie kicked off her shoes and heaved herself up onto a chair, taking great care not to step on her dress. It wouldn't do to fall into a crumpled heap on the floor. "Ladies and gentlemen," she called out. As no one seemed to hear, she tried again, this time much louder. However, everyone carried on talking. Connie looked down at her friends and shrugged. "I can't make myself heard above the chatter. I'll have to leave it for the moment."

"Not bloody likely! Shit, Connie, the place could be half empty before you get a chance to say anything," said Sadie. "You stay up there, I'll get their attention." Lifting her fingers to her mouth, she gave out a most piercing whistle.

"What the hell are you doing…?" Connie yelled. She broke off. The room had fallen silent and everyone was staring at her. She had been shouting at Sadie, when everyone suddenly stopped talking.

"You're on," hissed Sadie. "Get on with it!"

Connie smiled to hide her embarrassment and quickly began talking. "We… that is, I, on behalf of Divorcees.biz would like to make a couple of announcements." She coughed. She was making a mess of this. The well-rehearsed speech wasn't going to plan. She had been totally put off her stride when Sadie had whistled. That sort of thing wasn't done in polite society.

Taking a deep breath, she continued by thanking everyone for joining them. "The fact you are all here tonight must mean a dating agency especially for divorced people is needed." After telling them how she and her colleagues hoped this dating agency would be different from the rest, she went on to explain the reasoning behind the higher than normal fee. "We feel that the two-hundred and fifty pounds enrolment fee, will be a deterrent to those who aren't seriously looking for a partner and are simply joining the agency for a lark." Connie paused as there was a ripple of laughter from the floor. "But on a more serious note," she continued, "allowing us to arrange all the meetings, means that we know where and when they will take place and more importantly, who with. We feel this will be a simple, but effective precaution for everyone's safety. " She smiled. "However, it also means that at least one of us needs to be watching the website most of the time, which brings us to the extra fee of fifteen pounds every time you wish to arrange a meeting."

Connie quickly glanced around the room, trying to gauge the reaction to her comments. Most of the women were looking at each other and nodding their heads in agreement. It seemed the idea had gone down well.

"So, for those of you who would like to enrol," she continued, "forms can be found on the table by the door. Once you have completed the form, proceed to have your photograph taken by Terry, our photographer." She gestured towards Terry and he held up his hand. "He will print out a copy of the photograph for you to sign and attach to your form, this will ensure we know who is who when we add you to the website."

Connie concluded by stressing they wanted Divorcees.biz to be a reputable dating agency, which meant they needed everyone to be honest when they filled out their profile. "So please, no tinkering with the truth." After thanking everyone again, she stepped down from the chair.

"Thank goodness that's over," said Connie. She asked Jenny and Lucy to go over to the table, where a queue was beginning to form. Grabbing Sadie's arm, she steered her to a corner of the room. "Was that whistle really necessary? It certainly wasn't ladylike. I felt so embarrassed standing up there with everyone peering at me. They all thought it had come from me."

"Of course it was bloody necessary!" Sadie snapped. "How else would they have noticed you? Besides, you were the one shouting like a fish wife when everyone stopped talking."

Connie shook her head. It was amazing how swiftly Sadie could turn everything around so it appeared to be someone else's fault. "All right, let's drop it. But *please* watch your language when you're talking to our potential clients. Think before you speak, try to be diplomatic."

"Okay, okay." Sadie held up her hands. "Don't worry, I'll make all the right noises."

Connie wasn't convinced and would like to have said more, but seeing the others needed help at the table, she let the matter drop and hurried across to them. At the table, she gave a huge smile to the man nearest to her. "So you wish to join the agency?"

"Yes, my name is Brian Lomax." He looked around the room. "It seems you're off to a good start."

"Yes, indeed. We're delighted so many people have turned up this evening." Connie handed him a form. "Jenny is our treasurer, so when you have paid her, she'll give you a receipt. If you have any questions at all, please do not hesitate to ask." She held out her hand. "And now, may I welcome you to the Divorcees.biz Dating Agency."

"Thank you, my dear." Brian took her hand. "I hope to hear from *you* very soon," he winked, still holding her hand "Perhaps, when you check my form, you will find us to be compatible."

Connie smiled, weakly. "Perhaps," she said, pulling her hand away.

"Sounds like you have an admirer there." Sadie grinned, as Brian walked off towards Jenny.

"I hope not!" replied Connie with a shudder. Brian looked back at her and gave a little wave. Raising her hand, she wiggled her fingers. "Surely I can do better than that. He's eighty, if he's a day."

"You're exaggerating a bit, besides, he could be wealthy. He might even be a millionaire looking for someone to leave his money to." Sadie clapped her hands with excitement and her glasses slid down her nose.

"I don't care. There's more to life than money." Connie paused, as Sadie pulled a face. "Okay, I agree, money is important, but there's got to be more than money in romance." She was about to turn to the next person in the queue, when she thought of something else. "By the way, what makes you think he's wealthy? I recall you saying everyone wasn't what they seemed to be."

"Because he's the only one wearing a suit that actually fits him," Sadie said with a giggle. She turned back to the queue. "Okay, you guys! Who's next?"

Connie took a better look at Brian. Sadie was right. His suit was a good fit and looked expensive.

****

They were only half way through the evening and already the four friends were beginning to feel the strain. They had shaken countless hands and explained numerous times what they hoped their agency would achieve, yet the queue seemed to be never ending. Connie picked up a form to hand to the next person without even looking up. "Good evening, welcome to…"

"Good evening, Connie." A man's voice interrupted her.

Recognising the voice, she looked up quickly. "Andrew?" she hissed. "What the hell are you doing here?" She hurried around the table and came face to face with her ex-husband.

"I've come to join the new dating agency."

"You can't!" Connie steered him away from the table and across to where the waiter was standing. "Have a drink and then go." She took a glass from the tray and thrust it into his hand.

"Why can't I join?" he asked, sipping the champagne. "This is good stuff, not the normal run of the mill sparkling wine you find at some of these functions. You should try some."

"I jolly well hope it's good stuff. I'm paying enough for it." She paused and gestured towards her friends still busy at the tables. "Well, at least, *we* are."

"You mean this is your dating agency?" Andrew spluttered. "It can't be."

"Yes, it is. Which is why I don't think it's a good idea for you to join."

"Why ever not? The fact I'm your ex-husband shouldn't make any difference." He grinned. "In business you can't afford to be choosy."

"That's very true. Though it depends on who you're dealing with." Sadie chimed in. She had heard the last part of their conversation. "Hello Andrew, nice to see you. Sorry to interrupt, Connie, but have you got any more forms tucked away somewhere? We seem to be running short. Just tell me where they are, I'll see to it."

"Yes, there are lots in my bag under the table." She turned her head away, so Andrew wouldn't hear. "Get me out of this."

"Hello, Sadie," said Andrew. "How are you? I was very surprised to learn you ladies had set this up."

"Why was that, Andrew?" Sadie drawled. She took a glass of champagne from the tray. "Didn't you think a bunch of women were capable of doing something so…adventurous?" She watched him over the rim of her glass, while she took a sip of champagne. He was looking rather flustered.

"No! No, not at all. I…"

"So, you *did* think we were incapable?" prompted Sadie, pushing her glasses into place. "That's what they call sexist, isn't it?"

"No! Sorry, what I mean is, yes," Andrew bumbled.

"Yes, we're incapable, or yes, it's what they call sexist?" Sadie glanced at Connie, who had her hand over her mouth, trying hard not to laugh.

"Of course not… You're confusing me." Desperately looking for an escape route, Andrew pointed across the room. "Ah! There's what's-his-name. Must have a word, I'll catch you later." He hurried away and was lost in the crowd.

"Well done, Sadie. I didn't want to be stuck with him all evening." Connie laughed. "You certainly put him in his place. I don't think he believed I was capable of anything business-like. Only cooking and doing his dirty washing."

"Most men are the same, all they think about is having their creature comforts laid out for them," agreed Sadie. Though she didn't really think Andrew was like that. She had always thought him to be a very considerate man. She looked across the room to where he was now having a conversation with Quentin. She was sorry she had made him feel so uncomfortable.

Connie followed her gaze. "He was good in bed, though," she murmured.

"I wouldn't know," replied Sadie.

"Well someone did, otherwise we wouldn't be divorced!"

"I suppose that's something positive about him – being good in bed, I mean." Sadie sipped her drink. "Most men just think they are."

"We'd better get back to the table." Connie drew herself back to the matter in hand. "You said you needed more forms."

****

At last the evening came to an end. When the last person had departed out of the door, the four friends slumped into the chairs.

"I'm knackered!" Sadie threw her head back and closed her eyes.

"My hand has gone numb after greeting so many people this evening." Connie rubbed her right hand. "Why do men seem to think they have to grip so hard? Do you think it's a macho thing?"

"I don't know. Perhaps you're right. It could be their way of showing you how strong they are," said Jenny. "Anyway, it all went very well in the end and that's the main thing. At the last count I had two hundred and seventy-five forms, so at two hundred and fifty pounds a head, we should have over sixty eight thousand pounds. There may even be more when I do the final check."

"Not a bad start for a bunch of women," said Sadie. She opened her eyes and glanced at Connie. They both laughed.

"What's the joke?" asked Lucy.

"Andrew turned up and told me how surprised he was that we four had set this up." Connie explained. "Condescending so-and-so. Anyway, Sadie overheard, and by the time she'd finished with him, he didn't know what he was saying. You know what she's like when she gets going. Andrew scampered across to some friends as fast as he could."

"Did you know he joined our agency?" asked Jenny, cautiously. When he had handed her his form and photograph, she wasn't sure whether to accept them or not. However, as there had been a number of other people waiting in the queue at the time, she'd decided not to cause a scene.

"He did say he came here to join, but I wasn't sure it was a good idea and tried to put him off." Connie shrugged. "However, if he paid the fee, why not? He did pay, didn't he?" she added sharply. "I mean, he paid the full fee and didn't ask for a discount or anything?"

"Yes, he paid the full amount. In fact he paid cash," replied Jenny.

"Two hundred and seventy five people. I didn't think we would get so many here tonight," said Lucy.

Connie went across to the table where the remainder of the food was still waiting to be cleared away. "The food went well," she said, choosing a couple of sandwiches. "I'm starving. I didn't have anything to eat earlier. I was so nervous about the whole thing, I couldn't even think about eating, but now I could eat a horse. There's some food left if you guys are hungry, though you'll need to be quick. The staff will be along soon to clear it away."

"Not for me," uttered Lucy, wearily. "To tell you the truth, I'm shattered and just want to fall into bed. What time should we meet up in the morning? We'll have to go through all the forms and add the profiles to the website. It doesn't matter that it's Sunday. They'll all expect to log onto the site and see their profiles up there."

"We'll meet at the office at around ten o'clock," mumbled Connie, tucking into her plate of food.

"I'm going home, too," said Jenny. "Perhaps we could share a taxi, Lucy? See you both in the morning," she added over her shoulder.

"I'm not hungry either, Connie, and don't forget I'm coming home with you. You said you would put me up for a week or so." Sadie pulled her suitcase out from under the table.

Connie groaned. "Oh blast! I'd forgot about that. Yes, okay. If you don't want anything to eat, perhaps you could organise a taxi. I'll only be a couple of minutes." She screwed up her eyes. "What do you mean a week or so? I thought I said a few days."

"Whatever!" Sadie needed to keep Connie sweet for the time being, so she didn't want to push her luck by arguing about it now. Hopefully, the few days would automatically lead to a week and, if she played her cards right, a month or two. Finding something she could afford wouldn't be easy.

Back at the house, Connie pointed to the spare bedroom. "Hope you sleep okay."

"I'm so tired. I think I could sleep anywhere." She paused. "Thanks for putting me up, Connie. I promise I won't get in your hair."

"It's not my hair, I'm worried about," replied Connie. "You're just so untidy. I recall the last time you stayed with me, I spent most of my time clearing up after you."

"It'll be different this time, Connie. I promise to be more tidy."

"I'll believe that when I see it." Connie sighed as she left the bedroom. Sadie was a great girl, but she did tend to cause chaos wherever she went.

Sadie unpacked her case quickly and began hanging her clothes neatly in the wardrobe. "Blow this!" she mumbled, and flung the rest of the stuff over a chair. "I can start being tidy tomorrow." Undressing, she flopped down onto the bed. "Goodnight," she called out. "Give me a shout in the morning if I sleep in." If Connie made any comment, Sadie didn't hear. She fell asleep the moment her head hit the pillow.

CHAPTER TWO

"It seems we're the first to arrive. I thought the others would have been here by now." Connie was rather surprised to find the door to the office was still locked. She fumbled around in her bag for the keys. "We've just got to find out where the switch is for the landing light. It's too dim up here to find anything."

"I knew we'd be too early," grumbled Sadie. "I told you we could've had another hour in bed."

"You *did* have another hour in bed!" uttered Connie, pulling the keys from the depths of her bag. "If you remember, I was up and dressed an hour before you. You wouldn't budge. I had to resort to dropping a cold flannel over your face. If you'd got up earlier, we might have missed all the traffic at Marble Arch."

"Okay, okay," Sadie held up her hands. "I knew I'd get the blame for the traffic hold up at Marble Arch." She looked around the empty office. "So now we're here, what're we going to do? There's nothing we can do without Jenny. She has the forms and the cash and, if she has any sense, she'll still be curled up in bed. It's Sunday morning for goodness sake or hadn't you noticed?" She dropped her bag onto the floor and slumped into a chair. "By the way, has anyone ever told you your spare bed is uncomfortable? I hardly slept a wink last night."

"Andrew complained about it a couple of times, when I told him to sleep in the spare room after I found out about his affair with the floozy." Connie paused. "Anyway, if you couldn't sleep, why did I have so much trouble waking you up this morning?"

"I thought Andrew only slept with the floozy once – hardly what you would call an affair," Sadie replied.

"Once can become a habit," Connie said. "Besides, how do I know he was telling me the truth? He could have been shagging the wretched woman for months."

"True." Sadie yawned. "On the other hand, has he seen her since? It doesn't sound like it when he's resorted to joining a dating agency." She paused. "Our dating agency."

"Whose side are you on? Aren't you forgetting who you're relying on for a bed tonight?"

"I'm not on anybody's side. I'm simply looking at it from all perspectives." Sadie sighed. "And all I'm saying is, Andrew might not have seen the floozy again. It could have been a one off. He's a man, isn't he? He was out at a stag do and…"

"What was a woman doing at a stag party in the first place? It could have been a put up job. He might have invited her for a weekend away." Connie interrupted. She hoped that would silence Sadie – at least for the moment. Once her friend got started on something, she was like a dog with a bone. Gnawing at it for hours. This wasn't the first time Sadie had suggested Andrew's misdemeanour might have been a one off. Well Sadie could think what she liked, but as far as she was concerned, once, twice, or a regular habit, it was still a betrayal. "Listen! It sounds like someone's coming! I hope it's Jenny, then we can make a start."

The door flew open and Jenny bounced in. "Sorry I'm a bit late, but I slept in and then the traffic was bad around Marble Arch. I think there's a problem with a gas leak."

"We got caught up in that, too." Connie laughed.

Jenny opened her bag and pulled out four bundles of forms, all fastened with elastic bands. "I divided them into two groups this morning over breakfast. These are all men." She placed two bundles on the desk. "And these are women," she added, holding up the other two bundles. "We seem to have a fairly equal number of each."

"Yes, I noticed that last night when I looked around the room," said Sadie. "I'd been concerned we might have a surplus of one sex."

"Okay," Connie interrupted. "How're we going to do this? What I mean is, how do we set about getting them from here to there?" She pointed to the forms and then to the computer.

"Lucy is the computer buff, but she isn't here yet. So really we can't do anything until she gets here. She's set up the website and if we start messing around with it, we could lose everything." Sadie picked up the electric kettle. "Why don't we have some coffee while we're waiting? I'm sure she won't be long."

"Alright," said Connie, reluctantly. She was keen to get everything moving. Any clients logging on this morning would expect to find the site up and running, yet here they were, sitting around drinking coffee. "But once Lucy gets the names up there, we must sit down with her and learn how to do these things for ourselves. We each need to know how to set up a client and arrange meetings for them. We can't wait for Lucy every time someone gets in touch. It's not professional, and it's not fair on her."

Lucy arrived just as the kettle boiled. "Good to see you have your priorities in order. I'm dying for a coffee. I've been stuck at…"

"Marble Arch!" the others chorused.

"Yes! How did you know?"

****

"This is going to take forever," moaned Sadie, tossing another form on the pile in front of Lucy. "That's another form ready to be added to the site." She rubbed her right hand. "I don't think I've hand written so much stuff since I left school. I'm beginning to get writer's cramp."

When Lucy first set up the website, she had suggested they shouldn't include any addresses for fear of someone hacking in and sending unsolicited messages to their clients. Though it meant they had to write everyone's name and address together with a few details into ledgers, the others had agreed.

"I think some of these people are telling a few lies," said Connie. She held up a form. "For instance, this guy, Brian Lomax, has put his age at forty-nine."

"So?" asked Lucy, glancing up from the keyboard.

"Seventy-nine more like." Connie retorted. "Someone must have noticed him." She gazed at the blank faces. "For heaven's sake, Sadie, you saw him coming on to me. You even suggested he might be wealthy."

"Gosh, yes. I do remember him. He did look elderly, but I think you're exaggerating a bit." Sadie grinned. "I seem to recall, he rather fancied you."

"So, he came on to you, Connie?" laughed Lucy. "Perhaps I should arrange a date for the two of you?" Glancing at the others, she smiled and wiggled her fingers over the keyboard.

"Don't you think it would be good for our new company to get two people matched up on our first day?"

"Don't you dare!" Connie yelled.

"Andrew seems to have advanced even further in the world." Sadie held up his form. "I know he's Chairman of a large international company, but according to this, he is also a consultant for another two top firms. Drives a Bentley, a Rolls, and has a yacht moored in some French resort, and another in the Bahamas. It seems he has a mansion somewhere in the country and a large apartment in Park Lane."

"The lying toad!" Connie reached over and snatched the form from Sadie's hand. "I hope they all haven't told lies about themselves."

"How would we know if they had?" asked Jenny. "It's only because we all know Andrew rather well and you distinctly remember Brian Lomax from last night that we're even having this discussion."

"That's true. Nevertheless, we do know all this information on Andrew's form is rubbish. We can't upload it – it's fraud – isn't it?" Connie peered at the others over the top of her reading glasses. "Some unsuspecting woman is going to arrange to meet him and find out he's a lying cheat."

"But we can't alter things people have written about themselves," insisted Jenny. "That would be wrong. If you're unhappy about what Andrew has put on his form, then you should give him a call and discuss it with him." She paused. "The same applies to Brian Lomax. However, as for the others, we must upload the information they've given us." She looked across at Lucy. "What do you think?"

"I think you're right. There isn't anything we can do at this stage." Lucy suddenly had another thought. "Unless of course, someone makes a complaint after they've met up with a prospective partner and find things aren't what they read on the website. Then we would have the right to check it out and alter the profile accordingly."

"Perhaps we should have given the whole dating agency thing more thought." Connie sighed heavily. "We were relying on everyone being honest and telling the truth about themselves. It seems we were a bit naïve." She hesitated. "Perhaps we should just add Brian's details as he's written them. And as for Andrew…" She glanced back at Andrew's form. "I'll give him a ring later today and have a chat about what he's written here. I don't want to do it now. He's likely to talk for ages and I'd rather we finished loading these folks onto the site."

The women continued adding clients to the web database until Sadie suddenly realised how hungry she was. "If I don't have a break from reading all this stuff, I think my eyeballs will fall out and my stomach will declare war on me," she said. "Isn't it about time we had something to eat, it's gone three o'clock. I don't suppose anyone thought to bring anything?"

"I made a few sandwiches and bought some biscuits on the way here." Lucy rummaged around in her bag. "I thought we might be stuck in here for a while."

"Well done! I must admit Sadie and I didn't think about it." Connie reached for the kettle. "But once Sadie dragged herself out of bed it was too late to do anything, anyway."

"I thought it would be all my fault," Sadie snorted.

"Forget the kettle." Jenny giggled. She pulled two bottles of champagne from a cooler-bag she'd heaved into the office. "I saw them sitting on the table just before I left the Royale and took pity on them. They've been in my fridge all night."

"Great! Now that's more like it. I thought you'd brought a mountain of sandwiches in there." Sadie leapt to her feet. "I'll get the glasses." She paused. "Do we have any glasses? Or will we have to use the mugs?"

"Yes, of course we have wine glasses," Connie replied. "I brought some spare ones from home when we set up this office."

"I should have guessed," Sadie said. "I can't see you drinking wine or champagne out of a mug."

It took a while to clear a space where they could spread out the food and drink. The office was so small there was only room for two desks and four chairs. The women had to sit facing each other. A filing cabinet, which doubled for a small table for the coffee, tea, and mugs, stood in one corner, while a sink was squashed into another.

"We really must get a bigger office as soon as we can afford it. This is ridiculous." Connie carefully placed some of the paperwork onto the floor under the desk. "We can hardly move in here." She looked up at Jenny. "Will there be enough room now? I don't want to get these mixed up, especially as we have them into some sort of order."

"We would have a bigger office if we had taken the one in Ealing," said Sadie, almost tripping over her handbag. "It was three times the size of this poky hole. But you insisted we should be here on 'Park Lane'." She made quotations signs in the air.

"I simply thought that if we were going to be an upmarket agency, we should have an upmarket address," Connie explained. "Anyway, once we get the agency underway, we won't all be in here at the same time."

"Okay!" Sadie held up her hands. "I was only saying…"

"Stop arguing, you guys," Jenny interrupted. "I've poured out the champagne and Lucy has laid out the sandwiches; so cool it and let's eat."

****

"I didn't realise cheese and chutney sandwiches and champagne went so well together." Jenny popped the last morsel of sandwich into her mouth.

"I think champagne makes everything taste better," replied Connie, refilling their glasses.

"I agree," Sadie giggled, as she raised her glass to her lips.

"You've had enough," said Jenny. "Don't forget we still have lots of forms to go through this afternoon."

After finishing off the champagne, they went back to sifting through the forms.

****

"I think we might be coming to the end at last." Connie held up about half a dozen forms.

"Thank goodness! I have a splitting headache," Sadie moaned. "I thought we were going to be here all night."

"I must admit I didn't think it would take so long." Jenny passed another form to Lucy. She laughed. "You had too much champagne at lunch time, Sadie."

"I suppose we could simply have scanned the forms into the computer," said Lucy.

"What do you mean?" Sadie looked up sharply. "Are you saying there was an easier way to do this?"

Lucy explained what she meant by scanning.

"Well, why didn't we do that? Why have we been sitting here all day, going through everyone's life history, when we could have photographed each form and uploaded it?" Sadie flopped back into her chair and held her head. It was still aching. "Has anyone got any painkillers?"

"Because I thought it would look amateurish." Lucy explained, pulling some tablets from her bag. She passed them across to Sadie. "Here, try these. What I mean is," she continued, "they'd all have different handwriting, and some might have scanned worse than others and been illegible. This way, they all look the same. It's much more professional."

"I agree." Connie removed her glasses.

"Of course you do!" Sadie grumbled, swallowing the pills.

"For heaven's sake, Sadie. After spending all that money last night on an impressive launch, it would have been stupid to have a cheap looking website." Connie paused. "Lucy's done a good job. She's the one who's set up the site and typed up all the info. All we've done is sort out the forms into alphabetical order, read them through, and add a brief outline and email address to our registers."

"Yes, I suppose so," mumbled Sadie. She heaved a sigh and picked up her pen. "Sorry, Connie. But I just wish we were finished. I feel I know every single person intimately."

"Yes, I understand what you're saying." Connie held up the form she was working on. "For instance, this guy has detailed his whole life here. He even mentions what toffees he liked as a child."

Jenny laughed. "Yes, I've had a few profiles like that, too. Someone said how he wanted to join the Navy because he looked good in a sailor suit when he was a toddler."

"I can beat you all." Sadie held up a form. "This guy ends up by informing everyone he changes his underwear every day!"

They all burst out laughing.

"I think everyone misunderstood you last night. When you said 'be honest', they obviously thought you meant 'tell all'. It's not quite the same thing as telling the truth," said Lucy, when they had all stopped laughing.

Finally, the last form was checked and Lucy added it to the computer. "There we go!" she said, clicking the mouse. "Divorcees.biz is now up and running."

They all crowded around Lucy's desk to see the finished website. "We did it, girls! Isn't it exciting?" Connie clasped her hands together. "We're in business. Until last night, the whole thing had been a project. Something we were working on for the future. Now the future is here, our agency is out there on the World Wide Web." She paused and looked at the others. "But this doesn't mean we can sit back and relax and wait for the money to roll in; this is only the first step. From now on we must promote Divorcees.biz for all we're worth."

She recalled how they had given up their full time jobs to set up Divorcees.biz. Had they been too hasty? The money they received last night was good, but it wouldn't last forever. The Royale still had to be paid and the rent for this office was due on the first of every month and despite it being a rather pokey place, it didn't come cheap – nothing ever came cheap in Mayfair. What they needed now was for lots of clients to log on and ask for meetings to be arranged. That would bring in more income. And, hopefully once the word got around, new clients would register.

Sadie interrupted her thoughts. "What about Andrew? Someone will have to give him a ring and speak to him about his form."

"Damn! I'd forgot about him." Connie sighed.

"Would you like me to do it?" Sadie asked.

"No. If he had simply made an error, then it would have been okay. But since he has added all this… rubbish," she shook the form "I guess I'd better do it. However, I don't intend to stand for any nonsense. I'll make him understand Divorcees.biz is to be honest and above board and we won't tolerate lies on our site. I'll be calm and polite, but firm."

Andrew's phone rang several times before he answered.

"What's all this rubbish on your form?" Connie bellowed down the line. "You haven't got a Bentley, a yacht, or a mansion. What the hell are you talking about? And where did all these business consultancies come from? We can't put that up on our site; it's all lies."

"Hello, Connie, good to hear your voice. Lovely party last night." Andrew's smooth tone came down the line.

"Yes! Sorry! Hello, Andrew." Connie tried to calm down a little. "But like I said, what you've written is absolute rubbish."

"Perhaps we could meet up and talk about it," he replied.

"Talk about it?" Connie's voice rose again. "For goodness sake, what's there to talk about? We both know you've made it all up." She put her hand over the mouthpiece. "He wants me to meet up with him and talk about it," she whispered. "Can you believe it? No way." She swept her hand across her throat to emphasise the point.

"Of course it's rubbish, but it got your attention," Andrew continued, his voice remaining calm. "We could chat about my details over dinner. You could even help me fill in the form to your satisfaction. What're you doing this evening?"

Connie was speechless.

"Connie! Are you still there?" asked Andrew. His voice had lost a little of its calmness. "Connie?"

"Yes, I'm still here," she spluttered. "I'm lost for words."

"That's a first." Andrew laughed. "I'll pick you up at seven." He hung up before she could reply.

"What did he say?" asked Sadie.

"He's picking me up at seven." Connie replaced the receiver slowly, wondering what had just happened.

"That went well." Lucy grinned.

"What happened to 'I'll be firm' and 'no way'?" Sadie made quotation marks in the air again.

"I got screwed! That's what happened!" Connie shook her head vigorously. "He wrote all that nonsense because he knew I'd be the one to call him about it. Then he wound me up and put the phone down before I had time to refuse his dinner invitation." She slammed her fist down on the desk. "Why didn't I see it coming? Sadie should've made the call after all. She would have run rings around him."

"Too late to say that now." Jenny paused. "But look on the bright side."

"There's a bright side?" Connie raised her eyebrows.

"Of course there is." Jenny laughed. "You're fixed up for dinner this evening."

Connie groaned. "I've had enough for today. I think we should go home. The site is up and running, if anyone logs on they'll be able to check out their details for themselves. No doubt we'll hear if something is wrong." She turned to Lucy. "Would you keep an eye on the website this evening in case anyone gets in touch? However, tomorrow we'll bring our laptops and once you have uploaded the site details onto them, you can teach us how to work it. We can't leave it all to you."

Once everything was cleared away, they all left the office together. "Come on, Sadie, I can see our bus coming." Connie began to run towards the bus stop. "See you guys in the morning."

"What's so funny?" asked Connie. They were sitting on the bus and Sadie had burst out laughing.

"So you got screwed!"

Connie looked around at the seats behind. An elderly man smiled at her, while another man gave her a wink. "Keep your voice down, they'll think I'm a call girl. Anyway, what about it?"

"Nothing, it's just I was supposed to be the one with the colourful language!"

CHAPTER THREE

Connie was waiting for Andrew when he pulled up at the house. She knew he was always punctual, so she had made a point of being ready when he arrived.

"Enjoy your evening, both," said Sadie as she saw Connie out. "I won't wait up." She winked.

Connie was about to reply, but Andrew took her elbow and steered her down the path towards the car.

"Where're we going?" Connie asked as she clicked the seatbelt in place.

"It's a surprise," replied Andrew. He checked the traffic before pulling away from the kerb.

Connie shrugged. "Fine. But I better warn you, I've had a long, tiresome day and was looking forward to a soak in the bath followed by a quiet night watching television. Rushing home, having a quick shower, before getting dressed up to go out – especially with you – wasn't part of the plan. So watch out, I'm likely to be grumpy."

"That's okay. I can do grumpy."

"Tell me about it." Connie laughed. "You were always grumpy."

"No I wasn't," Andrew murmured.

Connie stopped laughing and looked away. "No, you weren't." Her voice was almost a whisper. She recalled how he had always been calm and patient during their marriage. Even when she did things that would make a parson swear, he would remain unruffled.

A short while later, Andrew stopped the car in front of a plush hotel. "We're here."

"The Condrew!" Connie exclaimed. "Pushing the boat out, aren't you? I thought we were simply going somewhere to sort out your form for the agency."

The Condrew was an expensive hotel in Cumberland Gate. Once you stepped through the doors, it was like entering a time warp. It had been built during the 1890's and though the hotel had been re-decorated over the years, none of its charm had been lost. You could almost visualise Sherlock Holmes strolling through the elegant drawing room. Connie adored this hotel. She and Andrew had come here often during their marriage. They had spent weekends at the hotel to celebrate their birthdays, wedding anniversaries and sometimes just for the sheer fun of it. It was their special place.

"For old time's sake." Andrew smiled. He handed the car keys to the man on the door. "Have someone park my car, please."

Inside the restaurant, the Maître d' led them to a table by the window and pulled out a chair for Connie. She sighed as she sat down. Andrew had even booked their usual table. "Nothing is going to come of this, you know? We're never going to get together again. Not ever!"

"*Not ever* is a long time. Can't we simply wait and see?" Andrew shrugged. "Now what would you like to drink?"

"A gin and tonic, please – a very large one. I need something to unwind."

"Unwinding sounds good." A gentle smile played around Andrew's lips. "I'll have the same."

****

In spite of her doubts about going out with Andrew, Connie was enjoying the evening. Everything at the Condrew was exactly as she remembered it. The food was delicious, the waiters, under the watchful eye of the Maître d', were attentive and the same pianist was playing the same soft music on the grand piano. She looked across the table at Andrew. Yes, even he hadn't changed.

Though wisps of grey hair were beginning to peep through, he was still a very attractive man. If anything, the grey made him look even more distinguished. Nothing else about him had changed at all. He still had those wonderful eyes. Eyes which were warm and sexy and made you feel so comfortable you wanted to melt into his arms. Then there were the tiny dimples that appeared in his cheeks when he laughed. And he had the same warm and friendly smile. It was his smile that had first drawn her to him all those years ago.

Connie recalled how, a little over eighteen months ago, they would have been upstairs in their favourite room tearing each other's clothes off by now. They had always booked their special room when they'd come here. It had a delightful balcony overlooking the edge of Hyde Park, where they would enjoy breakfast; watching everyone rushing to their places of work. She sighed. If only Andrew hadn't gone off with the floozy, they would still be together. They would still have their lovely home, still be making love by the pool in the moonlight, and would still… She scolded herself for raking up the past. He had betrayed her, and now they were divorced. It should be an end to it. Why had he brought her here? What was he trying to do? Did he think they would simply go upstairs to…?

"I've booked a room." Andrew interrupted her thoughts. She looked up. It was almost as though he knew what she was thinking. He had often done that when they were together. She would be thinking about something and he would suddenly start talking about that very same thing. She was convinced he could read her mind. "Our room," he continued. "I wanted everything to be the same."

"Nothing can ever be the same, Andrew. You blew it when you had the affair with that floozy."

"I didn't have an affair with the floozy." He shook his head. "Now you've got me calling her that. Nevertheless, I didn't have an affair. Well, not in the sense you mean. It was one night, Connie. One – damn – night! I swear if there was one thing I could remove from my life, it would be that one night."

"You never did tell me why you did it."

"I tried to, but you didn't want to know!" He slammed his fist on the table. The coffee cups rattled in their saucers and he looked around to see if anyone had overheard. No one appeared to be taking any notice, though. "Once you heard about it, you screamed for a divorce. I tried apologising. I tried telling you how I'd got drunk at John's stag do and didn't even know what I was doing. I can't remember anything about it. I might not have even touched the woman. Probably didn't. I wasn't really in any fit state to do anything even if I'd wanted to. All I remember is she was lying in bed with me when I awoke the next morning. She dressed and left without saying a single word. Maybe she was looking for a bed for the night without any strings attached and she thought I was a safe bet because I was so drunk. I tried to tell you all this, but you wouldn't listen to anything I said." He paused. "It was one night, Connie."

Connie's thoughts flew back to the conversation she'd had with Sadie earlier in the day. It was obvious she believed Andrew's side of the story. But then Sadie had always told her she'd made a mountain out of a molehill. Sadie was a tough cookie, she was untidy and her language wasn't always as polite as it should be, but she was a very shrewd lady. At least she could be, some of the time. Perhaps Sadie had been right. Had Connie really blown it out of all proportion because she'd felt so humiliated when Andrew confessed?

"Say something." Andrew reached across the table and took her hand.

"I don't know what to say," Connie mumbled. She was confused. For a moment, she wished she hadn't come here this evening; yet at the same time she was pleased she had. She moved her hand away and reached for her evening bag. She pulled out the form Andrew had filled in the evening before. "You said we could discuss your profile over dinner." Even to her it sounded ridiculous. Andrew was pouring his heart out and she was twittering on about a stupid form. But she was at a loss as to what else to say.

"You fill it in or don't fill it in. I don't care. I won't be using the agency anyway."

"Then why did you come to the launch? Why sign up? Why this?" She waved the form in front of his face.

"Because it was the only way I could see you again. You never answer my calls, or reply to my mail." He sighed. "I knew you were involved with Divorcees.biz. I knew you'd be there."

"Now I'm even more confused. You said you were surprised a bunch of women could set up such an agency!"

Connie shook her head. "You let Sadie walk all over you last night. Yet all the time…"

"I know, but I wanted to talk to you," he broke in. "I needed to speak with you – alone. But when I realised it wasn't going to happen at the launch, I suddenly decided to fill in the form with a bunch of lies. It was the only way I could get you to call me. I knew you wouldn't allow it to be added to the website the way it was."

Connie stuffed the form back into her bag. She wasn't sure what to say next. Even though she was looking down at the table, she could still feel Andrew's eyes burning into her. He was waiting for her to say something more. "Perhaps I could take a look at the room. It would be interesting to see if they've made any changes." She bit her lip. The words were out before she could stop them. She had only been wondering about the room. She hadn't meant to say anything.

"Yes, why not?" Andrew waved to the waiter for the bill before she could change her mind. "Will I order some champagne?"

"Champagne won't be necessary," said Connie.

Upstairs, Andrew opened the bedroom door and allowed Connie to enter first. Her feet sank in the rich, thick pile carpet. "It's exactly the same," she murmured, as she gazed around the room. "Nothing's changed." The heavy brocade curtains, the matching bedspread, the large ornate dressing table and the soft plush sofa in the corner, everything was as she remembered it. She walked over to the French windows and stepped out onto the balcony. The lights of London glittered far below. "This was always a lovely room."

"It's our room." Andrew had followed her.

"Did you bring her – the floozy – here? To this room?"

"No!"

"How can you be sure, you said you were drunk and couldn't remember anything?"

"If you recall, Connie, the stag party was held in Brighton."

She nodded. She felt stupid. Of course it had all happened in Brighton. If the party had been in London, Andrew wouldn't have stayed at a hotel. He would have taken a cab home and they wouldn't be in this mess now.

There was a tap on the bedroom door. "Room service," a voice called out.

Connie glanced at Andrew. A question hung on her lips.

"It'll be the champagne I ordered."

She opened her mouth to say something but Andrew was already moving towards the door. "I thought as we were up here, we could have a drink – for old time's sake." He turned and shrugged. "What harm can it do?" Opening the door, Andrew allowed the waiter to place the tray on a small table in the room before thanking him and dropping a tip in his outstretched hand.

The cork popped and Andrew filled two glasses. "To us," he said clinking her glass with his. "And for things to come."

Connie didn't reply. She took a sip of champagne and allowed her eyes to drift around the room. How easy it would be to slide back into Andrew's life. They'd had such fun together. Fabulous holidays on sun-kissed beaches, dinner parties, weekends away and evenings spent in this wonderful hotel – in this very room. The list was endless. Andrew's position in the company gave him an exorbitant salary, allowing them to do pretty much what they wanted. But even if he'd been penniless, she would have still loved him. Again, she glanced around the room: it was almost as though time had stood still and they were here on one of their usual evenings out. Yet…

"I've hired this room." Andrew broke into her thoughts. "It's mine… it's ours," he corrected himself, "to use whenever we want."

"Andrew!" She swung around to face him. "It must be costing you a fortune."

"I would pay anything to have you back." He took a sip of champagne. "What do you say?"

Connie walked back out onto the balcony and sank into a chair. Yes it would be good to have Andrew back. She couldn't deny she still loved him – well, not to herself, anyway. She might be able to fool Sadie and the others, but not herself. When she was younger, she'd had a few boyfriends, but none of them meant anything to her until she met Andrew at a dinner party. He was different. He was thoughtful, kind and attentive; even her parents were impressed by his quiet, polite manner and were delighted when they decided to get married. She recalled her father saying 'he couldn't have wished for a better husband for his little girl.' When she broke the news of Andrew's fling with the floozy, her mother had wept, unable to believe it.

She sighed and gave a sideways glance at Andrew. He still loved her, so why not give it a try? Getting back together might work. It *could* work, if… But then a picture of him with the floozy flashed though her mind and she closed her eyes tight shut, trying to block the wretched woman out. Could she ever forget his indiscretion?

"At least think about it, Connie. Please, say you'll think about it."

She glanced back into the room, towards the bed. "I am thinking about it," she murmured. "I am thinking about it."

CHAPTER FOUR

Sadie watched from the window as Andrew and Connie drove off. It would be good if they got back together again. Andrew was a great guy and anyone with half a brain could see he was still devoted to Connie. She honestly believed he had only played away one time, but as far as Connie was concerned, he'd had a wild passionate affair, which had gone on for months.

Sadie clucked her tongue and shook her head as she turned away from the window. Connie was a lovely lady and a good friend, but she could be incredibly stupid at times. Okay, she had been angry and very hurt when Andrew told her about the encounter, what woman wouldn't? If only Connie had listened to him, though, given him a chance to explain. On the other hand, why on earth had he mentioned it to her in the first place? If he had kept the whole episode to himself, they would still be together. She sighed; Andrew was too honest for his own good.

She went into the kitchen and poured a glass of wine. She was rummaging through the fridge hoping to find something for her supper, when the phone rang.

"Hi. It's me." Lucy's voice came down the line. "Is Connie there?"

"No. She's gone out with Andrew." Sadie hesitated. "Was it something important – can I help?"

Lucy laughed. "No, it's nothing important. It's funny really. I thought Connie might like to know Brian Lomax has requested a date with her."

"Brian Lomax?" Sadie squealed. "She'll go berserk!"

"Shall I set it up for a giggle?" said Lucy.

"No! I wouldn't advise it," Sadie replied. "Otherwise, once Connie learns how to work the website, you'll find yourself being paired up with unsuitable men for the next few weeks."

"True," said Lucy. She paused. "Would you like some company? I could bring the laptop around there for an hour or so. I could even bookmark the site on Connie's computer, give you the passwords and begin showing you how to add people as they join. It looks like a few people are logging on already."

"Good idea." Sadie glanced towards the fridge. "Have you got anything to eat? Connie's cupboards are empty and I'm starving."

"Not really. I haven't had a chance to do any real shopping for ages. How about we order pizza or something when I get there? We could have it delivered."

"Yes, we'll do that. Connie has some wine. I'm sure she wouldn't mind us having a glass or two to wash it down."

Sadie had no sooner put down the phone, than it rang again. This time it was Jenny. "I've sorted out the money ready for the bank, but it seems I have a couple of things which we all need to sign. Any chance of me popping in this evening?"

"Sure! Why not." Sadie paused. "You realise Connie isn't here? She's having dinner with Andrew, but Lucy's coming around shortly. We're going to order something to eat when she gets here."

"Sounds good. Make it for three. I'll be there in about half an hour."

****

A short while later all three were tucking into a monster pizza. "I hope Connie doesn't mind us using her house like this," said Lucy.

"Of course she won't." Sadie laughed. "Why would she? We're all here on behalf of our new company. The fact we're enjoying the evening is quite beside the point."

A sudden ping from Lucy's laptop told them another message had dropped into the mailbox of Divorcees.biz. This time, it was from a man called Michael Stone. It seemed he was keen on being introduced to a woman called Ann Masters. Lucy brought up Michael's face on the screen.

"Oh! That's the guy I rather liked." Sadie sniffed. "I thought he was rather dishy, but he spent most of the evening drooling over the tall elegant woman." She paused. "So who is Ann Masters?"

Lucy tapped the keys once more and another face appeared on screen. "She's the tall elegant woman." She glanced at Sadie. "Sorry, but it seems he's got past the drooling stage and wants to take it a step further." She looked back at the laptop as another message came in.

"This is beginning to get exciting," said Jenny peering at the screen. "I wonder who it is this time?"

"It's Michael Stone again," said Lucy, tapping the keys.

"Has he changed his mind already?" Sadie grimaced. "Sounds as though he's a bit fickle."

"No." Lucy paused and swung around to face the others. "He hasn't changed his mind, he's requesting meetings with Alice North and Jane Peters."

"Really?" Jenny swallowed hard. "Is that allowed? I know it's good for our business, money-wise, as he'll have three fees to pay, but he does sound a bit of a Casanova, doesn't he? I thought folks would be dating one person at a time – with a view to finding a substantial relationship."

"I think we all thought that," said Sadie. "I certainly don't think this is what Connie had in mind."

"Hang on, he's at it again." Lucy tapped the keys again. "He's now asking to meet Sue Long, Jane Porter, and… you, Sadie. He's booked himself up for every night next week."

"Bloody hell! No way!" Sadie leapt to her feet. "Did he think I wouldn't notice what he was up to? What a toe-rag."

"Perhaps he didn't realise you were a partner in the agency," said Lucy. "But on the plus side, it means he must have noticed you at the launch after all."

"If your comment is supposed to make me feel good, can I tell you it doesn't?" Sadie frowned. "He seems to have noticed everyone at the launch. At this rate, by tomorrow morning he'll have made a date with every woman on our website."

"No, he won't," Jenny decided. "We aren't going to set him up with anyone until we have all talked it through together. Connie should be told about this and whatever we do, it should be a joint decision."

"I agree," said Lucy. "What time will Connie be home?" She looked at her watch. It was eleven-thirty.

"I don't think she'll be coming home tonight." Sadie tapped her nose knowingly and laughed. "Not if Andrew has anything to do with it."

"If Andrew has anything to do with what?" Connie walked into the room and dropped her coat and handbag onto a chair.

They all jumped. No one had heard the front door open or close.

"Connie" said Sadie, her hand clutching her throat. "What on earth are you doing here?"

"I live here, remember?" said Connie, sinking into a chair.

CHAPTER FIVE

An awkward silence followed Connie's remark. It was Sadie who spoke first. "I kind of got the impression you'd be spending the night with Andrew."

"I think he was under that impression, too." Connie shrugged. "But here I am." She looked around the group. "So what's up? Has anything been happening on the site?"

Pulling herself together, Lucy quickly explained how Michael Stone had asked them to arrange meetings with several women at once. "Not all on the same evening, you understand," she added, hastily. "He's mentioned six women so far, including Sadie and wants to meet them on different evenings next week."

"You rather fancied him didn't you, Sadie?" Connie laughed

"Not any more," Sadie retorted. "Screw him! I made a big mistake when I hooked up with Alex. I don't need another jerk in my life."

Connie was about to reply, when another message came in. Again it was from Michael Stone. This time he was seeking a date with Jenny.

"What shall we do?" asked Lucy.

"I think he needs putting straight, right now. This is exactly the kind of thing we wanted to avoid. It's simply not on." Connie was angry. They had spent a great deal of time and money, setting up a decent agency and no way was she going to allow this sort of thing to happen. "If he isn't satisfied, then he can have his money back. We don't want *that* kind of clientele."

"Okay, tell me what to say." Lucy sat with her fingers poised over the keyboard, waiting for someone to dictate a message.

"We need him to know our agency is designed for ladies and gentlemen to meet up with like-minded people with a view to a committed relationship. We are not running some kind of seedy escort agency, where men can go through all the goodies on the shelf one after the other," Sadie said. She slammed her fist into the palm of her hand. "That should do it! What an oaf!"

"Ahem!" Connie coughed. "Let's keep it polite, shall we? Okay! Type this." She dictated a few words, explaining their policy for the agency. Once they had all agreed on the wording, Lucy pressed send and the message disappeared.

"Okay, I think I'm done!" Connie yawned. "I'm going to make some coffee, anyone want any?"

"Not for me. I better go home, it's getting late." Lucy glanced at Jenny. "Shall we share a cab?"

"Yes, good idea."

Once the two friends had left, Sadie went through to the kitchen to find Connie. "So what happened? Where did Andrew take you?" She hesitated, wondering whether it would be wise to enquire anything more, but her curiosity got the better of her. She coughed. "I really thought you would be away all night."

Connie sank into a chair. "He took me to the Condrew for dinner."

"The Condrew. Wasn't that your old haunt?"

"Yes. Andrew saw it one day a long time ago and noticed how the name of the hotel seemed to be taken from our joined names – Connie and Andrew. He booked us in for dinner that very evening. We loved it. Since then, we made it our favourite place."

"That is just so romantic," Sadie gushed.

"Yes – well." Connie sniffed. "Tonight he'd arranged for us to have our favourite table. And…" She hesitated a moment, wondering whether to go on.

"And what?" prompted Sadie. "You can't leave me hanging."

"He'd even booked our usual room – just in case."

"He'd booked your usual room? Just in case?" Sadie's eyes widened.

"Yes. He'd booked the room – our room."

"But you didn't stay?" Sadie waited for Connie's response.

"No."

"Why ever not?"

"I couldn't."

"You couldn't?" Sadie nodded. "Weren't you even a little bit tempted?"

"Yes, especially when I went upstairs to take a look at the room."

Sadie grabbed Connie's arm. "Oh my God! You mean you actually went upstairs to take a look at your special room and you still didn't stay the night?" Her jaw dropped. "How could you resist?"

Connie paused and took a sip of her coffee. "It seems Andrew has hired the room for the foreseeable future."

"Andrew's hired your special room?"

"Yes! Didn't I just say that? For goodness sake, why are you repeating everything I say?"

"Because I can hardly believe you went up to the room and didn't stay the night. Now you're telling me Andrew's hired the room, yet it still didn't sway you."

Connie looked down at the floor. "I can't get the floozy out of my mind. How could I sleep with Andrew, with her lying right there between us?"

"Gosh! The floozy wasn't there as well, was she?"

Connie pulled a face.

"Sorry!" Sadie pressed her lips together and sat down next to her friend. "Connie, you've got to get over it. Andrew's a good man. He loves you. Okay, he made a mistake with that woman. But I still believe him when he said it was only a one off. If only you could see…"

"I believe him, too." Connie began to cry. "He explained it all to me over dinner."

"So what the hell are you doing here?" Sadie leapt to her feet. "You're an idiot! You should be back there getting it together with Andrew." She was amazed at Connie.

"Because I couldn't stay."

"Why not?"

"Because the floozy… Oh for goodness sake, don't start all that again. You're freaking me out!" Connie dabbed her eyes with a tissue.

There was a brief silence, while Sadie sat down. "What're you going to do if Andrew starts dating another woman?

He's a young, successful man. He's going to want female company eventually. He won't wait forever."

Connie was taken aback by Sadie's question. If she had been asked the same thing a day ago she would have said she didn't give a damn what he did. However, that was then. Having spent the evening in Andrew's company and listening to his explanation, she now realised she would be unhappy if another woman was to take her place in his life. She opened her mouth to speak, but then the floozy popped into her mind. She was the reason for their divorce. That bloody woman would always keep popping up between them.

"Well?" Sadie tapped her fingers on the arm of the chair. "How would you feel?"

Connie stood up. "You're giving me a headache. I'm going to bed." She avoided answering the question.

"Okay, okay. I won't say another word." Sadie held up her hands. "Except this! You guys were made for each other, but you're so pig-headed you can't see beyond his one mistake. However, I'm not going to say anything more on the matter. Nevertheless…"

"What happened to I-won't-say-another-word?" Connie walked towards the stairs. "Good night, Sadie."

Muddled thoughts rushed through Connie's mind as she slowly climbed up the stairs. Why did Andrew ask her out? Okay, he explained that. So why had she gone out with him this evening? She could just as easily have said no when he arrived at the door. It might have been better if she had, at least she wouldn't be feeling so confused now. Yet she had showered and changed and then listened for his car to draw up outside. Was that because deep down she wanted to go out with him? No! Definitely not! Well – perhaps – maybe. Okay – damn it. Yes. She had wanted to go out to dinner with him. But why on earth had she gone up to the room?

Anyone in their right mind wouldn't have gone up to the bloody room.

She sank down onto the bed and thought about those dreadful moments before she left the hotel. Andrew had looked like a lost little boy when she'd insisted on leaving. He had pleaded with her to stay and, though she'd been sorely tempted, her pride hadn't allowed her to back down. Seeing her into a taxi, he had handed the driver a couple of notes to take her home, before disappearing back into the hotel. But as the taxi pulled away, she had glanced back through the hotel windows and seen Andrew walking into the bar.

****

Sadie sat in the kitchen for a few minutes after Connie had disappeared upstairs. She was dumbfounded. Connie hadn't answered her question. Did that mean she didn't know how to answer? Was she unsure of her true feelings? Connie could be so stubborn at times. Once she made up her mind about something, she never listened to anyone. If only there was something she could do to get them back together.

She sighed. It wasn't any good sitting here; she had to be up in the morning. They all had to learn about this damn program on the computer. She frowned. Computers were at the very bottom of her least favourite things. They never did anything she wanted them to, no matter how many times she tried. She could type, do filing, and man the phones with the best of them. She could even send and receive emails but that was as far as it went. She had absolutely no idea how the whole thing worked and didn't really want to know. She shivered. She would have to pay attention tomorrow otherwise she could lose important information inadvertently.

Sadie was still thinking about Connie's problem, when she slowly made her way up the stairs. There must be something she could do. She paused for a moment when an idea began to form in her mind. But would it work? First she needed to speak to Andrew; he would have to co-operate.

As she ran up the last few stairs and into her room, another thought crossed her mind. If her plan *was* put in motion, she would have to make damn sure Connie never found out she was involved or else all hell would break loose.

CHAPTER SIX

"You need to sign these forms, Connie." Jenny pushed the paperwork across the desk. It was the following morning and they were all back in the office. "The bank needs all our signatures as the account is in our joint names. Lucy and Sadie signed them last night. However, I've arranged it so only two signatures are needed for any transactions. It could be difficult to get everyone to sign an urgent cheque if a couple of us were on holiday in the Bahamas." She grinned.

"The Bahamas?" Sadie uttered. "When will I be able to afford a holiday in the Bahamas? I doubt I'll ever get much further than Brighton!"

"Don't be such a pessimist," Jenny replied. "You don't know what lies ahead."

"That's what I'm afraid of," said Sadie, gloomily. Her smooth forehead creased into a frown. "Nothing good ever lies ahead where I'm concerned. So I prefer to know what's coming, then I can be prepared for whatever is thrown at me."

"For goodness sake, cheer up. You'll have us all in tears in a minute." said Lucy. She turned to Connie. "Did Sadie tell you I bookmarked the Divorcees.biz website onto your computer while I was at your house last night? I was going to show Jenny and Sadie how it all worked, but…" She broke off as the computer pinged and a message dropped into the inbox. "Oops! It's Michael Stone. I think he's replying to the message we sent last night."

"What does he say?" Sadie leaned across the desk. "I hope he isn't going to be awkward about our message to him. Otherwise I'll…"

"He's apologising." Lucy swiftly interrupted. She glanced at Connie before looking back to the screen. "He says he didn't realise he couldn't set up a few dates at once and asks us to go ahead and arrange a meeting with Ann Masters." Lucy brought the photo of Ann onto the screen. "He's already paid the fee of fifteen pounds online. So what do you think, guys?"

"I don't think we have any choice," said Connie. She laid down her pen and clasped her hands together. "Now it is up to us to contact Ann and ask if she would like to meet up with Michael."

"But shouldn't we tell her what he was trying to do?" Sadie frowned. "I mean, shouldn't we tell her what Michael Stone is really like?"

"Do we know what Michael Stone is really like?" Connie sat back in her chair and made a steeple with her fingers. "He might be quite a nice guy. Though I must say I doubt it very much by the way he's presented himself to us. Nevertheless, it is not up to us to decide whom our clients should meet. We could get into all kinds of trouble if we start making remarks about any one person." She paused. "Anyway, we know Ann Masters met him at the launch, so at least she knows who the man is."

"Perhaps we could make a general recommendation on the site," Lucy said thoughtfully. "For instance, we could add a postscript to the main page advising our clients to meet up in a public place on a first date." In one way she agreed with Sadie. They should pass on any known information about the people they were setting up meetings for. But she also knew Connie was right. They could be accused of defamation of character if they were to make any negative remarks about someone.

"Good idea!" Sadie thumped her fist on the desk. "It's the least we can do."

"Okay," said Connie. "We'll sort out the wording, but in the meantime send a message to Ann Masters informing her of Michael Stone's request to meet up with her and see what she says." She pursed her lips. "I hope we don't need to have a full group discussion every time we're asked to arrange a meeting, otherwise it's going to take forever."

"By the way, what does Andrew want us to do with his enrolment form?" Lucy glanced at Connie. "Did you get a chance to mention it to him last night or were you too preoccupied?"

"Of course, I spoke to him about it," Connie snapped. She was still feeling very unsettled since seeing Andrew. "Isn't that the reason I met up with him?" She pulled the form from her bag and thrust it at Lucy. "Just put his name and that he is chairman of a large company. Look down his profile and add anything you know for sure. Forget all the other rubbish!"

"Oops, sorry," Lucy raised her eyebrows. "A little touchy this morning, aren't we?"

Connie sighed. "Sorry Lucy, but I'd rather not talk about last night, if you don't mind." She smiled. "Shall I put the kettle on for some coffee?"

****

During the morning, several people emailed the agency to arrange meetings.

"If this keeps up, we'll be millionaires," said Lucy, pressing the send button and releasing yet another a message into cyberspace. "Someone called Sue Hutchins rather likes the look of our Quentin. I have to say, I thought he looked rather dashing."

"So far, the only one of us to be asked out is you, Connie," said Jenny, wistfully. "The rest of us don't seem to have lit anyone's fire."

"Yes, well I can't really say I was excited about an invitation from Brian Lomax. He doesn't exactly light my fire." Connie grinned. "And you're forgetting about Sadie and yourself. The wonderful Michael Stone requested the pleasure of your company."

"But if you recall, we were way down his list," grumbled Sadie.

"Is there anyone you would like to arrange to meet, Sadie?" Lucy looked at the others. "That goes for all of you. I could write to them now."

"I think I'll wait a while and see how it all pans out," replied Sadie. One of the reasons she had agreed to get involved with this agency in the first place was to find a good, honest man. Someone as far removed from her ex-husband as possible. Yet, out of all those gorgeous hunks on the site, the only man who had shown her any interest was a jerk who wanted to hurl himself into a pool full of women before making a choice. "I'll sit back and learn a little more about the men on our books."

Jenny nodded. "Yes, I agree. I certainly don't want another husband like Rob. I really thought he was Mr Right when we got married, but as it turned out, he liked spreading himself around too much. After seeing how Michael Stone is working the system, I think I'll take things slowly, too."

Connie and Lucy both agreed to wait a while before choosing a man, though for different reasons. Lucy's ex-husband, Ben, had been very cruel both physically and mentally. She had only stayed with him for the sake of their son, Terry. However, once he'd been accepted for university, she'd immediately set about filing for divorce.

"Now I'm footloose and fancy free, I have no plans to rush into another liaison – unless Brad Pitt or Johnny Depp join our agency." Lucy grinned. "Either of them would make a big difference to my decision. Though I think I might get lost in the number of responses." She hoped the others would accept her answer without any questions. She had seen a couple of men, whom she rather liked and planned to write to them without her colleagues' knowledge. As they were each going to take a turn monitoring the site, there wouldn't ever be any secrets in the office and it would be most embarrassing to hear a rejection read out by any of them. Perhaps being part owner of a dating agency hadn't been such a good idea after all.

Connie, on the other hand, was still in turmoil over Andrew. She had tried to put him out of her mind; even accepting one or two dates over the last year. But since meeting him again the previous evening, she realised she was still madly in love with him. Therefore, her excuse was simply that she wanted to wait until the business got off the ground. "I don't think I could really concentrate on finding the right man at the moment."

Sadie remained silent, though Connie's unconvincing tone, together with the conversation they'd had the previous evening, revealed a great deal to her. It was obvious Connie needed saving from herself.

****

During the afternoon, Lucy uploaded the Divorcees.biz program onto each of their laptops and proceeded to show them how it worked. "You all know how to send an email etc, so what you need to get to grips with now, is the program itself." After tapping a few keys, a mass of letters, numbers and symbols appeared on the screen.

"What the hell is all that," screeched Sadie, taking a leap backwards.

"Ouch!" Jenny grumbled. "That was my foot. "There's no room to make sudden movements. Warn me the next time you decide to start jumping around."

"Sorry, but if you will creep up on…"

"They're the codes for all the things I've added to the site." Lucy continued. She closed her eyes. She had barely started showing her friends how the site worked; this was not the time for heated discussions. "This is you, Sadie," she pointed to the screen. "From here, I can add or delete anything on your profile. Watch carefully, I'll show you." She added a few words saying Sadie was a lady of many talents. She then brought up Sadie's page on the website and pointed to where the new words had been added. "You do the same thing if anyone wants to add or delete anything from their profile."

"Leave the comment up there, it makes me sound rather cool and mysterious," laughed Sadie.

"It's stretching it a little, though," said Connie, with a grin. "If you have any talents, they must be well hidden. I hâve yet to see them." She clapped her hands together. "That's it, a lady of many *hidden* talents."

Lucy promptly altered the wording. "Now you really *do* sound mysterious."

"I love it," squealed Sadie. "That should get the men flocking in my direction!"

Lucy then moved on to show them how to set up a new client and also how to delete one should they decide to leave the agency. She stressed they must take care they didn't add or delete something from the wrong person. "But, honestly, the whole thing is a doddle. It's much easier than it looks." She sat back in her chair and looked back at her friends' faces. "So what do you think?"

Sadie stepped back to her chair and flopped down. "I think you better count me out. There's no way I would dare do any of that. I'm happy to read the emails, arrange any meetings requested and be the general run-a-round in the office. But I refuse to delve into the works of the computer." She clasped her hand to her forehead. "My God! Don't you realise, I could mess up everything so easily and then where would we be?" She folded her arms. "Sorry guys, I mean it when I say I really can't do it."

"So, learning how to use the computer isn't one of your many hidden talents?" Connie laughed. She pulled her chair around and sat down beside Sadie. "Don't you think you should give it a try? We can't leave it all to Lucy."

"I'm warning you now – if I touch that thing, it'll all go wrong." Sadie stabbed her finger towards the computer. "Shit, Connie. You know darn well I'm not technically minded." She held up her hands. "And no amount of persuasion is going to change that."

"I guess it means Jenny and I will have to persevere and learn everything we can." Connie looked across at Jenny. "What do you say?"

Jenny was quite happy to give it a go. She was always keen to learn something new. "Sure, why not?" she said.

Sadie smiled. "Thanks, guys. Is there anything you would like me to do while you three are stuck at the computer?"

Jenny suggested she might like to go to the bank. "We shouldn't leave all this money lying around the office."

Sadie was quite happy to go out. She wanted to have a quiet word with Andrew and had wondered when she might get the opportunity. It would be difficult with Connie hovering over her shoulder both here in the office and at home.

****

Sadie hurried along Park Lane towards Oxford Street and quickly found a small café. After ordering a coffee, she pulled out her mobile phone and punched in the number of Andrew's firm and asked to be put through to his office. Several minutes passed and Sadie began to drum her fingers on the table. Why on earth was it taking so long for his secretary to answer?

"Who shall I say is calling?" the secretary asked, when she finally picked up.

"Tell him it's Sadie and please hurry."

"Sadie?" There was a pause. "Will Mr Somerfield know who that is?"

"Of course he'll bloody know," Sadie retorted. "Get a move on, I haven't got all day!" She glanced at the clock; the bank would be closing very soon.

There was a click and then Andrew came onto the line. "What is it, Sadie? Is Connie all right?" There was a note of concern in his voice. He had likely been alarmed when his secretary informed him he had a call from someone called Sadie. She had never rung him at the office before, so his immediate thoughts would have been for his ex-wife.

"Connie's fine." She assured him. "I can't talk long, I'm supposed to be at the bank right now. Connie has added your profile to our agency."

"Oh! I didn't think…"

"Don't interrupt, Andrew, let me finish." Sadie clucked her tongue and looked at the clock again. The minutes seemed to be ticking away faster than ever. "You need to do something to make Connie sit up and take notice. I think you should make her a little jealous by arranging a date with one of our other clients. And before you burst a gut," she added before Andrew could interrupt. "I don't mean you should go off somewhere and have wild, animalistic sex with some glamorous young model. Just choose someone fairly ordinary to accompany you to dinner or the theatre."

"I'm not sure that's a good idea." Andrew was less than keen. He wanted to get Connie back into his life, not make a bad situation even worse.

"For goodness sake, man, you're going to have to do something drastic or you may as well give up. This could really work." She hesitated for a moment before mentioning the conversation she'd had with Connie the previous evening. Was it fair to say anything or not? Was she breaking a confidence? In the end, she decided to tell him. "Connie was in a real dilemma last night. I think she really wanted to stay at the hotel with you."

Andrew remained silent. So Connie had told Sadie how he had almost begged her to stay. He felt a little embarrassed.

"I simply think she needs a little push." Sadie glanced at the clock again. "Look, Andrew, I have to go. The others think I'm at the bank and it closes in five minutes. Promise me you'll think about it."

"Okay, I'll think it over, but I'm not saying any more." Andrew hung up.

Sadie carefully deleted all evidence of the call on her mobile. It wouldn't do for Connie to pick it up by mistake and find she had been making secret calls to Andrew. Gathering her things together, she hurried out of the café, only pausing to drop some coins onto the counter to pay for the coffee.

****

After putting down the phone, Andrew sat back in his chair and looked up at the ceiling. His head had been aching all morning; he'd had far too much to drink the previous evening. After Connie left, he'd gone back into the bar and downed several large whiskeys before making his way upstairs to bed. He'd had such high hopes Connie would relent and stay with him. But she hadn't. Instead, she'd insisted on going home. And now Sadie's idea of how to win Connie back had made his headache ten times worse.

He had a meeting in half-an-hour. Right now he should be focusing on James Hargreaves, a very important man in the business world. He was very interested in the company and was thinking of investing a great deal of money. In this economic climate, anyone even hinting at putting money into the firm deserved his undivided attention. Yet Sadie's phone call was distracting him.

Could she be right? Should he try to make Connie jealous? But what if Sadie was wrong? It could be the end of any kind of relationship between him and his ex-wife. At least Connie was speaking to him now, a day or so ago, she would have stepped on him as easily as stubbing out a cigarette.

Connie was the love of his life. They had been married thirteen years before the divorce and he would marry her all over again without a moment's hesitation. There was no one else for him. She was the most wonderful woman in the world.

Though they'd both been disappointed when Connie found she couldn't have children, he hadn't dwelt on it. They still had each other and he was very happy to leave it at that. However, she hadn't taken the news quite so lightly. "Why am I so different?" she'd wailed at the time. "Why me? All my friends seem to have babies whether they want them or not!" But, being the tough cookie she was, she had learned to live with it.

Nevertheless, Connie had felt humiliated when he confessed his infidelity. The man who had vowed there was no other woman on earth for him had betrayed her. Her expression of sheer disbelief changing to one of horror was still imprinted in his memory. Perhaps he should have kept it to himself. She may never have found out if he hadn't told her. But he couldn't live with the knowledge that someone, somewhere, might have seen another woman leaving his room and could tell Connie. If she was going to hear about it at all, she had to hear it from him.

He sighed and drew himself back to the present. Maybe it would be best to forget about the phone call and leave things be. Nevertheless, even as his secretary ushered James Hargreaves into his office, Andrew was still thinking about his conversation with Sadie.

****

Sadie arrived at the bank just as the security guard was about to close the door. "I see one of the cashiers is still open and I only need to pay in these cheques." she gave him one of her most endearing smiles. "I promise it'll only take a few seconds." He relented and held the door open until she was inside. "Thank you," she said, giving him another big smile. "You're a star."

When she got back to the office, Jenny was making some coffee. "Would you like some?" she asked, reaching for another mug.

"Yes, please. Sorry I took so long, but there was a queue at the bank." Sadie crossed her fingers behind her back. It was only a little white lie. Surely it wouldn't hurt.

"We seem to be progressing with the website." Jenny handed a mug of coffee to Lucy. "At least, Connie is. I'm a bit slow on the uptake."

"Nonsense," said Lucy. "I think you're both doing well. Besides it's not as though you have to learn it all at once. Don't forget we're here every day." She took the coffee from Jenny. "The next time we get a new client, I'll watch while one of you sets up their profile."

By the end of the afternoon, several more people had been in touch to arrange meetings. Every time a message came in, Sadie's stomach turned over. Would this one be from Andrew? Though she still thought it was a good idea, she was a little apprehensive about Connie's reaction, especially if Andrew chose someone young and glamorous. However none of the messages were from him, so she was able to relax. Perhaps he had decided against her suggestion.

"We'll each take a turn at spending an evening with the computer" said Connie, putting on her coat. "I'm not doing anything this evening, so I'll see to it tonight."

"You'll need to take this with you." Lucy handed her the two ledgers containing email addresses. "I suggest we each make a copy of these to have at home. It would be better than carrying them back and forth every day."

Sadie swallowed hard as they all made their way downstairs. She had hoped Lucy or Jenny would look after the website tonight. If Andrew were to send a message this evening, Connie would be the one to pick it up and she might delete it without letting any of the others know. Any request from him would be better if it came during office hours when they were all present. She kicked herself for not thinking of it when she was talking to Andrew. She should have told him to send a message during office hours only. She shrugged. There was nothing she could do about it now, except sit with Connie all evening and watch as the messages came in. How boring was that?

Outside the building, they split up. Sadie and Connie hurried off to the bus stop, leaving Jenny to decide whether she would go straight home or wander around the shops. Lucy had already arranged to meet up with a friend who was visiting London for a couple of days.

"See you tomorrow," Connie called out as she and Sadie attempted to cross the busy road. "I don't know how they can say the congestion charges are working," she grumbled. "I can't see it's made any difference at all. There's still as much traffic as ever!"

CHAPTER SEVEN

Lucy made her way down Oxford Street, stopping occasionally to gaze at the displays in the shop windows. She was meeting Alice near the Palladium Theatre, and from there they were going on to a restaurant.

She was looking forward to seeing her friend again. Since Alice had moved to the north of England, they hadn't been able to get together very often, so they would certainly have lots to talk about.

Lucy looked at her watch. It was getting late. She was spending too much time drooling over the displays in the shop windows. She quickened her pace, but, hurrying around the corner into Argyle Street, she collided with someone coming her way.

"I'm so…" Lucy broke off when she saw her ex-husband glaring down at her.

"So we meet again!" Ben grabbed her arm. "What have you been up to?" he growled.

"Take your hands off me," yelled Lucy, having regained some of her composure. "It's none of your business what I'm doing."

Ben still held onto her arm. "Isn't it? I seem to remember paying you some money when we got divorced. I'd like to know who you spent it on.""You didn't give me any more than I was due!" Lucy wrenched her arm away from him.

"You treated me like dirt when we were married. I think you got off lightly." She tried to sound more confident than she felt. "I'm paying for Terry's education, if you must know. You never gave a damn about him!"

Ben pushed her into a shop doorway. "Think you're clever, don't you? But I know all about you and your precious friends starting up a dating agency." He sniffed. "Any money in it?"

"What's it got to do with you?" Lucy tried to break free, but his huge frame blocked her path. He had put on more weight since she had last seen him. She also noticed he was shabbily dressed. The grubby coat he was wearing had seen better days. That was very unlike Ben. He had always insisted his clothes were washed and ironed to perfection. She recalled the consequences if they weren't. "We're divorced, I lead my own life now." Lucy looked behind her, hoping to escape into the shop, but the place was in darkness. They had closed for the night.

Ben shoved his face closer to Lucy. "I thought there might be a little money coming my way. I don't have a job anymore, thanks to women like you." He wiped his nose on the back of his sleeve. "They said I was harassing them. But they were begging for it."

Lucy gagged. His breath reeked of stale alcohol. It was even worse than she remembered. "Get out of my way!" She attempted to push past him, but he was too strong for her and he shoved her back against the shop door. She banged her head hard on the wooden frame and, for a moment, she thought she was going to fall to the ground. But, somehow, she managed to stay upright. She knew once she was lying on the ground there would be no chance of her getting up.

"Don't be like that. We were married once upon a time. We have to look out for each other."

"When did you ever look out for me?" Lucy yelled. She looked over his shoulder, hoping someone would help her. But everyone continued to walk by. No one wanted to get involved. "You used to beat me up. What makes you think I would ever look out for you?"

"Set me up on your agency. Find me a woman – a rich woman. You could do that for me."

"Never!" Lucy growled. She was trying very hard to show she wasn't afraid of him, but deep down she was terrified.

His face contorted into a scowl and his eyes flashed wildly. He lifted his hand to strike her. "You dare talk back to me, you bitch!"

Lucy closed her eyes and waited for the inevitable. This had happened so many times before that she knew the drill. First he would knock her to the ground and then he would start kicking her. But, to her surprise, nothing happened.

"What the hell?" uttered Ben.

Lucy opened her eyes to see a woman hanging onto Ben's arm. "Get out of there, Lucy!"

Lucy didn't need to be told twice. She ran out of the doorway and grabbed Ben's other arm. "Thank God, you came when you did, Alice. I think he might have killed me this time."

"Get off me, you bitches," Ben yelled, as he tried to yank himself free.

By now the two policemen, who had been standing outside the Oxford Circus Underground Station, ran around the corner to see what all the noise was about. "What's going on here?" one of them demanded as he got closer.

"This man was accosting my friend," said Alice, still struggling with Ben's arm. "He had her pinned inside that doorway."

The other policeman took out his notebook. "Okay! Name?" he said, looking towards Ben.

"These women were bothering me!" Ben pulled his arm free from Lucy's grip. "I was minding my own business, when they started asking me for money."

"You lying bastard." Lucy screeched back at him. She turned to the policemen. "This is my ex-husband, Ben Anderson." She went on to explain how they had bumped into each other on the corner. "Ben was trying to intimidate me because I wouldn't give him any money."

"I see," said the policeman, nodding his head. "What about you? Did you hear all this going on?" he asked Alice.

"I came just in time to hear Ben calling her a bitch, then I saw him lift his arm to hit her. That's when I grabbed him and tried to pull him away." Alice glared at Ben. "He's an evil man and should be locked up."

"That's for a court to decide, Madam," replied the other policeman, calmly. "I'll call a car to take you all down to the police station. You can sort it out there."

"But Alice and I are going to a restaurant," Lucy argued. "We haven't seen each other for ages. Our evening will be ruined. Goodness knows how long we'll have to spend at the station."

"If you'd rather not press charges, we can leave it as it is," the policeman said. He shut his notebook with a snap.

Ben gave Lucy a triumphant smile. "I guess you're not going to press charges, then. You could never bring yourself to sign the papers, could you?"

"However," added the policeman, prodding Ben on the chest with his forefinger, "that doesn't mean you can run around the streets accosting women. I have your name in my book. Therefore, if you are involved in any further disturbances, I shall remember you. Do you understand?"

Ben shuffled his feet. "Yes," he muttered. He scowled at Lucy before scurrying up the road towards Oxford Street like the rat that he was.

After leaving the policemen, Alice and Lucy went straight to the restaurant. Lucy was still shaking when she sat down. "Once the divorce came through, I thought I was rid of that beast forever."

Alice suggested they both needed a strong drink to calm their nerves. "Has he been following you?" she asked after placing an order for two large gin and tonics.

"No, I don't think so." Lucy paused and thought it through. Could he have been following her? If he had, then he would know where she lived. Her stomach flipped over when she thought he might be watching her every move. But her more rational side took over. If he knew where she lived, he would have caught up with her long before now. He would probably have even broken into her flat. "No, I'm sure he hasn't. I believe it was purely by chance we bumped into each other this evening. Yet, he knew I was involved with the Divorcees.biz dating agency." She shrugged. "But I suppose he could have heard that somewhere along the grapevine. I was so relieved you showed up when you did; no one else came to my rescue."

"Well, you know me; I always stand up for the underdog." Alice smiled. "But seriously, you need to be careful. If you see him near your flat, call the police immediately."

Despite the bad start to the evening, Lucy enjoyed meeting up with her old friend. They had so much to talk about. Alice hadn't changed at all. She still had the same bubbly personality she had when they worked together a few years back. It also appeared she had retained her love of beautiful clothes. Tonight she was wearing a blue cocktail dress and matching shoes. She was also carrying the most wonderful clutch bag in the very same colour. Perhaps she had everything made for her. She did have a very good job in Newcastle.

"Would your new agency be any good for me?" Alice interrupted Lucy's thoughts. "I don't know much about dating agencies. I've always imagined them to be a sort of hotbed of lust."

"I suppose some of them are, but we want ours to be something special." Lucy paused. "That creep of an ex-husband of mine wanted me to enrol him for free and find him a rich woman." She looked down at the table.

"Forget about him." Alice could see that even thinking about the horrid man was upsetting Lucy.

"Looking back, I don't know what I ever saw in him. Though, he must have had something going for him, otherwise I'd never have married him." She thought back to the days before they were married. Ben had always come across as a kind person. Had it all been an act? Or had she been too crazy about him to see behind his good looks and disarming smile? "Thank God I was able to keep Terry safe. If Ben had laid a finger on him…"

"But he didn't, Lucy." Alice laid her hand on her friend's arm. "You saw to that. I only hope Terry learns what you went through to keep him safe."

"He already knows." Lucy pulled a handkerchief from her bag. "After the divorce he told me he'd heard his father and me arguing one night, a long time ago. He tried going back to sleep, but then he heard me cry out in pain. I gather he started to come down the stairs to find out what was going on. But, when he saw his father hitting me about the head, he ran back to his room and hid under the covers." She paused and dabbed the tears welling in her eyes. "Poor mite, he must have been terrified. Ben is a bully. He's enough to frighten anyone, let alone a little boy. After that, Terry closed his ears to anything he heard going on downstairs. Can you blame him?" Lucy took a deep breath. "You'll recall he became very withdrawn as he got older."

Alice nodded. "Yes, I remember. You were very worried about him."

"I thought he was starting to become autistic or something like that," Lucy continued. "However it seems he'd wrapped himself in some sort of cocoon to blot out what was happening around him. After he went to university and I got my divorce, Terry changed completely. He became much more outgoing. I guess it's because he knew we were both safe at last."

"You should have left the brute years ago," said Alice. "Oh I know you wanted to wait until Terry was older, but for goodness sake, Lucy, Ben could have killed you – and Terry."

"I realise that now. But my parents divorced when I was quite young. I guess they just fell out of love. But I saw my father regularly over the years and I loved him." Lucy wiped a tear from her eye. "I remember wishing they hadn't separated. Why couldn't I be like all the other kids and have my parents living together? I always felt the odd-one-out at school. I thought I was doing the right thing for Terry. I didn't want him to feel different from the other children. But…"

"Let's have another drink," Alice broke in. She felt they needed to change the conversation. "We'll talk about your new agency and what it can do for me – and for you. You could find the man of your dreams. After all, you have all those delicious men at your fingertips." She signalled to the waiter who was hovering close by. "Shall we have a brandy to go with our coffee?"

"I'm sure you aren't short of men friends," laughed Lucy. "With your good looks and fine figure; you are gorgeous. You must have half of Newcastle panting after you. As for me, I don't want to rush into anything. I want to bide my time."

"But not many of those panting men are my type, darling." Alice giggled. "I don't want another loser like Graham. I got fed up with his gambling habit. He burned though his money and then started on mine. Anyway, I think it might be fun to join your agency."

By the end of the evening, Alice had agreed to sign up to Divorcees.biz. "I'll give you a cheque now and leave you to fill in the form for me. You know as much about me as I do."

Outside the restaurant, Lucy decided to share a taxi with Alice. Ben could still be lurking around the area and she had no desire to bump into him again.

"I may be down in London next month. If so, I'll give you a ring and we can do this again," said Alice, when they reached her hotel.

Lucy sat in the cab and watched Alice walk up the steps and disappear into the hotel, before asking the driver to move off. For one brief moment, she wished she could turn the clock back to the days when she and Alice had worked together. But then she remembered she'd been married to Ben at the time and there was no way she wanted him back in her life. Nevertheless, it had been good to see her friend this evening and she was looking forward to meeting up with her again. If only she hadn't bumped into Ben. She had never seen him in such a bad way. He really was down on his luck. Good! At last he was getting what he deserved. But Alice was right about one thing; she would need to keep a wary eye out for him from now on. She certainly didn't want to bump into him again.

CHAPTER EIGHT

"We had twenty people requesting meetings last night," Connie told Jenny, as she and Sadie strode into the office.

"That's great news," Jenny replied. "I know it's early days, but it looks like our venture into the business world is working out well. Hopefully we'll hear from more people today."

"It was only twenty people, Jenny." Sadie flopped into a chair. "Don't get too excited. We haven't hit the headlines of the *Financial Times*."

"There's no need to be so grumpy, Sadie. I was only saying it's good because it means we earned three hundred pounds last night." Jenny paused. "So what's eating you this morning?"

"Sorry, Jenny. I didn't mean anything. Yes, I suppose from that point of view it is good news."

"What other point of view is there?" Connie asked. "We're here to make money." She raised an eyebrow. "You do remember what that lovely stuff is, don't you?" She paused. "Anyway, what *is* up with you this morning? You even got out of bed without me having to yell at you umpteen times."

"I'm fine, really, I am," Sadie insisted. "I'll put the kettle on. Lucy will be here in a few minutes, then we'll have some coffee." She was only too relieved to change the subject. She was still a little on edge about whether or not Andrew would request a date through the agency website. She had spent most of last evening peering at the laptop over Connie's shoulder. Every time a message dropped into the inbox, she had reared up from behind to check it out in case it was from Andrew. No way did she want Connie to delete it without someone seeing it. It was also for that same reason she'd leapt out of bed the moment the alarm went off. She hadn't wanted Connie to switch on the laptop without her being there.

"I was wondering whether we should start promoting the website again," said Jenny, changing the subject. "I don't mean we should have another massive party," she added quickly, having seen a look of horror forming on Sadie's face. "I simply mean a few adverts in some of the newspapers outside London. We want this to be a nationwide agency, don't we?"

"Yes, we do. Good thinking," said Connie. "We've only concentrated on this one area up to now. Now we've got the agency off the ground, we ought to spread our wings further afield."

"Morning, everyone." Lucy entered the office and closed the door behind her.

"Hi, Lucy," said Sadie. "Coffee will only be a minute. Did you enjoy your evening with your friend?"

"Yes, I did." Lucy hung her coat on one of the hooks by the door. "The time flew by. We had so much catching up to do." She pulled a cheque from her bag and handed it to Jenny. "Alice decided to join our dating agency. She asked me to fill in her details for her."

"I'm pleased you had a good evening," Sadie said. She chewed her lip for a few moments before continuing. "But what is it you're not telling us?"

"What makes you think I'm not telling you something?" Lucy looked up sharply.

Sadie shrugged. "I don't know. But there's definitely something you're keeping quiet about."

Lucy hesitated. She wasn't planning on mentioning that she had a run in with her ex-husband. She was still trying to put the whole episode out of her mind. But she should have known Sadie would pick up the vibes. There was something uncanny about Sadie. "It's Ben," she said at last. She explained how she had bumped into him on her way to meet Alice. "He was horrible." Tears welled in her eyes, as she described the events of last evening; how he had pinned her in a doorway and demanded money. "He even wanted me to add his profile to our site and set him up with a rich woman." She pulled a handkerchief from her handbag and dabbed her eyes. "I refused and he would have struck me if Alice hadn't arrived and grabbed his arm."

"The bastard!" Sadie slammed her fist down onto the desk. "You should have called the police and had him arrested!"

"Actually, the police arrived. They'd been outside the tube station when they heard the commotion." Lucy explained how she and Alice would have had to accompany Ben to the police station to press charges. "I didn't want to waste our whole evening there, so I left it. Though, one of the policemen took his name and gave him a warning."

"It was a cop out, more like!" Sadie cursed. "They should have arrested him and asked for a statement later. It makes my blood boil to think people can be accosted in the street, yet the perpetrator just walks off. Where's the justice in that?" She thumped the desk again.

"Sadie! For goodness sake, calm down." Connie went across to Lucy. "We all know the police can't just arrest anyone. In this day and age, they have to have witnesses, statements, and everything else that holds up the whole justice system." She sighed. "I'm so sorry your night was spoiled, Lucy. I know how much you'd been looking forward to meeting Alice."

"It wasn't all spoiled, Connie. We still had a good time chatting about the old days. Though, I admit it was marred a little by Ben's untimely arrival. Anyway, let's forget it and talk about something else." Lucy switched on the computer. "Why don't you set up Alice's page, Connie? I'll give you her profile and watch as you add the details." She was about to make room for Connie to join her at the computer when two messages dropped into the inbox.

"Who are they from," asked Jenny.

"The first one is from Alan Peterson. Wasn't he the guy who came with Quentin?" Lucy opened the message. "He wants a meeting with Ann Masters."

"She's doing well, she had two requests for meetings last night," remarked Connie with a grin.

"The other one is from someone called Jack Benson." Lucy paused. "Gosh, he's seeking a date with Ann Masters, too. Lucky lady. I'm afraid none of us are getting a look in." She was rather surprised that Jenny hadn't caught someone's eye.

Sadie heaved a huge sigh of relief – or was it more of disappointment? Since yesterday, her stomach had flipped a somersault every time the computer pinged. Would *this* be the message from Andrew requesting to meet up with another woman? The very message that would bring Connie to her senses and have her calling her ex-husband right away to say she couldn't live without him and promising never to leave him again. Well – something like that anyway. So why the hell didn't he hurry up and get on with it? If he hung around much longer, she was going to be a nervous wreck. Had he decided against her idea after all?

CHAPTER NINE

It was two weeks before Andrew finally sent an email to the dating agency. He had spent most of the fortnight agonising over Sadie's suggestion. In principle it was a good idea, but what if it all went wrong? Connie might never speak to him again. In the end, he had logged onto the website and waded through the sea of clients, dismissing each one, until he came to a familiar face. He sat back in his chair and stared at the photograph on the screen. If he were going to do this at all, then this lady would be his choice.

****

Sadie was so sure Andrew had decided against her idea of trying to make Connie jealous, she had started to relax and forget about it. That is to say, her stomach had stopped doing a somersault every time a message found its way into the inbox. So when Lucy called out that Andrew had sent an email, she almost choked on her coffee.

"You okay?" asked Jenny.

"Yes," Sadie spluttered. "Coffee went down the wrong way." She pointed vigorously to the coffee mug

"What does he want?" asked Connie.

"The subject heading reads 'Request Meeting'," Lucy replied. She kept her eyes glued to the screen, not daring to look at Connie.

"Oh!" Connie gasped. She was rather taken aback. She had half hoped the email was a message for her. Andrew had told her he wouldn't use the dating agency, so why else would he contact them? Yet here he was requesting to meet someone. "Err… who does he want to meet?" She tried to keep her voice slow and casual. "It's probably the lovely Ann Masters," she added, giving half a smile.

However, despite the casual tone and the forced smile, Sadie detected a tinge of despair in Connie's voice. Afraid of giving away the slightest hint she had anything to do with Andrew's sudden interest in dating anyone, she shrugged and looked down at the ledger in front of her.

"Are you really sure you want to know?" asked Lucy. Perhaps it would be better for Connie not to know about Andrew's arrangements.

"Of course I bloody want to know. Open it!" Connie coughed. Ah well, so much for trying to sound casual. She shook her head. "Just open the damn thing."

Sadie held her breath, waiting for Lucy to click on the mouse.

"Well! Who is it?" Connie drummed her fingers on the desk. She was bursting to know whom Andrew had asked to meet.

Lucy clicked on the message and burst out laughing. "It's my aunt. Andrew is requesting a date with my Aunt Agnes. He would like to take her out to dinner."

"Your aunt?" Connie said.

"That's nice," said Sadie. She was relieved Andrew hadn't chosen Ann Masters or anyone even slightly resembling her. The plan was simply to make Connie a little jealous, not have her raging around the office with daggers drawn. "Lucy's aunt is in for a treat, isn't she, Connie? I wonder where he'll take her."

"I'm going to give my aunt a ring and ask when she's free. She's got a laptop, but I can't wait until she switches it on. She's going to be so surprised. It's her birthday next week, so maybe he could take her somewhere to celebrate." Lucy picked up the phone and punched in the numbers.

"You're very quiet, Connie," said Jenny. "Are you okay?"

"Yes, I'm fine, "Connie replied quietly. "Why on earth shouldn't I be?" But she wasn't fine at all. Andrew was taking another woman out on a date. But why was it bothering her so much? He had a right to arrange a date if he wanted to. If someone asked her out, she would go – wouldn't she? Of course she would. Hadn't she already had a few of dates since her divorce? But on reflection, she had only accepted a date because she believed Andrew had been having a wild passionate affair. Though, quite truthfully, she hadn't really enjoyed any of them. But would she accept an offer now that she knew the truth about Andrew's love affair? She pulled out her handkerchief and blew her nose.

Sadie watched in silence. The plan was having the right effect.

"Aren't you going to say something, Sadie?" asked Connie.

"What do you want me to say?" Sadie stretched her arms in the air and yawned. "Andrew's a free agent and can do as he pleases. I hope Lucy's aunt enjoys her night out. I'm sure he'll be very courteous and give her a good time."

"My aunt is absolutely thrilled," said Lucy. She replaced the receiver and swung around to face the others. "It's made her day. She says she's free every evening next week except Saturday." Lucy grinned. "She didn't actually say so, but I have a feeling Saturday is her Bingo night." She swung her chair back to face the computer. "I'll get online and arrange a date with Andrew then let my aunt know the details. I'll try to make it for her birthday." She noticed Connie staring at her. "What?" she asked, raising her eyebrows.

"Nothing," snapped Connie, picking up some mail still waiting to be opened. She was being stupid. What did she care about Andrew having a date with Agnes? Lucy's aunt was an older woman for goodness sake. It was never going to be a permanent arrangement. Deep down, she knew he was only doing this to make her jealous. So in that case, why the hell was it working?

"I've sent a message to Andrew saying Agnes Anderson would be delighted to meet him for dinner and could he possibly make it the twenty-fifth. We'll see what he says. I've also written to Ann Masters telling her about Alan Peterson's request to meet her. Now, Connie, would you like have a go at setting up a page for this new client?"

Sadie watched Connie go through the motions of setting up a new page on the site. Though she seemed to be fooling the others, Sadie could tell she was irritated about Andrew taking someone out to dinner – even if the woman was old enough to be his mother.

She was itching to give him a call and tell him the plan was working, but, at the same time, she didn't dare do anything which might arouse Connie's suspicions. The twenty-fifth was still a few days away. It was going to be interesting to see how Connie behaved between now and then.

"I think it's time for coffee." Sadie felt she couldn't sit still any longer. She went across to fill the kettle. "Pity we don't have any cream buns."

"I can't eat cream buns," said Lucy. "I'm trying to lose some weight."

"Really? Wasn't it you who was stuffing your face with sandwiches and biscuits yesterday?"

"Yes, well – that was yesterday. I got on the scales this morning and I was horrified to find I weighed…" Lucy cast her eyes downwards. "Never mind what I weighed, but suffice to say I was heavier than I'd like to be."

"That's all very well, but I really enjoy having something nice to eat with my morning coffee." Sadie sniffed.

"So do I," grumbled Lucy. "That's the problem. If I were a stick insect like you, I wouldn't need to worry, but I'm not, so…"

"Okay, okay." Sadie interrupted, holding up her hands. "Forget the cream buns. Maybe we can get some plain slimming-type biscuits to keep in the office. It's just nice to have something to nibble on. I find a drink is too wet to have on its own." She had hoped someone would suggest she popped out for something to eat, giving her a chance to telephone Andrew, but no such luck.

A few more emails requesting meetings with various clients drifted in during the morning, but not as many as Connie had hoped. "We really need to have a steady flow. It's a bit hit and miss at the moment."

"It's early days," said Jenny. "However, like I said the other day, I think we need some new clients. Most of the people we have on the website were at the launch. They all met and summed each other up that evening. Alice is the only person we have on our books who lives outside the London area. We need to get our presence known elsewhere."

"Would anyone like to pop out and get a few newspapers from the stand on the corner?" asked Connie. "Perhaps a few magazines, too. We could give them a ring and ask about their advertising rates."

"I'll go!" Sadie leapt to her feet almost before Connie had finished speaking. "I need a breath of air," she added, realising she had volunteered a little too quickly. "Does anyone else want anything while I'm out?"

"You can call in at the bank with the cheque that arrived in the post this morning." Jenny waved the bankbook at her. "Might as well keep the bank account healthy. We'll be getting the bill for the Royale shortly."

"While you're out, I'll check online for newspapers outside London," Lucy said. "Jenny's right, we need to advertise ourselves nationwide."

Once she was outside, Sadie pressed the buttons on her mobile phone. "Choosing Lucy's aunt was a brilliant move," she said when Andrew came on the line. His secretary had recognised her voice and transferred her call quite quickly this time.

"How did Connie take it?" he asked. "I wasn't sure I was doing the right thing – I'm still not, actually."

"She was very quiet. In fact she's been quiet ever since your message came in. It's certainly ruffled her feathers." She laughed. "By the way, it's Agnes's birthday on the twenty-fifth, so a nice bunch of flowers wouldn't come amiss. Lucy said her aunt was thrilled to bits she had a date."

"Let me know if Connie gets upset."

"Yes, of course I will. I'll be your eyes and ears. I'm staying with her at the moment, so I won't miss a thing. I suppose she told you that when you met up?"

"Yes, she mentioned it. I have to go now. I have a meeting shortly." He paused. "I hope all this doesn't come back to haunt me."

After deleting all trace of the call on her phone, Sadie continued on her way to the bank. Andrew was such a lovely man. Connie was so lucky to have someone like him. Her own ex-husband, Alex, was a rat. She had realised he was a bit of a waster shortly after they met. He was a guy who was always on the lookout for easy money. He saw himself as one of the big 'wheelers and dealers' in London's backstreets, but he wasn't clever enough. Everyone knew that, except him. In the past, the police had always knocked on his mother's door if there was the slightest bother in the area. It was their first port of call.

So knowing all that, why on earth had she gone ahead and married him? Sadie sighed as she walked into the bank. Sadly, it was the same old story. She had thought she could change him. Make a man of him. Make him see how he could smarten himself up a bit and get a proper job – a job which brought a pay cheque at the end of each week. But had it worked out? Like hell it had! She'd been a fool to even think it might.

"Good morning."

Sadie was so deep in thought, she failed to see the security guard standing by the door. "Good morning," she replied. She grinned. He was the same nice man who had allowed her into bank the other day just as they had been about to close.

Glancing at the clock on the wall, he gave her a warm and friendly smile. "You've made it with plenty of time to spare, today."

Sadie laughed. "Yes, I didn't want to be the last customer twice in a row." She wished she had worn something better than her faded jeans and baggy top. She recalled Connie's frown when they had set out for the office that morning. 'Couldn't you have worn something a little more elegant? We *are* working in Mayfair,' she'd said. 'If someone calls into the office, I shall introduce you as the cleaner!'

"It's a lovely day." He nodded towards the door. "Too good to work indoors."

"Yes, it is. That's why I volunteered to do a few errands. I wanted to get out of the office." He seems very pleasant, she thought, as she strode across to the nearest counter and handed the cheque to the cashier. She wondered what he thought of her. At least he remembered her; she must have made some sort of an impression.

Through the glass panel separating her from the assistant, Sadie saw the security man's reflection; he was looking in her direction. She noted he was quite tall, rather good-looking in a funny sort of way, and was wearing a smart uniform. His hair was cut quite short, but she supposed it went with the job. He was carrying a bit more weight than was healthy, but didn't all fellows who worked security? Letting her mind wander a little further, she wondered what he was like in bed.

Still watching his reflection, she saw he had started walking towards her. Oh my goodness, was he coming over to speak to her? She came over all flustered and her breathing became rapid as he got closer. Yes, he was definitely coming to talk to her. She cast her eyes downwards, wondering what she should say if he asked her for a date? 'Yes, please! I'm free any night this year,' immediately sprung to mind. But it would make her sound too desperate. If Connie were here, she would tell her to act calm and be polite. Okay, Connie, I can do calm and polite. She pressed the palms of her hands down hard on the counter top to steady her nerves.

Glancing back at his reflection, she saw he was almost behind her. Quickly, she formed a plan in her mind. First, she would smile sweetly, before saying she would need to check her diary. Then, after rummaging through her bag, she would go through the motions of checking her busy schedule before saying, 'that would be very nice, thank you.' Right, that sounded good. Even Connie would be impressed.

"Excuse me." His voice was right behind her.

She took a deep breath and swung around. "Yes?" She gave him her sweetest smile.

"You dropped something when you pulled your bankbook out of your bag." He reached down and picked up a business card.

"Oh!" Sadie fought hard to hide her disappointment. "Yes… Thank you." Feeling very embarrassed, she took the card from him and turned back to face the cashier. Her face was getting hot. She must look like a beetroot now. But why should she be so embarrassed? Neither the security man, nor the cashier could possibly know what she had been thinking. Yet, once the cashier had finished stamping the bankbook, she grabbed it and hurried towards the door.

"I'll look forward to seeing you next time. I'm Michael, by the way," the security man called out after her.

"Oh! Err. Yes. Thank you… Michael." Sadie waved and threw him a smile and scurried away. Outside, she ducked around the corner and leant against the wall for support. Next time – if there ever were a next time – she wouldn't be so presumptuous.

****

"You look a bit flushed, are you feeling all right?" Connie asked, as Sadie burst into the office.

"Yes, I'm fine. It's a bit warm outside, that's all." She dropped the papers and magazines in front of Connie and flopped into her chair. She'd been so deep in thought when she left the bank, she'd almost forgot to get the newspapers.

She'd been half way up the stairs before remembering them and had run back to the kiosk on the corner of the road. "Anything happen while I was out?"

"We got a phone call from the Royale," said Connie.

"The Royale? What do they want? We haven't had their bill and forgot to pay it, have we?"

"They wanted to know what to do with the cake."

"What cake?" Sadie raised an eyebrow.

"*The* cake." Connie sat back in her chair and waited for the penny to drop.

"Oh my goodness, you don't mean the cake we ordered for the launch?" she added, suddenly remembering the cake at the reception. "The beautiful rich fruit cake laced with brandy that cost us a small fortune?"

"The very same," said Connie. "It seems we forgot to cut it on the night, so it's been sitting in one of their tins waiting for us to collect it."

"Shit! What a waste of money." Sadie dropped into her chair.

"At least you'll have something to eat with your coffee for the next few weeks." Lucy grinned. "But apart from that, we've only had a few more requests for meetings." She picked up one of the newspapers. "*The Times*! Isn't that a bit highbrow for a dating agency advertisement?"

"Not at all." Connie looked up from the *Good Housekeeping* magazine she had been flicking through. "Intellectuals read *The Times* and they're the sort of people we're looking for? How much do they charge for an ad?"

Lucy handed the paper to Connie. "I'm sure it'll depend on the size of the advertisement. Isn't that how these things work?" She paused. "You should know. It was you who organised the last lot."

"Did you find anything online?" Sadie asked.

"Yes," said Lucy. "We've arranged to have an advert in a number of local papers in Yorkshire, Northumberland, and Cumbria."

By the end of the afternoon, Connie had arranged for an advertisement to appear in several other national newspapers. They would all appear the following week. "I think we'll call it a day," she said, folding up the papers and dumping them in the bin.

"I'm not doing anything this evening, so I'll take website watch tonight if you like," said Lucy, turning off the computer.

"That's a good name for it," laughed Jenny as she went out of the door. "Website watch, I like it."

"You're very quiet, Connie," said Sadie. By now, the two of them were on the bus going home. "Is there something wrong?" She knew perfectly well Connie was still thinking about Andrew's forthcoming date with Lucy's aunt. But she wanted Connie to admit it.

However, it seemed Connie had no intention of discussing her thoughts with Sadie. "I think we exhausted all conversation in the office. We don't really have anything new to talk about." She paused. "Except, have you started to look for a place of your own?"

"I haven't had time." Sadie was hoping she might stay with Connie for a while longer. Rents in London were outrageous.

"We had all those newspapers in the office today. We could have helped you to look for something."

"Couldn't I rent the room off you? I promise to keep it clean and tidy and help pay for the food etc. I'll pay a proper rent; you could even give me a rent book."

Connie sighed. She hadn't really envisaged having a lodger. However, she had to admit it had been nice having some company during the evenings over the last few days and Sadie had been much tidier this time – well, a little tidier. "I'll think about it," she said at last.

"That's great! I'll look around and get myself a few things to make my room look more like my home."

"I said I would think…" Connie shook her head. What was the use? She could see Sadie wasn't listening. She was probably thinking about rushing down to Oxford Street the following morning to buy cushions and bedspreads.

CHAPTER TEN

One evening as she stepped down from the bus, Jenny noticed someone lurking outside her flat. She called it a flat, but in reality, it wasn't much more than a bed-sit. Rob had taken it upon himself to keep the flat they'd shared during their marriage, despite the fact it was he who'd had the affair. Looking back, Jenny knew she'd been stupid to let him off so easily. She should have fought for her share of everything. But being so upset at him cheating on her, yet again, she'd simply wanted him out of her life as quickly as possible.

Keeping her head down, she moved a little closer to her home. She intended to give the man a wide berth until she could see who it was. You couldn't be too careful these days. Too many people were being mugged on their own doorsteps simply for a few pounds. But when the man called out to ask her the time she recognised his voice. It was Rob, her ex-husband.

"What're you doing here," she asked, fishing around in her bag for the door key.

"I want to talk to you. Can I come in?" Rob shuffled from one foot to the other. "Please, Jenny, I need to talk to you. Can I come in?" he pleaded.

"Okay, but only for a few minutes. I'm going out." She wasn't really going anywhere, but she didn't want him to know that. Let him think her life had been one big party since they'd split up.

Upstairs, in her tiny room, she threw her bag onto the table. "Okay what do you want to talk about?"

"Can't we sit down and talk properly?"

"Why? Besides, like I said, I'm going out. I haven't got time for niceties." Jenny watched him lower himself into a chair. This wasn't the Rob she knew. He had several days' growth on his face and his hair gave the appearance he had just crawled out of bed. His suit was crumpled and his shirt looked dirty. When they were together, he had always been immaculately turned out. They might not have had much money, but Rob always made the best of himself when going to the office. He believed in making a good impression.

"I'm sorry, but I need to sit down." He rested his head on his hands "I made a mistake – a terrible mistake. I should never have left you for Angela." He looked up at her. "Will you give me another chance?"

Jenny flopped onto the only other chair in the room. She was speechless. That was the last thing she had expected him to say.

"Aren't you going to say something, Jenny?"

"I don't know what to say, Rob. You told me she was the one you loved. You said we had nothing going for us any more and I should step aside and give you your space. I was left with very little choice, as your fancy woman was standing on the pavement outside with all her baggage. You kept the bankbooks and most of the things we had bought together, leaving me with precious little and now you're telling me you made a mistake and want me to give you another chance. Just for the record, Rob, what did you expect me to say?"

"I know it looks bad, but I thought…"

"Looks bad! Looks bad? It looks bloody disgusting from where I'm sitting. Incidentally, where is the lovely Angela now?"

"Back at the flat. She refuses to move out." Rob looked down at the floor. "You and I… I thought we could start again."

"You damn cheat. You thought wrong!" Jenny leapt to her feet. "Now you'd better go."

Rob remained seated. "We were good together, Jenny. We could make it right."

"If you remember, it wasn't me who made it wrong. Now go." She pointed towards the door. Her hand was shaking with anger. "I'm going out and I need to get changed."

"I haven't anywhere to go."

"My heart bleeds for you. But now you know what it feels like to be turned out onto the street."

Rob rose to his feet. "Take some time. At least think it over."

Jenny looked away for one brief moment and then turned back to face him "Okay, Rob, I've thought it over and the answer is still no." She opened the door." If you don't mind, I need to get changed."

Jenny slammed the door shut behind Rob. She didn't want to give him the chance to swing around and hold it open. She was furious. The cheek of the man! Had he really crawled here thinking she would welcome him with open arms?

Angela hadn't been his first bit on the side. He'd had three flings with other dolly birds before she showed up and each time Jenny had forgiven him and taken him back. But when Angela came on the scene, she'd only to snap her fingers and

Rob sat up begging like a dog waiting for a treat. Now it seemed Angela had tired of him and he was on the prowl again, looking for somewhere to crash.

"Well, Rob, you've dropped yourself in it this time," Jenny murmured. "Damn-well serves you right." She went across to the window and looked down onto the street expecting to see Rob walking away into the night. But instead, she saw him hovering on the pavement below. Thankfully, her flat was on the second floor, so he couldn't force his way through the window. She watched him sit down on the wall outside the block of flats. Was he going to stay there all night?

The thought frightened her. Could he be going to start stalking her? She had planned on having a quiet night in, but with Rob waiting out there, perhaps it would be best if she went somewhere for an hour or so. Picking up her mobile, she rang Connie. "Will one of you be home tonight? Something's happened and I'd like to pop over."

"We'll both be here all evening," said Connie. "What's wrong?"

"I'll explain when I get there."

Rob was still waiting outside when Jenny left her flat. "I thought you'd have gone by now," she said, walking towards the bus stop.

"I need you." Rob ran after her. "Can't we just go back inside and talk quietly?

"I have nothing more to say to you." Jenny quickened her pace. "Besides, I've already told you I have plans for this evening." She glanced along the road and was relieved to see the bus trundling towards her. She stuck out her hand to make sure the driver saw her and didn't drive straight past. "Good bye," she called out over her shoulder.

Sitting on the bus, Jenny watched Rob turn and walk away slowly. A shiver ran down her back when she saw he was heading back towards her flat. Thank goodness she had been careful to make sure her front door was locked when she'd left. There was no way she wanted to come home to find him waiting inside.

****

"I couldn't believe it when I saw it was Rob standing there." Jenny had arrived at Connie's home and was telling them both how she had found a man hanging around outside her flat when she got off the bus. She took a sip of wine before continuing. "It seems there's been a falling out between him and Angela and he wanted me to take him back."

"I don't know how he had the nerve," said Connie. "I thought it was extremely generous of you to overlook his fling when it happened for the first time. But when it happened again, you shouldn't have forgiven him a second time. Or a third."

"I know," replied Jenny. "But I hadn't told my parents about his first affair; actually I hadn't told anyone. I felt so embarrassed about it. I even wondered whether it was my fault. Had I driven him to it? Then when it happened the second time, my father was so poorly I didn't want to worry him or my mother. I still didn't tell anyone – not even you guys. The third time…" Her eyes welled with tears and she pulled a handkerchief from her bag. "The third time it happened was when my father died. My mother was so distraught, I simply couldn't tell her." She wiped her eyes. "That's when I first told you. I had to tell someone. I felt so alone. Then along came the wonderful Angela and I was booted out. Of course, I had to tell my mother and the rest of the world about my failed marriage then. I couldn't hide it any more. Anyway, this evening, I refused point blank to have him back."

"And you merely held the door open when he left?" Sadie sniffed and pointed at Jenny's shoes. "If I had been wearing those winkle pickers, I'd have kicked him so far up his arse, he would have been spitting leather for weeks."

"Sadie!" Connie rolled her eyes. "That's not the way a lady talks."

"Maybe not, but I would've liked to have seen her do that!" said Jenny. "I have to say, it was a surprise to see him looking so pathetic. He always thought of himself as the boy wonder. He must have had to swallow his pride to call on me."

"Yes," said Connie slowly. She was thinking of Andrew. He had taken her to dinner and booked their favourite room. He must have been forced to swallow his pride when she had chosen to leave him and go home.

"Serves him right." Sadie folded her arms defiantly and peered at Jenny. "But there's more, isn't there?"

Jenny slumped back in her chair. "Yes. When I showed him the door, he left my flat, but he didn't actually go away." She sighed. "I allowed him to come inside on the understanding I was going out and could only spare him a few minutes. However, when he left, I looked out of the window and there he was, pacing around outside. I'm not sure what he was waiting for. Unless he was checking up on whether I was really going out. That's when I decided I needed to go somewhere this evening. Actually he was still there when I left."

"That doesn't sound too good," said Connie. "Perhaps you should call the police."

"And say what? I can't ask them to pop along to see if someone is waiting outside my flat."

"What about a neighbour? If you were to ring someone, would they take a look for you?" asked Sadie.

"I could try giving Ann a ring. She lives in the bed-sit above me. She might be out, though. She leads a full social life."

Ann was home when Jenny called. "Hang on. I'll pop over to the window." A couple of minutes later, she was back. "Yes. There's a man sitting on the wall. He's wearing a topcoat and has a mob of unruly hair. Is he dangerous?"

"He's my ex-husband. No, he isn't dangerous. At least I don't think he is. Anyway, just let him kick his heels out there. Thanks, Ann." Jenny clicked off her mobile phone. "You heard all that?"

Connie and Sadie both nodded.

"I don't think you should go home – not tonight, anyway. He could still be lurking around," said Sadie

"Where would I go?"

Sadie glanced at Connie before continuing. "You could bunk down with me"

"I can't…" Jenny began.

"Why not?" Sadie interrupted. "I'm sure Connie won't mind."

"No, of course I don't mind. I agree with Sadie. You certainly shouldn't go back tonight." Connie smiled. "We could all go to your flat tomorrow morning. I'm sure he'll be gone by then, but if not, then we'll threaten him with the police."

CHAPTER ELEVEN

When Jenny arrived at her flat the next morning, she was relieved to find Rob had gone. Even with Sadie and Connie to support her, she hadn't looked forward to meeting up with him again. As they made their way upstairs to her apartment, they met Ann hurrying down.

"I was hoping I would see you this morning before I went to the office," she said, her eyes glowing with excitement. "The police moved your ex-husband on late last night. I heard a bit of a commotion outside just before I went to bed and when I took a peek through the curtains, I saw John from across the landing talking with two policemen." She paused to catch her breath. "It seems the new lady on the ground floor had seen a man lurking outside all evening and was a bit nervous. She called out to John, as he came in and told him about it. He telephoned the police and they moved him on. I gather he was reluctant to go. He kept telling them how he was waiting for someone. But when they threatened to take him to the station, he moved away." She smiled. "It's the first piece of drama we've had here for a long time. I think everyone was watching from their windows. Even curtains across the street were twitching. Anyway, I must go. I'm going to be late for the office – again." She waved as she disappeared down the stairs and out of the front door.

"It's a good thing you stayed with us last night," said Sadie. "He might have still been outside when you got back."

"Yes, but what about tonight, or tomorrow night?" Jenny mumbled. She was beginning to feel a little afraid of Rob. What was he planning? Surely he didn't really think he could waltz back into her life after what he had done. "My guess, he's going to turn up again."

"Grab a few things," said Connie, briskly. "You can come and spend the next few nights with us."

"But I don't want to impose…"

"Jenny, I won't allow you to stay here with Rob hanging around," Connie interrupted. "You must come and stay with us. If he keeps showing up and sees you aren't here, he'll go away. If not, I'm sure the lady on the ground floor will have him arrested. She seems to be a no nonsense sort of woman."

"If you're sure." Jenny was grateful for the offer. "Of course I'll pay…"

"Nonsense! So that's settled. Now pack a few things and we'll go to the office."

****

"Did you guys sleep in?" Lucy asked. She had begun to wonder whether anyone else was coming to work that morning. "The website's been very busy. Four more people have applied to join and fifteen have asked for meetings to be arranged." She smiled at Sadie. "Someone wants to meet you."

"I hope it's not that womaniser, Michael Stone. I might be desperate, but…"

"No, it not Michael Stone." Lucy broke in. She didn't want Sadie to start raving about him again. She looked back at the screen. "Though, funnily enough, his name is Michael – Michael Beecham. He's one of the new people joining today.

Anyway, he looks rather cute. I would say it's worth meeting up with him."

Sadie peered at the screen over Lucy's shoulder. He did look very presentable. Clean-shaven, smart suit, pleasant smile… "Wait a minute, I know this guy," she yelled into Lucy's ear. "He works at the bank – he's the security guard!"

"Don't shout, Sadie. I'm not deaf." Lucy rubbed her ear. "At least I wasn't a few minutes ago."

"Oops, sorry." Sadie put her hand over her mouth. "But I know this man," repeated Sadie, a little more quietly. "Well, I don't exactly *know* him, but I've met him – twice. He's rather nice." She moved closer to the screen. "Can I read his profile?"

"I'll print it out for you then you can read it at your leisure. Besides, you might suddenly start shouting in my ear again." Lucy printed out the document and handed it to Sadie. "Let me know what you want to do. Unless, of course, you want to reply yourself."

Sadie took the sheet of paper and sat down.

"Well, there's a turn-up for the books. Our Sadie has got her first date since we set up the agency." Jenny laughed.

"I haven't agreed to meet him yet." Sadie glanced at Jenny. "I'm going to be very choosy this time around." She looked back at the sheet of paper in her hand. Obviously she wouldn't turn the security guard down. Men weren't exactly falling over themselves to meet her, so she couldn't afford to be too choosy. But she didn't want the others to know how desperate she was. She continued to read Michael's profile to keep up the pretence. "He says he went to university." She looked up. "I wonder why he's only a security guard at the bank and not the manager."

"Jobs are scarce, even for those with good qualifications," said Jenny. My cousin got a first in economics, yet she can't get a decent job at the moment. She's stacking shelves at her local supermarket."

"So, you never told me why you were all late this morning. Was it something exciting?" Lucy asked.

Jenny explained briefly what had happened and how she was going to spend the next few days with Connie and Sadie.

"Gosh, it seems we're all being harassed by our exes one way or another." Lucy looked at Connie. "Though in your case, I think Andrew is a very nice man. He's not really troubling you in the same way as our men are."

"Okay, I'll go for it." Sadie handed the paper back to Lucy. "He seems to be all right. However, don't write back to him for a couple of hours or so and then tell him I can do tonight or Friday. Tell him I'm very heavily booked all next week."

Connie raised her eyebrows. "Heavily booked? It's the first I've heard of it," she said. "Where are you going?"

"Nowhere. I'm not really booked up for anything. I just want him to think I am." Sadie sat down. "I don't want him to think I'm waiting anxiously by the computer for a man to give me the nod."

"But you are. You *are* waiting by the computer for a man to give you the nod – aren't you?" asked Jenny, smiling. "Isn't that why we set up this agency?"

"Well – yes. I suppose so. But there's absolutely no need for him to know that."

"Okay, I'll leave it for the moment," said Lucy. "But you better remind me, otherwise I might forget."

****

The rest of the day flew by. Connie took it in turns with Jenny to add the new people to the website. "I think we can safely say you are both up to speed on the site now." She paused. "Are you sure you don't want me to take you through it, Sadie?"

"No, thank you. I'll pass. But you can write to Michael Beecham now, Lucy. We'll see what he comes back with."

"He might not be able to log on until this evening, after he gets home from the bank," said Lucy, as she pressed send. "So don't be disappointed if he doesn't reply immediately."

Sadie hadn't thought of that. Since he'd asked to meet her, she had spent most of the afternoon going through her wardrobe in her mind's eye, figuring out what she would wear. She had kind of hoped he would reply immediately and make a date for this evening. However, if he were working all day, he wouldn't get back to her until later tonight, which meant she would have to wait another two days. She kicked herself. So much for playing hard to get!

Sadie watched the pointers move slowly around the clock. Every time a message dropped into the inbox, she wanted to rush across to see if it was from Michael. But she held back, not wanting to let the others see how impatient she was. It was almost five o'clock now. They would be packing up in a few minutes. It seemed she wasn't going to hear anything this afternoon.

"I have a message for you, Sadie," Lucy squealed.

Sadie jumped, she had been so lost in thought, she hadn't heard the computer's usual 'ping' when a message popped in. "What does he say?" she asked, leaping to her feet.

"He suggests you meet for dinner at Luigi's on Piccadilly at seven-thirty this evening." Lucy looked up. "Lucky you. It's a rather nice Italian Restaurant. Alice went there a year ago. She told me all about it."

"Seven-thirty! I'll have to get my skates on." Sadie threw her hands against her cheeks. "I don't know Luigi's. Is there a dance floor, or is it just a restaurant?"

"There's a small dance floor, but I think Alice said there wasn't any disco dancing. It was strictly ballroom," replied Lucy. "It's a rather swish place."

Despite having spent most of the afternoon thinking about what to wear, Sadie suddenly found herself at a loss. "A swish place. What on earth shall I wear? Oh my God, I don't know what to wear. Will you help me to decide, Connie? You're better at this than I am."

"Calm down, Sadie, otherwise you'll make yourself ill and won't be able to go!" Connie placed her hands on Sadie's shoulders and gently pushed her back into her chair. "First things first. You need to reply to Michael and tell him whether you'll be there this evening or not." She glanced at Lucy. "I think we've picked up the vibes that the answer is yes, so perhaps you could inform him Ms Sadie Grant will be delighted to meet him for dinner this evening at seven-thirty." Looking back at Sadie, she continued, "Why don't we shut up shop and get a taxi back to my house? We'll go through your wardrobe together. Jenny will be there, too, so I'm sure between the three of us, we'll get you sorted."

****

"Will I do?" Sadie gave a twirl. After a great deal of persuasion, she'd agreed to wear the green dress Jenny wore at the launch, instead of one of the gaudy creations she'd pulled out of the wardrobe. Even the white lace dress she'd worn at the launch met with their disapproval. "What if you step on it and you show off your breasts again?" Connie had said. "Michael might not be ready for a sight like that. Not on the first date, anyway."

On the way home, they had stopped off at Jenny's flat again. She'd forgot a couple of things when they were there earlier. Fortunately, while grabbing a couple of skirts from her wardrobe, she spotted the dress and thought it might be more appropriate for Luigi's than some of Sadie's stuff.

"You look lovely, Sadie." Connie nodded in approval. "That shade of green really suits you."

"Thank you for lending me the dress, Jenny. And you, too, Connie, for the evening bag, the makeup, and the perfume. Come to think of it, am I actually wearing anything of my own?"

"It's a pleasure. Just you be sure to have a good time," said Connie.

"What about my glasses? Should I take them off for the evening?" Sadie removed her glasses and squinted at her two friends.

"No!" Jenny and Connie chorused. "For goodness sake, leave your glasses on," added Connie. "You know darn well, you can't see a yard in front of you without them. You'll end up squinting at Michael all evening. He'll probably think you're pulling a face."

"Okay, okay. I'll leave the glasses on."

"And another thing," continued Connie, swiftly. "Try to behave like a lady. I realise it'll be difficult for you, but be polite and watch your language. At least on your first date."

Sadie grinned. "Yes, you're right. I shall be a picture of innocence this evening."

Connie shook her head. "That'll be a first," she mumbled. "Sadie a picture of innocence; pigs will fly across the London skyline before that happens."

"I heard that!"

"I think I can hear your taxi." Jenny went across to the window. "Yes, there's a cab outside."

"Have you got enough money?" asked Connie.

"Why?" Sadie had been on her way to the door, but she suddenly ground to a halt and swung around. "Won't he be paying?" She couldn't afford to pay the bill at a posh restaurant.

"I should think so. But if you have a row or you don't like him or if he tries something on and you don't want him to, will you have enough to get a taxi back here?"

"Yes, I have a few pounds in my purse." Sadie frowned. "I hope you haven't put a dampener on my night out. It never crossed my mind I wouldn't like him."

Jenny and Connie watched from the window, as the taxi pulled away from the kerb. "I hope she enjoys her evening out." Jenny closed the curtains. "I was surprised at you lending her your lovely evening bag. I was with you when you bought it and I recall it cost a small fortune."

"Oh, I don't mind lending it to her. I only hope she doesn't put it down somewhere and forget to pick it up. She can be such a scatterbrain." Connie laughed. "Besides, what else could I do? It was either lend her my bag or she would have taken that enormous thing she drags around the shops." She paused. "Thank goodness you thought of lending her your dress. Some of those things she wears are so, *quirky*, to say the very least."

Jenny grinned. "I know. But how do we go about telling her? I think she'll be terribly hurt if we actually come right out and say, Sadie, you have absolutely no dress sense at all."

"We'll have to work on that one; especially if Michael is going to stay on the scene." Connie glanced towards the kitchen. "But, in the meantime, what're we going to do this evening? Shall we eat in or out?"

CHAPTER TWELVE

Michael was waiting outside the restaurant, when Sadie stepped out of the taxi.

"I'll get that," he said, taking out his wallet.

"Thank you," said Sadie, smiling sweetly. "That's very kind," she added, recalling Connie instructions: be polite and watch your language. "I haven't been here before. It certainly looks very – nice." She had been going to say, posh, but thought better of it.

"I've only been here once myself, but I really enjoyed the evening. It was last Christmas and I was with some friends from the bank."

Stepping inside, they were met by a tall man in a dark suit. After checking the reservation he led them to their table. Sadie gazed around the large room and was overwhelmed. How nice of Michael to bring her to such a magnificent restaurant on a first date. Thinking back a few years, she recalled Alex had taken her for a pizza.

"Might I say how radiant you look tonight, Sadie?"

"Thank you, Michael." Sadie glowed with pleasure. Jenny had helped set her hair, while Connie applied her make-up. She'd hardly recognised herself when she'd stood in front of the mirror. Michael looked very smart in his evening jacket and bow tie. Should she remark on it? Did women usually compliment men on their appearance? She had never been in a situation like this before. Most of the men she had dated in the past had worn jeans.

"What would you like to drink?" asked Michael, beckoning the waiter.

"White wine, please." While Michael was ordering the drinks, Sadie cast her eyes around the sumptuous room. She wondered whether there would be anyone here she knew. How good it would be to see even one of her old friends; it would be good for them to see her with a man who thought enough of her to bring her to a place like this.

She was rather curious about why he had joined the dating agency. Obviously he was divorced, but what had made him decide to join Divorcees.biz? However she decided not to ask him about his private life. Not yet, anyway, perhaps later in the evening.

The waiter brought the drinks and left them to read through the menu.

"I think I'll have the soup, then the fish." Sadie closed the menu and took a sip of her wine.

"Sounds good, I'll have the same." Michael watched Sadie for a moment. "I joined the agency because of you."

"Sorry?" said Sadie. She thought she had misheard. It was almost as though he'd read her mind.

"I joined the dating agency because of you," he repeated. "I read the card you dropped in the bank before handing it back to you. Divorcees.biz dating agency, it said. I checked it out on the computer as soon as I got home that evening."

"Oh!" Sadie wasn't sure what else to say.

"I saw your photo on the screen and I read all about you. So I decided to join the agency and ask you out."

"Bloody hell!" gasped Sadie, slipping back into her more familiar language. "Are you telling me you paid two hundred and fifty quid plus another fifteen just to ask me out? You could have waited until the next time I came into the bank and saved yourself some cash – a whole lot of cash."

"Yes, I could. However, I didn't know how long I might have to wait. It could have been months before you showed up again. And if someone else usually does the banking, then you mightn't have come back at all."

"That's true," Sadie mumbled. "Jenny's the treasurer. I guess she'll see to most of the banking." She put her posh voice back on, hoping he hadn't noticed the slip-up earlier. "I'm so very flattered, Michael. To think you went to so much trouble and expense simply to ask me out." No one had ever done anything like that before. Alex had merely said 'Fancy a pizza?' in a take it or leave it sort of way.

Michael told her more about himself over dinner. It seemed his parents had been good people and given him an excellent education. He had lost his job as a financier a few years back, when the firm had gone under. "Total mismanagement," he said, thumping his fist on the table. "I told them countless times to cut back, but no one would listen to sense. They wanted to be among the big boys." He grinned. "There I go again, getting on my high horse."

Sadie smiled. "I bet the management came out of it with plenty of money and good pensions."

"Yes, they did. I had to change direction, as firms were cutting down their staff. That's why I went into the security business." He paused. "I'm not divorced."

"You're not?" Sadie uttered. What had she got herself into? Was he separated? Or even worse, was she his *bit on the side*? She swallowed hard. She might have done a lot of stupid things in her life, but being someone's bit on the side was not one of them and she didn't intend to start now.

"I'm a widower," he continued. "My wife died a few years back."

"I'm sorry." She tried not to show her relief.

He said that his wife had died of cancer and he had spent the last few years grieving. He would never forget her, but after bumping into Sadie, he realised he needed to get on with his life.

"But enough about me," he said, "tell me something about yourself."

"Not much to tell, really. I'm a funny sort of girl. Quirky, my friends call it. I think I drive them nuts, with my ideas and my…" She paused. She had been about to say her colourful language, but stopped herself in time.

"And your, *what?*" Michael prompted.

"Dress sense," she added, quickly. "I usually dress differently to the others."

"Like I said before, you look wonderful." Michael reached across the table and squeezed her hand.

"Thank you." Sadie blushed. Most of what she was wearing was either borrowed or had been applied by someone else. She would probably have worn her black and white zigzag striped dress and large orange earrings if the others hadn't talked her out of it. Glancing around the room, she was thankful she had listened to them. She would have stood out like a zebra crossing on a busy street.

"I was married for a number of years but, looking back, I don't know what I ever saw in him. He… never tried to make anything of himself." She fell silent. She had been going to say he was a no good, lazy son-of-a-bitch, but a picture of Connie popped into her mind's eye and she stopped herself. It was hard work trying to change the habits of a lifetime.

"Would you like to dance?" Michael pointed towards several couples waltzing around the floor.

"I'm afraid I'm not very good at ballroom dancing."

"I'll help you." Michael rose to his feet and held out his hand towards her.

She looked at the other dancers whirling effortlessly around the floor. "Erm, when I said I'm not very good at ballroom dancing, what I really meant to say was," she gulped, "I can't do it." She looked away. She felt so stupid. Here she was trying to sound as though she was part of London's high society and now she was being forced to admit she couldn't even dance.

"Then I'll teach you," said Michael.

She looked back to find Michael still holding out his hand.

"This is a waltz," he said. "Just follow me. You'll be fine."

Sadie rose to her feet and allowed Michael to lead her across to the dance floor. He took her right hand in his left and placed his right arm around her waist, before showing her the steps. "Back, together, close," he said. "Back, together, close."

Despite feeling awkward at first, she soon got the hang of it. Any dancing she had done in the past had been at discos, where it didn't really matter what you did. But she had a good sense of rhythm and was able to follow Michael quite easily. "This is cool. I'm actually doing a waltz," she exclaimed, as Michael whisked her around the floor. If only Connie could see her now.

****

"Why don't we go out somewhere nice for a meal?" suggested Connie. Sadie's cab had pulled away from the kerb and she and Jenny were wondering what to do.

Jenny nodded. Helping Sadie to get dressed up for her date had made her feel a little like Cinderella being left at home. "Why not?"

Connie grinned mischievously. "Let's change into something smart and go up to the West End. We'll treat ourselves."

"Sounds good, but nothing too expensive," replied Jenny. She was thinking of her bank account and how little money was in there at the moment.

"My treat." Connie held up her hands when Jenny opened her mouth to protest. "No arguments. Come on, let's change and get out of here."

Connie was dressed first. She had chosen to wear a rather striking low-cut red dress with matching shoes. While she was waiting for Jenny to put the final touches to her make-up, she decided to call a taxi. They could have taken a bus or even the tube, but this was a spur-of-the-moment outing, so why not go all the way.

"I think we should leave a note for Sadie in case she gets back before us," Jenny called out from upstairs.

"I doubt she will, but I'll scribble something and leave it on the table," Connie replied. "Are you nearly ready? I've got a taxi coming in about five minutes."

"Yes, I'm here. Will this do? Most of my evening wear is back at my flat."

Connie swung around to see Jenny wearing a black cocktail dress. She had dressed it up a little with a pretty gold coloured necklace and earrings. "You look very nice," she said.

"So do you." Jenny smiled and linked arms with Connie. "Watch out London, here we come."

Both women were still laughing when they climbed into the taxi a few minutes later.

"Where to?" asked the driver.

"London," replied Connie.

The driver took off his cap and scratched his head. "Yeah, you're already *in* London, lady. Whereabouts in London?"

The women looked at each other and started laughing all over again. "Drop us off in the middle of Piccadilly Circus and then we can decide where we want to go from there," Connie said at last.

"Okay." The driver started the engine and set off. It sounded like these two had hit the bottle already.

Connie's house wasn't too far from the West End, so it only took about fifteen minutes to reach the centre of London. After stepping out of the cab, Connie paid the fare. "Now, Jenny, which way?"

"Would it seem terribly awful, if we were to take a quick peek in Luigi's window?" she replied. "We might see Sadie with Michael."

"It does seem a bit naughty and she'll be furious if she sees us," said Connie. "But, what the heck, let's do it."

They hurried along Piccadilly. Neither could recall which side of the road the restaurant was on, so they had to check both sides as they went.

"There it is." Jenny pointed across the road.

Outside Luigi's they peered through the window. At first they couldn't see Sadie and wondered whether she and Michael had gone on somewhere else. But then Connie caught a glimpse of her on the dance floor. "Look! There she is – on the dance floor. I didn't know she could dance."

"She can't!" uttered Jenny.

"Well, she can now. Good for you, Sadie. Go for it." Connie stepped away from the window. "From the look on her face, I would say she's having a wonderful time. Her mood ring must be positively glowing at this moment. Perhaps we should go now." She had a sudden thought and grabbed Jenny's arm. "Did Lucy say she would watch the website tonight? Or are we supposed to be doing it?"

"I don't remember anyone mentioning it," said Jenny. "Shall I give her a ring?"

"No, forget it," said Connie after a moment's thought. "If she's out, she won't want to rush back any more than *we* do, and if she's in, she'll probably take a look anyway. I'll check it out when we get back." She paused. "Come on, Jenny, let's go and have some fun!"

CHAPTER THIRTEEN

Sadie's eyes sparkled as Michael led her from the dance floor. "I didn't think ballroom dancing could be so much fun." She put her hand over her mouth. "Sorry about treading on your foot. I hope I didn't hurt you."

"I didn't feel a thing." He smiled. "You're doing well, Sadie. You seem to have picked up the steps very quickly. We've gone through a waltz and the Foxtrot, now all you need to learn is the Quickstep. It can be a little tricky, but I'm sure you'll soon get the hang of it."

Sadie glanced around the room. Never in a million years had she expected to find herself on a date in a place like this. Since her divorce, any man who'd asked her out had taken her to a local pub. Even then, it was to watch him play darts or snooker with his mates.

She hid a grimace, when recalling how one man had even taken her to a football match. When they had arrived at the grounds, he yelled, 'Surprise'. She wondered where on earth he had got the idea that she liked football. Not having the heart to tell him she hated the game, she'd spent a very miserable afternoon, frozen half to death, on the terraces, trying to show some enthusiasm. She would have much rather been curled up in front of a warm fire, reading a book.

Michael was so different from any man she'd dated before. He knew how to treat a woman. He was very attentive:

holding her chair until she sat down, refilling her glass and, now, patiently teaching her how to dance. He reminded her a great deal of Andrew.

"Are you all right? You've gone very quiet." Michael interrupted her thoughts.

"Yes, I'm fine." Sadie paused. "Actually, I'm better than fine. I feel as though I'm walking on a cloud. Thank you so much for bringing me here tonight."

Michael smiled and rose to his feet. "May I have the pleasure of this dance?"

"I would be delighted," she replied, taking his arm.

****

"Okay, which road do we take?" said Connie. They were back in Piccadilly Circus. She pointed to each of the roads in turn. "Regent Street, Shaftsbury Avenue, Haymarket, What do you think?"

"I really don't mind, Connie. You choose."

"I know a nice place on Shaftsbury Avenue where they serve really good food. We could have a meal and then decide what else we want to do."

The restaurant was only half full when they arrived. However, the headwaiter, hovering by the door, said there was a table for two free in a corner at the back. "I'm not sure we want to be stuck right back there," said Connie, peering over his shoulder to see whether there was a more suitable table. "What about over there? It appears to be free." She pointed to a table much nearer to the front.

The headwaiter coughed. "We usually keep that table for couples."

"So, it's not actually booked at the moment?"

"No, Madam. As I said, we keep the table for couples."

"Perhaps we should just use the table at the back." Jenny hated causing a fuss.

Connie noticed him glancing towards the window. For a moment, she was puzzled, but then she had a thought. "Oh, I get it! If a couple pass by looking for somewhere to eat and see a handsome young couple sitting here enjoying a meal, then they'll think this is a great place to bring their date – or something like that. Well, tonight, any couples will have to look further back, because my friend and I are going to sit there."

"But…" the headwaiter began.

"But nothing," interrupted Connie. "If you forbid us to use that table, then I shall have this restaurant taken to court for discrimination!"

"Well," the headwaiter grumbled, "if you're going to be awkward…"

"Yes, you bet I'm going to be awkward!" Connie grabbed Jenny's arm and marched her across to the table.

"Discrimination against what?" asked Jenny after they had sat down.

"I've no idea, but with all the rules and regulations flying around these days, my guess is we would have found something very quickly. Besides, Andrew and I have been here countless times and I've never noticed any problem about seating arrangements before. If the regular guy had been on duty then he would've recognised me. Come to think of it, where is the regular guy?" Connie sighed. "He must have left or perhaps this is his night off. Anyway, let's look at the menu."

The headwaiter kept casting unpleasant glances in their direction. He was rather annoyed his authority had been questioned.

"So, who's the gorilla on the door?" Connie asked the waiter when he came to take their order.

"Albert," the waiter muttered, without looking around. "He's part of the new management. Joseph is off tonight. I think he's looking for another job. He isn't keen on the new rules since the place was taken over."

"Like keeping certain tables free for couples?"

"Yes, but that's only one of many." He shuffled his feet. "I better take your order."

"Don't let the miserable man by the door spoil our evening," said Connie after the waiter had disappeared into the kitchen. "The food here has always been wonderful. I doubt they've changed the chef. That would be pure madness, he's absolutely brilliant."

Just then two men walked in carrying briefcases. The headwaiter began to lead them towards the back of the restaurant, but one of the men pointed to the table next to Jenny and Connie. The headwaiter opened his mouth to say something, but, after glancing at Connie, he changed his mind. "Yes, of course, sir" he said.

"Good evening, ladies," said one of the men, as he lowered himself into a chair. "As we're going to be neighbours, so to speak, perhaps we should introduce ourselves. This is David Edwards and I'm John Hutchins."

"Good evening to you both. I'm Connie and this is my friend and colleague, Jenny."

"Enjoying a meal out this evening?" said David.

"Yes, it beats cooking and washing up," replied Connie, taking a sip of her wine. She nodded to the waiter, as he placed the starters in front of her and Jenny.

"Bon appétit." David smiled at Jenny before turning to the waiter to order his meal.

During the course of the evening Connie and Jenny learned the two men were in London to attend a business conference. "We go back to Peterborough tomorrow." David told them.

Connie explained how she and Jenny had set up a new online dating agency. "There are also two other friends involved. The whole thing is still very much in its infancy, but we're making progress every day," she said, handing them a card. "If you know anyone who is divorced and looking for a respectable agency, perhaps you could mention us."

Jenny tugged at Connie's arm. "For goodness sake, you can't go touting for business in every restaurant," she whispered.

"I'm not touting for business in every restaurant. I'm just mentioning it to these two…" She paused. "Gosh Jenny! That's a good idea, though. We were wondering how to get our agency known without it costing a fortune. That could be the answer. We'll get some leaflets printed and ask some of the better restaurants and clubs to display them on their counters."

Jenny agreed; it did sound a good way of getting the agency known.

"I guess we'd better be going now." Connie smiled at the two men. Since finishing their meal, she and Jenny had been discussing where to go next. Connie rather liked the idea of going on to a nightclub, a place where they could dance and have some fun. However, Jenny wasn't so keen. She said she would rather go to a cocktail lounge in one of the plush hotels. "I've never done that, so it would be a first for me."

After glancing at her watch, Connie agreed. It was getting rather late. A leisurely drink somewhere would round the evening off, though it wasn't what she would call 'having fun', which, to her mind, had been the whole point of going out that evening. However, she had enjoyed the meal, and chatting to the men on the next table.

"You never know, we might meet again somewhere." David leapt to his feet and helped Jenny with her coat.

"Yes, that would be very nice," Jenny gushed. "Thank you. I hope you enjoy the rest of your meal."

"Thank you, John," said Connie, as he held her coat.

At the desk, Connie presented her credit card to the headwaiter.

"I trust everything was in order," he said.

"No. Not quite."

"Not quite?" he repeated.

"Yes, that's what I said. Not quite." Connie paused, while she tapped her pin number into the machine. "Let me explain. Your waiter was both courteous and helpful," replied Connie, slowly. "The meal was excellent, which means you still have the same chef. However, I feel the man on the door needs to take a few lessons in manners. "

"The man on the door?" He looked through the window. "But we don't have a door…" He was scowling, when he turned back to face her. "You mean me!"

"Yes, I do. Good night!"

Outside, Connie burst out laughing. "I enjoyed that. Did you see those two women at the back straining to hear? I hope I spoke loud enough. They should do the same. I noticed they were ushered to the back very quickly when they came in. The nerve of the man."

"Do you realise you're beginning to act like Sadie?"

"What!" Connie shrieked, stopping in her tracks. "Me, behave like Sadie. Oh my God, I hope not. I must be spending too much time with her."

"Well," Jenny paused, "not exactly like Sadie. She would have used much more explicit language, but you're becoming a little – shall I say, quizzical – tying everyone in knots."

"Quizzical? Gosh, do you really think so?" Connie stared at her reflection in a shop window. "Please tell me I'm not really becoming too much like Sadie."

Jenny burst out laughing. "So, what did you think of David?" she asked, changing the subject.

"I thought he was very nice. He seemed to like you, Jenny. They were both very sweet, helping us with our coats in the middle of their meal." She looked up and down the street. "Okay, where shall we go for our drink? Did you have anywhere in mind."

"What about the Langley? And before you say a word, I'm sure it's expensive, but we could sit there with one drink and make it last. I'll pay for it."

"The Langley sounds good to me. The cocktail lounge there is lovely, though it's a while since Andrew…" She broke off. Why did she have to keep thinking about Andrew? "We'll get a cab," she added, waving down a passing taxi.

"Like I said, I've never been there," said Jenny, as she stepped into the cab. "But I've heard about it."

"Just you wait and see. You're in for a lovely surprise. And you must try one of their specials. They're all wonderful."

****

"Are you enjoying the evening?" Michael squeezed Sadie's hand as he led her back to their table.

"Enjoying it? Michael, this has got to be one of the most wonderful nights of my life." Sadie flopped into the chair. "I didn't realise what I was missing. I always thought ballroom dancing was something older folk did during the afternoon at their local dance hall. Yet, it isn't. It is so romantic." She blushed. Was she sounding too eager? Perhaps. Nevertheless, she was really enjoying Michael's company and wanted him to know how she felt.

He was a real gentleman; so thoughtful. She only hoped her occasional lapse into more questionable language wouldn't put him off. She had tried so hard to follow Connie's advice, but occasionally some forbidden word would slip through the net.

"We make a good team. We'll have to do this again." He looked at his watch. "It's getting late. Are you expected back? Is someone waiting for you?"

"Good God, no." Sadie kicked herself under the table. Come on girl, get a grip; you're beginning to sound too keen. He will think you're desperate. "What I mean is, I'm renting a room from my friend, Connie, at the moment and I have my own door key."

Michael smiled. "In that case what about another drink? And then we'll tackle the Quickstep again. I really think you'll get it the next time."

"Yes, please." Sadie smiled. She wondered whether she should offer to pay for something. She had seen the pricelist. Actually, she had almost choked when she saw the pricelist.

She guessed food and drinks wouldn't come cheap in a place like this. However, when she saw what they charged for a bottle of wine she thought it was an absolute disgrace. Michael was a security guard in a bank. True it was a large bank and it was a responsible job – he could get killed trying to stop it from being robbed – but, nevertheless, he was still just a security guard, not bloody Chancellor of the Exchequer.

All too soon the band played the last waltz and the evening came to an end. Sadie hovered from one foot to another when Michael went to pay the bill. She still didn't know whether she should offer some money.

Outside, Michael hailed a passing cab. "I'll see you home," he said.

"There's no need, I'll be fine," she said. It was late and Michael had to get home himself (wherever his 'home' was).

Nevertheless he insisted. "You never know who might be lurking around at this time of night."

She shivered as she thought of Rob hanging around Jenny's flat the other evening. "Michael." She hesitated. "I don't know how to word this, so I'll just come out and say it. Would you like me to put something towards the bill? I mean…"

He held up his hand and laughed. "Of course not. It was nice of you to think about it, though."

"Thank you," she replied. "I've had a really lovely evening."

It wasn't long before they arrived at Connie's house, "Would you like a coffee or something?" Sadie asked, as the driver pulled up at the door.

"No thank you, it's very late and I'm on duty early in the morning." He would love to have accepted her offer for coffee. They'd had such a lovely evening and he really enjoyed being with her so much, he didn't want to leave. She was like a breath of fresh air in his dry and dusty life. But this was their first date and he didn't want her to think he was being too forward. "Perhaps we could meet up again? See a show or a film?"

"Yes, thank you. I'd like that." Sadie tried not to sound over keen. But on second thoughts, neither did she want him going away believing she wasn't interested. "Wait! I'll give you my mobile number." She wrote down the number and handed it to him.

Michael leaned forward and pressed his lips against hers. His kiss was warm and gentle; everything a woman expected from a kiss on a first date. Yet, at the same time, it held the hint of a passion Sadie had only read about in love stories. All too soon, he drew away. "Good night, Sadie. I'll give you a ring," he said, before turning and walking back to the taxi.

For a moment, Sadie couldn't speak. She placed her fingers to her lips, trying desperately to relive the wonderful moment. "The office number is on the website," she called out at last. She watched until the cab reached the corner of the road, before turning the key in the door. "Hi guys, I'm back!" she yelled as the door swung open.

****

Michael waved as the taxi turned the corner at the end of the road, but he doubted Sadie had seen him. It was too dark. As the cab wound its way through the almost deserted streets, he sat back in his seat and recalled their evening together. For a first date, it had gone rather well, he thought. Sadie was quite a girl and he liked her a great deal. She was so unlike most of the other people he'd seen coming into the bank.

She seemed such a down to earth person. No airs and graces: what you saw was what you got and he had definitely liked what he had seen this evening. Yes, he'd really enjoyed her company and was looking forward to meeting up with her again.

****

"I wonder if Lucy is still up," said Connie, as she stepped out of the taxi. She and Jenny had arrived at the Langley.

Jenny glanced at her watch. "It's gone eleven. She could be in bed, sound asleep."

"Well, then let's wake her up and see whether she wants to join us." Connie pulled out her mobile phone and stabbed in the number. "It's ringing." She grinned at Jenny. "She can only say no."

"She can say a hell of a lot more than *no*, being woken up at this time of night."

"Hello, Lucy, is that you? You sound different. For a moment, I thought I had the wrong number." Connie put her hand over the mouthpiece. "She was brushing her teeth and had a mouthful of toothpaste," she whispered to Jenny. "We're outside the Langley – Jenny and I, that is, Sadie is on her date. Anyway, we're going for a drink in the cocktail bar and wondered whether you might like to come, too." She nodded at Jenny. "Great! Well hurry up, we'll meet you inside." She was just about to shut her phone, when she heard Lucy's voice. "What was that?" she asked. "Oh, just wear something smart. You'll be fine. We're only having a drink, not a banquet." She clicked off the phone. "She's going to get a taxi and should be here in about twenty minutes."

Inside the hotel, Connie made a bee-line for the ladies room. "I'm going to refresh my make-up. You never know who you might meet in a place like this."

"I'll do the same. Besides, I don't want to walk into the bar on my own."

"We look a million dollars," said Connie, as they left the ladies room. "It's amazing what a bit of lipstick will do for you."

"Oh my goodness," Jenny stopped in her tracks and her jaw dropped, when they walked into the cocktail bar. "I really didn't think it would be so grand." She had been overwhelmed at the hotel's sumptuous lobby, but this was something else.

"Close your mouth, Jenny. You could catch flies in it." Connie laughed. "But yes, it is wonderful." She pointed to a table across the room. "Let's sit over there, then we'll be able to see Lucy when she walks in."

Jenny sat down on one of the comfortable chairs and gazed around the room.

"Can I get you anything?" One of the waiters was hovering with a notepad in his hand.

"We're waiting for a friend," Connie replied. "She shouldn't be long."

"There she is now." Jenny waved across to Lucy, who was standing at the entrance.

"Could you give us a minute," Connie said to the waiter.

He disappeared back to the bar.

"What on earth made you decide to come here," whispered Lucy. She had sat down and was now looking at the drinks menu. "Have you seen these prices?"

"I have to admit it was my idea," said Jenny. "It's my treat, by the way, so I can only afford one drink, you'll have to make it last."

"Were you ready for bed?" Connie asked.

"Not quite. I'd been watching the site for most of the evening and was getting a little bored with it, so coming out was a welcome break."

"Gosh! Don't look now, but those two men we met at the restaurant have just walked in." Jenny quickly turned her head away.

"Restaurant! You mean you've been to a restaurant, too? Lucky devils." Lucy sighed. "I wish you'd invited me."

"It wasn't planned!" Connie broke in. "After getting Sadie ready for her date, Jenny and I thought we might like to go out rather than start cooking something."

"How did Sadie look when she left?" Lucy asked. "Did you manage to get her to wear something nice?"

"She looked great!" Jenny replied. "We persuaded her to wear my green dress. You know – the one I wore at the launch. I did her hair and managed to soften her tight curls a little, while Connie did her make-up."

"Thank goodness! I had visions of her turning up to Luigi's wearing one of those weird outfits she buys."

"She would have done, if we hadn't tactfully intervened," Connie laughed. "Okay, what would you like to drink?" Connie had seen the waiter coming back towards them.

They all decided to have a Singapore Sling.

"Good evening. So, we meet again."

They looked up to see David and John standing by the table. David was smiling down at Jenny.

"Hello," Connie introduced Lucy to the two men.

"Do you mind if we join you?" Without waiting for a reply, David pulled up a chair next to Jenny.

The waiter arrived with the drinks the ladies had ordered. "Put those on my tab," said David, without taking his eyes off Jenny. "And would you bring us our usual?"

Jenny glanced sideways at Connie. They hardly knew these men and now they were paying for their drinks – not just any old drinks, but these madly expensive ones. She hoped they weren't under the impression they were call girls on the pull.

"Thank you, David. That's very kind of you." Connie picked up her glass and took a sip. "This is lovely, Jenny." Without the men seeing, she nudged her friend and nodded towards the drink on the table.

"Yes, thank you, David." Jenny smiled. If Connie was okay about it, then so was she.

They chattered for the next hour. It seemed David and John were staying at the Langley. They would be heading back to Peterborough the following morning after spending the last three days in London. "The conference was only part of the reason we're here. Our company is keen to move the business nearer to London," John told them. "However, finding suitable and, more importantly, affordable premises in this economic climate isn't easy.

"But we think we might have come up with something worth looking into," added David. "If it all works out, we could be moving to London very soon."

Connie hadn't failed to notice David's obsession with Jenny. Who could blame him? Jenny was a very attractive lady. She glanced at Lucy, but her eyes were firmly fixed on John and he appeared to be taking more than a passing interest in her. She was beginning to feel a little like a gooseberry. She would have left her friends and gone home, but she knew they wouldn't let her go back alone and she didn't want to spoil their evening.

"I think we'd better go now." Jenny glanced at her watch. "It's very late. Besides, they must be closing shortly."

"Yes," said Lucy reluctantly. She wished she had met John earlier in the evening. She rather liked him and hoped he felt the same about her. He had kept looking in her direction, which had to mean something.

"Perhaps we could meet up the next time we're in London? John and I might be here again in the next two or three weeks, if the board is interested in the property we've found."

"That would be very nice." Jenny gave David a warm smile. "I'll look forward to it." She wondered whether she should give him her phone number. On the other hand, he might not really mean it. Once he was back on the road again, he could easily forget about her. However, the problem was solved when the suggestion to exchange phone numbers came from David.

Jenny jotted down two phone numbers. "The top one is Connie's number. I'm staying with her at the moment. I've added my mobile number as well."

John asked for Lucy's number, which she was more than happy to give. He gave her a card showing both his home and office number.

Outside, John hailed a taxi and the three friends piled in. "I'll be in touch," David called out as the cab drove off. "Me too," yelled John.

"Wasn't he wonderful?" gushed Jenny, still clutching the card with David's phone number on it. "I'm glad we decided to go to the Langley. I might never have seen him again if we'd gone to a nightclub."

"I'm only too pleased you called me to join you, otherwise I would never have met John at all." Sinking back into the seat, Lucy decided she was definitely going to lose some weight. She would start a new diet tomorrow and stick to it. If – no, she had to think positive here – *when* she met John again, she was going to be several pounds lighter.

"We'll drop you off first, Lucy." Connie broke into her thoughts. She gave the driver the address, before giving Lucy a prod. "Are you still with us? You seem to be miles away. What're you thinking about?"

"Losing weight."

Connie laughed. "Where have I heard that before?"

"I mean it this time! When John and I meet up again, I want to be slimmer." Lucy hesitated. "Do you think he meant it, when he said he would get in touch? I mean, look at me." She gestured towards her hips. "I must have looked like a beached whale compared to Jenny and you."

"Nevertheless, it was you he gave his number to." Connie smiled. "You know, you run yourself down too much. You aren't that overweight, Lucy. Certainly nowhere near being a beached whale, as you so eloquently put it."

"We're pulling into your road," said Jenny, glancing out of the window. She looked back at Lucy. "Connie's right. You do tend to criticise yourself too much."

The cab came to a halt outside Lucy's flat and she jumped out. "I'll settle up with you guys in the morning." She giggled. "It's morning now. Thanks for inviting me." She waved as the taxi pulled away.

****

"Hi, guys. I found your note." Connie and Jenny both nearly jumped out of their skin. They had been creeping along the hall so as to not wake Sadie and she had suddenly popped up from nowhere.

"Oh my God!" Jenny clutched her throat. "You nearly frightened the life out of me. We thought you'd be in bed and didn't want to wake you."

"I just got back a few minutes ago. I've put the kettle on," replied Sadie. "Where've you been?"

"We went out for a meal. After getting you all dolled up, we felt like going out ourselves." Connie paused. "Did you have a good time?"

"Yes, I had a lovely evening." Sadie waltzed around the kitchen and took three mugs from the hooks under the shelf as she passed. "Michael is wonderful, the restaurant was superb, the food was delicious. Michael is absolutely wonderful, the band was brilliant, the service was great – and did I mention how wonderful Michael is?"

"No, you didn't mention him at all. So, tell us, what do you think of Michael?" Connie winked at Jenny mischievously. "Is he any good?"

"Don't start her off again," Jenny groaned. "Otherwise we'll be here all night."

"Don't be like that, Jen. I've just had the most wonderful evening imaginable and I was bursting to tell you about it, but neither of you were here." Sadie took the tea caddie out of the cupboard. "Tea anyone?" she asked. "Where've you been, anyway?"

"We went for a meal at a restaurant in Shaftsbury Avenue. Then Jenny fancied going for drink at the Langley." Connie yawned. "I'm starting to feel tired."

"Pushing the boat out, weren't you, Jen? I don't imagine it's cheap there." Sadie handed out the mugs of tea.

"No, it isn't, but it's really lovely."

"Go on, then, tell her about the men you and Lucy met." Connie prompted.

"Men? Lucy? So Lucy went, too?"

"She wasn't with us at the restaurant." Jenny went on to explain they had first met the men while having dinner and how it had been a surprise when they turned up at the hotel. "By then, Lucy had joined us. John and David even paid for our drinks, so it didn't cost us a penny." She held up the card David had given her, with his home and office numbers. "John gave his to Lucy, so we might hear from them."

"Lucy's going on a diet," added Connie.

Sadie rolled her eyes. "Oh no! Not another one! Please save me from Lucy on a diet. I don't think I can stand the strain again."

"I think she means it this time." Connie yawned again. "I'm beat. I'm going to take my tea up to bed. See you both at around eight o'clock in the morning. I think we're all going to be late getting to the office."

"We better go to bed as well," mumbled Jenny.

Nevertheless, as Sadie and Jenny were still sharing a bed, they talked long into the night before finally falling asleep.

CHAPTER FOURTEEN

"Sorry I'm late. I overslept." Lucy bustled into the office and threw her bag onto the desk.

"Don't worry about it. We've only just arrived ourselves." Jenny laughed. "We all had a late night, didn't we?" She paused. "But it was fun."

"My aunt phoned as I was leaving. She's really looking forward to her date, but I think she's a little concerned Andrew might change his mind about taking her out, due to her age and everything, and simply not turn up. I assured her he wasn't the sort of person to do something like that." She paused. "He wouldn't, would he, Connie?"

"No, of course he wouldn't," snapped Connie. "Andrew isn't like that at all. Your aunt is a very lucky lady to be going out with him." Feeling guilty at her outburst, she quickly looked down at the pile of mail lying on the desk. Why had she yelled at Lucy? It wasn't her fault. She needed to get a grip. Yet the very thought of Andrew taking another woman out to dinner, no matter what age that woman might be, disturbed her.

Biting her lip, Lucy flashed a glance at the others. She wished she hadn't mentioned her aunt's call. She had wanted to follow it up by telling them she had also heard from John. Though they had only spoken for a few moments, it had been good to hear from him. It meant he hadn't forgot about her in the cold light of a new day. Connie's eruption had spoiled the moment. There was no reason why she should speak to her like that. If Connie wanted her ex-husband back, then she should have been more encouraging when they met a few days ago. Without another word, Lucy picked up her bag and walked out of the office.

"Was that really necessary?" Sadie leapt to her feet. "Connie you're a good friend to me and I'd do anything for you, but right now I have to tell you you're a real idiot!" Connie looked up sharply and opened her mouth as though to say something. But Sadie continued, not giving her chance to get a word in. "What Andrew does has nothing to do with Lucy – or you. If he wants to take Agnes out for a meal, he can. He doesn't need your permission. You and Andrew are divorced." She spelled it out. "D.I.V.O.R.C.E.D. That means he's his own man. He gets to go out with whoever he likes!" She looked towards the door. "I'm going after Lucy."

"No! Wait! You're right." Connie grabbed her coat and handbag. "I'll go after her. I'll take her for a coffee. Somewhere we can talk." Before rushing out of the door, she glanced at Jenny. "Check the mail. I think I saw an envelope with the Royale printed on the front. It might be their bill."

"Oops! Andrew taking someone out to dinner has really upset Connie more than she's saying," said Jenny, after Connie had disappeared down the stairs. She picked up the envelope Connie had mentioned.

"Yes, it has," replied Sadie thoughtfully. Her plan was working well, perhaps too well. She only wanted Connie to be a little put out at Andrew taking someone for a meal, not start ranting and raving at Lucy because the lady in question happened to be her aunt. Goodness knows what Connie would do if she learned Sadie'd had a hand in the whole affair. She looked across at Jenny, who was peering at the account from the Royale. "What's up? You look as though you've seen a ghost."

"Oh my goodness." Jenny shook her head. "Almost nine thousand pounds!"

"That's not too bad. I thought it might have been more. We had a lot of food…"

"Sadie! The nine thousand pounds is for the drinks alone! It seems we got through around one hundred and seventy bottles of champagne." Jenny looked further down the account. "The food comes to another…"

"Just tell me the total." Sadie interrupted, as she lowered herself into her chair. "But wait until I am firmly seated with something to hold onto."

"Twenty – five – thousand – pounds." Jenny spoke slowly so Sadie wouldn't misunderstand.

"Twenty five grand! I think I need to lie down." Sadie sank back in her chair. "I thought Connie said we got a deal on the food."

"We did."

"And it's still twenty-five grand?" She grinned. "Perhaps we'd have got another three thousand pounds discount if we had all shown our cleavage!"

"There's nearly ten thousand on the drinks bill." Jenny looked up at Sadie. "It seems we weren't only paying for the champagne. There are several other drinks on here as well. Gin, brandy, whisky…"

"Don't tell me any more." Sadie gasped. "I can't believe people were going to the bar and adding their drinks onto our tab when we had champagne flowing like water. They must have been drinking like fish all evening.""Thank God most of the people joined our agency on the night, otherwise we wouldn't have been able to pay the bill," said Jenny, nodding her head in agreement. "Then where would we have been?"

"In deep shit," Sadie retorted.

Jenny rolled her eyes as she picked up another envelope. "This one is from the photographer. He's charging us fifteen hundred pounds."

"We're in the wrong business, Jenny. Fifteen hundred pounds – for what? All he did was take a few photos, drink our champagne and eat our food." She cocked her head to one side. "It seems to me, we actually paid the guy to eat and drink our stuff. Nice work if you can get it."

****

Connie caught up with Lucy outside. "I'm sorry," she said, linking her arm. "I didn't mean to be nasty."

Lucy stopped walking and pulled her arm away. "Connie, if you want Andrew back, then you should meet up with him and tell him how you feel. Otherwise, let it go and get on with your life."

Connie looked down Park lane. "Shall we go for a coffee and a cake somewhere?"

"I'm on a diet!" Lucy retorted sullenly.

"Yes, of course… I forgot." Connie shifted from one foot to another. This wasn't going well. "Okay, then we'll just have coffee."

Lucy sighed. The last thing she wanted to do right now was to talk to Connie. But, realising they had to work together, she needed to get over it. "Okay. Where do you want to go?"

They found a table in Starbucks on Oxford Street. Connie told Lucy to sit down, while she went to the counter. "I'm sorry, Lucy," she said, when she returned with the coffee. "I know my problem has nothing to do with you or your aunt and I shouldn't have snapped at you. Of course Andrew won't let her down." Connie placed her elbows on the table and sank her chin into her hands. "My life seems to be in a muddle at the moment."

"Muddle? Listen to yourself, Connie. We're all divorced and hoping to find our Mr Right. Yet at the same time, we're scared to take the plunge again for fear of ending up with the same type of person we divorced. It turns out that Jenny's ex was a womaniser and now seems to be stalking her, while Sadie's is a loser and hanging out with a prostitute simply to get back into the flat. Which, incidentally, I think Sadie was paying for, because Alex never contributed much money to anything. How low can a man get? My ex-husband is a bully. He used to beat me up because he drank too much and it made him feel like a man. Can you believe that? The bastard felt like a man because he could beat up a defenceless woman. The other night he shoved me into a doorway. For a moment I thought he was going to kill me until my friend intervened. No one else gave a damn!" She looked away and shook her head. "Can you believe that? All those people walked past and not one gave a damn whether someone was being murdered a couple of feet away." She shivered. Even now, here in the safety of this café, she could see Ben towering over her, his fist poised ready to strike. She turned back to Connie. "You haven't got a clue about the real world. Andrew worships you, he always has. But you know that already. Yet you can't seem to be able to get his one indiscretion out of your mind. That's okay; it's up to you. It's your decision. However you can't blame me or any of your friends if he decides to move on."

"So? What's your point?" asked Connie. She had allowed Lucy to talk without interruption, but she wasn't sure what she was supposed to gain from it.

"What's my point? What's my point? Haven't you been listening to a word I've said? My point is this: Your life isn't in a muddle, Connie – not really. Your problems are of your own making. You simply need to get a grip, sit down and think hard about where you want to go from here. If you decide Andrew is out of the equation, you need to forget about him and move on. But, if you want your husband back, then for goodness sake, do something about it before someone else snaps him up." She grinned. "Someone like my aunt. She isn't an old lady who knits socks all day. She might be getting on a bit, but she's still quite an attractive woman. And I'm telling you she's bought herself a new dress for her evening out with Andrew!"

Connie bent her head and looked down at the table. Lucy was right; Sadie was right. She should meet Andrew again for a drink somewhere and have a long talk. Yet she couldn't get past the floozy. She simply couldn't get her head around the fact Andrew had played away. And as long as she felt like that, then what was the point?

"I hear what you're saying, Lucy. Sadie keeps telling me the same thing. I know you both want to help, but I just can't bring myself to accept what Andrew did." She sighed. "Perhaps one day I'll come to terms with it and then we'll take it from there."

"Perhaps by then it'll be too late." Lucy drained her coffee cup and placed it back on the saucer. "I think we better head back to the office."

"Yes." Connie stood up slowly. Lucy's last remark was ringing in her ears. 'By then it'll be too late'. She was right. One day it would be too late. One day Andrew would tire of waiting for her and walk out of her life forever. She sighed. Maybe it would be for the best if he did. Then she could put him out of her mind altogether and look for another man on the agency website. After all, that was what they had set it up for in the first place.

They left the coffee shop and walked back to the office in silence.

****

"Get a load of this!" Sadie picked up the account from the Royale and waved it at Connie and Lucy the moment they entered the office. "Twenty-five grand! Twenty-five grand for one evening! I don't know how the Royale has the nerve."

Taking the bill from Sadie, Connie sat down and began to read through it.

"Most of the money was spent on drinks. It seems some folks helped themselves at the bar," added Jenny.

"Okay, there's nothing we can do. There's no alternative, we'll have to pay them." Connie sighed heavily. "I really didn't think everyone would guzzle champagne all evening. A couple of glasses during the evening was what I intended. But to have gone through almost a hundred and eighty bottles, that's an awful lot of champagne. I'm surprised the hotel had so many bottles in the cellar."

"I expect they increased their order, when they realised we were serving champagne all evening and not changing to something cheaper after the first few bottles." Jenny sniffed. "Still we'll know what to do the next time."

"The next time?" Sadie screeched, leaping to her feet. "What next time?"

"Calm down, Sadie, it was only a figure of speech," Jenny added, quickly.

"Anything else?" asked Connie.

"The photographer has sent in his account, too." Jenny handed her the bill. "He's asking for fifteen hundred." She glanced at Sadie. "Do you think we should speak to them both about their accounts being so high?"

"No. I think we should simply write out the cheques and get it over with." Connie wasn't in the mood for arguing about money right now. Her mind was preoccupied with the conversation she'd had with Lucy. If Andrew were out of her life forever, would she be able to settle down with another man? Or would she still be wondering about what he was doing? Who he was seeing?

Jenny broke the silence. "I heard from David this morning on my mobile," she chirped. She had wanted to burst out the news to everyone at the office earlier, but the bust up between Lucy and Connie had rather spoilt it.

"You got a call from David?" Sadie uttered. "You and I have been sitting here together all morning and you never mentioned you got a call from David. What did he say?"

"Not a lot. He and John were waiting for the train. He simply wanted to say hello."

"Hello? And that was it? Just hello?" Sadie frowned.

"Yes. Well, he said a couple of other things, but then the train came in and he had to go." She paused. "But he rang and that has got to be a good sign." She looked at her friends. "Well, hasn't it?"

"Yes, of course it's a good sign." Connie was pleased the conversation had moved on from the two rather large accounts they were faced with. It also gave her something else to think about other than what Andrew was up to.

"John called, too," said Lucy. "The call came as I was leaving home, which is another reason why I was late this morning. He was at the station with David, so he couldn't talk long. But he did say he would be in touch this evening when he got back home. Both he and David were going straight to the office when they reached Peterborough."

"That's great, Lucy, and you, too, Jenny. It means they weren't messing around last night," said Connie. "What about you, Sadie? Have you heard anything from Michael?"

"No, not yet, but he did say he would like to meet up with me again." Sadie's eyes glazed over as she thought about the night before. "He's really very nice and certainly knows how to treat a lady. Not like some of the scum-bags I've met."

"A couple of messages have dropped into our inbox." Lucy clicked the mouse to open the first one. "This one is from Michael Stone. He wants us to introduce him to Charlotte Strong."

"He's putting it about it a bit, isn't he?" Sadie laughed. "Still, it's money in our pockets, so why should we complain?"

"As long as he continues to ask for meetings to be arranged one at a time." Connie was still unsure about this man's intentions. She could have kicked herself for not setting down a few ground rules when they first formed the agency. "I was wondering whether it was too late to make a few rules. Obviously, it would've been better if we'd given the whole idea more thought at the outset." She shrugged. "But we didn't. Is it too late now?"

"I'm not sure." Lucy looked at the blank faces of her friends. "If some people aren't happy with any rules we make, they may want to leave and ask for their money back."

Connie hadn't thought of that. It would be a blow if people decided to ask for refunds. They needed their money to pay the two massive accounts they'd received that morning. "In that case, one of the rules would have to state there would be no refunds if clients decided to leave."

"That goes without saying, doesn't it?" Sadie frowned. "What I mean is, I hope our clients aren't expecting their money back if they decide to get married and have no further use for the agency."

"No way," said Connie. This was going from bad to worse. "We need to have something to that effect on the site."

"Don't worry. I'll add a few words in a minute. But, getting back to the emails for the moment, the other is from Brian Lomax." Lucy smiled. "He seems to have given up on you, Connie. He's now asking to be introduced to Ann Masters."

"She's welcome," laughed Connie. "Write to her and see what she says."

The rest of the day went smoothly. Several new messages came in requesting meetings with other clients, while a curt reply from Ann Masters told them she was declining Brian's offer.

"Can't say I blame her," said Lucy as she typed a message to Brian Lomax informing him of Ann's decision. "However," she added as she clicked the send button, "I do feel sorry for him. So far everyone has turned him down," She glanced at her watch. "If no one minds, I'm going to shoot off now. I promised my aunt I would call in to see her new dress." She bit her lip. Perhaps she shouldn't have said why she was leaving early. Clearly Connie was still smarting about Andrew's date with her aunt.

"That's okay. I'll keep an eye on the site." Connie tried to sound brighter than she felt. "I'm not going out this evening, so I'll do Website Watch tonight." At least it would give her something to keep her mind occupied.

At that moment, the phone rang. "It's for you, Sadie." Lucy passed over the receiver.

"Hello," said Sadie cautiously. "Michael!" she squealed, after the caller revealed who he was. "Lovely to hear from you."

The others looked on, while Sadie listened to what Michael had to say.

"Yes, I would love to," she gushed. "Oh! Wait a minute, I better ask if Connie needs me with the Website Watch tonight." She gave Connie a pained expression, which clearly said 'you don't really need me, do you?'

But Connie was already flapping her hands. 'Go,' she mouthed.

"It's okay. Connie doesn't need me." Sadie paused. "That's great, I'll be ready." She was beaming when she put down the phone. "It seems someone has a couple of tickets for a show in the West End and now they can't go, so Michael bought them from him." She clasped her hands together. "Isn't that wonderful?" She hesitated and pulled a face. "I didn't mean it to come out like that. Obviously it's a shame for the people who can't go, but it's good news for me. If you see what I mean."

"Stop while you're ahead," said Lucy. She had hung back to hear what Michael had to say. "Anyway, enjoy your evening. I'd better be off."

The others listened as Lucy's high-heeled shoes clattered down the stairs.

"For the money they charge us, and all the others in this building, you'd thing they would carpet the stairs instead of just painting the wooden steps a dull grey colour," moaned Jenny.

"Yes, well." Connie didn't want to get embroiled in an argument about the premises. It was she who had wanted a Mayfair address and she had got one – albeit the office was far too small and way too expensive.

****

Connie switched on her laptop and brought the Divorcees.biz website onto the screen. She, Sadie, and Jenny had arrived back home and she wanted to make sure no one had tried to contact them since they left the office.

Meanwhile, Sadie, who had rushed upstairs the moment she burst through the front door, was pulling clothes from the wardrobe and throwing them in a heap on the bed. "We're going for a meal before the show and Michael will be here very soon," she yelled down to her friends. "What do you think I should wear?"

Jenny and Connie looked at each other and smiled. "We're coming," they chorused.

CHAPTER FIFTEEN

Once Sadie disappeared out of the door, Connie and Jenny flopped down onto the sofa. While Sadie had been in the shower, they'd checked through her clothes, desperately trying to find something suitable for an evening at the theatre. In the end, they'd managed to persuade her to wear Jenny's black cocktail dress, together with a gold necklace belonging to Connie.

"If Sadie is going to carry on seeing this guy, then we've got to take her shopping!" uttered Jenny. "We're running out of clothes fast."

"You know something?" laughed Connie, "a short while ago, she wouldn't have been seen dead in the sort of clothes we wear. Fortunately, you and Sadie are about the same size, otherwise she'd have been really stuck." Connie was a size larger than either of them, so borrowing her dresses, though appropriate for any occasion, was out of the question. "I think we'd better get ourselves something to eat," she continued. "After that, I'm afraid it's Website Watch for me." It wasn't the most exciting thing in the world, but at least it would take her mind off Andrew's forthcoming date with Lucy's aunt. Agnes was taking the whole thing a little too seriously for her liking. The woman had even gone to the expense of buying a brand new dress for the occasion.

****

Sadie was enjoying another wonderful evening with Michael. There were times when he made her laugh, but there were also moments when he was serious about the very same things she thought were important. It was as though they had a single belief. Where had this lovely man been all her life?

After finishing their meal, they made their way to the theatre. It was a warm evening, so they'd decided to walk. London was beginning to come alive. People spilled out of restaurants, talking and laughing, while taxis shot back and forth, ferrying passengers from one engagement to another. However, Sadie was oblivious of it all. Her arm firmly linked through Michael's, she hung onto his every word as they strolled towards the theatre.

****

"The lady in the shop helped me to choose it." Agnes slipped effortlessly into her new dress; the soft silky material sliding easily over her narrow hips.

Lucy had been rather surprised to find her aunt had chosen something very stylish and expensive for her evening out with Andrew. It was most unlike the clothes she normally wore.

"The assistant was very helpful," Agnes continued. "I would've asked you to go with me, but I know you're extremely busy with the new business." She straightened the sleeves and pulled the neckline into shape. "What do you think?" Her eyes shone as she did a pirouette on the spot. "I've even bought some new shoes to go with it."

Lucy thought she looked fantastic. Her aunt hadn't piled on the pounds around the hips like so many women did when they reached a certain age. She had retained her slim figure and smooth complexion. It was only the odd tell-tale wisp of grey hair, which gave away the fact she was a little older than you might first think.

"You look wonderful. But..." Lucy shifted uneasily from one foot to another. She was about to remind her aunt this was probably a one off outing; she doubted Andrew would be asking her out again. But how could she possibly add a downside, especially when her aunt seemed so happy. "You look absolutely fabulous!" she said.

However Agnes hadn't failed to notice the flash of concern in her niece's eyes. Smiling, she reached out and took her arm. "Don't worry, Lucy. I'm not so naive as to believe this meeting is going to lead anywhere. You're forgetting I know exactly who Andrew is, and I also know he's still very much in love with his wife." She patted Lucy's arm. "I might be an old lady, but I'm not stupid. I still know how many beans make five." She grinned. "However, on my birthday I have a handsome man coming to take me out to dinner and if that doesn't give me a reason to splash out on a lovely new frock, then I don't know what does. Besides, you're forgetting I'm still a member of Divorcees.biz. I might even get to wear it again."

"Oh, Aunt. I don't think you're an old lady, I think you're wonderful, kind, and witty. I hope you have a lovely evening with Andrew." Lucy reached into her handbag. "And to prove it, I brought you a present to wear for the occasion."

Agnes opened a small box to reveal a strap of pearls. "My dear they're lovely. But you shouldn't have…"

"They're not real, Aunt." Lucy added hastily. "I couldn't afford real pearls, but they're the next best thing. Here, let me put them on for you."

Tears welled in Agnes's eyes as she gazed at her reflection in the mirror. When she was young, she had longed for a necklace like this, but money had always been tight when she was growing up. Even when she was older, there was always something else needed more urgently. Her family always came first. "They're perfect, Lucy – absolutely perfect."

"When our new agency gets going, I'll buy you the real thing."

"No! These are exactly what I always wanted." Agnes hugged her niece. "I shall treasure them."

****

"You look deep in thought. What are you thinking about?" asked Jenny.

"Nothing really." Connie looked back down at the laptop. "I was wondering whether we would get any messages tonight," she lied. She certainly didn't want Jenny or anyone else to know she was still thinking about Andrew and Agnes. She knew she was being stupid. Why should she give a damn what he did? But, she still couldn't get the matter out of her mind.

Thankfully, a message dropped into the inbox. "There's something here from Brian Lomax," Connie said, opening the email. "He wants to know why no one is taking him up on his offers to meet." She sat back in her chair and looked at Jenny, her hands clasped behind her head. "How can I tell him he's asking to meet the wrong people? If he was to choose someone more his own age, I'm sure he'd get a better response."

"Can't you simply say that?" said Jenny. "I agree, you'd need to be tactful, but he's asked us a question relating to the agency, so he should be told the truth. I think Lucy said he'd tried asking six women out to dinner, but not one has agreed to go."

Connie sighed. "Okay, I'll try to word something. Why do I get all the rotten jobs?"

"Because you're good at dealing with people. You seem to be able to say the right things." Jenny laughed. "We couldn't possibly leave something like this to Sadie. She would simply tell him to stop cradle snatching and start meeting people his own age."

"Damn right!" uttered Connie. "Sadie doesn't know the meaning of the word tact. We'd lose all our clients in an instant if we left it to her."

During the evening, Jenny received a call from David. He told her a little more about himself and how he and John would be back in London in a few days. "The company is keen for us to learn more about the premises we found," he told her. "If we like what we hear, we're authorised to put in an offer on the spot. Hopefully you and I can meet up. Perhaps we could make a foursome with John and your friend and go somewhere for dinner."

Jenny's eyes were sparkling when she put down the phone. She burst into the sitting room to tell Connie about it. "Isn't it exciting?" she said, when she had relayed most of the conversation. "A chance meeting like that. It could be the start of something big. It's almost like that old movie, *Brief Encounter*."

"If you recall, the female character in the film went back to her husband," Connie laughed.

"Well, that isn't going to happen to me. Even if nothing comes of this 'encounter'," Jenny made quotation marks in the air, "I won't be going back to Rob. How're things going with you?" She pointed to the laptop.

"I've been kept quite busy," said Connie. "Several more messages have come in requesting meetings and most have accepted the invitations. However, there're a few I still need to hear from. Perhaps they haven't picked up their emails yet. Anyway, we've made a tidy sum this evening." She grinned.

"I've also had a reply from Brian Lomax. Thankfully, he seems to have taken my message in the right spirit, because he's going to have a rethink. I'm assuming he's going to go through the whole website very carefully."

"Well, that's something." Jenny sat down next to Connie. "He could have got a bit shirty and asked for his money back. It's not easy telling someone they're too old for the people they're choosing." She cocked her head on one side. "Did that make sense?"

Connie nodded. "Sort of." She snapped the lid of the laptop shut. "It's getting late. I think I've had enough of this now. I'm going to have a cup of tea, and then I'm going to bed." She clasped her hands together above her head and stretched. "Sitting here, watching this thing all evening has made me stiff."

"I offered to take over, but for some reason, you wanted to do it yourself."

"I know, Jenny, but once I got going I thought I would stick with it. Your turn will come and then you won't be so keen." Connie glanced at the clock again. "I wonder how Sadie's getting on."

CHAPTER SIXTEEN

"Did you have a nice evening?" asked Lucy.

It was the following morning and Sadie and the others had arrived at the office.

Sadie didn't answer. She hadn't even heard Lucy's question. She was miles away.

"Is she okay?" Lucy glanced at Connie.

"She's fine. Though we can't get any sense out of her," said Connie. "She's been like this since she got up this morning. You have to either nudge her or yell at the top of your lungs to get a response."

Lucy laughed. "She's in love. Good for her."

"Sorry, did you say something?" Sadie looked up.

"I asked whether you'd had a nice evening, but I think I've got the picture."

"Yes, I did. We went to see *Love Never Dies*. It's a great show. Michael's going to call me later today."

"John called me last night. He's coming to London sometime next week and wants to meet up with me."

"David called me last night and said the same thing," Jenny squealed. "He suggested we could go somewhere as a foursome. What do you think?"

"You didn't tell me David called," Sadie chirped. "I asked you whether anything had happened while I was out last night and I don't recall you saying anything about David."

"Yes, I did. But the glazed, far away look in your eyes told me you'd switched off the moment the question left your lips." Jenny grinned at Connie. "You seemed to have dropped out of our world and…"

"Okay, okay!" Sadie held up her hands. "I get the message. I'll try to keep focused. But you know I've never been out with anyone like Michael. He wants to take me to lots of nice places. This is a whole new experience for me. He's going to ring me here sometime today." Sadie hesitated when she saw Jenny and Connie imitating a yawn. "Okay, so I've told you already."

The others nodded and smiled. "Yes, you have," said Connie. "But we don't mind."

"I've been thinking," said Connie.

"Oh dear! That doesn't sound good." Jenny pulled a face.

"It's nothing really." Connie smiled. "We need to talk this over, but as the agency is running smoothly, do we all need to come into the office every day? The original plan was for us all to be here every day for a few months, and then we'd decide whether two of us could manage at any one time. However, I feel we've got it sussed already. What do you think?"

"I'm not so sure." Jenny glanced nervously at the others. "I think there're a few things we really need to get sorted before we go down that road." She had hoped someone would break in at this point, agreeing with what she had said so far. But they all remained silent. "Take last night for instance," she continued. "Brian Lomax sent a message…" She broke off for a moment when Sadie groaned. "No. Wait a minute,

Sadie. The man wasn't asking us to arrange a meeting with someone. He wanted to know why no one ever said yes to his invitations."

"We all know why no one says yes to him. Surely the silly man could have figured it out for himself." Sadie closed her eyes and sighed heavily. "So what's the problem? If I had picked up the message, I'd simply have told him to look in the mirror and..."

"That's exactly the problem, Sadie!" Jenny broke in. She threw her arms up in the air. "You would've jumped in with both feet. He could have taken umbrage at your remark and left the agency. Not only that, he could have asked for his money back or worse – compensation. We can't afford to give money back. No! When we get asked something like this, we need to have a polite answer ready, not leap into the firing line with guns blazing." She shook her head at Sadie. "As it turns out, Connie was looking after the site, so it fell to her to reply. She was tactful and sympathised with him, but she was able to tell him what the problem was. He replied, saying he was going to take another look at the profiles online." She paused. "What I'm trying to say here is we need to be together until a range of these questions comes in and we have answers we can pull off the top of our heads. Okay, we might need to tweak them a little to fit different circumstances, but at least we'd have a template." Jenny fell silent. Everyone was staring at her. Did they think she was being stupid? Why didn't someone say something? "Aren't you going to say anything?" she asked at last.

Lucy spoke first. "Yes, I can see where Jenny is coming from and I tend to agree with her." She saw Sadie flash a scornful glance in her direction. "I'm not saying Sadie can't be tactful when she needs to," she added quickly. "No, not at all. If we think before we speak we can all come up with the right answers." That didn't sound too much in Sadie's favour either. She never thought about what she was going to say. She always said the first thing that came into her head. "Can I simply say I think we should stay together for a while longer?"

"Okay." Connie shrugged. "If that's what you all think, it's fine with me."

"But it doesn't mean to say we all have to be here together every second of the day." Jenny paused. "We could take it in turns to go out shopping or something. We all have things we need to do."

"Sounds good to me." Sadie smiled. "In that case, do you mind if I pop out for a few minutes? I'd like to do a little window-shopping. I might need to buy a new dress."

"Okay. But perhaps you might like one of us to come with you before you actually decide to buy anything," said Connie. "You know – a second opinion."

Sadie knew exactly what she meant. In another time, another place, she might have thrown a tantrum, demanding to know what was wrong with the outfits she chose. However, since meeting Michael, she agreed her own clothes weren't at all suitable for the sort of places he was taking her. She would have felt so embarrassed on the first two dates if Connie and Jenny hadn't intervened. "Yes, thank you. I'd be grateful for your advice."

"Well, there's a turn-up," Jenny uttered when Sadie had clattered down the stairs. "For a moment I thought you were taking your life in your hands. There was a time when she would have cut off your ears for even suggesting her choice in clothing was questionable."

Connie winked. "Ah! Yes. But that was before she met the lovely Michael."

****

Sadie wandered down Oxford Street, stopping occasionally to look in dress shop windows. She reached Oxford Circus and was about to return to the office when her mobile rang.

"Hello," she said cautiously. It wasn't a number she recognised. However, her face broke into a smile when she heard Michael's voice.

"I rang your office, but someone told me you were window shopping." He paused. "Are you nearby? Have you got time to pop into the bank for a few minutes?"

"Yes," replied Sadie. She glanced down the street; the bank was only a couple of minutes walk away. "I'm quite near, so I'll be there in a tick."

Michael was waiting by the door when she arrived. "I'm due a break. Shall we go to the coffee shop on the corner?"

Sadie nodded. "Yes, that would be great."

"I wondered whether you liked going to discos," he said when they were seated in the coffee shop.

"Yes, I do. I used to hang out in those places all the time." She cupped her hand over her mouth. "I used to go to discos quite a lot," she corrected herself. It was difficult trying to keep up the pretence of talking posh all the time.

Michael laughed. "You were okay the first time." He paused. "I wasn't sure whether to suggest going to somewhere like that, because you look… well, you look above such places. You know the kind of thing I mean. Loud music, gyrating around the floor, and everything else that goes with discos and night clubs."

"You've got to be kidding me! I adore loud music and I absolutely love gyrating around the floor. I'm the original upbeat girl!" She hesitated. "What do you mean, I look above all that? Look at the outfit I'm wearing today." She pointed to her black and white skirt and red and white striped top. "And then look at my glasses." They had black and red striped frames.

"I love it!" Michael enthused. "I adore it. You look superb."

"Bloody hell!" Sadie couldn't believe her ears. Not expecting to meet Michael today, she had worn one of her more outrageous outfits. "Oops! I mean, you do?"

"Of course I do. You're great, Sadie." He held up his hand when she tried to interrupt. "Let me get this off my chest." He took a deep breath. "Yes, sometimes I like to go out to dinner at nice places, but I also like letting my hair down occasionally, so to speak." He laughed, rubbing the top of his head. His hair was cut quite short. "Be yourself with me, Sadie. I asked you out because I liked you when you first walked into the bank. The second time, you came in I knew I simply had to ask you out. At first, I thought perhaps you were too good for me, but I think we rub along okay. What do you say?"

For a moment, Sadie was lost for words. Here was she thinking she would have to change, not only her ways, but also her language and her dress sense to keep Michael interested in her. Yet, it now seemed he was trying to alter his ideals to get her interested in him. "Okay." She pointed both index fingers at him. "Let me get this straight. You like me for what I am. My bizarre dress sense, though that's only my friends' opinions, I absolutely adore my clothes. Then there's my choice of language, which my friends hate, and there's the fact my kooky opinion on anything counts for nothing." She paused, waiting for Michael to respond. But he remained silent. He continued to gaze at her with his chin resting on his cupped hands. "Well, aren't you going to say something?" she added

"What do you want me to say? I've said it all. I think you're great. You're witty, quirky, and whatever else you set out to be. I love the way you're dressed today. I love the way you say what you mean. And I love your sense of humour."

"Oh Michael…" Sadie felt so happy. "You like the way I dress and my colourful language and…"

"Yes. Didn't I just say that?" Michael interrupted, his eyes twinkling.

"Yes, sorry. I must stop doing that. Connie gets so annoyed when I keep repeating everything she says."

Michael laughed. He took her hand. "I don't mind. Are you free tonight? We could go to a disco or something."

"Yes! I'd love to."

He leaned across the table and kissed her. "I'd better get back to the bank. No need for you to rush away. Enjoy the coffee. I'll call for you at about seven. We'll have something to eat and decide where to go from there." He grinned. "Casual dress."

"You bet!" Sadie winked. "You haven't seen anything yet."

Sadie was on cloud nine as she walked back up Oxford Street. Wait until the others heard about this.

****

"A message has come in from Ann Masters. She said her date didn't turn up last night." Lucy had opened one of the three messages, which had dropped into the inbox. "It sounds as though she's furious with us because she had cancelled something else to meet up with the guy."

"That's not our fault. How can she be furious with us?" said Connie. "We can't be held responsible for someone not showing up." She paused. "What are the other messages about?"

Lucy opened the emails. "Oh, more people wanting to meet Ann Masters." She pulled a face. "She's certainly getting her money's worth for her fee. We could make money from this agency on her alone."

"Do I detect a little jealousy there?" asked Connie.

"No, of course not!" Lucy replied. She sighed. "It just seems so unfair. We set up this agency so we could get our pick of the handsome hunks, yet no one has asked us out."

"Don't forget about Sadie. She was chosen by two different Michaels."

"And one of them turned out to be a womaniser, the kind of man we didn't want to attract." Lucy shrugged. "I guess the second one must be okay," she added grudgingly. "I'm sure Sadie would have dropped him like a hot brick by now if he hadn't come up to scratch."

"What about John?" Connie said. "He seems to want to see you again."

"Yes," she replied slowly. "We'll see." It was true, John had said he would be back in London shortly and would give her a call. But somehow, she couldn't get really excited about it. Not in the same way Jenny was about David. Something in his tone had given her cause to doubt he was genuine. "Besides, he didn't appear through the agency."

Connie was about to reply, when Sadie suddenly burst into the office.

"I have something to tell you all." She didn't wait until she was seated before she began. "Michael rang my mobile while I was out. He asked if I could meet him for a quick coffee and you'll never guess what he told me!" She paused and looked at each in turn.

"Well, go on then, tell us. You can't leave us dangling in mid-air," said Connie impatiently. "What did he say?"

"He says he likes me for who I am and…"

"But he doesn't know who you are." Lucy interrupted. She laughed. "Not the real you, anyway. He's only seen you all dressed up in someone else's outfits and trying to put on a posh accent."

"I know that!" Sadie said. "Give me a bloody chance to finish! Don't you see? That's the whole point! He saw me in this clobber today and he said he loved it. Actually, he said he *adored* it." She corrected herself. "So you see: I don't need to borrow your clothes any more. He says he likes quirky. *And* we're going to a disco tonight. It seems he loves all that crazy, loud music, too. Isn't that great?" She clasped her hands together and sank into her chair. "Sounds like we were made for each other."

Connie looked at the others and rolled her eyes. "I don't believe it," she uttered. "And I thought Sadie was beginning to get some dress sense at last."

CHAPTER SEVENTEEN

Connie slowly opened her eyes. She had been dreading this day for the last week, but now it had finally dawned. This evening Andrew would call on Agnes and whisk her off to dinner at one of the best restaurants in London.

She closed her eyes tight and pulled the duvet over her head. If only she could stay tucked up in bed until the whole thing was over and done with. She knew this one date wasn't going to lead to anything – if you could call it a date. So why was she allowing herself to get so uptight about it? Yet, try as she might, she couldn't blot it out of her mind.

No doubt Lucy would be talking about it all day. Well, perhaps not all day, but it would sure as hell seem like it. And then they would go through it all over again tomorrow, because Jenny and Sadie would be anxious to hear every little detail of how Agnes had enjoyed her 'date' with Andrew.

She slowly pushed the duvet to one side and crawled out of bed. There was nothing else for it; she was going to have to get dressed and face the world.

"You're late getting up this morning," said Sadie over her bowl of breakfast cereal. "It's not like you. I hope you aren't going down with something – especially something catching." She knew exactly what was eating Connie. But she wanted her to suffer. If this was going to work, Connie had to feel really upset. Upset enough for her to realise she desperately wanted Andrew back in her life.

"I'm fine. I simply felt tired this morning."

Sadie shrugged. "Okay, if you say so." She hid a smile and continued eating her breakfast. This was going to be a very long day for Connie.

****

The day turned out exactly as Connie had feared. It began with Lucy bursting into the office full of apologies for being late.

"My aunt rang this morning," she said breathlessly. "She told me she wouldn't keep me long, but in the end she was on the phone for three quarters of an hour. She's so looking forward to this evening, especially as it's her birthday today. I wouldn't care, but she knows I'm stopping by this evening before I go home." She glanced at Connie; suddenly realising she was there. "Well, I suppose I'd better get down to some work," she added hastily.

"Perhaps you should leave a little earlier and help your aunt to get dressed," said Sadie. She didn't want the conversation to end there. She wanted it to drag on for as long as possible. "I mean, it *is* her birthday and you'll want to see her before Andrew arrives and he's always very punctual." She cast a sideways glance at Connie. "She might even want your opinion on how she looks before she leaves. What do you say, Connie?"

"Erm, yes, of course." Connie looked up from the letter she had been trying to focus on without much success. She forced a smile. "Good idea."

"Thank you. I'll leave around four if everything is okay here in the office," said Lucy.

Connie nodded, hoping that was the end of it. Surely everything had been said on the subject of Aunt Agnes's 'date'. Yet, for some reason, Lucy's aunt seemed to pop up from nowhere all throughout the day. It wouldn't have been so bad if the website had been busy. Who was going out with whom usually caused quite a buzz of conversation, but strangely it was very quiet today.

By two o'clock Connie couldn't stand it any longer. She stood up and reached for her bag. "I'm just popping out for an hour for a little retail therapy. Does anyone want anything?"

"Do you think we've gone on a bit too much about my aunt?" Lucy said, once Connie was out of earshot.

"I don't know," said Jenny, cautiously. "Perhaps when she comes back we shouldn't say anything further.

"No!" Sadie slammed her hand onto the desk. "For goodness sake, that's what she needs. A constant reminder of what she's missing. Shit! A good kick up the backside wouldn't go amiss either. She's her own worst enemy."

Jenny and Lucy stared at her. They were lost for words.

"What?" Sadie asked, holding up her hands.

****

Connie wandered aimlessly around the shops. What she really wanted to do was to sit down somewhere out of sight and have a good cry. But the streets and shops of London were too busy. She would have to get a grip on herself, and force back the tears.

She tried to concentrate on a new line of dresses displayed in a shop window. Usually when she was feeling low, such a sight would snap her out of the doldrums and she would hurry into the shop to try something on. But today even that wasn't working. Besides, why bother buying anything new? She had plenty of clothes already and it wasn't as though she was going anywhere special. Life was very boring at the moment. She recalled the days when she and Andrew were together. Back then they had seldom been home. There was always some wonderful function or another to attend.

'Stop it!' she told herself, walking away from the shop window. She'd come out of the office to get away from the constant chatter about Andrew, but he had followed her out here.

She called into a café and lingered over a coffee and a large, sticky cake, before finally deciding to make her way back to the office. It was no good; she might as well go back. This jaunt wasn't doing anything to help her. It had been foolish of her to think it would.

****

"That didn't take long," said Sadie when Connie returned. She noted Connie wasn't carrying any shopping, which meant she hadn't bought anything. Things must be really bad for Connie not to spend any money, especially while on retail therapy.

"No, I'm fine. I stopped off for a coffee on the way back. Did I miss anything?"

"Not really." Lucy looked up from the computer. "We've had a few people requesting meetings, so I suppose that's a plus. I was beginning to think our clients had deserted us."

"I had a quick call from Michael," added Sadie. "There's a new disco opened and he wondered whether I might be interested."

"And are you?" quizzed Connie, although she knew what the answer would be.

"Of course I'm bloody interested," Sadie laughed. "I told him I'd be ready and waiting when he called to pick me up."

Just before four o'clock, Lucy gathered her things together. "I'm off now," she said, walking towards the door. "I'm so excited. You'd almost think it was me who was going out this evening." She sighed. "But no such luck."

"Your turn will come," Sadie replied. "John will be here soon. Meanwhile, tell your aunt to have a lovely evening and don't forget to say that we want to know all the gory details tomorrow. Don't we, Connie?"

Lucy nodded. She still wasn't sure about John. Only time would tell. She glanced at Connie who looked as though she was about to say something. "Bye," she said and quickly disappeared out the door. She had no intention of waiting to hear whatever it was Connie was going to say.

****

"Ta-da! How do I look?" Sadie bounced through into the sitting room. They were back at Connie's house and she had changed into some disco gear.

"Terrible!" said Connie. "You aren't actually going out dressed like that?" She closed her eyes and opened them again hoping she had been dreaming. But no, she'd seen it right the first time. Sadie had chosen to wear a bright pink skirt. It was far too short and much too tight. She had teamed it with a skimpy black top, which showed her midriff, and a pink leather jerkin. The outfit was finished off with a large black and white necklace and matching earrings that hung down to her shoulders.

"Good! That must mean I've got it right." Sadie glanced at her reflection in the mirror above the fireplace. "It's a disco we're going to, not some posh hotel. People wear all sorts of things to reflect their mood."

"I can't imagine what your mood must be."

"Can't you tell? I'm happy! In the pink! I think it all looks cool." Hearing a car pull up, she hurried across to the window. "He's here! I'll see what he thinks."

Connie heard Michael telling Sadie how wonderful she looked, before he was dragged into the lounge.

"I'd like you to meet Connie. She's one of the partners in the agency. Connie, this is Michael."

They shook hands, but before either could say a word, Sadie pulled Michael back towards the door. "Got to fly, Connie, the meter's running. See you later. Cheerio!" With that, they were gone.

****

Meanwhile, in another part of London, Andrew was heading towards Lucy's aunt's house. He was still uneasy about doing this, but he had made the arrangements and there wasn't anything he could do about it now. At least he had chosen someone Connie couldn't really get jealous over – or could she? If there was one thing he had learned over the years, it was that women could be very unpredictable, especially his ex-wife.

He was taken aback when Lucy opened the door. What was she doing here? He'd hoped his visit would go unnoticed, especially by any friends of Connie's. But, upon reflection, why wouldn't she be at the house? Lucy and her aunt were very close and it *was* Agnes's birthday.

"Hello, Andrew. Please come in. My aunt will be down in a few minutes."

"Thank you," he said, stepping into the hallway. Feeling a little embarrassed, he fiddled with the knot in his tie and was relieved when Agnes appeared. "Good evening," he said, handing her a bouquet of flowers. "May I wish you a happy birthday?"

"How very kind. They're beautiful. Thank you." she replied, as she accepted the gift. "Perhaps Lucy will put them in water for me."

"Of course I will." Lucy took the flowers, while Andrew helped Agnes with her jacket.

"Might I say you're looking very lovely this evening, Agnes." He paused. "I've booked a table at the Ritz, I hope that's to your liking."

"How wonderful. The Ritz has such a lovely restaurant." She tried to make it sound as though going to the Ritz was something she did on a regular basis, though she had never been there in her life. Out of the corner of her eye, she saw the quizzical expression on Lucy's face and gave her a look that clearly said 'don't you dare say a word.'

Once Andrew and her aunt had gone, Lucy began to arrange the flowers in a vase. "Dinner at the Ritz," she mumbled to herself. "I should be so darn lucky."

****

Connie bit her lip as she glanced at the clock. This was going to be a long evening. In a way, she wished Sadie hadn't been going out tonight. At least she would have had someone to talk to.

Andrew and Agnes would be having dinner by now. She wondered where he had taken her. Might it be the Condrew? She hoped not and pushed the idea to a small corner at the back of her mind. That was *their* place; hers and Andrew's. Surely he wouldn't take Agnes there.

****

Andrew had prepared himself for a long and dull evening. Agnes was old enough to be his mother. What on earth would he talk to her about? He didn't know anything about her. Well, not much, anyway. Their lives were worlds apart. When Sadie suggested he take out another woman from the agency, he hadn't been keen on the idea, until he spotted Lucy's aunt among the clients. Yes, it was possible to date another woman with Connie's knowledge without her thinking he was flirting. But it could mean he would be in for a rather boring evening. However, he was turning out to be greatly surprised. Agnes was a charming, witty lady who made him chuckle constantly.

Meanwhile, Agnes was having the time of her life. The restaurant was wonderful, the food was out of this world, and Andrew had even ordered a bottle of champagne to celebrate her birthday. This was an evening she would never forget, and she couldn't wait to tell her friends about it.

When she set out with Andrew earlier in the evening, she hadn't failed to notice the curtains twitching at numbers twenty-seven and twenty-nine, while Mrs Duffy, in number thirty-three had pulled the curtain completely to one side to get a better look. Mrs Duffy was the original nosey parker and liked to know everyone's business. Agnes had been tempted to give her a wave, but thought better of it. Let the old witch think she hadn't seen her. No doubt she would find some excuse to call tomorrow morning to find out where she had been and who the lovely young man was.

She glanced at her watch and was surprised to see it was so late. They would have to leave shortly. What a shame. She was having so much fun. But she had been on this earth long enough to know that all good things came to an end.

CHAPTER EIGHTEEN

The next morning, the moment Connie opened her eyes, she crossed her fingers and made a resolution. Every time Agnes or Andrew's name was mentioned, she was going to switch off completely. Pull the plug; shut her ears or even bury her head in the waste paper bin if need be. As long as it blocked out any conversation about those two people.

But like all resolutions, it fell by the wayside the moment she entered the office. She and Sadie were hardly through the door before Sadie asked Lucy how her aunt had enjoyed her date.

Connie tried her hardest to look unconcerned. She sat down at her desk and began to open the mail.

"She had a lovely evening," said Lucy. "She sounded thrilled to bits when she rang me this morning. I was there last night when Andrew called for her. He'd brought the most enormous bouquet of flowers. I heard him telling my aunt he had booked a table at the Ritz. Though she tried to hide it, I could tell she was excited about it. I gather Andrew even bought some champagne to mark her birthday." She paused. "It was near midnight when he took her home. I'm surprised she was up so early this morning." She smiled. "So, how did Website Watch go?"

Connie had tried hard not to listen to Lucy, while she was relating the story of her aunt's evening with Andrew. Keeping her head bent over the desk, she continued to open the mail. She told herself she didn't want to know anything about it – yet, deep down, she did. She wanted to know every tiny scrap of detail.

She heaved a silent sigh of relief, when she learned Andrew had taken Agnes to the Ritz. At least they hadn't gone to the Condrew. But he *had* escorted her home. Of course he would take her home. She was an old lady, wasn't she? No gentleman would leave a lady to find her own way home at midnight, and Andrew was certainly a gentleman. But what happened when he took her home? Did he go in for coffee? Did he sit there half the night? Did Agnes show him how she had decorated her bedroom? She wanted to scream out these questions. So much for her resolution!

She looked up for a moment and saw Sadie watching her.

"So! It sounds as though your aunt thoroughly enjoyed her evening," said Sadie, her eyes still firmly glued on Connie. She could read her like a book and knew exactly what was going through her mind. "Did she invite Andrew in for coffee to round off her birthday treat?"

Lucy laughed. "Good heaven, no." She frowned. "At least I don't think so. Aunt said he was very gallant right up to the end of the evening. He insisted on seeing her up to her front door and even gave her a kiss on the cheek before she went inside. I think she would have said if she had made coffee for him."

"That is so sweet," said Sadie. "Andrew is a very nice man. Your aunt must have had a wonderful evening." She sighed. "Ah well, I suppose we should bring ourselves down to earth and see what's been happening on the site overnight."

Sadie looked down at the ledger on her desk, but her mind was elsewhere. She needed an excuse to get out of the office for a few minutes and give Andrew a ring. She had to tell him the plan was working. Okay, Connie had kept her head down believing no one would notice what she was doing. But Sadie had been watching her closely. She had seen the telltale signs – the taut lips, the brief pause while slitting open an envelope when Lucy mentioned the champagne, but most of all, the clenching of her fists when she heard Andrew had escorted Agnes to her front door. Connie could say whatever she liked, but Sadie knew she was as jealous as hell.

"You look a bit agitated, Sadie. Are you all feeling alright?" Lucy burst into her thoughts.

"Yes – no." Sadie put a hand on her head. Lucy's question had given her a chance to escape for a few minutes. "I've got a bit of a headache. I'll just pop out to the chemist."

"Would you like me to go for you?" said Jenny. "The heat outside won't help your poor head."

"No – thank you, I'll be fine. The fresh air might help." Sadie shot out of the door before anyone could stop her.

"Is it just me or does anyone else think Sadie's been acting a bit strange of late?" Connie walked across to the window and looked down to the pavement below. She could see Sadie hurrying along the road towards Oxford Street. "I wonder what she's up to?"

****

"So, that's it. She's definitely jealous. We're getting somewhere." Sadie had barely left the building before stabbing her fingers on her mobile. Though Andrew's secretary had told her he was in a meeting, she wasn't about to be put off so easily. "This is very urgent," she had screamed down the line. "Put me through or consider the consequences." 'Trumped up know it all,' she'd thought, tapping her foot on the pavement while she waited for Andrew to come on the line.

Andrew wandered across to the window of the boardroom, as Sadie told him about Connie's reactions. He listened carefully, only glancing occasionally at the group of people seated around the large oval desk. Though it heartened him to know Connie was upset about him dating another woman, he didn't dare believe she might come back to him. She was a proud woman, the sort of woman who never backed down. If he was going to win her back, then he needed to humble himself. Yet he had tried that already. He had booked a table at the Condrew. He'd even hired their special bedroom for the unforeseeable future. He'd almost got down on his knees and begged her to relent. But she had still taken a taxi back home.

"I guess I'll just have to wait and see what happens next." Aware he had an audience, he chose his words carefully.

"You need to date someone else," replied Sadie.

"I'm not sure that's a good idea!" Andrew was mortified. If this were to become a habit, Connie might start doing the same thing to get her own back. He wasn't sure he could cope with that. She could even find a man she liked.

"You've got to, Andrew – at least one more time. For goodness sake, be a man. You can't give up now!"

"I need to think it over. I'd better go, but thanks for letting me know." Andrew returned to his place at the table. "Sorry about that," he said, pointing at his phone, "but it was a matter of some urgency."

****

"Are you feeling better?" asked Lucy when Sadie arrived back in the office.

"Yes, thanks. The pills are starting to work. I could do with a cup of tea, though." Sadie filled the kettle and switched it on. She had very nearly forgot to buy the headache pills, only remembering at the last minute. She had even pulled two from the blister pack and tossed them down a drain for fear Jenny or Lucy saw the packet. All this cloak and dagger stuff was wearing her down. She certainly wasn't cut out to be a spy.

It was late in the afternoon when Lucy suddenly announced they had received two emails. She gave a quick glance in Connie's direction, before looking back at the screen. "One is from Andrew. He wants to have a date with… Sadie!"

"Sadie!" squealed Connie. "You're kidding me, right?"

"No, I'm not. That's what he says."

Connie sank her head into her hands, while Lucy and Jenny looked at each other. Neither knew what to say.

Sadie, who had been in the restroom, came back to find them all sitting staring at each other. "What's up?" she asked.

"Andrew has requested another date," said Lucy quietly.

"So?" Sadie shrugged. "What's the problem?" She tried to sound casual, but secretly she was delighted, though somewhat surprised Andrew had responded so quickly. He had certainly sounded very doubtful when she'd spoken to him only a little while ago. "He's a free agent." She walked across to her desk. "Who does he want to meet?"

"You," replied Jenny, before Lucy could say anything.

Sadie spun around. "Who? Me! Seriously?" she screeched. "He's asked for me to go out with him?" Her mind was in turmoil. How could she go out with Andrew on a date now she was in a serious relationship with Michael? On the other hand, how could she turn Andrew down, when the whole idea of him requesting to meet someone was her idea? If she didn't go, he probably wouldn't ask anyone else. "Okay." She ran her tongue along her bottom lip. "Okay, when does he want to meet up? I like Andrew, it should be fun."

"You mean you're going?" Connie looked up quickly. She could feel the colour draining from her face.

"Yes, why shouldn't I?" Sadie shrugged. "You don't seem to want him."

"He asks if you can make it this evening?" said Lucy.

"This evening," Sadie repeated. "He wants to meet me this evening?" She looked up at the ceiling and breathed out heavily. How on earth was she going to explain this to Michael? She was supposed to be meeting him this evening.

"Okay, tell him yes," she said, suddenly realising Lucy was waiting for an answer. "Ask him where he's taking me," she added. Andrew wasn't a disco person so what on earth could she wear? She had already borrowed Jenny's gear twice. Connie's clothes would be too big. Though she could hardly borrow something from Connie to go out on a date with her ex-husband, even if they were the same size – yet on the other hand, why not? Connie and Andrew were divorced. What should it matter to her, unless she was jealous? Which, after all, was the whole point of the exercise.

But, right now, a bigger problem was hanging over her. Somehow, she needed to get in touch with Michael and explain what was going on. He was due to pick her up at seven o'clock. Between now and then, she must contact him and put him off. This meant she had to find another excuse to get out of the office. She wouldn't be able to talk freely with Connie listening to her every word. This was turning into a bigger deal than she first thought. What the hell had she got herself into?

She leapt to her feet. "I need a new lipstick!" she declared. "The one I bought yesterday won't do at all for a night out with Andrew. It's too… too…" She flapped her hands around. "Too gothic." She didn't give anyone a chance to say anything. She grabbed her bag and headed for the stairs.

"That was a bit sudden, wasn't it?" Jenny stared at the door.

Lucy shook her head. "She's been in and out like a fiddler's elbow all day. I do wonder about her sometimes."

"Didn't you say there were two emails?" asked Connie. "Who's the other one from?"

"Yes. I forgot about it with all the excitement." replied Lucy. "It's from Brian Lomax. "I wonder who he's chosen this time."

****

"Is that you Michael?" Sadie hoped he wouldn't get into any trouble for receiving phone calls at work. She would have to make it up to him the next time they met. But she had to stop him from calling at Connie's house that evening to pick her up. "Something's come up. I can't make it tonight." After she told him the reason, there was a long pause. "Are you still there?" she asked.

"Yes, I'm still here."

"I've got to go out with Andrew. You recall I told you I was trying to get him and Connie back together. Well, the plan is starting to work. Connie is beginning to get rattled." She paused. "Last night he took Lucy's aunt to the Ritz and I told him he should fix up another date. Well, he has, and this time he's chosen me. You do understand, don't you? I mean there's nothing going on between us." There was no response.

She bit her lip. Was he upset at the idea? How on earth had she got herself into this situation? Michael was the first good thing to happen to her in a long time. She wasn't about to lose him. She would put Andrew off before she would allow her relationship with Michael to fall apart. Suddenly, she had an idea. "Michael, why don't you come with us? Connie would never know, she'll just think I'm with Andrew. We'll all go for dinner somewhere. Obviously Andrew will have to pick me up, as Connie will be there to see me off. But we could all meet up at a restaurant. What do you say?"

"Okay. No problem. It's a shame I won't be meeting the real you again this evening." He laughed.

"And I was looking forward to showing you more of my gear," said Sadie." She laughed. "Now I'm going to ring Andrew and put him in the picture. Once I know where we're going, I'll send you a text and you can meet us there." This was beginning to get more complicated by the minute. She could feel a real headache coming on now.

She telephoned Andrew's office. "Pick up the damn phone, Andrew," she yelled, after his extension had rung a few times. A couple of people walking past her stopped and grinned. She smiled briefly, before turning her attention back to the phone. Finally, she heard a click and Andrew came on the line. She quickly explained what was going on.

****

As it turned out, he didn't mind Michael joining them at the restaurant. In a way, he was relieved. If the whole thing backfired, he would be able to tell Connie there was a third party with them the whole time. He still couldn't believe he was taking marital advice from Sadie, of all people. She was the zaniest person he had ever met. He still didn't fully understand how Connie and Sadie had ever become such good friends. They were like chalk and cheese. Sadie was from the East End of London. Her parents had worked hard and played hard. He'd only met them once some time ago.

They were friendly enough, but he quickly learned they were people who spoke their minds, calling a spade a spade. Sadie was exactly the same. The niceties of life had passed her by. In contrast, Connie's family was fairly well to do. She had gone to the right schools and met the right people. She knew how to conduct herself on all occasions. But this didn't mean she was a snob. She could ease herself into any situation and mix with all types of people. That was one of the things he loved about her.

****

Once Sadie had finished speaking to Andrew, she sent a text to Michael's mobile, giving him the necessary information before sinking into one of the chairs outside a café. Why had her life suddenly become so complex? At one time, everything had simply rolled by like a gentle breeze on a summer's day. She had been quite content to let that happen, only getting more involved when it suited her. Now, here she was, deceiving one of her best friends by interfering in her marital problems. Though, to be fair, she was only trying to help. Nevertheless, she seemed to be getting herself into deep shit in the process.

She saw a waiter heading her way, so she stood up quickly and made her way back to the office.

****

"Have I missed anything?" Sadie asked, as she bounced back into the office.

"Yes," said Jenny. "There's been quite a flap on here, while you've been out. We had another message from Brian Lomax – he wants to meet up with Lucy's aunt."

"But that's good, isn't it? Why the flap?"

"Because I'm not sure I like the idea," said Lucy, before Jenny could reply. "He's asked to meet several women, all of them younger than himself and now, quite suddenly, he wants to meet my aunt."

"It's not quite suddenly, though, is it?" said Sadie. "Isn't that what we told him to do? Find a woman more his own age. Have you informed your aunt yet?" Sadie asked. "I mean, it is really up to her, isn't it?"

"That's what I said!" said Connie. "Anyway, we've sent a message to Agnes and we're waiting to hear from her."

The computer pinged again. "Two messages," said Lucy, "and one is from my aunt. She says she's going to accept the invitation."

"Good for her." Sadie clapped her hands. "So who is the other one from?"

Lucy looked back at the screen. "Ann Masters. She's still going on about the man who didn't turn up. I don't know what she expects us to do about it. She didn't even pay for the meeting; he did."

"Forget about it," said Connie. "We don't have to do anything. Anyway, there might be a good reason why the guy didn't show."

"So, getting back to your aunt, she's going to take the old man on, is she?" Sadie laughed.

"Looks like it." Lucy frowned.

Sadie was rather surprised at Lucy's attitude. "Why are you so against it? He might be an okay guy. Where's he taking her and when?"

"He's calling for her tomorrow evening at seven. They're having dinner at Anthony's." Lucy hesitated. "I'm worried she might like him and they get together permanently."

"So what if they do? Good luck to them both, that's all I can say. From what you've told me, your aunt could do with someone in her life." Sadie sat down. "What's the big deal?"

Lucy ran her fingers back and forth across the keyboard. "I'm thinking about my uncle. What would he think if he was still alive? He and my aunt were really good together. They thought the world of each other. Should she be going out with another man?"

"Lucy, you've got to get yourself a life, girl. If your uncle were still alive, she wouldn't be thinking about a date. She wouldn't even have joined the agency." Sadie heaved a sigh. "Your aunt knows there'll never be anyone to take the place of your uncle. But for heaven's sake, she's still alive and well, and trying to get on with her life. Do you really want her to spend the rest of her life alone, because you can't get your head around it?" She stopped abruptly and shook her head. She could feel an argument brewing. Normally she wouldn't give a damn and would continue to give her opinion, whether it was wanted or not. However, Lucy was a friend and a partner in the firm. Besides, having just spent half an hour on the phone trying to sort out her own tangled problems for the coming evening, she might end up saying a lot more than she ought. "We best drop it."

Connie nodded. She had wanted to say something similar, when Lucy was raving on about it earlier. Okay, she could have found the words, but she would have been too tactful. She might not have got through to Lucy. Sadie could always be relied on to hit the right spot.

Lucy turned back to the computer. She knew Sadie was right. Her aunt was entitled to a bit of fun now. She had nursed her husband for several years before he died. But what if she chose the wrong person?

Yet, who was Lucy to judge anyone? She had made a bad choice when she'd decided to marry Ben. Both her mother and Aunt Agnes had tried to make her wait and see how the romance panned out. But she'd been stubborn, maintaining they were both wrong and had gone ahead and married the horrible man. More fool her. He had been a waste of space and a bully.

"Anyone want a coffee?" Jenny broke the silence. She plugged in the kettle.

"Yes, please," Lucy looked up and glanced at Sadie. "Yes, I know you're right, it's just I don't want her to make any mistakes."

"She won't," laughed Sadie. "Your auntie is a tough cookie. I reckon she'll let Brian know exactly what she thinks of him after their evening out." She tapped Connie on the shoulder. "Okay. What do you want me to do now?"

CHAPTER NINETEEN

Sadie decided to wear one of her own dresses that evening. After all, her real date was with Michael; Andrew's presence was simply to make Connie jealous. They were going to a nice restaurant. It wasn't anywhere too formal, but she knew it would be smart, so she chose one of her less outrageous outfits.

"Andrew's car has arrived." Connie called out from the bottom of the stairs.

"Okay, nearly ready." Sadie sat on the bed and waited until Andrew rang the doorbell. Actually, she had been ready for sometime, but she wanted Connie to open the door. It would be good for her to meet up with Andrew again, however briefly. With Jenny still on a shopping spree in Oxford Street, there wasn't anyone else to let him in.

"You'd better come in. Sadie's still upstairs." Connie's voice drifted up the stairs. "I don't know what she's doing. She's been up there ages."

The moment Sadie heard Andrew and Connie go through to the sitting room, she crept to the top of the stairs. Her plan was to leave them alone together for a few minutes, but at the same time, she didn't want to miss a thing.

****

Downstairs, Andrew shuffled from one foot to another. He had hoped to see Connie, while calling for Sadie. He had even given a great deal of thought as to what he would say to her. However when she opened the door, his well-rehearsed speech flew out of his head. "You're looking good, Connie," was the best he could come up with.

"Thank you," Connie replied. "You're looking well yourself." She sat down and picked up the newspaper. She wasn't really reading it. Nothing in the news interested her these days. It was usually doom and gloom on every page. But she wanted Andrew to believe she wasn't even slightly concerned about him dating other women.

"I hope you don't mind me taking Sadie out this evening. I mean, you're not upset by it, are you?"

"Me? Upset? No, of course not. Whatever gave you that idea?" Connie shook the newspaper and made a big thing of turning the page.

"I mean, you don't mind me coming here to pick her up? I'm not unsettling you, am I?" Andrew fidgeted with his tie – something he always did when he felt himself in an uncomfortable situation.

"I don't care what you do. What makes you think I'm unsettled?"

"Nothing," said Andrew. "No, nothing at all." He grinned. "Except you're reading the newspaper upside down."

Tossing the paper to one side, Connie closed her eyes. She felt such a fool. She wanted Andrew to think she couldn't care less about him. She even tried to reassure herself she didn't give a damn what the hell he did. Yet, she did care. She cared deeply. It had been bad enough when he'd met Lucy's aunt. But tonight he had called here to pick up Sadie. Sadie was more his age. Sadie would make him laugh. Sadie would… She didn't want to think any more about what Sadie might do. She wanted to stop all the thoughts hurtling around inside her head. She screwed up her face, and tears squeezed their way through her eyelids and rolled down her cheeks. She loved Andrew. She would never love another man the way she loved him. She wanted to fling her arms around him, yet… there was still the floozy to be reckoned with. That wretched woman was always going to pop up between them.

"Are you all right?" Andrew squatted down beside her. "Perhaps I should call Sadie?" He patted her hand, his face etched with lines of concern.

"No!" Connie opened her eyes and reached for a tissue. "I'm all right." But she wasn't all right. She was far from all right. Sadie would be down in a few minutes and then the two of them would disappear out the door and into the night, leaving her sitting here alone and miserable. Damn Sadie! Damn the floozy for starting all this in the first place!

Andrew swallowed hard. He wished he hadn't come here tonight. He shouldn't have made the arrangement with Sadie in the first place. But coming here to pick her up was a bad idea. Connie looked awful.

****

Sadie sat at the top of the stairs, listening to every word. This was working out even better than she had hoped. Was there something else she could do to push Connie into admitting she had made a mistake? Then she had a brilliant idea. She leaped to her feet and ran back to her bedroom. She dragged several outfits from the wardrobe and threw them onto the bed. At last she found everything she was looking for. She pulled off the dress she was wearing and quickly changed into some different gear. Looking at herself in the mirror, she decided it needed something else and began yanking stuff out of the drawers. "There" she said out loud, gazing at her reflection, "perfect."

When she reached the sitting room, she found Connie staring down at the floor with Andrew squatted down beside her.

"I'm ready," said Sadie, bursting through the door. "What do you think?" She did a twirl on the spot.

"You look very…" Andrew gaped at her and swallowed hard, "nice."

"Oh my God!" Connie had looked up to find Sadie wearing a very short, black, red and white jazzy striped skirt. It was skin-tight and she had hitched it up so high they could almost see her knickers. She had teamed it with a yellow and black spotted top and a fluorescent pink and green boa was flung over one shoulder. The most enormous black and gold earrings dangled from her ears. To finish, she was carrying a bright orange jacket over her arm. "For heaven's sake, Sadie. You can't go to a good restaurant dressed like that." She glanced at Andrew. "You don't want to be seen with her in that outfit, do you?"

"Of course he does. Andrew needs a little excitement in his life." Sadie strode across to the mirror. "Anyway, what's wrong with it?"

"What's right with it, you mean? It's not the sort of thing you wear to go to Benedict's. And the heels on those shoes are too high. You can't even walk in them. You're going to make Andrew look ridiculous."

"What do you care?" Sadie replied haughtily. She didn't turn around; she was still preening herself in the mirror. "Andrew, do you think I should wear my black and white feather boa with this dress or does this one look good? I wanted something to jazz up my outfit a little." She could see Connie's reflection and was delighted at how horrified she looked.

"No! No. Forget the boa altogether." Connie leapt to her feet. "Andrew, you're going to be a laughing stock."

"You aren't interested in Andrew any more, so why are you getting yourself so worked up about what he and I are doing – or wearing?" She swung around. "If you think I'm not dressed well enough to go to Benedict's with Andrew, then why don't *you* go with him instead?"

Connie stared at Sadie for a moment. "I'm not dressed," she whispered. She was still wearing the suit she had worn in the office.

"I'm sure Andrew will wait." Sadie's tone was brusque. She still needed Connie to believe she was annoyed with her for interfering in her choice of dress. "But if you aren't interested, then we'll go." She looked around. "I've forgot my bag, hang on a moment."

"Please don't tell me you're taking that huge thing you tote around the shops." Connie snapped.

"Why not? It's got stripes all over it. It'll match my skirt. I'll show you, Andrew." Sadie hurried out of the room and galloped upstairs. She hovered around on the landing hoping to hear what Connie said.

"I don't mind waiting for you to change, Connie." Andrew took her hand.

Connie looked up into Andrew's eyes. They were pleading with her. Even *she* wouldn't want to be seen with Sadie tonight. Her outfit was outrageous. No, it was more than that; it was hideous. She smiled. "I'll be as quick as I can." She had almost reached the door when she thought of Sadie. "But what about Sadie? She's going to be as mad as hell with me."

"You go and get changed. I'll speak to Sadie. I'll make it up to her." Andrew smiled as his ex-wife left the room.

The moment Sadie heard Connie close her bedroom door she hurried back downstairs. She had swiftly changed into something a little less over the top, when she'd heard how things were going. Okay, she liked bright colours, but even she wouldn't like to be seen in anything so appalling. "Okay." She grinned. "So how're you going to make it up to me?"

"I'll think of something," laughed Andrew.

"I'm going to meet Michael now. I'll get a cab. Did you book for three at Benedict's? If so you need to cancel one place, before Connie gets there."

"No I left it booked for two. I was sure they would find another chair on the night." Andrew paused. "Thanks, Sadie." He kissed her on the cheek.

"I better go before Connie comes down and finds I've changed. Tell her I've gone clubbing or something. I'll give the door a slam so she'll think I'm a bit fed up. Bye, Andrew. Have a great time."

Sadie hurried along to the end of the street, pulling out her mobile phone as she went. "Change of plan, Michael," she puffed. "I'll tell you about it later." She hailed a passing taxi. "Where do you want me to meet you?"

****

"Did I hear the door close?" Connie had changed and was back downstairs.

"Yes. Sadie said to tell you she's gone clubbing."

Connie pulled a face. "Best place for an outfit like that." She sighed. "We better get going otherwise they'll give our table away." Before leaving the house, she left a brief note for Jenny telling her where everyone was.

****

"I didn't expect to be going out this evening, so it's a nice surprise, said Connie as Andrew pulled into the car park behind Benedict's restaurant.

"It's a nice surprise for me, too." He smiled.

"What on earth made you decide to bring Sadie here in the first place? You know the kinds of things she wears."

"I thought a little of your dress sense might have rubbed off on her, especially as she's living with you at the moment." He laughed. He knew it would take something really serious to change the way Sadie thought or dressed. But he'd had to take her somewhere nice. The arrangements were being made through the agency and Connie knew Andrew wasn't a fan of discos or rowdy nightclubs.

She took Andrew's arm, as they walked into the restaurant. It felt good to be with him again. She took a deep breath. She must really try to forget about the floozy and enjoy the evening.

CHAPTER TWENTY

When Sadie arrived home, the house was quiet. She crept upstairs and found Jenny was already asleep. She changed into her night things, before tiptoeing along the landing to take a peek in Connie's room. The bed was empty.

She began to make her way back to her room, but realised she was still too excited to sleep. She'd had another wonderful evening with Michael and felt she needed to unwind a little before going to bed. Perhaps a mug of hot chocolate might help.

While she was waiting for the milk to heat, she recalled her evening. She and Michael had lost all track of time at Zak's Wine Bar and Disco. It was only when they sat down to catch their breath they'd noticed how late it was. Why on earth couldn't she have met Michael before she'd married Alex? Her life would have been so different. She could be living in a pleasant house in the suburbs. She might also have a couple of kids by now. Michael would have made such a loving husband and a doting father. Still thinking about it, she tipped the warm milk into the mug of chocolate powder and sank into a chair.

And yet it could still happen. If he felt the same way about her, as she did about him – yes, it could still happen. She was still young enough to have children. She'd always wanted to be a mother and she knew her own mother was crying out for grandchildren.

It was Alex who had said no. "Selfish bastard," she muttered, slamming her fist down on the table. His lame excuse had been, 'children will come between us, Sadie'. But she'd realised too late it was because she would have had to give up her job, which meant the lazy blighter would have needed to find decent employment.

Michael was so different. He was polite, he was kind, and his face lit up when he saw her. For a moment Sadie felt sad when she recalled his wife had died of cancer. The big C, as John Wayne used to call it. Michael had told her how he sat with his wife until the end.

Sadie cupped her hands around the mug and reminded herself how delighted he had sounded when she phoned to say she would be meeting him on her own after all. Later, when she explained what had happened, he'd seemed pleased Andrew and Connie might be getting back together. "Life is too short to carry a grudge," he'd told her. "Whatever happened in the past should stay there. Connie needs to put it behind her." Then he'd smiled that lovely smile of his before continuing. "You're quite the little match maker aren't you? Or perhaps I should say peace maker in this case."

She looked down at her swollen feet. She had danced her socks off all evening and hadn't felt a thing. But, now she was sitting comfortably in a chair, they were beginning to protest. Michael had liked her outfit. Though it hadn't been as zany as the one she had worn to get Connie rattled, it had been very different to the ones she had worn on their first two dates.

They hadn't had a chance to talk much because of the loud music, but on the way home in the taxi Michael had kissed her. It was a warm, gentle kiss, the kind of kiss which left you panting for more. She touched her lips. She could still feel the tingle of his lips on hers. And then, when he had seen her to the door, he'd kissed her again, saying he would ring her sometime the next day.

Sadie swallowed the last of her hot chocolate and glanced at the clock. It was very late and Connie still wasn't home. She must be having one whale of a time.

****

Benedict's was a lovely restaurant. The food there was always delicious and so well presented. There was only one drawback; it didn't have the intimacy of the Condrew. Connie felt at home at the Condrew. She had very nearly suggested they cancel the dinner reservation and go there instead. But perhaps Andrew might not have felt comfortable about it, especially after what had happened the last time.

During the drive to the restaurant, Andrew had decided to play the evening with caution. He wasn't going to say or do anything to rush their relationship. At first, it had crossed his mind to cancel Benedict's and go to the Condrew. But, recalling their last visit there, he quickly dismissed the idea.

"Would you like to dance?" he asked. The restaurant had a small dance floor and the band was playing a waltz.

Connie smiled. "Yes, please," she whispered.

It felt so good being in Andrew's arms again. She had thought of him a great deal over the last week. She hadn't wanted to. Yet, how could she not think of him? His name had popped up in the office almost every day and each time, she had felt a stab of pain that she wasn't with him. But then the spectre of the floozy would rear up from a black cloud, reminding Connie she was still there, hovering between them.

"Thank you for coming with me this evening." Andrew smiled. "I don't know what Benedict's would have made of Sadie's outfit."

"Sadie has a crazy sense of dress. When we held the launch, we all spoke to Sadie in turn, asking her what she might be wearing. I think she was beginning to get a complex – if it's at all possible for Sadie to get a complex about anything. Fortunately for us, she didn't throw a tantrum. Instead, she bought something respectable. Well, very nearly respectable. Her dress was so tight she could hardly walk." She laughed. "I won't tell you what happened to her on the way to the Royale. Suffice to say, she gave one London bus driver the ride of his life." Connie cast her eyes around the elegant room. Most people were in evening dress. "The maitre d' might have thrown her out – and you, too." She laughed. "Though, she wouldn't have cared. She'd have stuck two fingers up, stood up at the microphone and told them all what she thought, before storming out. But it would have looked bad for you. You bring clients here, don't you?"

"Yes, I do. But it didn't happen. You saved the day and my reputation." Andrew bit his lip. He shouldn't have said that. It would remind Connie of his one indiscretion, just when the evening was going so well.

However, Connie merely smiled. At this moment, she was too happy to let anything spoil it.

The hours passed all too quickly and now the band was playing the last waltz. The dance floor was packed and Connie snuggled up to Andrew as they rocked back and forth in time with the music. "That's it, I'm afraid," said Andrew, as the band played the final chord. "I hope you've enjoyed your evening."

"Yes, I have," mumbled Connie. She was sorry it had all come to an end. There was so much she wanted to say to

Andrew, but somehow the time had slipped away too fast. They had talked at length about the dating agency and Andrew's work, among many other things. Yet they had skirted around the real issues. How they felt about each other and what they were going to do about it. No! That was wrong – what *she* was going to do about it. Andrew was already trying very hard to get back into her life. "It's been wonderful, Andrew. It's been like… old times."

"Yes, it has." Andrew sighed. It *was* like old times, except now he would be taking her back to her own home. His thoughts drifted to the room at the Condrew. It was all ready and waiting for them, if only… But this wasn't the right time. Maybe after a few more dinners and more wine – lots more wine…

"I was wondering," Connie broke into his thoughts. She hesitated.

"What were you wondering?" Andrew prompted.

"Nothing. It wasn't anything." Connie shook her head as she slipped her arms into her jacket. She was doing it again! Holding back. Why the heck didn't she simply say what she wanted to say and be done with it? "Except… I was wondering whether we might have a drink at the Condrew to round off the evening." She looked at her watch. "But perhaps it's too late. You have to be at the office tomorrow morning."

"A last drink at the Condrew sounds good to me," said Andrew quickly. "If we hurry we should catch the bar before they close." He wondered what gave her the idea, but he wasn't going to ask. It might spoil the moment.

There were only a handful of people in the bar at the Condrew. Most of the guests had probably gone to bed. "I'm afraid I'm closing, sir – unless of course you're staying at the hotel."

Andrew was about to tell him they weren't, but Connie spoke first. "Yes, we're staying here for the night," she said. "I'll have a gin & tonic. What will you have, Andrew?"

During the short journey to the Condrew, Connie had wondered whether she was doing the right thing. Her heart was fine with the idea – in fact her heart was ecstatic. It was beating like a bass drum, telling her this was the way to go. It was her head that was causing her grief; constantly reminding her of Andrew's mistake. Pointing out she should get over Andrew and move on. But move on to where, and who with? No other man would ever live up to Andrew.

Sadie was right; he was a very sexy man. Okay, she hadn't actually used those words. What was it she had actually called him? Handsome and virile – that was it. But for heaven's sake it was the same thing, wasn't it? So now it was make your mind up time. Put up or shut up! Which in layman's terms meant she either needed to be firm with her head and get over the floozy or shut Andrew out of her life forever.

Her remark took Andrew by surprise, though he tried to hide it from the barman. "Make mine a malt whisky." He showed Connie over to a table in the corner. "Did you really mean it or were you only saying it to get a drink?"

"I don't know." Connie shook her head. "Let's see how it plays out, shall we?"

CHAPTER TWENTY-ONE

Jenny gave Sadie a prod. She had just opened her eyes and saw that it was half-past nine. "Wake up, Sadie! We've slept in." She scrambled out of bed and ran towards the bathroom, only pausing to bang on Connie's door as she passed. "Wake up! We've all overslept."

Sadie rolled over and squinted at the clock. Surely it wasn't morning already. It only seemed like a few moments ago when she closed her eyes. "I'll get some coffee organised while you're in the shower," she called out, dragging herself out of bed. "I'm next in the bathroom, Connie," she added, when she passed Connie's door. "So don't you go creeping in there before me."

Once Sadie had set out the cups and put the kettle on, she dashed back upstairs. She met Jenny coming out of the bathroom. "Have you heard anything from Connie?"

"No," Jenny replied. "But when I'm under the shower I can't hear anything."

Sadie banged her fist on Connie's door before going in. "She's not here." She smiled to herself. If Connie was where she thought she was, then her plan had really worked.

"Do you think she's all right?" asked Jenny. Her face creased into a frown. "She might have had an accident or something."

"Didn't you read the note Connie left for you? It was on the hall table. She was going out with Andrew. I saw it last night when I came in."

"No, I didn't. I thought she had simply popped out with a few mates. Anyway, weren't you going out with Andrew?"

"Yes, I was, but then…I wasn't." Sadie decided to choose her words carefully. Jenny didn't know about her plan to get Andrew and Connie back together and she had no intention of telling her now. "Andrew was here when I came downstairs last night. Connie almost had a seizure when she saw what I had chosen to wear, so…" Sadie paused. Jenny's frown was turning into a puzzled expression. "Forget it. It's complicated."

"Everything about you is complicated," said Jenny, walking back to the bedroom she shared with Sadie. Suddenly she stopped and swung around. It had dawned on her what Sadie had been trying to say. "Please don't tell me you were going to wear one of your crazy dresses to go out with Andrew." One look at Sadie told her she was right. She clasped her hands to her cheeks. "You were! Oh my goodness, you were going to wear something outrageous. Little wonder Connie had a fit." Her expression of horror changed into a grin and her hands slid down from her face. "You crazy kid. Gosh! I wish I'd been here."

Sadie was thankful Jenny hadn't been here. The whole thing had only worked because she wasn't here to let Andrew in when he'd called. She glanced at the clock. "I'm going for a shower. Talk later." She'd got out of that tricky situation for the moment.

****

"Where have you been?" Lucy was alone in the office, when Sadie and Jenny finally arrived. "The mother ship's been going berserk." She pointed towards the computer. "The phone hasn't stopped ringing either. I've been running back and forth like a scolded cat." She peered behind the two girls. "Where's Connie?"

"She went out with Andrew last night and didn't come home," replied Jenny.

"But I thought Sadie was going out with Andrew."

"Yes. It seems she was and then she wasn't." Jenny sighed. "Don't let's get started on that."

"Suffice to say, my choice of outfit did not meet Connie's approval," Sadie interrupted. "Shall I open the mail?"

At that moment, the phone rang again. It was Sadie who picked it up.

"Hi, it's me." Connie's voice came down the line. "I know it's a bit short notice, but I'm taking a few hours off today."

"Okay. No problem. But exactly how many hours are you…?"

"Twenty four." Connie broke in. "I'm sure you'll all be able to cope." She hung up without another word.

Sadie tried to contain her excitement. If she was right, Connie and Andrew had gone to the Condrew last night and were going to spend the day there. Everything was going to plan. *Now it's up to you, Andrew*, she thought as she slit open another letter. *And for goodness sake don't do anything to cock it up!*

"Who was it?" asked Lucy.

"It was Connie. She's decided to take a few hours off today." She grinned. "Something's come up."

****

Connie looked down at Andrew. He was still sleeping. She was tempted to wake him, but decided against it. Why not let him enjoy his long lie in? Instead, she allowed her thoughts to drift back to the evening before.

The previous evening, downstairs in the bar, they had sipped their drinks slowly, without saying a word. One by one, the other guests retired to their rooms, until there were only the two of them left. The barman, still drying the glasses, kept flashing suspicious glances in their direction. Obviously he thought they weren't residents after all and had lied so he would serve them drinks.

Eventually, he'd sidled up beside them. "Can I get you something else?" he asked.

Again, it was she who replied. "Yes. Could you have a bottle of champagne sent to room one hundred and nine?" Even to her, her voice had sounded a little strained. The barman had probably thought they were both married and playing away.

Andrew, who had been fidgeting with his empty glass, looked up quickly. Once the barman moved away, he reached across the small table and took her hand. "Are you sure about this?" he asked quietly.

She nodded and made her way across the reception area towards the stairs, leaving Andrew to settle the bill. Glancing back, she saw the barman smile broadly as he pocketed a couple of notes. Andrew had been generous.

The moment she had entered the bedroom, she'd fixed her eyes on the bed, fully expecting to see the spectre of the floozy rising up to haunt her. But to her delight, all she saw were the crisp white bed sheets. Andrew followed her into the room and placed his arms around her. And there they had stood, motionless, until a tap on the door told them the champagne had arrived.

Andrew popped the cork, filled two glasses and handed one to her. They stepped out onto the balcony and listened to the light hum of the late night traffic. She watched Andrew as they sipped their champagne. It was obvious he wasn't quite sure what to do or say. But he didn't need to say anything; his eyes spoke volumes. She looked into the bedroom and then at the bed, half expecting to see the floozy suddenly materialize from beneath the sheets. But no, it didn't happen. What she did see, as she stared at the bed, was Andrew's love for her. He had hired this room. He was paying a small fortune for it, and it was all for her.

At that very moment, her love for him overwhelmed her and, setting her glass down on the small table, she flung her arms around his neck and kissed him. "I love you, Andrew," she gasped. "I've been such a fool. Forgive me." Smiling, Andrew swept her up in his arms and carried her into the bedroom where…

The sound of Andrew stirring broke her thoughts and she turned back to face him.

He opened his eyes. For a moment, he wasn't sure where he was, but then he saw Connie smiling at him and he remembered everything.

"If you were due at the office at nine o'clock, then you're nearly two hours late," said Connie, gently twisting a strand of his hair through her fingers.

"There's nothing so urgent it can't wait," he replied. He reached out and pulled her closer to him. "What about you? Don't you have an office to go to?"

"I've already telephoned and told Sadie I'm taking the day off."

"That's all right, then. We can spend the day here." He kissed her. "We have a lot of catching up to do."

"That's exactly what I hoped you'd say," she replied.

****

The phone in the office rang again. This time it was David, wanting to speak to Jenny. A date had been set for him to go back to London and he was hoping they could meet up. He coughed. "I'll be on my own this time… John has a couple of other things he needs to see to."

Jenny glanced across towards Lucy. She would be disappointed when she heard John wasn't coming after all. "I'm looking forward to seeing you. I'll try to arrange to have some time off," she added, before putting down the phone.

"Just my luck!" Lucy grimaced, when Jenny told her the news. "I meet someone nice and then he dumps me before our first date!" She'd had a terrible feeling this was going to happen. John's calls had become very infrequent. Even on the occasions he did ring, he'd sounded distant. His whole attitude seemed to have changed. Nevertheless, it was a blow having to learn from Jenny that he wasn't interested.

"David didn't say he was dumping you," said Jenny. She felt awful at having to tell her friend the news. John should have telephoned Lucy and told her himself. "He just told me John had a couple of pressing engagements."

"But that's what he meant." Lucy pointed at the computer as another email dropped in. "All these people on the website are getting asked out, yet no one has asked to meet me." She paused. "Even Sadie has met someone new."

"Don't you start getting at me, Lucy," Sadie chided. "And what do you mean by, 'even Sadie has met someone new'. I'm not a freak, you know!" She shook her head. "You need to get out there and find someone for yourself, instead of sitting here waiting for someone to come knocking on your door." Sadie threw down the letter she had opened. "Look,

Lucy, I'm sorry for snapping at you, but you've got to get yourself a life. You were a dormouse when you were married to Ben and although you're now your own woman, you're still a dormouse. Don't just sit there waiting for someone no one else wants to suddenly give you a call, because I'm telling you that person is going to be trash. Go through the website and choose someone for yourself, someone who sounds good and kind. Someone like yourself."

Lucy didn't reply. She stared down at the keyboard.

Jenny glanced at Sadie. Had she had gone too far this time? If Sadie had spoken to Connie or her in that manner, they would have snapped back at her, saying she should mind her own damn business. But Lucy was different. Taking the brunt of Ben's cruelty for so many years had left her a rather insecure person.

"Do either of you mind if I go for a walk? I really need to have a think," Lucy said. "I'm sure one of you could arrange the meeting for whoever has contacted us." She picked up her jacket and handbag and headed for the door.

"Lucy!" Sadie grabbed at her arm. "I'm sorry. I really shouldn't have spoken to you like that. I always say too much. You know me well enough now to realise I don't mean anything nasty."

"No, it's all right. You're probably right." Lucy smiled weakly. "I just want a little fresh air."

"Your tongue can be really sharp sometimes," said Jenny, after Lucy had left. "Why on earth did you go off at her like that? You know what she's like."

Sadie looked away. She felt bad at being so short with Lucy. But she was just trying to make her see that she needed to pull herself together. "I know," she said at last. "However, she really needs to sort herself out. Hopefully she's wrong about John and he'll get in touch with her. It does seem a little strange, though, to suddenly pull out of the trip to London." She paused and took a deep breath. "I think we'd better see what the email was about."

"I'll do it." Jenny went across to the computer. She didn't want Sadie to send any messages at the moment; not in her present mood. "Oh my goodness. It's from someone called Paul Holloway." She looked up. "He wants to meet Lucy."

Sadie leapt to her feet and ran to the top of the stairs. "Lucy! Lucy!" she called out. But there was no reply. "It's too late, she's gone. We'll have to wait until she comes back," she said, walking back into the office.

CHAPTER TWENTY-TWO

Lucy stood on the pavement outside. Tears welled in her eyes and rolled down her cheeks. She heard Sadie call out, but ignored her. 'Stuff you,' she thought, wiping her eyes with the back of her hand. 'I'll come when I'm good and ready.'

She sighed as she walked off in the direction of Hyde Park. Miss Sadie know-it-all didn't know everything. She *had* tried making a date on the website – twice! One person had responded by declining her invitation. He had been very polite about it, but at the end of the day, it was still *thanks but no thanks.*

The other had been more positive, agreeing to meet up with her for a meal. She had worn her very best dress. At least it was one she could get into and didn't make her look like a pudding overflowing its basin. She'd taken care with her make-up and had even splashed out on some expensive perfume. She'd arrived at the restaurant in good time, not wanting to keep him waiting and then hung around for ages before realising she'd been stood up. How could he do that? How could anyone be so cruel as to leave her standing there – humiliated?

She had noticed a man hovering on the other side of the road for a few minutes, but then he'd disappeared. At the time she thought he was waiting for someone, who had turned up when she wasn't looking, but now, thinking back, she wondered whether he had been her date and had changed his mind once he saw her.

She shivered as she went through the gate leading into the park. Thank goodness she hadn't told the others she'd approached anyone. They would have wanted to know all the details. How could she have told them she'd been stood up? She could feel her cheeks heating up even just thinking about it. And now John had done the same thing. None of them had even given her a chance. Little wonder she saw herself as a person no one wanted.

Now you are your own, woman, but you're still a dormouse, Sadie had said. The words were still ringing in her ears. Sadie was right about that. She *was* a dormouse. Yet she hadn't always been so quiet and put upon. There had been a time when she'd been the life and soul of any party she attended. And my God, she had been to a number of parties. She grinned to herself as she recalled her youth. Oh, what fun she'd had. The lovely young men she had dated…but all that had been a long time ago. Long before she'd met Sadie and the others; they had never met the real Lucy. Back then she had been something like Sadie – well, perhaps a little like Sadie. Surely nobody could possibly be really like Sadie. The grin on her face disappeared.

It had been at one such party that she'd met Ben. At first he'd seemed like a nice young man. Yes, he'd been a little sharp with her at times, but she had simply dismissed it, believing it to be the strain of his job. So when he asked her to marry him, she'd said 'yes' before the words were fully out of his mouth.

But, after the wedding, he swiftly changed from Mr Nice Guy and the real Ben began to show through. He was demanding; a complete control freak, and he wouldn't allow her to meet anyone once she had left her place of work. Her whole personality changed and she became a recluse. And then when the beatings began. She lost all confidence. If it hadn't been for her son, she couldn't have gone on. Terry needed her, and he was all that mattered.

She shook her head and dragged herself back to the present. Enough! Now she needed to get a grip, be more forceful. For a moment, she trembled at the thought. It wasn't easy for a leopard to change its spots simply because it happened to fancy being a lion for a change. Or was it?

She sniffed and blinked her eyes rapidly, forcing back the tears trying to well up in her eyes again. She took a deep breath. Yes, it was easy, because here was one cute little chick who was going to prove it. She slammed her fist down into her hand. She would buck up her ideas, get herself a new man and get on with her life. When she got back to the office, she would trawl through the photos and profiles of men her own age and see who popped up. And she would suggest a meeting. Good work, Lucy, she thought. How forceful is that?

But to play safe, she still wouldn't say anything to the others. Not likely! Okay, she was going to turn herself around and be brave, but not *too* brave. Once she had something positive, then she would tell them. In the meantime it would be her secret.

Deep down, she still felt bitterly disappointed John had changed his mind about her. After all, in this instance, it was *he* who had made the first move, so she'd thought she was in with a chance. For goodness sake, there must have been something about her he liked when they'd met. But, whatever it was, it had certainly fizzled out very quickly.

She strolled down to the lake and bought an ice cream from a van. It had been a long time since she'd last visited the park. She sat down on a bench and watched people rowing small boats across the water. Some looked experienced, while others struggled to pull the oars. She smiled when one of the oars missed the water completely and the man in the boat fell backwards off his seat.

The time passed swiftly and it was only the sound of a clock chiming somewhere in the distance that made her glance at her watch. She leapt to her feet and walked quickly back up the path towards Park Lane. She hadn't meant to stay out so long. But she'd enjoyed wandering around on her own, and at least she had come to a decision about her life.

"Where've you been?" Sadie had heard Lucy's footsteps on the stairs and was waiting by the office door.

"Hyde Park." Lucy took off her coat. "Why? Is there a problem with that?"

"No, not at all. But I was worried about you." Sadie glanced at Jenny. "Anyway, the message that came in before you left was from someone called Paul Holloway. He wants to meet you, Lucy." Sadie's eyes sparkled as she spoke. "I called out for you, but you'd already gone."

"Yes, come and take a look." Jenny swung the screen around. "As you weren't here, we took a look at his profile and he seems to be a very nice."

Lucy screwed up her eyes suspiciously. Had they done this? Had the two of them begged someone to ask her out to make her feel better? She wouldn't put it past Sadie to do something like that. How embarrassing. But then she recalled there'd been a message in the box when she left and Sadie *had* yelled down the stairs. So perhaps it was the real deal. Anyway, the email would show the time it came in, so she would know whether it was a fix-up or not. "Okay, I'll take a look."

She flung her coat on a chair, and sat down in front of the screen. The email was genuine. It had arrived *before* she'd left the office. So there were no shenanigans going on. "Yes, he does seem to be rather nice," she said at last. "If he's telling the truth here." She pointed towards the screen.

"Go for it, Lucy," said Sadie. "You'll only learn more about him by taking the plunge." She paused. "I know we all said we weren't going to rush into another relationship, but when someone rears their head like Michael and David and now Paul, why not give it a whirl?"

"Yes, I will," said Lucy. "Jenny, would you do the arrangements? Just say I've agreed to meet him. We'll see what happens next."

Jenny tapped out the message and pressed send. "That's it. All done. It looks like you'll have a date very soon."

Lucy didn't reply. She was determined not to get too excited until the meeting was arranged. He could be like John, and call it off, or even the other man, who hadn't bothered to show up. However, she had to admit his photograph did look rather nice and his profile read well. But only time would tell. The only problem now was that Sadie and Jenny knew about the arrangement. So much for keeping it a secret

It was an hour later when a reply dropped in the inbox. Lucy read it out to the others. "He says he's delighted I've agreed to meet him and suggests having dinner tomorrow evening. He mentions a small restaurant just off the Haymarket."

"That's wonderful, Lucy," said Jenny. "It's crowded around Haymarket so it should be safe to meet him there. He won't try anything on with so many people about. I think you're in for a really nice evening."

"Let's wait and see." Lucy turned back to the screen. "Another message here. It's from Ann Masters." She paused while she opened the message. "She wants to meet Andrew."

"Ann Masters is asking to meet Andrew!" Sadie screamed. "Oh my God! No way. If Connie finds out, she'll lay an egg. Perhaps we should delete it." Already she could see all her hard work getting them together going down the pan.

"We can't delete it! Andrew will have to be told. It's up to him what he says to her." Jenny peered at the screen over Lucy's shoulder. "Besides, if he and Connie are really back together, then there won't be a problem. No doubt he'll ask us to remove his profile from the website."

"Sounds reasonable, I suppose." However Sadie still wasn't sure Connie would see it that way.

****

Connie and Andrew were enjoying a light lunch on the balcony of their room. Both were wearing bathrobes supplied by the hotel. Connie had worn a full-length evening dress the night before and hadn't anything to change into. She had told Andrew that she couldn't go anywhere until the evening otherwise she would look stupid.

Andrew didn't mind spending the day at the hotel. He was enjoying having his wife back and being able to spend some time alone with her. It had been well after lunchtime when they had showered and put on robes, by which time they were both feeling hungry. The waiter, who delivered their lunch, had been discreet. He didn't raise an eyebrow when Andrew opened the door dressed only in a bathrobe, while Connie sat out on the balcony wearing the same.

"It's so good to have you back in my life." Andrew reached across the table and squeezed Connie's hand.

She smiled. She was happy she had finally overcome her obsession with the floozy. It was seeing the sheer look of horror on Andrew's face when Sadie bounced downstairs dressed like a pearly queen that had made her realise how much she loved him. She couldn't allow him to be so humiliated.

"How do you feel about moving in here for a few days?" she asked. "We could each bring a few things from home and stay here until we sort our lives out."

Andrew had been thinking about how to bring up the subject of what they were going to do next. He was keen they should live together again, but didn't want to rush Connie into anything. Despite the wonderful night they had spent together, it was early days and she could be so unpredictable. "I think that's a great idea," he said. "We can come and go as we please."

Connie was feeling so happy. The floozy had fizzled out like a puff of smoke. Andrew was back in her life and they were going to spend some time here in their special room at the Condrew. What more could she want? But then she suddenly thought of the agency. Did she want to be involved with it anymore? Not really. But the whole thing had been her idea, so she couldn't simply opt out. The others were relying on the business for an income. They needed her. And not only that; half her business partners were relying on her house for a place to live. That very fact alone was the reason she wanted to move in here.

Yes, she wanted Andrew back in her life, which meant she wanted to sleep with him – but certainly not with her two friends sleeping in the bedroom next door.

CHAPTER TWENTY-THREE

"My aunt is meeting Brian Lomax this evening." It was the following morning and Lucy was telling her friends how her aunt had telephoned her earlier. "Gosh, yes. I'd forgot he'd asked her out." Sadie grinned."She sounded quite excited on the phone and told me joining the agency was one of the best things she'd done." Lucy smiled. "You were right, Sadie. She should enjoy her life. My uncle would have wanted that." She paused. "Brian is taking her for a meal somewhere."

But Sadie wasn't listening. She'd heard Connie coming up the stairs and was waiting by the door when she walked in. "So, is it safe to assume all is well between you and Andrew?" she asked.

"Yes, you could say that." Connie tried to sound casual, as she manoeuvred her way between the desks towards her chair, but she didn't convince anyone. Her broad smile gave away her true feelings. She had thought she might bump into either Jenny or Sadie when she went home to pick up some clothes the evening before and had prepared herself for the confrontation. But, as it turned out, neither of the girls was there at the time, so she'd quickly gathered her belongings and hurried out. "I'm going to be staying at the Condrew for a little while. But you girls can use the house."

"I think it's about time I moved back into my own flat," said Jenny. "I've called my friend a couple of times and it seems Rob came back one night, but the lady downstairs called the police again and had him moved on. He hasn't been back since."

"It's up to you, Jenny." Connie shrugged. "If you want to stay on for a few more days, then it's okay by me." She looked across at Lucy. "So what's been going on at the agency? Any new people?"

Lucy brought her up to date. "I did the Website Watch last night and another four people joined, so that's another thousand pounds in the bank." She paused. "And guess what?" She stuck out her hands, palms upwards. "Ta-da! I have a date this evening."

"Oh, are John and David back in London already?" Connie raised her eyebrows. "I thought there were still another couple of weeks to go."

"No, they aren't here yet. David is coming in about two weeks to meet up with Jenny, but John…" Lucy broke off. She didn't want to talk about John. She was still smarting over how he had dumped her. "John isn't coming. Anyway, this evening I'm meeting someone called Paul. He asked to meet me through the agency." She brought up Paul's profile on the screen. "What do you think?"

"It's not what I think, honey. It's what you feel." Connie peered at the photograph. "You know, I think I spoke to this man at the launch," she said thoughtfully. "Yes, I remember him now. He was on his own and looked rather shy, so I offered him another glass of champagne. I thought it might loosen him up a little. He seemed a very polite, quietly spoken man." She looked around at the others. "Is there anything else I should know?"

The three women looked at each other.

"Okay. What's happened? Have we been issued with a writ or something?" Connie tapped her fingers on the table. Obviously her friends had something to get off their chests.

It was Jenny who spoke first. "Anne Masters has requested a meeting," she said after a long pause. "She wants to meet Andrew."

"Andrew? You mean *my* Andrew?" Connie gasped. "Are you telling me Anne Masters wants to meet my Andrew?" She glanced at Sadie. "Oh my God, Sadie, you've got me doing it now."

"Doing what?" Sadie stared at her. "I'm just sitting here. I haven't done anything."

"Repeating myself. You've got me repeating myself." She shook her head. "There I go again."

"Nothing to do with me." Sadie shrugged.

"Yes, *your* Andrew." Jenny butted in. "Anne Masters is asking to meet Andrew."

"Well I suppose you'd better tell him." Connie sighed. "Send him an email. He'll be at the office all morning." She reached for a pen. "Use this address," she added, scribbling on a piece of paper.

"Okay, if you say so," said Lucy. She typed out a message and pressed send. "I think that's all the news for the moment, so you're up to speed."

It wasn't very long before a message from Andrew winged its way into the inbox. "He's politely declined Anne's request and has asked us to remove his profile from the agency." Lucy looked up from the screen. "He also says to inform Anne Masters he has already met the woman of his dreams." She sighed. "That is so romantic."

Connie's face glowed with pleasure as she continued to open the mail. Andrew was back in her life and she was determined nothing would ever come between them again. She had already told him that if he ever went to any kind of stag do away from home again, she would don a trouser suit and wig and go with him!

"Okay, what's next?" asked Lucy, though she really didn't give a damn what was next. In her mind she was already trying to decide what to wear this evening. She could wear the same dress she wore the evening she met John. But on reflection, perhaps it might be a bad omen. She wasn't really superstitious. Yet, did she really want to risk the possibility of Paul ditching her at their first meeting?

There was also the dress she wore at the launch, but then Paul might have already seen her in it. Did men usually take note of that kind of thing? She sighed. He probably hadn't even noticed her at the launch. If he had, he might not be asking her out.

CHAPTER TWENTY-FOUR

Lucy left the office early. She wanted time to go through her wardrobe properly. There might be something tucked away at the back she had forgot about. But even if there were, would she be able to squeeze into it? Her diet wasn't going too well. She hadn't lost any weight over the last two weeks. In fact, it seemed she had gained a pound when she'd stood on the scales this morning. It was so unfair. Some people could eat what they liked and not put on even an ounce, while she had to almost starve herself before the pointer on the scale moved a fraction downwards.

She heaved a sigh and thought back to when she'd been much slimmer. But that was before Ben started beating her up and she'd lost all respect in herself and her appearance. Now it seemed she was stuck with it.

She pulled dresses from the wardrobe one at a time and put them back. Those she knew would fit fairly comfortably were rather dowdy, while others, which looked as though they actually had a waist somewhere, were too tight. She sank down onto the bed. It was no good; she was going to have to wear the same dress she wore at the launch. If Paul were a typical male, he wouldn't even notice. But did she want a typical male? Not if he was anything like Ben, she didn't.

She glanced at the clock. She wasn't due to meet Paul at the restaurant until about half past seven, so she still had plenty of time. He had offered to pick her up, but she made an excuse, saying she needed to call somewhere else first. She wanted to see how they got on before giving him her home address.

While soaking in the bath, Lucy recalled his photo on the website. He looked rather nice and his profile showed his wife had left him for another man. Was that good or bad? Had he divorced his wife because she flirted with any man she came up against? Or was it because he was a rotten guy and she had left because she couldn't stand living with him for a moment more? She sighed. This was the downside of a blind date. Could she really rely on what Paul had said on his profile? He could have written a whole bunch of lies about himself. It would be up to her to decide when she met with him. If there was one thing she had learned, it was that nothing in life was straightforward.

****

Paul was already waiting outside the restaurant when she arrived. He looked genuinely pleased to see her. She had been a little concerned that when he met her in the flesh and realised there was a lot of flesh to meet, he might disappear into the night. The photo she had used on the site was the real deal. She had asked her neighbour to take it a few days before the launch. But he had manoeuvred her into rather a flattering pose, which seemed to have hidden many of her bulges.

"Thank you for agreeing to meet me," he said, shaking her hand. "I wasn't sure you would come."

"Thank you for asking me. I was absolutely delighted to receive your invitation." Lucy bit her lip. Did that make her sound as though she was desperate for a date?

"Shall we go in?" Paul smiled and held the door open for her.

Lucy found Paul to be charming. At first he had seemed a touch shy and unsure of himself. However, as the evening wore on, he opened up a little more. It seemed Paul's wife had been having an affair with his best friend for months, before he found out about it. "I was gobsmacked when I finally discovered what was going on. He was my best mate, for God's sake! We'd gone to school together as kids." He slammed his fist down on the table, causing the cruet set to rattle.

Lucy looked away. Even though he had been divorced for two years, it was obvious he was still very upset about it. Did this mean he was still in love with his ex-wife?

Paul reached across the table and took her hand. "I don't love her any more, if that's what you're thinking. My love for her died once I learned of the affair. No! I'm angry because the whole thing was going on under my nose and I was foolish enough not to see it. I loved and trusted her." He paused. "I didn't want another relationship. I was so let down by my wife and my best friend. I couldn't bear the thought it might happen again. But recently I decided I should pick up the pieces and move on. That's why I joined the agency." He smiled. "I saw the advertisements and made up my mind to go to the launch. That was when I first saw you. I was going to speak to you, but someone beat me to it. The other evening, I took a look through the website and found you on there and decided to send a message."

A wave of relief surged through Lucy. He had seen her at the launch party and liked her even then. He didn't seem to mind she hadn't the hourglass figure of Jenny or matchstick lines of Sadie. He liked her for the way she was, bulges and all. And, in turn, she liked him. Though he wasn't the dashing young man on a white steed she always thought would charge in and save her from a boring life, he was quite attractive and had a great sense of humour.

She told him about her marriage to Ben and how he would beat her if he came home in a bad mood. "So you see, I, too, was a little cautious when it came to deciding what to do with the rest of my life."

"What you went through makes my problems seem insignificant," he said. He moved his chair closer to hers and put his arm around her. "Let's both forget our former partners and pretend we're starting our lives all over again."

Lucy laughed. "I think that's a brilliant idea. We're two young people without a care in the world, meeting up for the first time." She paused. "But I think you should know I have a son. He started university this year and has digs in Cambridge, but he puts in an appearance now and again."

"Cambridge! He must have had good grades to get there."

"He did. I encouraged him to work hard at school. I didn't want him to turn out to be a nobody like his father." Lucy smiled. "But we aren't going to talk about our spouses all night, are we?"

"No, we aren't. And it's okay about your son. I would like to have had a son. Julia didn't want any children. She was afraid it would ruin her figure." He grinned. "And that's it," he said holding his hands up. "No more talking about our ex-partners."

At the end of the evening, Paul asked Lucy if she would like him to see her home. "I'm not expecting an invitation in or anything like that. I'd just like to make sure you get home safely."

Lucy hesitated. While she was sure Paul was the genuine article, she still didn't want him to know her address. Not yet, anyway. Better to be safe than sorry. "That's very kind, Paul," she said at last. "But I'm not going straight home, I'm staying with a friend at the moment." It was the first thing to spring into her mind.

"Fine, I'll see you safely there," he said, helping her on with her coat.

For a moment she panicked. Where on earth could she go? But then she thought of Connie's house. Hopefully one of the girls would be there to open the door. "Thank you, that would be nice," she replied.

All too soon, the taxi pulled up at Connie's home and Lucy stepped out. Paul followed her and asked the driver to wait, while he saw her to the front door. Just as she was about to press the doorbell, he took her hand and, pulling her close, he kissed her gently.

A wave of excitement ran through Lucy when their lips touched. It had been a long time since anyone had held her like this. He was so gentle, yet so passionate. Completely unlike Ben, who simply grabbed her and forced her onto the bed. There had never been any passion in their lovemaking, only lust and brutal force.

When Paul released her, she gazed up into his eyes. Now the time had come, she didn't want him to leave. It had been stupid to say she was staying with someone tonight. Had they been standing outside her flat right now, she would have dragged him in and rushed him into the bedroom. She kicked herself. Now she would have to wait until another time.

"Thank you for a wonderful evening," she whispered when he moved away.

"There's always tomorrow," he replied, smiling.

Impulsively, she reached up and put her arms around his neck and kissed him again. Stepping back, she rang the doorbell. "You'd better go, your taxi's waiting."

"Have you forgot your key again?" Jenny's voice could be heard from behind the door. "What would you have done if I'd gone out?" she continued as she pulled the door open.

"Yes, sorry about that, Jenny, but I was in such a hurry this evening, I forgot to put it in my bag." Her eyes danced from side to side as she spoke. She was trying desperately to tell Jenny to play along with her.

Jenny smiled awkwardly. She wasn't sure what was going on here. Lucy looked extremely flushed. Had Paul been trying it on? Should she grab Lucy and pull her inside before slamming the door and calling the police? But then she saw the taxi waiting at the roadside. Paul must be leaving. "It's okay. I'm just teasing you." She opened the door a little wider, before walking down the hall towards the kitchen. "I'll put the kettle on."

"So, what was that all about?" Jenny asked when Lucy finally shut the front door and joined her in the kitchen.

"I feel like an idiot." Lucy flopped into one of the chairs around the table. Before she could say anymore, she heard the front door slam shut.

"Have you got the kettle on? I'm gasping for a cup of tea." Sadie's voice rang out along the hall. "Or have you gone to bed?"

"Yes, the kettle's on. We're in the kitchen," Jenny called out. "If I'd been in bed, I'd be wide awake by now anyway."

Sadie peered cautiously around the kitchen door. Who was 'we'? Please don't say Connie had stormed home again. She was relieved, though somewhat surprised, to see Lucy sitting there. "What're you doing here? Did you have a problem with that guy; what's his name – Paul?"

"No." Lucy closed her eyes. "As I was just about to tell Jenny, I think I've just shot myself in the foot." She explained how Paul had wanted to see her home, but she had put him off, saying she was staying with a friend.

"So?" Sadie cocked her head on one side. She wasn't sure what Lucy was getting at. Had he been a monster? Had he tried to assault her?

"So, when he kissed me goodbye outside the door, I kissed him back."

"You kissed him back?" Sadie glanced at Jenny.

"Yes. I liked it."

"You liked it." Sadie shook her head.

"Yes, I kissed him back because I liked it. For goodness sake, stop repeating what I say."

"Okay. Let me get this straight," Sadie counted on her fingers. "The guy kissed you outside the front door. You liked it. Then you kissed him back. So what's your problem?" She shrugged. "Why have you shot yourself in the foot?"

"Because, if I hadn't been so cautious and told him I was staying with a friend, he would've taken me back to my flat and I could've asked him in for a coffee." Lucy replied.

"Why did you want to be so cautious in the first place?" asked Jenny

"When he wanted to take me home, I wasn't sure I wanted him to know where I lived – not yet anyway. I was afraid he might be a stalker or something. That's why I made the excuse I was staying with a friend." She slammed her fist on the arm of the chair. "Why has my life got to be so damn complicated?"

"Only because you make it that way," Sadie said. "So if you had gone to your flat, you would have hurtled him into the bedroom."

"I didn't say that." Lucy turned her face the other way. Sadie could be so spot on at times. It was uncanny.

"But that's what you meant. He must have hit the right spot." Sadie grinned.

"When he kissed me, it felt so wonderful. So gentle, so…"

"Are either of you going to drink your tea?" Jenny intervened. She pointed to the two mugs on the table. "It's getting cold. And have you decided what you're going to do now, Lucy? Are you going to stay here or are you going to get a taxi back to your flat? It's getting rather late." She winced. Ouch, that had sounded much harsher than she'd meant it to. However, it appeared Lucy hadn't noticed as she replied quite calmly.

"I think I'd better go home." Lucy spoke slowly. "I haven't any clothes here and I can't go to the office in this long dress." She pointed to the cocktail dress she was wearing.

"We could look in Connie's wardrobe." Sadie peered at Lucy. "She has a couple of… loose dresses…that might fit. I know she wouldn't mind. You could even sleep in her bed."

"No, but thanks all the same. I'll call a taxi." Lucy swallowed the last drop of tea. "I was a fool, wasn't I? I mean, I should have allowed Paul to take me home."

Sadie nodded. "Yes, I would say so." She shrugged. "Still you've done it now. No use going on about it."

However, Jenny was a little more sympathetic. "Perhaps you did the right thing. It was a first date and you didn't know you were going to click after one kiss."

Lucy was waiting by the door when the taxi arrived. "I'll see you guys in the morning. Thanks for listening to me."

"Well, after all that, how did you get on with Michael?" Jenny asked when Lucy had left. "Did you have a nice evening? Or do you have a problem you need to discuss with Agony Aunt Jenny?" She laughed. It was meant to be a joke, so Sadie's reply took her by surprise.

"As a matter of fact…"

CHAPTER TWENTY-FIVE

"That was David on the phone," Jenny called out, as she put down the receiver. Buzzing with excitement, she hurried into the kitchen to find Sadie. "He's coming to London next week. I gather the first few days will be taken up with sorting out the firm's new premises, but then he's taking the rest of the week off."

Sadie, who was buttering the toast, looked up. "Slow down, Jenny. You're talking so fast I can hardly make out what you're saying."

Jenny repeated her news more slowly.

"That's great, Jenny," Sadie smiled. "At last you guys will be able to get to know each other better." But, thinking of Lucy, she grimaced. "Did David say anything about John?"

"No. He didn't mention him at all. Not even a message for Lucy."

"What a toe rag. John could have had the decency to give her a call and tell her he'd backed out. For all he knows, she could be putting her whole life on hold, waiting for him to get in touch." In her mind's eye, Sadie could see Lucy firmly planted in an armchair, knitting socks for various worthwhile charities. "You know the kind of thing I mean? Something like Miss Havisham in *Great Expectations*."

Jenny laughed. "For heaven's sake, Sadie. You *do* exaggerate. I can hardly see Lucy sitting in some dusty old room somewhere, waiting for John to put in an appearance."

"Well no. Not now she's found Paul, or at least he found her. But something similar might have happened. She can be such a little mouse when it comes to men."

"What about you, Sadie? You think you know it all. Yet, you came home in a dither last night wondering whether to invite Michael to spend the night with you or not."

"Oh I wanted to, there's absolutely no doubt about that. I really fancy him rotten and I think he fancies me. But…"

"But what? You wouldn't say anything more last night and now you're closing down again. If you both like each other so much, what's the problem?"

Sadie sighed. "I don't think he knows how to ask me. Or he might even think I'll be shocked at the thought of sex before marriage." She placed her head on one side and laughed. "Me, shocked? Can you believe it?" She sighed. "But I don't like to ask him, because he might think I'm… you know." She gestured wildly with her hands.

"Forward," said Jenny.

"Yes, forward." Sadie had been thinking more on the lines of 'a bit of a tart', but she didn't want to call herself that, even in fun. "He saw me home last night and, when he kissed me, I wanted to open the door and fling him inside."

"A bit like Lucy and Paul?" ventured Jenny. "She said exactly the same thing."

"A hell of a lot like Lucy and Paul," said Sadie. "I thought we women were supposed to be liberated, yet here we are, wondering how to get a guy into bed without looking… too forward."

"I'm surprised at you, Sadie. I mean I'm surprised at Lucy, too, but for a different reason. Like you said, she's always been the little mouse, so for her to want to rip the guy's clothes off is a complete turn around. But you're such a go-ahead woman. I can't understand why you're holding back this time around."

Sadie shrugged. "I don't want to mess up a good thing. I'll see what happens this evening. We're going out again." She glanced at the clock. "We're going to be late for the office again; we'd better get a move on."

****

By the time they reached the office, Lucy and Connie were already there. "Lucy was telling me she'd spent a lovely evening with Paul." Connie said.

"Yes," interrupted Lucy. "I'll tell you both about it later." She hadn't told Connie about her detour on the way home last night and hoped the others would pick up the vibes not to give it away now.

"How was your evening with Andrew?" Sadie winked at Connie. "Or shouldn't we ask?" She gave a knowing nod to Lucy, reassuring her she wouldn't mention seeing her the previous evening.

"Of course you can ask, but that doesn't mean I'll tell." Connie smiled. There was no way she would discuss any intimate moments between Andrew and herself with anyone. "All I'll say is, I'm really very happy and he's suggested we buy another house somewhere. His bachelor flat in town is nice, but rather small for entertaining."

"So does that mean I'm on the move again?" asked Sadie. She placed her hand against her forehead. The thought of looking for another place to live in or around London filled her with horror. She could end up sleeping in the office.

"No. Well, not immediately anyway. I'm quite happy for you to continue renting a room there, though I think I'll need another tenant to share it with you."

Sadie was relieved to hear she wasn't about to be evicted. Connie's house was very comfortable and she had got rather used to living there over the last few months. But she hoped she would be allowed to vet the new tenant. It would need to be someone she could get on with. "Thank goodness! I had visions of me wheeling my suitcase around London looking for a place to rest my head." She paused and glanced at Jenny. "Anyway, Jenny has some news. Go on, tell them, Jen."

"It's about David. He rang this morning to tell me he's coming to London a little earlier than planned. He arrives on Monday." Jenny avoided looking at Lucy as she went on to explain how he would be here for a week. "I understand he'll be tied up for a couple of days, but when he's free, I'd like to be able to spend some time with him."

"Of course you must." Connie replied. "Take all the time you need. You both have a lot of catching up to do." She looked at the others. "It seems we've all found our feet again. Perhaps it would be a good idea for us to go out for a meal together sometime – you know, the eight of us. What do you think?"

"That's a great idea!" Sadie was quite enthusiastic. She had never wanted to ask Alex to any dinner arrangements that involved Connie and Andrew. He wouldn't have fitted in at all. His idea of a good evening with friends was to see how many pints he could drink before he fell to a crumpled heap on the floor and had to be carried home. But Michael was a different man altogether. She would enjoy introducing him to her friends.

Like Sadie, Lucy had never introduced Ben to Connie and Andrew. He was such a brute; she'd never wanted any of her friends to meet him. Especially Connie. She would have been horrified that she had stooped so low, as to marry such an evil man. However Paul was completely different. He would mix in perfectly. "Yes, I'd like that," she agreed.

"If you're interested, Jenny, we could try to organise something when David's in London." Connie paused.

"I'll speak to him about it when we talk next," said Jenny. "Like I said he's going to be around for a few days, so I'm sure we could fix something up."

"Okay, we'll try to make a date for one evening next week," said Connie. "Once we've decided on the evening, I'll make a booking somewhere for dinner."

"Fine! But don't you go booking somewhere too expensive," replied Sadie. "Not everyone earns as much as Andrew."

"Yes, I agree," Lucy, added. "I've no idea what Paul does for a living. We talked about all sorts of things, but I don't think we got around to where he works."

"Okay, no problem." Connie sat down. "We'll talk about it once we have a date in our diary."

"Gosh! There's been a great deal of interest in the website while we've been discussing our own arrangements." Lucy swung the screen around so they could all see for themselves. "People are queuing up to join the agency. There're ten here, and look," she pointed to the bottom of the screen, "all these are messages from our clients. They're probably asking for meetings to be arranged." She clapped her hands. "We're in the money!"

"Obviously word of our agency is getting around," said Connie.

"If it carries on like this, we'll be millionaires!" Sadie laughed.

"Or we could sell the agency and walk away with a handsome profit."

There was a deathly silence. Connie cast her eyes around the bewildered faces of her colleagues and wished she had kept her mouth shut. They were all looking back at her in horror. "It's only a thought," she added. But she could see the damage was done.

"Sell up?" said Sadie. "You're suggesting we sell the agency?" She took a deep breath and released it slowly. "I'd never thought of that."

"Neither had I," said Jenny slowly. "We'd have to get a jolly good price for it to be split four ways. Don't forget, we all gave up good jobs to set this up. It might not be so easy to find work now. Good jobs are becoming so scarce."

"I wouldn't expect to let it go for peanuts," said Connie. "Obviously we'd want the best price we could get. But the agency is up and running and it seems to have taken off. Someone might see it as a good income."

"*I* see it as a good income!" uttered Sadie. "And I'm reluctant to let it go." She looked at Lucy. "You haven't said anything yet. What do you think?"

Lucy honestly didn't know what to think and said so. "It's not as though I wouldn't get another job somewhere. Being a computer programmer usually means there is work out there. But I rather like being my own boss for a change."

"Exactly!" Sadie chirped. "Being your own boss is definitely an upside." She glanced at Connie. "Anyway, what brought all this on? I seem to recall the whole thing was your idea in the first place and now you suddenly want out."

Connie shrugged. "I don't know." How could she admit that she had lost interest in the agency because she was back with Andrew?

"I bet I can guess!" said Sadie, excitedly. "Now you and Andrew are back together, you're more interested in your life with him than you are about us and the agency." She paused. "I can't say I blame you, but where does that leave the rest of us?"

"Sadie's right." Jenny was thoughtful. "Okay, say we get around forty thousand pounds for the agency, out of that we would have to pay legal fees etc so that would leave us with less than ten thousand each. It might sound a lot, but if you think about it, it won't last very long."

"And as we wouldn't have jobs, we would be relying on that money until we find some sort of employment." Sadie sank back into her chair. "It would be spent in no time." She paused. "But if you really want to leave, perhaps the three of us could buy you out."

"I'm not sure we could afford it," said Jenny. "We have some money in the account, but we might need that to fall back on, should there be an emergency."

Connie felt awkward. Everything Sadie and Jenny said was true. "Look, just forget I said anything. It was a dumb idea. I hadn't thought it through." She was relieved the phone rang just then, and they were able to change the subject.

"That's great news," Lucy squealed into the phone. She put her hand over the mouthpiece and turned to the others. "It's my aunt. She says she enjoyed meeting Brian Lomax last night." She turned back to the phone. "Actually, I thought you might find him a bit of a bore."

"Not at all," her aunt's voice drifted down the line. "We got on really well. Like me, he's widowed and looking for some company. I'm seeing him again this evening. He's going to try to get some theatre tickets." She paused. "I won't keep you. I just thought you'd like to know."

"Well, there's a turn-up," said Lucy replacing the receiver. "It seems they're meeting up again this evening. It just goes to show, you can never predict the future."

"If you remember, you didn't want them to meet," said Connie. "Did you ever mention your thoughts to your aunt?"

"No. I didn't say a word. Like you all said, it was up to her to make the decision." Lucy glanced at Sadie. "You've gone very quiet. I thought you would have had something to say."

Sadie smiled. "I'm glad your aunt enjoyed her evening. It'll do her good to get out a bit more and mix with different people." She had still been thinking about Connie's suggestion to sell the business. She hadn't believed her when she said she had only just thought of it. Connie didn't suddenly come up with things as important as that, without thinking them through first. No, this had been on Connie's mind for at least a couple of days.

Despite them all agreeing to forget the matter, it was uppermost on everyone's mind for the rest of the day. Sadie didn't say a great deal all afternoon, which was so unlike her. She usually drove everyone mad with her constant chatter. Lucy only spoke occasionally and even then it was only to inform them of a new client or someone wanting a meeting arranged. It was only when they were packing up for the day that their enthusiasm returned.

"Well, I'm off now," said Lucy excitedly. "I'm meeting Paul at seven-ish and I still have to decide what to wear."

"Enjoy your evening. By the way, where're you going? I don't think you mentioned it this morning."

"We're going for dinner at a quiet little restaurant, then we can decide what we want to do next." Lucy replied, hurrying across to the door. "Bye everyone. Have a good evening, whatever you decide to do."

"It's good to see Lucy looking so happy. I hope this Paul character is the real deal. I would hate to see her upset. She deserves a break." Connie watched Lucy disappearing down the stairs. "Well, I think that's it for today. I hope you both have a good evening. Andrew and I are off to the theatre."

Outside the office, Sadie and Jenny waved goodbye to Connie, before hurrying across the road to catch the bus. "What're you doing this evening?" Sadie asked once they were aboard.

"I don't know. I suppose I'll be on Website Watch – again." Jenny paused. "You know, once we're all settled with men in our lives, I don't think any one of us will want to stay home keeping an eye on the computer. Connie could be right about selling the company."

Sadie didn't say anything. She was thinking through what Jenny had said. Okay, she couldn't set up clients on the website, but she could send and receive emails, so she would be expected to take her turn on Website Watch during the evenings and weekends. That could mean up to two nights a week listening for that all-important 'ping' telling her another email had popped in. Was that what she wanted? Is that what any one of them wanted to do? She doubted very much it was the end of the subject.

CHAPTER TWENTY-SIX

"You seem a little down this evening. I thought you wanted to go to the theatre." Andrew was trying to fasten his cufflinks. "Have you changed your mind?"

Connie pulled on her dress. "No, I'm looking forward to seeing the show." She hesitated for a moment, wondering whether to say any more. "I sort of put my foot in it today at the office," she added at last.

"You sort of put your foot in it?" Andrew cocked his head on one side and grinned. "Either you put your foot in it or you didn't."

"Actually I think I dropped my whole leg in it." Connie turned around and indicated for him to fasten the zip on her dress. "I suggested selling the agency."

"Sell the agency?" Andrew, still fiddling with Connie's zip, paused for a moment. "I take it your suggestion didn't go down well."

"No, it didn't. There was a rather embarrassing silence during the rest of the afternoon." Connie sighed. "I thought they might at least have discussed the idea, but it was voted down straightaway. I didn't expect that."

Andrew shook his head and smiled. "It's not always a good idea to go into partnership with friends, especially when you're all going to be working together so closely. Luckily, it has worked out fine, so far. If I were you I'd put it out of your mind. I'm sure the others have forgot it already." He kissed her.

"I love you, Andrew." She put her arms around his neck and kissed him.

"It's rather a pity we're going out," said Andrew. "It might be more fun to stay here."

"Save it for later." Connie smiled as she reached for her jacket.

****

"You're very quiet this evening. Is it me? Have I done something to upset you?" Michael took Sadie's hand. "You'd tell me if you had grown tired of me, wouldn't you?"

"Oh, Michael, I'm sorry. No you haven't done anything wrong and again, no, I definitely haven't tired of you." Sadie sighed. "It's not you, it's Connie."

"Okay, what's she done now?" Michael laughed. "I thought she was happy, now she and her ex-husband are back together." He paused. "Or have they split up again?"

"No, they haven't split up. She's very happy. In fact that's the problem." Sadie went on to explain how Connie had suggested selling the agency "I know it's because she and Andrew are back together and she doesn't need the income anymore. But the rest of us do, so naturally we disagreed. For a start, we'd all have to find new jobs. The money we'd get from the agency wouldn't last forever."

"So, what's the problem?" Michael scratched his head. "If you all disagreed, Connie would have been out-voted. That means you won. You got what you wanted – didn't you?"

"Yes and no."

"You know something? I don't think I'll ever understand women." Michael grinned. "What do you mean, yes and no?"

"Yes, it's good because we're all still in business." Sadie sighed. "But there's a downside. Jenny said something on the way home, which set me thinking. She mentioned how we'd all have to take it in turns to watch the site evenings and weekends. We need to do this because that's when most of the messages drop in. It's the only time most people can browse through the online profiles." She looked at Michael. "So it would mean I'd be stuck indoors with the laptop two nights a week."

"But don't you realise lots of people work shifts these days? It's a different world now. Days of nine till five, five days a week, have long gone. Jobs often include unsocial hours. I'm sure we could work around it." Michael grinned. "Here was me thinking you'd gone off me."

"Actually, I'm falling in love with you." Sadie quickly lowered her head. She hadn't meant to say it out loud. The thought had run through her head, but then changed into words and tumbled out before she'd had time to stop it. She had wanted to be more sure of his feelings towards her before saying anything. Now it was too late – she had laid all her cards on the table. What would he do now? Was he ready for such a relationship? Would he take her home at the end of the evening and leave, not even mention meeting up again? "Sorry, I shouldn't have…"

Michael placed a finger over her lips. "I'm falling in love with you, too. I never thought I would ever say that again to anyone… until I met you. You're so good for me. I liked you from the first moment you walked into the bank, but when I got to know you better…"

Sadie could hardly believe it. She flung her arms around his neck. "You mean it? You actually mean you could love me, with all my quirks, my impossible dress sense and my… well, the way I tend to say what I mean?" "Yes, Sadie, I adore it all." Michael kissed her.

"Come on, let's get out of this noisy place and go somewhere we can talk properly." Sadie rose to her feet and grabbed her jacket off the back of the chair.

"Okay, where would you like to go?" Michael beckoned the waiter.

"I don't know. Just somewhere quiet. Somewhere we can hear ourselves breathe." Sadie would have suggested going back to Connie's but Jenny would be at home on Website Watch.

"Would you like to have coffee at my flat?" Michael suggested. He handed the waiter some money and told him to keep the change. "Or would you prefer…"

"Coffee at your flat would be great." Sadie bit her lip. She was doing it again: leaping in with both feet. "Unless you'd rather…"

"My flat it is, then," Michael broke in. He laughed. "If one of us doesn't make a decision, we'll be here all night."

Michael's flat was south of the Thames. It was on the second floor of a small block. Inside, Sadie found it to be very comfortable and surprisingly tidy, for a man living on his own.

"Make yourself at home," said Michael. "I'll put the coffee on."

Sadie wandered around the flat. As well as the sitting room and kitchen, there were two bedrooms and a bathroom. She strolled into one of the bedrooms. It was obvious Michael used this one, as some of his clothes were draped over a chair in the corner. She sank down onto the bed and slowly ran her hand across the navy blue bedspread.

"How do you like your coffee?" Michael's voice drifted through from the kitchen. "Black or white?"

Impulsively, Sadie slipped off her shoes, swung her legs onto the bed and stretched out. "Forget about the coffee, I've changed my mind," she called out. She slid out her mobile phone and quickly sent a text to Jenny.

Michael hurried through the flat to find her. "Are you leaving? I thought you wanted to talk."

"We can talk here." She patted the bed beside him. "Or not… We might have already said everything that needs to be said."

Michael sat down on the edge of the bed. "Are you sure about this?" he asked.

"Aren't you?" Sadie raised an eyebrow.

"Yes, I… I am," Michael stuttered. "I just don't want you to think I suggested we came here because…" The rest was left unsaid as Sadie grabbed his tie and pulled him down beside her.

****

"You're looking very nice, Lucy," said Paul, as he helped her out of the taxi.

"Thank you," Lucy replied. She had tried on every dress in her wardrobe, before deciding on this one. Though she could squeeze into them all, this one had slipped over her hips the easiest and didn't show her lumps and bumps quite so much. It was strange, because when she had tried this dress on a couple of days ago, it had felt tighter. Perhaps the diet was working after all. "You're looking very smart, too." She glanced at the restaurant. "I haven't been here before."

"Neither have I," Paul replied. "A friend recommended it a little while ago, so I thought, why not give it a try?"

Lucy was relieved Paul hadn't been here with his ex-wife. She didn't really know why. Perhaps it was because she didn't want the spectre of his wife peering over her shoulder all evening – a bit like Connie with her dreaded floozy.

"What else do you like to do? I know you enjoy dining out, but I need to know what other things you do in your spare time." Paul asked. They were now seated and had placed their order with the waiter. "What I mean is, do you like the theatre? Or do you go dancing? I'm just trying to learn what sort of things you do to unwind."

Lucy was stumped. She didn't really do very much at all. She couldn't afford to go to clubs and bars, and, as for the theatre, they were far too expensive. It wasn't easy bringing up a son without much support from his father. Even though Terry was at university now, she had to help him out. She didn't want him to go out into the world owing a huge debt. "I'm afraid I don't go out much," she said at last. "I can't afford to go partying and hitting the high spots." She decided telling the truth was the best option. "I still help out my son whenever I can."

"No, I don't go out much either." He grinned. "In my case, I don't want to go anywhere on my own." He reached across the table and took her hand. "But now we have found each other, we can go out together. Have some fun and enjoy ourselves." He paused. "So what sort of things do you enjoy?"

Over dinner she told him how she used to love the theatre. "Just because I can't afford to go, doesn't mean I don't like it. Drama, musicals, I love them all. I also enjoy music. I once went to the Proms. It was a long time ago, but it was an experience I'll never forget. It was absolutely brilliant. I like walking, watching tennis. I like a good movie, and I used to love partying with my friends." She paused. "But enough about me. Tell me about yourself and the things you like to do."

"It seems we like doing the same things. I enjoy doing everything you've mentioned. We're going to get along fine together." He went to tell her how he worked for an insurance company in the city. "I'm not chairman of the board or anything like that. Just one of a team."

Lucy didn't care what he did. He was nice, considerate, kind, *and* he had a regular job. That was enough for her.

After dinner, they strolled down Oxford Street hand in hand. It was a warm evening and there were still a number of people about. "What shall we do now?" Paul asked. "Would you like to go on to a club?"

"Not really," Lucy answered. At the moment, she was enjoying having Paul to herself and the last thing she wanted to do was to go to a noisy club. She felt him squeeze her hand and she squeezed his back. She wanted him to kiss her, right there in the middle of Oxford Street, exactly as he had kissed her outside Connie's door the evening before. "Do you?"

He shook his head. "No."

They walked past the tube station and for one brief moment, Lucy recalled the evening she had encountered Ben. She glanced over her shoulder half expecting to see him looming up behind her. But he wasn't there. He was probably lying drunk in a police cell.

"Are you warm enough? I thought I felt you shiver," Paul asked.

"I'm fine. I was just laying an old ghost to rest," she replied.

Paul stopped walking and turned to face her. "Are you sure you're all right? Tell me the truth."

Lucy told him about the evening she had met Ben unexpectedly. "He frightened the life out of me. He would have hit me if Alice hadn't arrived and grabbed his arm."

"The bastard!" said Paul harshly. "Don't worry, I won't let him touch you ever again." He leant forward and kissed her.

It was the same way he had kissed her the previous evening, soft and gentle. She felt as though she would melt in his arms. He was about to pull away, but she wrapped her arms around his neck and held him, his lips pressed against hers. Eventually, they moved apart. For a moment, they gazed into each other's eyes and then Paul pulled her to him and kissed her again.

Lucy didn't want him to let go. Here they were, in the middle of Oxford Circus, kissing as passionately as if they were in bed together. She could hear people walking past. Some were tut-tutting, others were wolf whistling, while another called out, "Go for it, guys." But she didn't care. She had never felt this way before and didn't want the moment to pass.

"We better move on," said Paul when they finally tore apart from each other. He smiled. "We might get arrested." He grasped her hand tightly as they continued walking down Oxford Street. He hadn't felt this way about anyone since he had first met the woman who was to become his wife, but then he recalled how that had ended. No! He didn't want to go there. Not all women were the same.

He glanced at Lucy. He was still clutching her hand. He wanted to ask her back to his flat. But was it too soon? They had only met the evening before, for goodness sake. Yet, already he felt he had known her for much longer. She was sweet, and so down to earth. Her head wasn't in the clouds like some of the women in his office.

Lucy felt Paul's eyes rest on her for a fleeting second. She wondered whether he was thinking what she was thinking. Right now she was thinking about inviting him back to her flat. His kiss was still burning on her lips and she wanted more. But at the same time, she didn't want to sound too eager. What would Sadie suggest if she were here now? Stupid question! Sadie would tell her to go with her instincts. Connie would probably say, see how it goes, while Jenny would… well, there was no point in asking Jenny. She would miss three buses going her way if a decision had to be made about which one she should get on. No, Sadie's advice would be the best option… She had no idea Sadie had been going through the same dilemma the night before.

"You've gone very quiet." Paul interrupted her thoughts.

"I was just thinking."

"So, what were you thinking about?" He laughed. "It must be very serious to make you shut down like that."

"I was thinking about whether to invite you back to my flat." She paused. Had she been too bold? "You know, for coffee or even tea. I have both," she added quickly, trying to make it sound as though she wasn't going to rip off his clothes the moment he entered her door. "My flat isn't very big, but I do have a couple of chairs and a table." Now she was gabbling. But as Paul hadn't said a word, she felt she should keep going. Why couldn't he say something?

"Actually, I was going to suggest you come to my place for a drink, but I wasn't sure how you'd feel about it," Paul said at last. "You might have taken it the wrong way and thought… well, you know what I mean."

"Yes, I'd like to see your place, Paul. Thank you." She was relieved he hadn't thought her too pushy.

Paul lived in a flat just off the city centre. It was on the top floor and had spectacular views of London from the large windows. It was also quite spacious and well furnished. Lucy was quite taken aback. "How on earth can you afford something like this? It's beautiful."

"My grandfather gave me some money a year ago. You see, Granddad was a shrewd man and he made quite a lot of money on the stock exchange many years ago, and though he always made sure his family was okay, he never indulged any of us. He said we should stand on our own two feet; learn that life is a challenge. But after my marriage broke down and the divorce was finalised, he saw how desolate I was, so he gave me the money for this flat. He felt the time was right." He paused and pointed towards the window. "I love looking out over London, especially at night when all the lights are glowing. Take a look while I pour some drinks."

Lucy moved across to the large window and looked out over the landscape. It was a wonderful sight. Paul joined her and handed her a glass. "Would you like to hear some music?" She nodded and he moved across the room to select a CD. They sat together on the sofa sipping wine and listening to the music.

Paul slipped his arm around her and she snuggled up against him. He kissed her and she responded. The wave of excitement she had felt earlier in the evening, rushed through her again.

"Would you like another drink?" Paul asked when their lips parted.

"No, thank you." She was flushed and sounded breathless. "Do you?"

"No." He kissed her again. "Lucy… would you like…?"

"Yes," she whispered without allowing him to finish.

****

Back at Connie's Jenny was answering the email requests for meetings and enquiries about joining the agency. There were so many she'd hardly had time to stop and have something to eat. David rang, but she was so tied up, she couldn't talk long. "I'll ring you back when Sadie gets home," she'd told him. "She can look after the site for a little while and give me some space."

Suddenly her mobile phone buzzed. It was a text from Sadie: '*not home 2night ☺☺ c u 2morrw.*'

"So, you're not coming home after all," she muttered, flinging the phone down onto the sofa. "So much for having a few minutes to myself!"

CHAPTER TWENTY-SEVEN

"I assume you had a good evening with Michael," said Jenny as Sadie burst through the door into the office. She was wearing the same dress she'd worn the evening before.

"Oh, Jenny, we had such a great time," Sadie replied. She twirled around the cramped room, stumbling into chairs and desks. "I don't suppose you thought to bring me another dress?" she asked when she sat down. "I didn't have time to go to the house this morning."

"No! I didn't think to bring you another dress!" Jenny snapped. She stood up from the computer desk. "I was absolutely fed up last night. I was stuck on the wretched website all evening. It was so busy, I couldn't do anything else."

"What else did you want to do?" Sadie asked. "I didn't think you were going anywhere."

"I wasn't, but that's not the point."

"Well, what *is* the point?" Sadie peered at her. "If you weren't going anywhere, why are you getting your bowels in an uproar about being on Website Watch?"

"Because if I *had* wanted to swan off for the night, I couldn't have, could I?" Jenny paused. "I hardly had time to talk to David when he called. The blinking laptop was pinging away all evening."

"Oh, so that's it. David telephoned and you're taking it out on me because you couldn't talk to him."

"Yes! No, I don't mean to take it out on anyone. I was just fed up at the time." Jenny sank back down at the computer.

"So what were you fed up about?" Connie walked into the office in time to hear the end of the conversation.

"Nothing," mumbled Jenny. She looked up sharply. "No! It's not about nothing. Just because the three of you have men in your lives again, doesn't mean I'm going to sit at home with the laptop like a modern day Cinderella. You guys have got to take your turns."

"David called her last night and she was so busy working on the website. She couldn't speak to him," Sadie explained to Connie. She turned back to Jenny. "If it had been me, I would've switched the thing off until I was ready to turn it on again. We can't let it take over our lives."

"I'll take over tonight," said Connie. She could feel a row brewing and wanted to put a stop to it before it got too out of hand. She was itching to know exactly how much money they had made the previous night, but she didn't think this was quite the right time to ask. "By the way, where's Lucy? Has anyone heard from her this morning?"

Sadie shook her head. "I haven't." She fumbled around in her bag for her phone, wondering whether she had missed a call from Lucy. But she hadn't.

"Someone's coming up the stairs now. Perhaps it's her," said Jenny.

"Sorry I'm late." Lucy burst through the door. After spending the night with Paul, she had dashed home to change, before coming to the office. However, due to the traffic, it had taken longer than she thought. She smiled at Jenny. "Would you like me to take over now?"

"About bloody time!" said Jenny, moving away from the computer.

Lucy stared at her. What had she done to deserve that? Jenny seldom used such language. "Shall I go out and come in again?"

Jenny grimaced and waved her hands in the air. "Sorry. I don't mean it. I'm just feeling sorry for myself." She hadn't meant to be nasty to anyone this morning, but she couldn't help feeling a little jealous. They had all found partners and she hadn't. She had tried to reassure herself David was coming to meet her the following week. He had seemed very nice when they met a few weeks earlier, but until they met up on a proper date, she couldn't really call him her boyfriend.

"Okay." Lucy sat down without another word.

An uneasy silence followed. Connie began to open the mail. She pushed two enrolment forms towards Sadie and asked her to add their names and addresses to the register. "When you've done that, Lucy can add them to the site.

Sadie pulled the register from the filing cabinet and added the names to the list. She glanced at Jenny, wondering whether to ask her for the list of people who had joined the agency the evening before or leave it until later. Perhaps she might have calmed down by then. She turned away, but then looked back at Jenny again. This was ridiculous. Why were they all pussyfooting around her? It wasn't their fault she hadn't spoken to David. She didn't have to watch the website every single minute last evening, for goodness sake. Now she was sitting there playing the martyr, while they trod on eggshells around her. "Would you like me to add the names and email addresses of the new clients to the register?" she asked. "Or do you want to do it yourself?"

"I'll give you the list," said Jenny. "I've already added their profiles." She glanced at Connie and Lucy. "There were thirty new members and forty five emails asking for meetings to be arranged."

"Thirty new members!" screeched Connie.

"Seven and a half thousand pounds," Jenny informed her. "Plus the six hundred or so for the meetings."

"That's brilliant," uttered Connie.

"Not when you're stuck in a room all evening on your own."

"For goodness sake, you've made your point, Jenny, give it a rest." Sadie flung down her pen. "You're driving me nuts."

Jenny opened her mouth to say something, but, instead, she burst into tears.

"Jenny, I'm sorry. I didn't mean to upset you." Sadie looked at Connie and grimaced. "Come on, Jenny. You know me. I always open my mouth and put my foot in it."

"No, it's not you." Jenny wiped her eyes. "Or any of you. It's me. I shouldn't have kept on about it. But I was feeling so sorry for myself last night. All of you were out having a great time and I was stuck at home. And then when Sadie sent me a text to say she wouldn't be home, I just snapped." She rose to her feet. "If no one minds, I'm going out. I need some air."

They sat in silence as Jenny gathered her things and left the office. Connie was the first to speak. "I suggest we make up a proper roster for Website Watch. When our turn comes around, we'll have to take it whether we like it or not." She paused. "Also, we're each going to have to spend some time away from the office. The four of us have been friends for many years and we've never ever argued as much as we have since we started this agency. Especially Jenny. She usually takes everything so calmly. We must be spending too much time cooped up together in this little office."

"You're right about setting up a roster," said Sadie. "Last night, when Jenny and I were on our way home, she talked about what you had said regarding selling the agency. She'd been thinking it through and pointed out the downside if we carried on. How we'd have to make our personal arrangements around Website Watch. I must say it made me realise what was involved.

"So are you now saying you want to sell?" Connie asked.

"No, but nor am I saying that I don't want to sell," replied Sadie. "Truthfully, I don't know what I want. When I mentioned all this to Michael, he pointed out that lots of people have to work some sort of a shift pattern, which is true. I'm just not sure I want to do it." She paused. "And as for your other statement about being cooped up here together, I agree. We've been friends for years. We've laughed and cried together, we've been on holidays together, yet Jenny has never reacted to anything like she did this morning. She has always been the calmest of us all. I think the quicker she meets David again, the better for us all."

Lucy had remained silent, though she had been listening very carefully. "When we started this venture, we didn't have men in our lives," she said. "Now that we're dating again, we're seeing the whole thing from a different perspective. I feel the same as you, Sadie, however, I'm still not sure I want to sell. This is a good business. There are lots of dating agencies out there. Some of them are free, while others you pay a fee to join, but then it's a free-for-all. People log on, find someone they like the look of, and then go for it, as email addresses are visible to all members. Then there is Divorcees.biz. Our agency. It isn't cheap, but it has class and the word is getting out there. So, should we really think of selling up simply because we don't want to take a turn at watching the site?" She paused. "I don't want to put a dampener on either of our new relationships, but Sadie, I think we should bear in mind it is early days for us. Michael and Paul could make a bolt for it at any time, so we might need the agency to keep us going. Jenny is a different matter." She hesitated. "I don't like to say this and it's just a suggestion, but do you think David might have dropped out of the loop?"

Sadie nodded thoughtfully. She hoped David was still there for Jenny. Heaven forbid Michael should leave her now. He was the best thing to have entered her life in a long time. Last night had been wonderful. Michael had been a gentle, yet exciting lover. But, over the years, she had learned good things don't always last, so, yes, she had to agree it was early days. She dragged her thoughts back to the problem in hand. "You mean, Jenny could be making it all up?"

Lucy nodded. She hoped that wasn't the case. She reflected on her evening with Paul. She had hardly given him time to ask whether she would like to stay the night with him, before saying yes. They had made love and then talked for a while, before making love again. Neither of them had heard the alarm clock this morning. It hadn't mattered to her, but she was concerned for Paul. Unlike her, he wasn't his own boss. He had kissed her and told her he would ring during the day, before bolting out the door with his briefcase in one hand and a slice of toast in the other. For him to dump her now would be horrible.

Connie understood what Lucy was saying. It *was* early days for their new relationships. Lucy had only met Paul a couple of days ago, though Sadie and Michael had been together a little longer. As for Jenny… She sighed. Only time would tell what was going on there. "The best thing that could happen for Jenny is for David to come to see her – and the sooner the better for all of us."

****

Jenny flounced down the stairs and out of the building. She leaned against the wall wondering what to do next. She felt such a fool. Why had she come out here? She had to go back to face them all again later. It would have been better to have sat in the office and smoothed everything out. Sadie was right; she could have switched off the laptop and had a proper talk with David. She didn't have to sit with the wretched thing all evening as though they were joined at the hip. But that wasn't the real problem, was it? Deep down, she was jealous of Sadie and Lucy. Though she would never admit it to either of them. She hardly wanted to admit it herself. She wasn't normally a jealous person. She was always happy for her friends when things were going right for them. And this was no exception. She was very happy for them, but at the same time something was nagging away at the back of her mind. Could he be leading her on? Did he have another girl somewhere? He had told her his job used to take him all over the world. Perhaps he had a woman in every town. She didn't need another Rob in her life. One bad marriage was enough.

She moved away from the building and ambled towards Oxford Street. David would be here shortly. At last they could go out together, all this waiting was getting her down. She still didn't know much about him. Only what he had told her on the phone, and that was precious little. Once they met up properly, he might decide she wasn't the girl for him after all. Or vice versa. Perhaps it would have been better if they hadn't met at all. She could have got on with her life instead of hanging around waiting for his calls.

She went into a small café on the corner of Oxford Street and ordered a coffee. Impulsively, she pulled out her mobile phone and pressed the numbers of David's office. She had never called him at the office before, always imagining him to be bogged down with work. But today, she felt she needed to talk to him. Something needed to be sorted out. "Hello, David," she said, when she finally heard his voice.

"Jenny, how nice to hear from you," he replied. "Is everything okay? You sound a little strained."

"Yes, I'm fine." She paused. "I just wanted to talk to you." Now he was actually on the other end of the line, she didn't quite know what to say. She took a deep breath. "David, do you really like me? What I'm trying to say is, you haven't seen me for a few weeks and even when we met, it was very briefly. So what I want to know is, are you really interested in me or are you just keeping me dangling?" It had all come out in a rush. Would he understand the question? Thinking back over her words, even she didn't understand the question!

"Jenny, I can hardly wait to see you again. I'm hoping the firm will send me to London this weekend. They might need me there first thing on Monday morning to sign some contracts. I expect to hear their decision later today. I haven't mentioned it before, because nothing was settled." David paused, for a moment. A thought had popped into his mind. "Have you found someone else? Is that it? Has someone new come into your life?"

"No. No, it's nothing like that." Jenny was delighted to learn David was serious about seeing her again, but at the same time, she wished she hadn't phoned him. Perhaps she shouldn't have been so hasty. "I'm really anxious to see you again." Now she was beginning to sound desperate. She needed to slow down. "But, you see, I had this awful feeling you might not be so keen. You could be leading me on and already have a girlfriend… or a fiancée somewhere… and… and… " Now she was bumbling. He would think she was some kind of an idiot. She should get off the phone – quickly. "I'm sorry, I shouldn't have called." She clicked the off button and slowly laid the phone on the table.

She took a sip of her coffee. That was stupid. Why on earth had she phoned him? What had she hoped to gain? She had set out her feelings on a stall and now he knew she was anxious to see him. He knew she was worried in case she wasn't the only woman in his life, which meant she was desperate for him and goodness knows what else he had picked up from her call.

Her phone started to ring and vibrate on the table. One glance told her the call was from David. She didn't want to pick up, but it kept on ringing. She watched as the phone travelled slowly across the table with each vibration. Any second now it would stop and go to voice mail. She could listen to whatever he had to say later.

****

David heard a click and then the phone went dead. "Jenny!" he leapt to his feet and yelled into the phone. "Jenny, are you there?" By now everyone in the office was staring at him, but he didn't care. Jenny had gone; she had hung up on him.

Slowly, he lowered himself into his chair, ran his fingers through his hair. He thought back over the last few weeks to the night he had first laid eyes on her in the restaurant. She had looked so exquisite, so elegant. He had been drawn to her in that instant. When they chatted during the dinner, he had found her personality to be so utterly charming. How disappointed he'd been when she and her friend left before them. He recalled wishing they'd met on his first evening in London. At least they would have had a little more time to get to know each other. But then it seemed as though fate had taken a hand when they met up again at the hotel. Since then he had been counting the days to when he could get back to London and see her again.

But perhaps she hadn't felt the same about him. After all, such an attractive young woman living in the capital must meet lots of men every day. Or could it be that she had considered him to be a man like John, who had suddenly backed out of meeting Lucy?

He had felt really bad about that, especially as it had been left to him to break the news that John wouldn't be coming to London. Did Jenny now think him to be the same type of unscrupulous person as John, and was simply leading her on?

Looking at it from that point of view, he couldn't really blame her. She didn't know very much about him at all. Only what he'd told her during those few snatched conversations on the phone, and that was precious little. He'd much preferred to talk about her. He should have gone back to London before now. He could have taken the train and gone for a weekend. Jenny only had his word that he was coming back to see her at all. He should have seen this coming. Why on earth hadn't he seen this coming?

He took a deep breath. He couldn't leave it like this. He had to talk to her again. He had to make her understand that he really wanted to meet her. Picking up the phone, he thought about what he would say, then he stabbed in her number.

****

Jenny stared down at the phone. Any second now it would stop ringing and David would leave a message. But would he? Or would he switch off, thinking she didn't want to talk to him anymore? Is that how she really wanted it to end? She grabbed the phone and pressed the answer button.

"Hello, hello. Jenny, are you there?" David's voice came down the phone. He sounded tense.

"Yes, I'm here," Jenny replied.

"I didn't think you were going to pick up. I'm coming to London for the weekend, regardless of what my firm is planning," said David. "I've got to see you. I haven't been able to stop thinking about you since we first met. I really need to see you again. I'll catch a train on Friday evening after work and phone you when I get to Kings Cross." It all came out in a rush. But he didn't want to give her the chance to hang up before he said everything he needed to say.

Jenny didn't know whether to laugh or cry. "David," she yelled. "I'll be there to meet you." She glanced around the café; suddenly aware everyone's eyes were fixed on her. "I'll be at the station to meet you," she repeated, lowering her voice. "No matter what time it is, I'll be there."

****

"Feeling better now?" asked Sadie.

Jenny had arrived back at the office. She nodded. "Yes, thank you." She paused. "I'm sorry for making such a fuss earlier. I…" She wasn't sure what else to say.

"Forget it," Connie replied for them all. "Least said – soonest mended, was what my grandmother used to say. I'm sure you're going to feel a whole lot better once David comes to see you."

Jenny couldn't help noticing Connie's swift glance towards Lucy and Sadie. What was that all about? Surely they didn't think she was making up stories about David's calls. "I've spoken to David and he's coming to London on Friday evening, so hopefully you'll all get a chance to meet him over the weekend," she said.

"That's good news, Jenny," said Sadie.

"Yes." Jenny crossed her fingers behind her back, hoping nothing would come up to change to David's plans. "I can't wait to see him."

CHAPTER TWENTY-EIGHT

Jenny was waiting on the platform when David jumped down from the train. She noticed he was dragging an extremely large suitcase. Was this a sign he was going to be in London for more than a few days? She waved as he approached. Though he had told her his train wasn't due to arrive until seven o'clock, she'd been hanging around Kings Cross station since around six. She'd been far too excited to sit quietly at Connie's house watching the hands move slowly around the clock.

"It's so good to see you again, Jenny," he said. He dumped the case and wrapped his arms around her and kissed her. All those weeks of waiting were over and he was here at last. "I could hardly wait for today to come." He pointed to his case. "I'm in London for two weeks. I have to sign the documents and oversee the change over, which should take about three days, the rest of the time is mine or should I say, ours."

Jenny's eyes sparkled as she gazed up at him. He was even more attractive than she remembered. "I was looking forward to seeing you again," she said. "I'm taking some time off from the office so we can be together."

David picked up his case and they walked out of the station and into the street. "I have a room booked at the Langley. We'll go there first and once I've checked in, we'll have dinner somewhere." He hailed a cab and shortly afterwards they were walking into the hotel.

"Tell me a bit more about yourself, Jenny." David had checked into the hotel and they were having a pre-dinner drink in the bar. They had decided to have dinner in the Langley.

"What more can I tell you?" She laughed. "I've already told you my life history on the phone." She stood up suddenly and gave a twirl on the spot. "This is me! What you see in front of you is all there is. I have no secrets." It was true, she had told David everything about herself during their phone conversations. She had wanted him to know of her marriage and divorce. She had even told him about how Rob had hung around outside her flat until the police moved him on. There was no point in hiding anything, as it was bound to come out sooner or later, probably when she least expected it. "Tell me something about you. You never said very much about yourself on the phone."

"Where would you like me to start?" he asked.

"At the beginning!"

"I can't even remember the beginning of my life!" David laughed. "I do remember being a boy scout, going off to camp and all that stuff. But then my mind takes me to the firm I work for. I seem to have been there forever."

"It was your first job?" Jenny asked.

David nodded. "Yes, I went there as a junior in the office when I left school and I've been there ever since. I worked hard, as I wanted to make something of myself. And then when I got the chance to travel on behalf of the firm, I jumped at it. The money was great." He paused. "But my wife didn't like me being away so much and in the end she had an affair. She could have come with me, though. She didn't have to stay at home." He took a sip of his drink. "She told me she didn't like globetrotting, but, looking back, I think she liked playing at being single."

"And now? Do you still travel to far flung places?" Jenny asked.

"No. A year ago I decided I didn't want to live out of a suitcase any more. So I was upgraded and now I only travel around the British Isles, but not very often."

At that moment, they were called into dinner.

****

"We have one more to see." Connie and Andrew were viewing houses. She had taken the afternoon off and visited several estate agents, before meeting up with Andrew. So far, they hadn't viewed anything which had the 'wow factor'.

"Does it really have to be a house?" Andrew asked. "What about a nice apartment?"

Connie pondered for a moment. She hadn't thought of an apartment. Perhaps one of the new large places facing the river might be a nice option if the housing stock didn't come up to scratch. An apartment with all mod cons, close to the shops, and close to the office did sound appealing. "Okay, but we'll have to take a look at this one. We've already made the appointment."

It turned out the house wasn't what they were looking for. Even Andrew thought so and he wasn't half as fussy as Connie. "If we take a taxi, we should get back to the estate agents before they close," he said. "We could grab a handful of sales leaflets and look through them this evening."

"Sounds like a good idea. I'm on Website Watch tonight, so we're stuck in the Condrew, anyway. Sadie and Lucy are both out with their respective boyfriends and Jenny is meeting David at Kings Cross."

"How are Sadie and Michael getting on?" Andrew asked as he hailed a taxi. He hoped Sadie had found the right man this time. Connie had mentioned something about them all getting together for dinner one evening.

"The vibes I've picked up from Sadie are good. He's definitely better than her ex-husband." She paused. "But then anyone has to be better than Alex. I only met him twice and that was enough for me. I'll never understand why she married him, he was a loser from the word go." She went on to explain how Michael had qualifications in the financial world, though he was working with the security team at the bank their agency used. "That was how Sadie came to meet him."

The taxi dropped them off outside a large estate agent. "Okay, let's see what they have to offer," said Connie, striding up to the door

****

"You've lived a very exciting life." Jenny and David had finished dinner and were walking along the embankment. The moon peeked out between the clouds and the Thames flowed silently past them.

"And it's far from over, you know," laughed David.

"I didn't mean you were old or anything." Jenny flushed. "I just meant…"

"I know what you meant. I was joking." David leaned down and kissed her on the cheek. "You're so lovely, Jenny."

"Do you miss travelling?" Jenny asked. "I mean, do you find living the quiet life boring?

"Not really. I thought I would, but I don't. Perhaps I *am* getting old, after all." He glanced at her out of the corner of his eye.

"No, you're not!" squealed Jenny. She laughed and punched him playfully on the arm. "You're teasing me again."

They continued to walk along the embankment, hand in hand. Jenny was surprised how much she liked David and how comfortable she felt in his company. Despite being pleased to see him, she had been a little apprehensive when they met on the platform at Kings Cross. Was she doing the right thing? What on earth would they talk about? They knew very little about each other. Yet, she was finding him most charming and so easy to get along with.

"I better see you home," said David. "It's getting late." He paused. "I'll call for you tomorrow morning and we can spend the whole day together. You can even show me the tourist spots."

"Yes, I'd like that," said Jenny. She was disappointed the evening had passed so quickly. Tomorrow wouldn't come fast enough. After her divorce, she had promised herself she wouldn't leap on the first man she met. So determined to be more careful this time around, she had decided to take any future relationship very slowly, even going so far as to work out a plan. After four or five dates, she would invite him back for coffee when she knew her neighbours would be at home. Then after several more weeks, she might hint about him spending the night with her.

Yet, here she was, as excited as a teenager, hanging onto David's every word and not wanting to leave him for a second. But this wasn't just any man, she told herself. This man was kind, considerate, and extremely attractive.

"Sadie!" Jenny called out, when she opened the door to Connie's house. There was no reply. Sadie mustn't be home yet or else she was staying over at Michael's again. "Would you like to come in for coffee?" David was standing behind her. He had insisted on seeing her to the door.

"Yes and no," he replied.

"What does that mean?" Jenny asked.

"It means, yes, a coffee would be good, but no, I'm not angling for you to ask me to stay the night." He pulled a face. "I don't think that came out quite as I wanted it to. What I meant was…"

"I know what you meant." Jenny laughed. She wished she knew for certain that Sadie wouldn't be home. Despite all her plans, the way she was feeling at the moment, she was more than happy for David to stay the night. "Make yourself comfortable. I'll start the coffee." In the kitchen, she quickly sent a text to Sadie asking if she was coming home that evening. She put on the percolator and set out the cups on a tray. Just then, her mobile vibrated. '*No nt cming hme – go 4 it!*' Jenny felt her face warming. She had hoped Sadie wouldn't pick up what she was actually getting at. How foolish to even think it. Sadie always picked up on everything!

"I'd better be making a move." David glanced at his watch. "It's getting late."

"Would you like another coffee before you go?" Jenny asked. She picked up the percolator, but it was empty. "I can make some more."

David laughed. "I've had four cups already. I feel as though I'm swimming in the stuff."

"Yes. Me, too." She put down the percolator, unsure what to say next.

David looked at her for a moment, then wrapped his arms around her and kissed her. Jenny melted into his arms. She couldn't remember ever feeling like this before.

"I better go," said David, moving away from her. "I didn't…"

She put a finger to his lips and pulled him towards her. "No. Stay," she whispered.

CHAPTER TWENTY-NINE

The next morning, Jenny and David strolled through Hyde Park. David had suggested she show him some of the sights of London, so, as it was bright and sunny, she'd thought the park would be an ideal place to start.

"If you look over there, you can just about see our office window." Jenny pointed across the park to one of the buildings on the other side of the road. "Up there; the tiny window at the very top. And at this very moment a couple of my colleagues will be in there bringing the ledgers up to date after last night's Website Watch."

"Website Watch?" David raised his eyebrows.

Jenny explained how someone needed to be on duty most of the time to arrange the meetings and install new members. "That's how we make our money. So we call it Website Watch. Then the ledgers in the office need to be brought up to date."

"I see," said David thoughtfully. He took another look at the tiny window and laughed. "If the room is as small as the window, it must get very crowded in there at times."

"Yes, it does," she replied. "It sometimes gets very heated, too, when we have the occasional argument."

"I can't see you ever arguing with anyone, Jenny. You have such a lovely nature. That was the second thing I noticed about you. You have a warm and positive attitude to everything and everyone."

"Oh, I get annoyed sometimes, but not often." She thought back to earlier in the week, when she had been rather short with Sadie. "So what was the first thing you noticed about me?" she asked, changing the subject slightly.

"How pretty you were, or, I should say, you *are*," said David without a moment's hesitation.

Jenny blushed and looked away. "Oh," was all she could say.

****

"What would you like to do today?" Paul asked. He and Lucy had just finished washing the breakfast dishes and were putting them away.

"I don't know." Lucy frowned. "It's been so long since I had a Saturday off, I've lost track of what goes on at the weekends." She paused. "You choose."

Paul scratched his head. "Well, there's a football match on at..." He broke off and laughed when he saw the pained expression on Lucy's face. "Only joking." He thought for a moment. "Isn't there some art exhibition you wanted to see?"

"Gosh, yes there is. I'd almost forgot about that. It's at the Gallery in Trafalgar Square."

"Okay, we'll go there and then have something to eat in a little bistro somewhere. After that, we'll play it by ear."

"Sounds lovely." Lucy clasped her hands together in delight. "But are you okay with art exhibitions?"

"Art and I have never been very passionate about each other," said David with a grin. "But we manage to get along together on the few occasions we meet, so the Gallery it is."

"You're crazy." Lucy looped her arms around his neck and kissed him. "You don't have to go with me. I can go alone. You can do something else. Something you're more passionate about – like football."

"I am passionate about you, Lucy," said Paul. "I'd like to come with you. Besides, you might like to instruct me on how art and I might get along better in the future."

"Okay," said Lucy. "Let's get our coats and go. Lesson number one on the wonders of art, coming up."

****

"So, where do you want to go next?" asked Jenny. They had reached an exit from Hyde Park.

David glanced up at the sky. There had been endless blue skies earlier in the morning, but dark clouds were now beginning to form. "I think we might need to look for something under cover. Any ideas?"

"What sort of things are you interested in?" she asked, throwing out her hands in despair. "You'll recall, I don't know much about your likes or dislikes."

"Oops, sorry. Yes, well… I think I'll like anything you do. How about that for starters?"

"You're an idiot!" Jenny exclaimed. "Okay, how are you on art galleries?"

David pulled a face. "Not a lot. But if that's your thing, then why not?" He shrugged. "I'm happy to give it a go."

"Okay, then the art gallery it is. It's cheap and it's quiet, so, culture, here we come."

It started to rain the moment they reached the gallery. "Just in time," said Jenny, as the first few drops of rain began to fall.

****

"I wonder what they're doing now," said Connie.

"Who?" Sadie asked absentmindedly. She was busy adding a new client to the register.

"Jenny and David, who do you think?"

Sadie looked up and laid down her pen. "Probably still in bed if they have any sense."

"What makes you think Jenny will have rushed David into bed? She hardly knows the man. They only met last night. You can't count their encounter at the Langley. Jenny isn't the sort who does something like that without some thought." Connie paused. "Actually, Jenny isn't the sort to do anything without giving it a lot of thought."

"Well, in that case, my guess is she'll have taken all of two seconds to think about it, and then rushed him into bed." Sadie giggled. "Besides, she contacted me last night and asked if I was coming home. Why else would she have done that, if it wasn't because she was desperate to get David into my half of the bed?"

"You could have put that a little more delicately." Connie grimaced.

"For goodness sake, Connie. Whichever way I said it, it would have meant the same thing. Why beat about the bush?" She picked up her pen again. "I hope Lucy is enjoying her Saturday off. I suppose we've been lucky up till now that Lucy hasn't minded doing a Saturday morning because Michael has been on duty at the bank and Jenny was still waiting for David to show up."

Connie had been thinking that very same thing. It *had* been very convenient. But now the bank was shutting its doors at the weekend and Jenny would be seeing more of David, which meant she and Sadie would have to take their turn. The weekends were the busiest time for the agency. Last weekend, they'd made seven thousand pounds. No, they couldn't possibly afford to close the site for two days.

****

The art gallery was very busy. Jenny had forgot there was a special exhibition this weekend. "I should have remembered. Lucy mentioned it last week."

"Not to worry," said David. He smiled. "It might not be quiet, but at least it's dry."

They wandered around the gallery, pausing occasionally whenever they saw something they particularly liked.

"That could be us," said David, putting his arm around Jenny. "What do you think?"

She looked to where he was pointing and saw a small statue of a young man and woman. The man's arm was around her waist and the woman was looking up into his eyes while he gazed down at her, his face filled with love and admiration.

Jenny smiled. "Yes, it could," she whispered.

They moved away from the statue and carried on walking around the gallery when suddenly they came face to face with Lucy and Paul. "I should have guessed you'd be here, Lucy," said Jenny, once they had all introduced themselves. "We came here to get out of the rain."

"We were thinking of going for something to eat," said Lucy. "If you're finished in here, how about we make a foursome?"

Jenny looked at David and he nodded. "Yes, why not? It sounds like fun."

****

"So, what do you think about Paul?" asked Lucy. Her eyes were flashing with excitement. They had finished lunch and the two ladies had gone to the restroom to freshen up. "David is really sweet. He's just your type, Jenny."

"Yes, he is," Jenny whispered. For a second, she allowed her mind to drift back to the evening before, when they had made love. He had been so gentle. "I like Paul, too. You both seem made for each other," she added, dragging herself back to the present. "Fingers crossed that both our futures will be brighter from now on."

"I second that," said Lucy. She glanced towards the door. "I wonder how they are getting on out there. I mean, do you think they'll be talking to each other or will they be sitting in silence until we get back?"

"Oh, I think they'll have found something in common to talk about. Men usually think of something to say." Jenny thought for a moment. "Work! I mean men often talk about work – their jobs – what they do."

"No," said Lucy slowly. "Paul doesn't talk too much about work when he's away from it. What about beer?"

"I'm not sure. I haven't seen David drink beer yet. So what else is there?"

The women looked at each other and laughed. "Football," they chorused as they left the restroom.

"I still think it should have been a penalty." David's voice drifted towards them as they returned to their table.

"I agree," said John. "I couldn't understand how the ref didn't see it."

"We were right!" said Lucy, with a small giggle.

****

"Lucy and Paul are very nice," said David. He and Jenny were now back at the Langley hotel. He had been a little concerned John's name might have come up during the conversation over lunch. But, thankfully, it hadn't. On the other hand, why should it? Lucy was with another man and they both seemed very content together.

"I've known Lucy for a long time. We met several years ago when we both worked for the same firm. However, today was the first time I'd met Paul and I thought him to be very pleasant. I'm glad she's found someone like that. Her first husband, Ben, was a brute." She hesitated. "So what happened to John? I thought he liked Lucy when he met her. She was quite hurt, you know?"

David sighed. "John is a bit of a lady's man. He seems to drift from one girl to another. But I really thought he liked Lucy. He talked about her all the way back to Peterborough. I thought perhaps he'd found 'his' girl at last, but it wasn't to be."

"Well, if he's like that, then I think Lucy's had a lucky escape. A Casanova is the last thing she needs in her life." John reminded her of Rob. He had flitted from one woman to another after they were married. Perhaps he'd even been doing it before the wedding, how was she to know?

"You've gone very quiet, are you okay?" David asked. He slid his arm around her.

"Yes, I'm fine." She looked up at him and he kissed her.

"Jenny," David said. "What are your plans for this evening?"

"I haven't any," she replied, smiling. "What've you got in mind?" But she already knew the answer.

CHAPTER THIRTY

Jenny felt on top of the world when she arrived at the office on Monday morning. She floated across to her desk, totally oblivious to the stares from her friends. After spending a wonderful weekend with David, she'd almost had to tear herself away from him that morning, when he'd had to rush off to finalise the deal on the site of his firm's new offices. He'd lingered in bed too long and had been forced to dress hastily and rush out of the door after snatching a quick kiss from Jenny. "See you back here later," he had called, before slamming the door behind him.

She needn't have come into the office at all. No one was really expecting to see her until David went back to Peterborough. However, when she left the Langley, her feet had started walking in the direction of Mayfair and she hadn't even noticed where she was until she found herself outside the office.

"Hello, is anybody there?" Sadie waved her hand up and down in front of Jenny's face. "Mother ship calling, is anyone there?"

"What?" Jenny looked up at Sadie and smiled. "Sorry. I've had the most wonderful weekend and haven't quite come down to earth yet."

"Yes, we can see that! Lucy told us you were blissfully happy when she met you on Saturday." Connie laughed. "We weren't expecting you to be here this morning."

"No, neither was I. However, my feet seemed to take over, so here I am." Jenny gazed at her friends. "But once David finalizes the deal, I'll take a few days off to get to know him. It should all be settled by Thursday."

"It strikes me you must know pretty much everything about him by now," said Sadie, grinning.

"Yes, well…" Jenny felt her cheeks warming. Why did she have to blush when she felt embarrassed? Surely she could feel awkward without everyone having to know about it.

"Okay!" Connie frowned at Sadie. "I think we should get back to sorting out these ledgers, don't you?" She turned to Jenny. "Business is booming! Several more people wanted to join the agency over the weekend, so we have lots of new details to add to our books. Not only that, there's been heaps of messages requesting meetings." She pointed to the pile of envelopes. "There might even be a couple of cheques in there. More than one person said they didn't like giving their details over the internet."

"Okay, I'll make a start with the mail. If there're any cheques, they'll need to be banked." said Jenny.

When all the post was opened, Jenny held up a bundle of cheques. "Guess what?" she squealed. "We have five thousand pounds worth of cheques here. Most of them are people paying the enrolment fee, but there are a few who are simply paying for a meeting to be arranged. It seems there are more people who prefer to pay by cheque than we first thought."

"Bloody hell!" spluttered Sadie. "That's brilliant!"

"Yes, it is," agreed Connie. "Five thousand pounds plus the money we received online over the weekend gives us around eight thousand. Gosh, we're really getting noticed." She was so delighted with the news she didn't even pick up on Sadie's language.

"Would you like me to take it to the bank for you?" asked Sadie. "I wouldn't mind having a stroll down Oxford Street."

Jenny laughed. "What you mean is, you want to meet your lovely Michael for a coffee if he can get away from the bank for a few minutes." She picked up the paying-in book. "Okay, I'll sort out the banking now and you can be off."

The rest of the day ran smoothly. A few more people joined the agency, while others asked for meetings to be arranged. They each felt quite excited about how well their business was doing. Connie offered to look after the website that evening. "I'm not going out tonight. Andrew has a business dinner and won't be back till late."

The other three were pleased to let her carry on. None of them really wanted to stay home that evening. Life had suddenly become far too exciting.

****

Back at the Condrew, Connie threw the laptop onto the bed and switched it on. The last thing she wanted to do was sit in front of the computer all evening. It was true she wasn't going anywhere, but she would have preferred to take a long soak in the bath, slip into something comfortable and read a book or watch TV. A large gin and tonic would have figured in there somewhere, too. Now she was going to be stuck in front of the laptop. Okay, she could still have the G&T, but the rest of her leisurely evening had been blown out of the window.

She strolled out onto the balcony and looked across Hyde Park. It was a lovely evening and people were meandering through the park on their way home. She thought this was one of the best views in London. It was such a shame they couldn't live here permanently. Well, they could if they wanted to, but it cost too much. However, she had liked the apartment they looked at a few days ago. It was a penthouse with views of London all round. Andrew had set about getting a mortgage from his firm and they were waiting to hear the decision. Meanwhile, she hadn't told her friends about it. She thought it would be best to wait until everything was settled.

The laptop pinged, which meant there was a message from someone. Connie sighed as she went back into the room. It was starting already. She was about to open the message when Andrew hurried in. "Sorry I'm late, but everything seemed to erupt at the office and I couldn't get away. How are you placed this evening? A couple of my colleagues can't make it for dinner and I kind of hoped you would stand in. Ron is going to bring his wife and…" He frowned as the laptop pinged again. "Oh, I see you're on duty again so you won't be able to…"

Connie quickly snapped the lid of the laptop shut. Having dinner with Andrew was far more preferable than Website Watch. "I would love to join you for dinner."

"But think of all those lonely people out there, desperately waiting to hear from you." Andrew grinned.

"You make me sound like the Samaritans," Connie said, kicking off her shoes. "How long have I got? Where are we going and what time is the dinner? I need to check out my wardrobe, I haven't a thing to wear."

Andrew rolled his eyes. "Here we go again," he murmured to himself. "Connie darling, you look great in anything you wear, just pick something out of the wardrobe."

"Men!" said Connie, disappearing into the bathroom. "You have no idea…" the rest of her words were lost as she shut the door and ran the shower.

Andrew poured himself a drink and opened the laptop. He downloaded the messages for Divorcees.biz and watched in amazement as they all dropped into the inbox. He knew each message was worth at least fifteen pounds and counted up to as many as twenty before he slammed the lid shut. "Three hundred pounds," he muttered to himself. "The dating agency business is booming."

CHAPTER THIRTY-ONE

Connie was the first to arrive at the office. She was hoping to have a few minutes to herself to catch up with the emails on the agency website before the others turned up. She had planned to glance through some of the messages the previous evening when she and Andrew returned from dinner. But they had lingered over the meal and she had drunk a little too much wine and then Andrew had…

"Oh my goodness," Connie clapped her hand to her forehead. There were eighty-two emails in total. Andrew had told her he had taken a peek while she was getting ready and found twenty, but now there were eighty-two. She had only managed to reply to around fifteen before Lucy bounced through the door.

"Hi, Connie. Is everything okay with you this morning?" said Lucy cheerfully. Her evening at the theatre with Paul had gone very well and she was still feeling on top of the world.

"No, it isn't!" Connie snapped as she stabbed her finger on the send button. She sighed heavily and looked up. "Sorry, yes it is. I went out with Andrew last night and this morning I found eighty-two emails waiting to be answered." She held up her hand when Lucy opened her mouth to speak. "I know exactly what you're going to say. Yes, I said I would take Website Watch, because I wasn't doing anything. But there was a change of plan when Andrew's business dinner was at stake. He needed me and I wasn't going to say no." She looked back at the computer and opened another email. "Someone else wants to be a member of the agency. They say a cheque is in the post."

Lucy didn't say anything. She filled the kettle and plugged it in, before switching on the main computer. Once the website appeared on the screen, she leaned across to Connie. "I'll start from the bottom of the list, and we'll meet in the middle."

"Thanks, Lucy. I'm sorry I was so short with you. I was simply amazed to find so many emails. We should be delighted, as each message means money; well, most of them do anyway. But it's going to be a little tiresome if someone has to be watching the website twenty-four hours a day."

They were still going through the emails when the others arrived. Connie noticed Sadie wasn't looking her usual bubbly self. He eyes didn't have the sparkle they usually did after an evening out with Michael. And she seemed a little distant. However, she dismissed it, believing Sadie had probably had a late night.

"I've got the post here." Jenny dropped a pile of letters onto the desk. "The postman was delivering as we came in, so I said I would save his legs."

"You both look very busy," said Sadie, taking off her coat. "Are the emails piling in already?"

"Yes – no. Some have come in this morning, but most are from last night. I went out with Andrew, so I didn't get a chance to check them out."

"Shit, Connie! I thought you said you were staying in last night to look after the site." Sadie threw her coat onto the hook. "All those people might have been sitting there waiting for someone to get back to them, while you were swanning around some posh restaurant with Andrew!"

"Don't you talk to me like that!" Connie spat, leaping to her feet. "If I remember rightly, it was *you* who advised Jenny she should leave Website Watch if something better came up. Well, last night something better came up for me!" She sniffed. "Anyway, I didn't say I would stay home and watch the site. I said I hadn't anything *planned* for the evening. There's a difference!"

"Whoa! Calm down!" Jenny flapped her hands up and down. She was alarmed at what was happening. Things were beginning to get very heated. "For goodness sake, get a grip, both of you."

"Well, I was just saying…" Sadie looked huffed.

"Yes, we all heard what you were saying…" Jenny frowned. "Does all this huffing and puffing mean you've had a row with Michael?"

"No! Of course I haven't had a row with Michael!" exclaimed Sadie, still glaring at Connie. "I simply thought that…"

"Sit down, Sadie!" Lucy thumped her fist on the desk. "Sit down both of you! What's going on here? Okay, so Connie went out. What's the big deal? Why are you getting on your high horse? For goodness sake, Sadie, you would have done the same thing. We would all have done the same thing. So don't start getting high and mighty here."

"I'm just saying…"

"We heard you, Sadie. We know what you were saying. So what's ruffled your feathers?" Lucy screwed up her eyes. "It *is* Michael, isn't it?"

"Nothing's ruffled my feathers! Everything's fine." Sadie snapped. She closed her eyes and took a deep breath. Everything wasn't fine at all. Her lovely new world was falling apart and she couldn't do anything about it. Her eyes brimmed with tears and she slumped into her chair. "I bumped into Alex last night when I was out with Michael. That tart he brought to the house all those weeks ago was draped over his arm, and he'd been drinking. He made himself known to Michael and said some pretty nasty things about me. None of them were true, by the way. Then he went on to tell Michael how good I was in bed. I could have died with embarrassment. Especially when he gave Michael a wink and said 'but I guess you already know that'."

"Is he still standing?" Jenny asked. "Alex, I mean, not Michael. Knowing you, he could be lying senseless somewhere."

"I wanted to. I wanted to smack him on the mouth, but I held back. I don't know how I managed to stop myself, but I did. Perhaps by then I was too stunned to move." Sadie looked at Connie. "I'm sorry. I shouldn't have gone off at you, but I'm so upset about last night." She swallowed hard.

"Didn't Michael say anything," asked Jenny uneasily. "Surely he said something?"

"No, not a word. He simply pushed Alex to one side and we walked off. But he didn't say anything. Not to me or to Alex. Heaven knows what he was thinking. Even when he finally did speak, it was about something trivial. As it turns out, I'd already told him I would be going back to my room at Connie's house that night, as I really needed to do some washing, get more clothes, you know, things like that. Anyway, he dropped me off at the door and didn't come in for coffee."

"I'm so sorry," said Connie. She reached out and stroked her friend's arm. "But I'm sure Michael will be fine. He probably got a shock at Alex suddenly looming up. Let's face it. Alex looming up from nowhere is enough to knock the wind out of anyone."

"I don't know. Surely he could have said something to Alex for humiliating me like that. 'Piss off,' springs to mind." Sadie sighed. "But he didn't say a word. I'm telling you here and now, if my relationship with Michael is finished, I'm going to join an order of nuns. I really love that guy. There is no way I'm going to go through all this pain and sorrow again." She closed her eyes for a moment and reflected on the strange expression on Michael's face, when he walked away from her last night. But then, shaking her head, she picked up the post. "Okay, do you want me to start opening these?"

"No. Leave it. I'll see to it," said Jenny. "Why don't you make us all a nice cup of coffee?"

"The kettle's been boiled," added Lucy. She was relieved the row between Connie and Sadie had been resolved. But Sadie's comments had set her thoughts in motion. What would Paul's reaction be if he were to meet Ben on the street? She had told him all about her ex husband, not wanting anything to suddenly rear up out of the blue and he'd taken it all in his stride. But if he actually bumped into the brute, it might prove to be another story altogether.

Sadie set about making the coffee. "How did your evening go, Jenny? Did you go out anywhere?" she asked.

"Yes, we had dinner in the Langley then went to see a film. You'll have guessed I stayed the night with David, as I didn't come home." Jenny blushed when she thought back to their lovemaking. She wished it was Thursday and then she and

David would be together for a few days before he had to go back to Peterborough.

"I might simply have thought you'd moved back to your own flat," Sadie winked. "But I didn't. I knew where you were." She was trying desperately to sound cheerful, though her stomach felt as though it was tied up in knots. "So how much money have we made today?" she asked, setting a mug down beside Connie.

"We haven't finished yet, but at the moment we have nearly twenty thousand pounds." Connie took a sip of her coffee. "Ugh! You put sugar in mine."

"Sorry. I think I've given you mine." Sadie changed the mugs around and was about to take a sip of her coffee, when she suddenly realised what Connie had said. "Twenty thousand pounds!" she gulped over the top of the mug. "Are you sure?"

"Yes, of course I am." Connie glanced at Lucy. "That's right, isn't it?"

"Yes." Lucy glanced at the pile of mail. "And who knows, there might even be a little more money in one or two of those envelopes."

Sadie fell silent as she thought it through. This was like a dream come true. Their business venture was actually making money. They were on a roll and it could only get better. She should be feeling on top of the world, yet she wasn't. She could only think of Michael and what he might be doing or thinking at this very moment.

Okay, she had only known the guy a matter of weeks, six at the most. But she felt as though she had known him all her life. What if he never wanted to see her again? What if what happened last night had made Michael rethink their relationship? What if…? She had to stop thinking about

Michael. After all, nothing permanent was ever discussed. Nothing was written in stone. Sadie sank into her chair. She slammed her fist onto the desk and her coffee slopped over the top of the mug and onto one of the files. If only they hadn't met Alex. Everything had been fine until they bumped into that miserable idiot!

"Are you okay?" Connie asked cautiously. She glanced at the others. "Would you prefer to go home? We can manage here."

"And what would I do back there, all by myself? No I need to be here – among friends."

As it turned out, it was very busy in the office and Sadie didn't have time to dwell on her problems. The phone never seemed to stop ringing, emails flooded into the inbox, and there were so many enrolment forms and cheques in the mail, they hardly had time to stop for lunch.

"We need to bank all these cheques," said Jenny. "Best get them cashed before anyone has a change of mind." She looked at Sadie. "Do you want to go to the bank or would you prefer me to go."

"You go," Sadie replied quietly. Any other day, she would have jumped at the chance of even catching a glimpse of Michael, but not today. "If I met Michael, what on earth would I say to him? What could I say to him?"

"I never thought I'd see the day when you'd be lost for words, Sadie," said Connie. "I've known you to talk your way out of a situation even though the whole thing was your fault in the first place."

"Yes... well... this is different." Sadie looked away. It *was* different. What *could* she say? Perhaps she should have made light of the whole thing last night after they strode away from Alex and his tart. But she hadn't said anything. For God's sake what could she have said? How could she have defended herself after marrying a rude, horrible man like Alex? "I'll put the kettle on while you're away and make some coffee when you get back."

Jenny put on her coat and stuffed the cheques into her bag. "I won't be long," she said, walking towards the door. However when she opened the door, she heard footsteps on the stairs. "Someone's coming." She stood back, waiting to see who would appear at the top of the stairs.

"You have got to get yourselves a lift here." The voice came from a man.

"Oh my goodness!" uttered Sadie. "That's Michael's voice. Tell him I'm not here." She flew into the corner where she was partly hidden by one of the filing cabinets. She hoped he wouldn't see her.

"We can't do that," hissed Connie. The footsteps were drawing close. "He's sure to see you standing there."

Sadie crouched down and pulled a chair across in front of her.

Jenny looked around at the others. "I'm off now. See you guys later," she said, before heading down the stairs. It was a cop out, but if there was going to be a scene, she wanted nothing to do with it.

"Good afternoon, how can we help you?" asked Connie when Michael stepped into the office.

"I came to see Sadie." he paused. "I really need to see her urgently."

"Well… she isn't here at the moment," said Connie uneasily. Out of the corner of her eye, she could see Sadie crouched in an uncomfortable position, struggling to stay hidden. They needed to get rid of Michael as soon as possible. She glanced at Lucy, hoping she would help by saying something, but Lucy was tapping away at the computer keyboard. "Can I give her a message?"

"No! This is something I must do myself." He heard a slight sound and looked sharply towards the door, as though expecting Sadie to walk in any minute. But there was no one there. "I really need to talk to her. It's very important I see her." He was about to continue, but he heard another movement close by. He swung around. "Sadie!" he cried.

Sadie stood up and moved the chair away. She grinned sheepishly at Connie. "Sorry, Michael, but I wasn't sure I could face you today – at least, not in front of my friends." She swallowed hard and drew herself up to her full height. "If you've come here to run me down, then forget it. I've already told them what happened last night." She paused. "I left nothing out."

Michael looked down towards the floor. "That's what I want to talk to you about. I should have done something there and then, but I was afraid it might all get out of hand. I wanted to knock the guy flat and rub his face in the pavement." He looked up. "But what if I injured him? Where would we be now?" He sighed. "Once we walked away, I felt I had let you down. No. More than that, I *knew* I'd let you down. I wanted to say something to you – I wanted you to understand why I hadn't hit him. But I couldn't think of the right words. So I said nothing." Sadie was about to interrupt, but Michael held up his hand. "Let me finish. I need to say what I came here to say." He sighed. "Sadie, you're the best thing that's happened to me in a long time. I love you. But if I had taken a swipe at that guy last night, then I could easily have said goodbye to any future we might have together."

Michael fumbled around in his jacket pocket and pulled out a small box. "This is not how I meant it to be. Last night, I was…I was planning to go down on bended knee and ask you to marry me. I wanted it to be perfect, just the two of us, sitting on a bench by the river in the moonlight. But the mood changed when that oaf… " He hesitated and glanced at Connie and Lucy as though suddenly remembering they were still there. "What the heck! If this is what it takes, then I'll do it here and now." Michael lowered himself onto one knee. "Sadie, will you marry me?" He opened the box, and held up an engagement ring.

"I don't know what to say," said Sadie.

"For goodness sake, say yes and put us all out of our misery." Connie pulled out a handkerchief and dabbed her eyes.

Sadie held out her left hand. "Yes, Michael. I would love to marry you."

After he had slipped the ring onto her finger, Sadie flung her arms around his neck. "It's beautiful, Michael. I'm so happy. After last night, I thought… Never mind what I thought."

Lucy came from behind the desk and hugged Sadie, while Connie shook Michael's hand. "This is wonderful. We've got to celebrate. I'll pop out and get some champagne."

"I can't stay. I've got to get back to the bank," said Michael. "I told them I had some personal business to attend to and would only be gone a short while." He placed his arm around Sadie. "Walk downstairs with me."

"I'll do more than that." Sadie picked up her bag. "I'll walk down to the bank with you." Outside, they met Jenny. "Look at this, Jen." Sadie held out her hand to show off her engagement ring. "Isn't it beautiful?"

"I'm so happy for you," Jenny gushed. "Both of you." She hugged Sadie, then was going to shake hands with Michael, but changed her mind and gave him a hug, too.

"You have some good friends, Sadie." Michael said as they strolled off towards Oxford Street, holding hands.

****

"I met Sadie and I don't think I have ever seen her looking so happy," said Jenny, bursting into the office. "I gather Michael proposed to her." She wished her relationship with David was as far gone. She had only spent a couple of days with him, but she felt he was right for her.

"Yes. He went right down on bended knee and asked Sadie to marry him. It turns out the whole episode last night was a big misunderstanding." Connie smiled. "We should have a celebration. You know, all of us go out for a meal somewhere. We were planning to do it, anyway, so why not sort something out now?"

"That sounds good. We could easily work something out."

"That's settled then. We'll talk to Sadie when she gets back. In the meantime, I'm going out to get a bottle of champagne. I won't be long." Connie picked up her bag and went down the stairs.

"I wish it was me," said Lucy wistfully.

"Well, why didn't you say?" Jenny raised her eyebrows. "I'm sure Connie wouldn't have minded you going out to get the champagne."

Lucy laughed. "Not that, silly. I wish I was the one getting engaged."

"Oh, yes." Jenny laughed, too. "Of course! I don't know what I was thinking." She paused. "But you know something, Lucy, I think you're doing okay. Paul seems a really nice man; he's certainly quite taken with you. It was obvious."

"Thank you, Jenny." Lucy beamed. She looked at her watch, wishing it were time to go home. She recalled how when she was married to Ben, she longed to hold the pointers back. She hated going home to him. But things were different now. Paul was always so pleased to see her. He always asked how her day had been. He listened to her when she talked to him and was always ready to help her with whatever she was doing. If only she had met Paul the first go around.

****

Sadie was treading on air, as she walked back up to Park Lane. She kept lifting her hand and spreading her fingers to get a better view of her lovely ring. This was the first engagement ring she'd had. Alex hadn't gone in for such niceties. He had much preferred his idea of splashing out on a party. However, the kind of party he had organised was nothing short of a colossal booze-up. She recalled feeling so embarrassed when her friends arrived. By then, Alex was already plastered and couldn't even stand. His friends or mates, as he called them, were no better. All they could do was make suggestive remarks to Connie and Jenny and several other people she had invited. She should have walked out on him there and then. She should have realised things could only get worse. But she hadn't. She had gone ahead and married the creature. She looked down at her ring again. This time it was going to be different. This time it was going to work, because this time, she had met the right man.

When she arrived back in the office, a bottle of champagne was waiting to be opened and small dishes of nuts and crisps were spread out on the desks. "Congratulations!" her friends chorused as she walked in the door. Her face was glowing. She couldn't remember ever being this happy.

CHAPTER THIRTY-TWO

A few weeks had passed since the day Michael asked Sadie to marry him. Connie had suggested they should all get together for a proper celebration, but because David had been flitting to and from Peterborough, they'd had to postpone the event until now. Connie had booked a table at a nice hotel. Not her first choice, but Sadie insisted the venue shouldn't be too expensive. "Not everyone can afford the places you and Andrew frequent," she'd told Connie firmly. Now the big night had arrived. Connie planned she and Andrew would be the first to arrive. She wanted Andrew to order some champagne to be put on ice.

"Your friends are costing me a fortune," he laughed.

Connie slipped her hand into his and squeezed it. "I've never seen any of them look so happy for a long time. Sadie is positively glowing." She thought back to the time Sadie married Alex. She hadn't really wanted to go to the wedding - if you could call it that – a few words said in the local registry office, but she had made the effort to support Sadie. She recalled the whole thing had been over in a flash. Then the registrar had rushed across the hall to write a certificate for someone's death. Maybe that's the reason the marriage had been doomed from the start. It certainly didn't send positive vibes. "I think she's made a good choice this time. Michael really loves her and he's good for her."

"What about the others?" Andrew asked. "Jenny and Lucy. How are their relationships going?"

"Jenny is on cloud nine. According to her, David is the best man in the universe." Connie paused. "I haven't met him, so I only know what she tells me. But Sadie has met him briefly a couple of times, when he's called at the house and Lucy met him at the art gallery the day they all had lunch together. They both say he's a nice guy. Talking of Lucy, she's been very quiet over the last couple of days." She sighed. "Oh, she's still seeing Paul, at least, I assume she is. She certainly hasn't said anything about them breaking up, but I know there's something bothering her. Anyway, we'll meet him tonight, so we can judge for ourselves."

"We can't judge him, Connie. He's Lucy's choice and who she sees is up to her, we can't interfere." Andrew paused. "You didn't try to interfere when Sadie was marrying Alex, did you?"

"No, I didn't. Under the circumstances, it might have worked out better for Sadie if I had. But in Lucy's case, I'm a little concerned Paul might be another Ben. Then where would she be? However, Jenny assures me he's very nice. The four of them had lunch together a few weeks back and she said they all got on very well." Connie heaved another sigh and picked up her evening bag. "Okay, I'm ready."

****

At the restaurant, Andrew asked the waiter to put some champagne on ice. "Do you want something to drink now, Connie?

"No, thank you. I'll wait for the others to arrive." She watched Andrew pay for the champagne. How could she have been such a fool to walk away from the most generous, loving man on the planet? At one time, she couldn't get the floozy out of her mind. Now she hardly gave the wretched woman a thought. It was almost as though the whole thing had never happened – except, if she ever did bump into the woman who had caused her so much pain and grief, she would punch her right on the nose.

"I paid for the champagne, otherwise it might have gone on the bill and I think you want it as a gift."

"Yes, I do. Thank you, Andrew." She paused. "I was wondering, do you think it might be a good idea for us to get re-married?" She put her hand over her mouth and giggled. "Oops, isn't it the man who should do the proposing?"

Andrew smiled. "It's okay for you to do it this time. If you remember, I did it the first time around." He took her hand. "And I accept."

"Should we tell the others or keep it to ourselves?" Connie asked. "At least until we decide on a where and when?"

Andrew was quite happy to go along with whatever Connie wanted and said so. "Though, I think you'll find it difficult to keep it a secret for too long."

"Then we won't leave it too long." She laughed.

"We aren't last, are we?" Sadie appeared in the doorway and looked around to see whether anyone else had arrived.

"No. The others haven't turned up yet, but it's still quite early." Connie glanced at the rather ornate clock on the wall. "Andrew has ordered some champagne, so would you mind waiting until the others come?" She was relieved Sadie hadn't worn something totally unsuitable for the venue.

"No problem." Sadie threw herself down onto a seat next to Connie. "Andrew, I'd like you to meet Michael. Connie has already met him, though it was very briefly." She gestured to Michael to sit next to Andrew. "Actually, Michael used to be in finance, so you guys might have something in common."

She so wanted the two men to hit it off. Though Michael always said he liked his job in security, she hadn't failed to notice how he spoke rather wistfully about his years in the financial world. She guessed he was missing his true vocation more than he cared to admit. She knew Andrew would never offer anyone such an important job in the company unless he really thought the applicant was right for the position, which is why she hadn't asked him outright. But if Andrew began chatting to Michael about various monetary matters and found out how good he was at finances, then he might find he liked him and…

"Indeed!" said Andrew.

"Yes, and the company would still be operating, if they had listened to Michael."

"Ahem!" Michael coughed. "I'm sure Andrew doesn't want to talk business, Sadie."

"Actually I don't mind talking business," said Andrew.

"I think business is Andrew's passion," Connie laughed.

"No. You're my passion, Connie. Business comes second."

Connie blushed when the others laughed. "This has got to be a first, Sadie," she said, changing the subject. "You're usually last to turn up for any get-together." Connie laughed.

"Yes, well, you have Michael to thank for that. He doesn't like to be late for anything and keeps hurrying me along." Sadie smiled at Michael and then lowered her eyes to the engagement ring on her finger. "But I don't mind, really. He has so many other endearing qualities."

Connie coughed. "I don't think we need to go there."

"Go where?" Jenny and David had arrived in time to hear Connie's comment.

"Nowhere," replied Connie. "Just a figure of speech." She looked towards the door. "I thought Lucy would have been here by now."

"Do you think they'll come this evening? Jenny asked. "Oh, I know she said they would be here, but she seems to have been very distant lately. I was worried things weren't well between her and Paul."

Connie glanced at Andrew. "Just what I said earlier," she murmured.

However, a few minutes later, Lucy and Paul arrived. "Sorry we're late," she said, "but it's all my fault. I couldn't decide what to wear."

After the introductions were made, Andrew signalled the barman, indicating it was time to bring the champagne.

"Andrew, you're spoiling us," said Jenny. "But I love it."

Connie stood up.

"Are you going somewhere?" asked Sadie.

"No, of course not. But I want to tell you all something before we burst into conversation."

"Couldn't you tell us while you were sitting down?" Sadie grinned.

"I could, but I wanted to tell you standing up – alright? Now do you want to hear what I have to say or not?" Connie frowned. Sadie could be so irritating at times.

"Well, get on with it then!"

"I think I've gone off the boil now." Connie flopped back into her chair.

"Come on, you can't leave us in suspense." Lucy glanced at Sadie. "For goodness sake, let Connie tell us in her own way."

Connie stood up again. "Andrew and I are getting married – again."

"I thought you were going to keep it a secret," laughed Andrew.

"Well, I did – for about fifteen minutes," Connie replied. She had intended to wait a while, but she was so happy. She couldn't leave it a moment longer or she would burst.

Sadie leapt to her feet and hugged her friend. "About bloody time! I'm so pleased for you both." When she finally let go, she hugged Andrew. "That is wonderful news."

"Yes, it is." He pulled her closer and whispered in her ear. "And I owe you one. Your advice paid off."

Once everyone had congratulated the couple, Sadie raised her glass and proposed a toast. Connie held her breath for a moment, hoping she wasn't going to say something outrageous or even mention why they had got divorced in the first place. However, she needn't have worried, Sadie simply wished the happy couple all the best for the future.

Sadie was grinning when she sat down. She had been tempted to tell Andrew not to be a naughty boy this time, but changed her mind. Connie was in such good spirits; it would be a shame to spoil the moment. "Where and when are you going to tie the knot?" she asked.

"I have no idea. We only decided to get married a few minutes before you walked in." Connie looked at Andrew. "However, I think it would be nice to go off somewhere, just the two of us."

He smiled and nodded. He was happy to go along with whatever she wanted.

"But you must have some idea?" Sadie persisted.

"I really don't know." Connie paused. "Hawaii might be good, or better still, one of those lovely islands in the Indian Ocean. Somewhere romantic."

"That sounds good to me." Andrew broke in. He leaned back in his chair. "Yes, somewhere in the Indian Ocean."

"It sounds beautiful," said Jenny.

Sadie was doubtful. Connie didn't usually throw any party without fanfares and trumpets, let alone a wedding – especially her own. She would be very surprised indeed if they sneaked off together to get married. But she kept her thoughts to herself.

"Where did you get married the first time around?" Lucy asked. She hadn't known Connie back then.

"Essex," Connie replied. "Both our families lived in Chelmsford, so we were married there." Draining her glass, she nudged Andrew for a refill. He waved to the barman, while she continued. "But this time around, I think we'll do it our way."

The barman brought another bottle of champagne and refilled everyone's glass.

Connie was delighted at how well the evening was going. Those new to the group seemed to be mixing well. It was good they were all getting on together. She rather liked David. Though she had only just met him, he came across as very reliable and so very easy to talk to. He was also besotted with Jenny. Any fool could see that.

She glanced at Lucy. She hadn't said very much at all since they arrived. Paul seemed like a nice man, but, again, she had only met him once. Perhaps there was a something about him that was causing Lucy to have second thoughts. Connie sighed. No doubt Lucy would tell them all when she was good and ready. In the meantime, they would simply have to wait and watch and be there for her if something went wrong.

****

"Are you going to talk business all night?" asked Connie. Dinner was over and they were all relaxing in the lounge. Andrew and Michael were deep in conversation about financial matters, having picked up from where they left off earlier. "This is supposed to be a social occasion."

"Sorry, darling," Andrew smiled at Connie. "I guess we're going to have to get together another time," he added, turning back to Michael.

"You're very quiet this evening, Lucy," said Sadie. She would have mentioned it earlier, but Andrew was taking such an interest in Michael, she hadn't wanted to stop the flow. "Is something up between you two?"

Connie flashed a look of horror at Sadie. Trust her to butt her nose in. This wasn't the time to upset Lucy further.

"No, nothing's up." Lucy glanced at Paul. "It's Terry," she added, finally.

"Your son?" said Sadie. "So what's wrong with Terry."

"Nothing."

"What do you mean, *nothing*? You've just this minute said there was something up with Terry."

"Well, there isn't anything up with him… it's just… he's coming home on Saturday," said Lucy.

"But that's good isn't it?" Sadie quizzed. "I thought you'd be delighted to see your son again."

"Yes, it is – I am." Lucy paused. "But he doesn't know about Paul." She reached out and took Paul's hand. "Well… yes… of course he knows Paul is in my life. I told him how well we were getting on. What I mean is, I haven't told him about us sleeping together."

"For goodness sake, Lucy." Sadie burst out laughing. "Terry is a grown man. He knows how many beans make five. He'll have already guessed that much."

"You think so?" Lucy's eyes widened.

"I know so," replied Sadie. "Terry's at university, Lucy, he hasn't entered a monastery. He'll have had his eyes opened the moment he walked through those hallowed portals." She laughed. "That makes it sound a bit like a monastery, doesn't it? Anyway, he certainly won't be thinking you two shake hands every night before going your separate ways."

"No. I suppose not," said Lucy slowly. She looked at Paul. "It's just I tried hard to bring Terry up to be good man. I didn't want him to turn out anything like his father." She hesitated. "And his coming home for the weekend is so sudden, I wonder whether he disapproves of me going out with another man."

"He won't turn out like his father," said Connie. She patted Lucy's arm. "He hated how Ben treated you. I would be more than surprised if he ever wanted to see his father again. You must look on the bright side. He's probably coming home to meet this new man in your life and to give you his blessing." She looked at the others and, though they nodded in agreement, she could tell they weren't entirely convinced.

****

Jenny and David were on their way back to the Langley when he asked about Lucy. He had noticed the shadow of doubt sweep across Jenny's face when Connie tried to re-assure Lucy.

"You'll recall me mentioning Ben, her first husband?" Jenny paused and looked at David. When he nodded, she explained how he used to come home drunk most nights and then beat her up. "I don't know how she stuck with him for so long. But she didn't want to break up the home for Terry's sake. Truthfully, I think Terry would have been better off without his father, but Lucy didn't see it that way. She held on until Terry went to university."

"I see," said David. "So you think Terry might be coming home to check out the new man in Lucy's life?"

Jenny nodded. "But more than that, Terry might be coming home to warn him off. Tell him to move on." She paused. "And I can't blame him for being a little cautious. After everything his mother went through with her first husband, Terry's father, he'll want to make sure she isn't about to make the same mistake again. However, Lucy is very happy at the moment, so Terry suddenly arriving and hurling himself into the ring to warn Paul off might be the last thing she needs."

"Yes," said David thoughtfully. "It's a tricky situation and I can see why you're concerned for your friend. But it's something the three of them are going to have to sort out between them."

"Yes, you're right," she sighed. "Yet, it'll be her friends who'll have to pick up the pieces if the situation explodes."

CHAPTER THIRTY-THREE

By the time Saturday came around, Lucy had almost chewed her nails down to the quick. Despite re-assurances from her friends, she was still tormenting herself over Terry's sudden homecoming. Of course, Sadie was right. Her son would have worked out she and Paul were sleeping together, but that was no reason for him to drop everything and rush home so early in the term.

Thinking back, it had been unwise of her to inform him of Paul's existence so quickly. She should have dropped hints gradually, rather than yelling down the line, 'I have a new man in my life,' and almost deafening him at the same time. But she'd been so excited and so happy, the words had simply shot out on their own.

She glanced at the clock. Terry would be here shortly. She really needed to get a grip. If only Paul were here, too. At least she would have had some support. But he had said he would wait until later in the afternoon. "It'll give you both a chance to talk quietly," he had told her gently. "If he finds me sitting here when he walks through the door, he might get the impression I have taken over and resent me from the outset." She sighed. He was right, of course, but it would've been good to have him to lean on.

A car pulling up outside interrupted her thoughts and she hurried across to the window. She watched Terry step out from the taxi. He slammed the door shut and paid the driver, before walking towards the apartment block. Usually, when he came home he would look up at the window and smile. But today he kept his head down.

Her stomach flipped over and she sank into a chair. She was still sitting there when Terry walked into the room.

"Hello, Mum," he said. He threw his overnight bag onto a chair and walked across to where she was sitting.

She rose to her feet and hugged her son. "Terry, how nice to see you. But should you really be missing out on your studies so early in the term?" She tried to keep her voice calm. She didn't want him to know she was feeling so tense over his visit.

"I had to come home." Terry took a step back from his mother and looked towards the kitchen. "Is he here?"

"No. Paul is at work," Lucy explained cautiously. "You'll meet him later." Terry nodded and Lucy thought he looked slightly relieved. "He's looking forward to meeting you," she added.

"And I want to meet him!"

Lucy winced. Had she detected the hint of a threat in his tone?

"But I wanted to have some time with you first," Terry continued. "Alone!" He hesitated. "I need to know that this guy is okay, Mum. I want to hear the truth, but with him hanging around, you might not have dared to answer my questions truthfully."

"Well, we're on our own. Paul won't be here until this evening." Lucy watched her son shifting from one foot to another. He appeared to be feeling as uncomfortable as she was. "Why don't we sit down and you can ask me whatever you like." She took Terry's arm and steered him across to the small sofa.

"I spent all last night and most of the ride here this morning trying to find the right words, but, now I'm here, everything has disappeared from my head. So I'm just going to come right out and ask." Terry took a deep breath before continuing. "Is this Paul character safe? Does he drink a lot?" He paused and glanced at Lucy. "What I mean is, have you got yourself involved with another bastard like my father? I couldn't do much to help you when I was younger, but I'm sure as hell not going to let you go through all those beatings again."

"Paul is nothing like your father, honey! He's a kind and generous man." Lucy took her son's hand. "How could you possible believe I'd choose another man like Ben?"

"Some women can't help themselves. They seem to look on being bullied as a way of life," mumbled Terry.

"Not me!" declared Lucy. "Once my divorce came through, I made up my mind I was going to find myself a nice man and enjoy the rest of my life. Mind you, I hadn't quite worked out how I was going to do it. When you have a figure like mine, men seem to keep their distance." She laughed. "But I found Paul." She paused. "No, that's not strictly true – Paul found me through our new dating agency and since then I've felt like my life has become a whole new chapter still waiting to be written. I can't wait to turn each page and find out what's going to happen next. Paul has taken me to theatres, clubs, cinemas, it's like living in a whirlwind and I'm loving every minute." She paused to catch her breath. "Tonight, he's taking the three of us to a restaurant and then a show. And tomorrow – well tomorrow is another day, we can decide what we want to do when it comes."

Terry smiled for the first time since he had arrived. "I'm delighted you're so happy, Mum. I was pleased when I heard you'd met someone. But then I got to thinking everything might not be as good as you were making out. And the more I thought about it, the more concerned I became. In the end, I decided I had to come and check this guy out for myself." He hesitated. "So, what show are we going to? I can't remember when I was last at a theatre."

"I took you to see *Peter Pan* when you were ten years old." Lucy grinned. "I bought tickets and hid them, otherwise your father would have ordered me to take them back and ask for a refund." Her expression changed to one of sadness when she remembered how much Terry had enjoyed the show. There had been too few such days when he'd been young.

"Yes, I remember." Terry laughed. "I used to try to fly."

"That's right!" Lucy clasped her hands together. "I even made you some paper wings and fastened them on the back of your shirt with a safety pin." She smiled. "I hate to disappoint you, but we aren't seeing *Peter Pan* this evening. We have tickets for *Love Never Dies*. Sadie saw it recently and thought it was brilliant."

"Sadie. How *is* Sadie these days? I always liked her. She's such a fun person."

"*Fun* person! Zany, more like. She's as crazy as ever. She's got herself a new boyfriend – fiancé," Lucy corrected herself. "I've only met him a couple of times, but he absolutely adores her."

"Tell me some more about Paul." Terry feared the conversation was moving ahead too quickly. There was still so much he needed to know about this man. "Where does he work? Has he moved in here?"

"No. He hasn't exactly moved in here," said Lucy slowly. "You see, I've kind of moved in with him. He has a lovely apartment and there are some tremendous views over the city." She hesitated. Terry looked as though he was about to break in, but he remained silent. "I came back here today so you and I could talk more freely. I didn't want you to feel uncomfortable at being in unfamiliar surroundings." She went on to explain where Paul worked and how he came to have such a nice apartment. "He isn't wealthy, by any means, but he works hard and earns a good salary." She fidgeted with her necklace for a few moments, wondering whether to continue. Perhaps it would be best to come clean and bring her son right up to date. "I think I am in love with him, Terry, and I really believe he feels the same way about me. And before you say a word, I do realize I haven't known him very long, but I hope you'll at least try to understand."

There was a long, awkward silence before Terry spoke. He was still mulling over the whole idea in his mind. If his mother were ever to marry Paul, he would then have a stepfather. Did he want a stepfather? Hadn't he managed well enough without a father until now? During the early years of his life, he'd stayed well away from his real father out of fear. So why would he want to have another one thrust upon him now? He glanced at his mother. She looked worried and was still fidgeting with her necklace. She deserved a new life and if this Paul was as good as she said he was, what right had he to stand in her way? He took a deep breath. "Well, I suppose I should meet the guy," he said at last.

Lucy smiled. She was relieved the ordeal was over – at least for the time being. Once Terry met Paul, she was sure any doubts still lingering in her son's head would be blown away. But if not, what would happen then? Would Terry insist she give up the lovely new man in her life? Then it would be down to her to choose between Paul and her son. She pushed the idea out of her mind. Hopefully she wouldn't have to go down that road. She glanced at her watch. "Gosh, look at the time. Paul shouldn't be too long. He's leaving the office early and is picking us up before going to his place to get changed. I thought you might like to see his apartment. You just have time to freshen up a little."

She crossed her fingers behind her back and watched Terry pick up his bag and walk through to the bathroom. With a little bit of luck all would go well this evening and by the time Terry went back to university, he and Paul would be the best of mates.

****

The evening did go well – much better than Lucy thought possible. Paul, with his light and easy manner, soon had Terry chatting to him as though they were old friends. There had been a slightly awkward moment when Paul first arrived at Lucy's flat. After walking in and greeting Terry, he had pulled Lucy to him and kissed her – something he did every evening when he returned from the office.

Terry had stood by and watched without saying a word. In all the years he had lived with his parents, he had never once seen his father show even the slightest affection towards his mother. When he arrived home from the pub or the betting shop, he simply yelled at her for no reason at all. Sometimes it didn't stop there. The shouting would be followed by physical abuse. At least this guy was showing his mother some love and attention.

For that one brief moment, Lucy had been under the impression Terry was feeling a little left out or even jealous. His expression had been hard to work out. But then he had smiled warmly at Paul and after that, it had been plain sailing.

Now the show was over and they clambered into a taxi. "Where do you want to go from here?" Paul asked.

"I don't know about you two, but I'm bushed." Terry yawned. "I was up at the crack of dawn because I had a couple of tutorials this morning before I left Cambridge. I think I'll have to call it a night."

"And they say it's the young who have all the get up and go," Lucy laughed. "Okay, we'll go back."

"I'll drop you both off and…" Paul began.

"Hold on!" Terry interrupted. "What about we all go back to your apartment? Earlier I noticed you had two bedrooms. Can I crash down there?" he glanced at his mother. "It's much more comfortable than Mum's and I absolutely love the views."

"You cheeky monkey!" Lucy slapped his arm. "My flat is…" She looked at Paul and grinned. "Okay, I admit it, my flat's a dump."

"Sure, Terry, why not?" Paul replied. He kept his tone even, but deep down he was delighted. To him this was a sign he had been accepted. "We'll stop by Lucy's flat and pick up your bag." He squeezed Lucy's hand when Terry wasn't looking. "Then we'll all have a couple of drinks and gaze across the London skyline before turning in."

****

The following day Lucy and Terry spent a lazy day at Paul's apartment. Terry told them he needed to spend the morning studying his notes in readiness for his lecture on Monday afternoon. "But could I possibly watch the football match on TV this afternoon? England is playing away and I know Mum hates football, so I guess it's down to you, Paul."

"You know something?" said Paul. He swiftly glanced at Lucy, but she didn't fail to notice the twinkle in his eye. "I was hoping to watch that game, too. So what do you say,

Lucy? Can we lads sit together on the sofa with a couple of beers and enjoy the match?"

She laughed. "It seems I'm outnumbered. Yes, okay. I have a few things I need to do before I start dinner. So you guys can whoop it up or whatever it is you do while watching football." Secretly, she was thrilled. It couldn't have worked out better. This was a chance for the two men to get to know each other without her hovering around.

Three o'clock was kick-off and both Terry and Paul yelled and cheered when their team took to the field. During half time, they discussed how the game had gone during the first half.

Terry couldn't believe how much he enjoyed Paul's company. Only yesterday he had asked himself whether he really wanted a stepfather. Today, he wouldn't even have contemplated the question. Paul was great fun. Thinking about it now, he realized it must have been as difficult for Paul to meet him, as it was for him to meet Paul.

He should never have doubted his mother's choice. But on the other hand, if he hadn't, he wouldn't have come here and spent such a lovely weekend with them both.

CHAPTER THIRTY-FOUR

"So you see, we all had a wonderful time," Lucy gushed. Back in the office on Monday morning, she was telling the others how the weekend had gone. "Terry and Paul got on well together and before he left, he told me that he hoped everything would work out well for me."

"I'm delighted for you, Lucy." Connie hugged her friend. "So all the worry about Terry's reaction to Paul was for nothing."

Lucy nodded, as the others crowded around her. Tears welled in her eyes. "I was so stupid, wasn't I?"

"Welcome to the club. I think we've all joined the 'stupid' club at some time or another." Sadie made quotation marks in the air. She gave a quick glance in Connie's direction, before stepping forward to hug Lucy. Drawing herself away, she looked Lucy up and down. "Lucy!" she squealed. "Are you losing weight? I swear there's less of you than there was the last time I gave you a hug."

Lucy looked down at her hips. "Gosh, yes, I think I must have lost some weight. I put this dress on this morning without a thought. I didn't notice how easily it slipped on; I was in a bit of a rush. But now you mention it, the last time I tried this on, I took it straight off again because it was showing all my bulges."

"Well, they aren't showing now, girl," said Sadie. "Those hips are disappearing fast."

"Just goes to show what a good man in your life does for you," added Jenny.

"Well, you'd better be careful, Jen," said Lucy with a chuckle. "If you lose weight because of the good man in your life, you could very easily slip away to nothing. The same applies to you, Sadie, perhaps even more so. A couple of pounds off you and you'll dissolve completely."

The sound of the computer brought them back to the real world. "This thing has been going berserk since I switched it on," said Connie. She stretched across the desk to check the message. "One, two, three… Gosh, during the short time we have been congratulating Lucy, we've had ten messages. I think we have a little gold mine here." She glanced at Lucy. "Are you up to sorting them out or would you like me to carry on for a while?"

Connie sat down at the computer when Lucy said she was still too excited about her weekend to think about matchmaking for anyone else. "I'll make some coffee."

"I think we're becoming addicted to the stuff." Sadie laughed. "At the end of every conversation, someone reaches for the kettle."

"Oh my goodness!" Connie gasped. "I don't believe it."

Sadie swung around. "I was only joking about being addicted, Connie. No need to get yourself worked up about it."

"What?" uttered Connie. She looked up from the computer and shook her head. "No, not that, silly – this." She flapped her hand in front of the screen.

"So, what's happened now?" said Jenny. "Please don't tell us Michael Stone is up to his tricks again."

"No, nothing like that." Connie swung the screen around. "Look at this. You too, Lucy, before you disappear. It's good news. We've all been invited to a wedding."

"Bloody hell! Someone has beaten us to it," said Sadie, peering at the screen. "While we've all been wringing our hands over our love lives, someone out there has simply thrown out the bait, hooked her man, reeled him in and is already half way up the aisle."

"Yes," said Connie. "I suppose you could put it like that." She brought up the woman's profile on the computer. "She's called Elizabeth Hudson and was asked out by someone called Alan Johnson on the very first day of our agency." She looked up at the others. "It seems they got on so well, they're getting married and we've all been invited."

"It's really nice of her to ask us," said Lucy. "But I'm not sure why. They don't know any of us."

"Perhaps it's because we introduced them," said Jenny. "We got them together."

"But getting people together is what we do. It's a business and they've already paid us." Lucy shrugged. "Anyway, that's only my opinion."

While Lucy was setting out the mugs, the others mulled over what she had said. "I think you're right, Lucy," decided Sadie. "We can't start going to the weddings of all our clients. For one thing, it would cost a fortune in presents and outfits."

"And for another, what if we were asked to a couple of weddings on the same day," added Jenny. "We'd have to choose. How could we choose between two happy couples?"

"Yes, I suppose you're right," agreed Connie reluctantly. At first she had thought it a wonderful gesture and had even started thinking about an outfit in the new dress shop on Regent Street. But the others did have a point. It could all get out of hand. They could even have to spend most weekends at weddings. "Okay, I'll think about how to word our apologies and get back to her later. Meanwhile, I'll start setting up meetings for these other people. A few more requests have dropped into the box, so I guess it's going to be a busy day."

****

It was a hectic day. They hardly found time to drink their coffee. It also seemed new clients were beginning to find their way to the office.

"That makes twelve people who've called into the office today," Sadie gasped, after the last one disappeared out of the door. "I'm not sure why they need to come to see us personally, unless they simply want to check us out. "But as they've all signed up and have each paid two hundred and fifty pounds for the privilege, I think I can live with them dropping in. Though I think we'll have to get a bigger office if this keeps up." She coughed. "I'm losing my voice with talking to them all."

"Sounds like Michael's in for a quiet evening for a change," Jenny laughed.

"Don't you worry about that," said Sadie. "By the time I've had a warm bath and sucked a couple of lozenges, I'll be a new woman and raring to go."

"Where'll you be raring to go to this evening?" asked Connie.

"I've absolutely no idea, but I'm sure Michael will have everything in hand."

"I bet he will, too." Lucy winked.

"Saucy!" said Sadie. "Though you could be right. We seem to have been out every night over the last week. Perhaps it's time for us to stay in – and…" She paused and went all dreamy-eyed.

"Yes?" chorused Lucy and Jenny. Both had stopped what they were doing, and were waiting for Sadie to continue.

"… watch some TV!" Sadie laughed.

CHAPTER THIRTY-FIVE

Several weeks had passed and the agency was continuing to grow. Connie and Andrew had settled into their new apartment and had thrown a housewarming party; inviting as many of their friends as they could squeeze in. Sadie kept talking about her wedding, though no date had been set, while Jenny and Lucy were still settling into their new relationships.

Lucy was blissfully happy with Paul. He was so attentive. What more could she want?

After feeling a little out of sorts for a few days, Paul insisted she make an appointment with her doctor. "You can't be too careful," he'd told her.

"I think Paul is making a mountain out of a molehill, so I'm only here to keep him happy," she told Doctor Wright when she arrived in the surgery. "I've probably eaten something which doesn't agree with me."

"That could be true," the doctor replied. She smiled. "But as you're here now, I might as well check it out."

The doctor was very thorough and Lucy began to feel a little alarmed, especially when she was given a specimen bottle and shown the way to the ladies room. Could there be something seriously wrong with her after all? She prayed that wasn't the case. "I can't possibly be ill," she muttered on her way back to the doctor's surgery. "I won't allow it! Not now

I'm so happy." She glanced at the specimen bottle in her hand. It looked fine to her. Right colour – well, she supposed it was. She wasn't in the habit of checking what colour her urine was. Was anyone? Did people usually check what colour their urine was every morning?

Back in the surgery, Lucy watched anxiously as the doctor tested the sample with what looked like an ice-lolly stick.

"Well," said Doctor Wright, turning to face Lucy, "it seems you are going to have a baby."

Lucy couldn't speak. A baby! My God, she was having a baby. She hadn't even thought of it. Why hadn't she thought of that?

"Are you alright?" The doctor leaned forward and took Lucy's hand. "Did you hear what I said?

"Yes!" Lucy gulped. "Are you sure? Could there be some mistake?"

"I'm absolutely sure. No mistake." Doctor Wright grinned. "You're about two months gone, so you can expect your baby early next year." She worked out the date and scribbled it down for Lucy.

Outside on the pavement, Lucy stared down at the piece of paper in her hand. She was still unable to take it in. "Oh my God! I'm going to have a baby." She hadn't realized she'd spoken out loud until someone passing by gave her a thumbs-up. She grinned back at them before digging around in her bag for her mobile phone.

Her fingers trembled as she began to stab in the numbers of Paul's office. But then she pressed *cancel.* Perhaps she should wait until this evening, when they were together. She winced. That would mean she had to keep the news to herself all day. She couldn't possibly tell her friends until she had spoken to Paul. He should be the first to know.

Just then she saw a taxi rolling towards her. In that instant, she decided to go to Paul's office and tell him there and then. She flagged down the cab and gave the driver the address. She breathed out heavily as she sat down. How would Paul take the news? Was he ready to become a father? Well, whatever his response, there was no going back now.

****

"Are you alright?" Paul was concerned Lucy had come to his office. He knew her appointment with the doctor was for that morning. Was there something wrong? Why else would Lucy have travelled halfway across London to see him?

"I saw Doctor Wright and she gave me a thorough examination." She swept her tongue around her bottom lip.

"And?" Paul prompted. He feared the worst by now.

"And… I'm going to have a baby! We're going to have a baby!" Paul didn't say anything for a long moment. He simply stared at her.

Lucy was beginning to panic a little. She had assumed Paul would be as happy as she. But perhaps he didn't want a family.

"We're going to have a baby," Paul said a last. The news was only just sinking in. "Wow!" he let out a yell and punched the air. "I'm going to be a father." He grabbed Lucy and hugged her close. "That is absolutely the most wonderful news." He turned his head and looked at the other people in the office. "Did you hear, guys? I'm going to be a dad!"

Tears welled in Lucy's eyes and spilled down her cheeks. "Paul, I'm so happy." She grabbed a tissue from her pocket and wiped her eyes. "For a moment I thought you might be…"

"Lucy! I'm absolutely delighted! You can't believe how happy I am." He had to shout to make himself heard above the noise behind him. By now everyone in the office was crowding around to congratulate them both.

****

Lucy ran up the stairs to the office to tell her friends the news. She hadn't even mentioned she was going to see the doctor; she had simply said she was going to take a stroll around the shops.

"I have the most wonderful…" She stopped mid-sentence when she saw what Sadie was wearing. "Oh my God, Sadie. What on earth have you got on?"

Sadie was decked out in the most outrageous outfit she had ever seen. Lucy looked her up and down from the short luminous pink skirt, the silver sequined top, complete with gold bolero, right down to the black lace tights and red boots. A bright red feather attached to a green band around her forehead completed the scene. Lucy stood there, mortified, unable to say a word.

"Do you like it?" Sadie did a little twirl on the spot. She would have walked up and down as though on a catwalk if there had been enough room. "I bought this lot today at that new boutique just off Piccadilly. What do you think?" She shot a glance at the others. "Connie says it's too much and Jenny thinks it's a little over the top." She narrowed her eyes. "Well, say something, Lucy, for goodness sake. It isn't that bad – is it?"

"I think they're both right – but more." Lucy gulped. "*Far* too much and *well* over the top. Sadie, I almost need sunglasses to look at you."

"Shit!" Sadie uttered. "I knew you'd agree with them. I don't know why I bothered to ask you." She heaved a sigh and twirled around again. "Take another look. You might decide differently this time."

Lucy blinked her eyes three times. "No. Sorry. It doesn't do it for me. But," she added, trying to sound more positive, "maybe it's because you're wearing all those colours together. What if you wore the skirt with something not so… glaring? You know, something to tone it down a little. You'd then have the silver top to go with… say, a black skirt." She looked at the others for some support.

"Exactly!" said Connie. She thumped the desk triumphantly. "That's what I was trying to tell her when you came in. But you know our Sadie; she has to be the world's all or nothing girl. Anyway," she continued, suddenly realising Lucy had stopped mid-sentence when she'd come in, "what's your news?"

"Oh, it's nothing really." Lucy slung her bag onto a chair and took off her coat. Somehow, after seeing Sadie swirling around in her new outfit, the moment had been lost.

"No. Come on, tell us," said Jenny. "You sounded excited when you came in."

Sadie sat down, her head on one side. She had an idea about what Lucy was about to say, but this was Lucy's big moment. She had to tell them herself.

Lucy shrugged. "Well, I wanted you to be among the first to know," she took a deep breath. "I'm going to have a baby."

"What!" Connie shrieked. She leapt to her feet and squeezed herself between the desks to reach Lucy. "Oh my God. That is the most wonderful news. Have you told Paul – about the baby, I mean? Yes, of course, you've told Paul. Silly me. He had to be the first to know."

By now, Sadie and Jenny were beside Lucy. "You must both be very happy," said Jenny. Tears flowed down her cheeks as she spoke. Even Sadie was blinking her eyes rapidly in an effort to hold back tears.

"Yes, we are," said Lucy, fumbling for a handkerchief. "I was going to ring Paul from outside the doctor's surgery, but then changed my mind and took a taxi to his office. He's thrilled to bits. He was yelling, '*I'm going to be a dad,*' all around the office."

"All this brilliant news, and there was me prattling on and on about this stupid outfit," said Sadie, throwing her arms around Lucy. "You should have told me to shut up." She pulled away and took a step backwards. "I'm going to get changed and then I'm going out to get a bottle of bubbly. I think we need a small fridge to keep a supply of booze in here." She was on her way to the lady's room on the landing, when she swung around. "Are you able to drink? I mean, now that you're pregnant, should you be drinking?"

"No. I suppose not," said Lucy. "But I'll have a small one to celebrate and then it's no more booze for me until after the baby's born."

Everyone's attention was drawn towards the computer when they heard it sound. "I'll see to it," said Connie, scrambling across to open the new message. In her haste she stumbled over a chair. "There goes another pair of tights," she wailed, running her hand up and down her leg. "That's the second pair in as many days." She tossed the chair to one side. "We haven't got room to move in here without falling over something." She looked at Lucy, who was clenching her lips together, trying hard not to laugh, while Jenny was calmly replacing the offending chair into its rightful place. "Okay." Connie spread out her hands. "I know having this cupboard as our office was all my idea, but, how was I to know how much smaller it would become when we put the desks in and…" she broke off having glanced at the computer screen. "Eek!" She stabbed her finger at the screen. "Look at all the emails."

It seemed while they were congratulating Lucy on her pregnancy, the rest of the world had been carrying on oblivious to anything. There were at least twenty emails waiting to be read – if not more.

Connie sank down onto the chair in front of the computer. "Twenty-four. I'm not sure I can cope with all this. Some of these people are new. They want to join the agency."

"I'll take over," said Lucy. She shooed Connie out of the chair. "You go and get the glasses ready for the bubbly." After a few moments, she looked up from the computer. "Hey guys, there are twenty-four emails and," she clasped her hands together, "they *all* want to join. Wow!"

Jennie was already doing the sums. "That's six. Thousand. Pounds!" she said slowly. "As you say, Lucy, that's definitely a big wow."

"Agreed," said Connie, setting out the glasses. "And when those twenty-four people start asking for meetings to be arranged, there'll be even more lovely money floating into the bank."

"You were right, Connie," Jenny looked up from her calculator. "All those divorced people out there were waiting for an agency for divorcees to be set up. But how amazing that it was us who actually went ahead and did it. It could so easily have been someone else."

"Well, thank goodness it wasn't!" Connie said briskly. "The whole thing could have turned out quite tawdry in someone else's hands. We took a different road." She held her head high. "We created something with – class."

"Yes – well," said Lucy. She coughed. "It seems we have another email. This one is not wanting to join or asking for a meeting – well, I suppose it is, but not in the sense…"

"For goodness sake get on with it, Lucy." Sadie, having returned in time to hear the latter part of the conversation, was waiting impatiently to open the bottle.

"It seems someone wants to buy our agency." Lucy looked back at the screen.

"Some two-bit low-life, I expect," said Connie. "I wouldn't let our agency go to anyone who's expecting it for nothing and then turning it…"

"Eh… No." Lucy interrupted. She was still reading the message. "He's offering to pay us handsomely if our accounts are to his satisfaction."

Sadie sank into a chair. The bottle slipped from her fingers and would have crashed to the floor if Jenny hadn't caught it in time.

"Are you sure he's for real?" asked Connie.

He's spelled it out that he is very serious. He's mentioned offering up to two hundred thousand pounds for the company if it is what he is looking for," Lucy explained.

"Who is it?" Jenny whispered. "Who's offering us that kind of money? It's got to be some joke."

"Why are you whispering?" Sadie asked. "Do you think someone is listening to us?"

"I don't know." Jenny shot a glance at the door, as though half-expecting someone to swing it open and yell, 'fooled you,' as they bounded in.

"The message is from the owner of a large company, which conducts most of its business online," said Lucy. She was still reading the email. "It seems they were planning to set up a new internet dating agency for people who are divorced, but found there was already one up and running – ours." She looked across at the group and raised her eyebrows. "Well, that's certainly given us something to think about."

"It has indeed," uttered Connie. Her brain was working overtime. She was still keen to sell the agency, though she understood why the others were hesitant. However, a cool fifty thousand pounds each wasn't to be taken lightly. Surely the others would agree to sell now they had been offered so much money. "So, what are you all thinking?"

CHAPTER THIRTY-SIX

"And that's where we left it." Back at their new apartment, Connie was telling Andrew about the offer to buy their agency. "The others wanted the opportunity to talk it over with their partners." She gave Andrew a sideways glance. "You're very quiet. What're you thinking?"

Andrew shrugged. "It's not up to me. However, if you want my opinion, I think it's a good offer." He put down the glass of wine he was holding and sucked his cheeks in.

"But?" Connie nodded her head for him to continue. "There's a but in there somewhere, isn't there?"

"I'm just wondering whether it's worth more."

"More than two hundred thousand?" Connie was incredulous.

"If they are offering that amount straight off the cuff, then it has got to be worth more." He picked up his glass and took another sip of wine. "You said yourself, twenty four people asked to join today. That's six thousand pounds you made in one day, not to mention any money coming in from people asking for meetings. Who knows how many will log on tomorrow and want to be members."

"Put like that..." Connie nodded her head thoughtfully.

"There's no other way of putting it. And if Michael's as good with figures as I think he is, he'll be telling Sadie the same thing."

Before Connie could reply, the phone rang and she reached over to answer it. "Hi Sadie. What's up?" She glanced at Andrew while she listened to what Sadie had to say. "Andrew has just said the same thing to me. We need to regroup and think it through." She paused for a moment. "Would you both like to come here this evening? I'll give the others a ring, too. Perhaps we could all put our heads together."

"They're all coming at around eight o' clock," said Connie, as she put the receiver down after the last call. "All the men appear to be thinking along the same lines as you." She laughed. "I'm not sure Lucy was too eager to leave the nest this evening. She and Paul were talking about baby clothes."

****

It was the first time Paul had met the others since the news of Lucy's pregnancy. So it was only when lots of congratulations and backslapping was out of the way, they finally got down to business.

"Since I spoke to Connie, Michael and I have given the whole thing more thought," said Sadie. She ran her fingers over her short skirt to smooth it down, before continuing. "Michael agrees with Andrew. He thinks the business is worth more money. But I'm concerned: if we push for more money and they don't want to pay, couldn't they simply choose to open up a new agency of their own?"

"Yes, I thought of that," said Jenny, taking up the reins. "We could find ourselves with some hefty competition."

"But they'll have the same problem." It was Michael speaking now. He glanced at Andrew. "They won't want the competition any more than Sadie and the others," he continued, gesturing towards the four ladies. "Your agency is established and doing well. They would be the new guys on the block trying to break into the market. You already have a clientele who know and trust you. You four have set the standards and the word has got around. Anyone else would always be one step behind; trying to keep up with you."

"Very true," said David. "I agree with you and Andrew. What about you, Paul?"

Paul laughed. "I'm still trying to get my head around being a dad, but, yes, I think you all shouldn't be too quick to accept the offer." He looked at Lucy. "How did you end this afternoon? Did you reply to the offer? And if so, did you leave yourselves room to manoeuvre?"

"We sent back a standard type of reply saying we would need to think it over as selling hadn't ever been part of the equation."

"That's good," said Andrew. "If they come back to you, it means they're keen to buy you out. But don't reply immediately. Let them think you're not interested. Give them a chance to up the offer."

"To what?" asked Connie. "We're new to this game of cat and mouse. How much should we be looking for?"

"I'd say at least three hundred thousand, even if they meet you half way, that's an extra fifty grand," Andrew replied.

Michael nodded in agreement. "Absolutely! You girls are onto a winner. They know if they don't pay, someone else might jump in and that's the last thing they want."

"Bloody hell!" uttered Sadie. "Wow and bloody hell again!" She glanced at Connie. "Oops, sorry I…" she began, but she could see Connie and the others were as gob-smacked as she was.

"For once, you've got it right, Sadie." Connie swung around to face Andrew. "Are you serious?" Andrew nodded. "Bloody hell!" she punched the air with delight.

"I can't believe it," Sadie said at last. She looked from Andrew to Michael and back to Andrew, her head twisting from side to side. "Are you sure you guys aren't having a laugh at our expense?"

"I can assure you Andrew never jokes about money," said Connie.

"We're not saying you'll get that amount." Andrew looked at Michael for confirmation. "But they should certainly pay more than their starting offer," he continued when Michael nodded.

"I need to sleep on this. It's too much to take in all at once." Jenny gave David a nudge. "You've gone very quiet. What do you think?"

"I agree with the others," said David. "If you really want to sell, then you need to hold out for more money. It's a thriving business and the guy who wants to buy it, knows it."

Later that evening, Andrew called Michael to one side for a quiet word. He told him that the head of their finance department was taking early retirement. "So you see, there will be a vacancy very soon. Would you be interested in applying for the position?"

"So, what did you say?" asked Sadie. By now, she and Michael were in a taxi on their way back to his apartment and he had told her what Andrew had said.

"I told him I would think it over," he replied, slowly.

"And…" Sadie pressed him for more information.

"And, I'm thinking it over," he said, with a wink.

****

"My aunt is getting on well with Brian Lomax. He's asked her to move in with him." Lucy made the announcement the moment she walked into the office the next morning.

"Gosh! Really? So soon?" said Sadie. "How do you feel about that?"

Lucy shrugged. "I don't know. I don't think it's sunk in yet. I phoned to tell her about the baby and once she had congratulated me and made all the right noises, she told me her piece of news. I don't even think she knows what to do herself."

"Let me know when it's sunk in and I'll clear off somewhere. I don't want to be around when the shit hits the fan," laughed Sadie.

"I wish you wouldn't use that kind of language, especially in this office." Connie raised her eyebrows. "It's not good for business."

Sadie glanced around the room. "But there's only the three of us here."

"Well, you never know. Someone could be about to knock on the door, but decides this is not the kind of agency they want to be associated with when they hear you saying something like that," replied Connie

"Saying something like what?" said Jenny. She had arrived in time to hear the end Connie's statement.

"Never mind." Connie rolled her eyes. "Don't let's go through it all over again.

"My aunt might be moving in with Brian Lomax," Lucy told Jenny.

"Oh, I see – well – no I don't really," said Jenny. "Why shouldn't Lucy say her aunt might move in with Brian Lomax? What's the problem with that?"

"That's not the problem! Give me strength." Connie clenched her fists and shook them in the air. "Can't we just leave it? We've more important things to think about. Like, whether or not this company will get back to us today and what we're going to do about it if they do."

"Keep your hair on!" Sadie wagged her finger at Connie. "It's no good you getting your bowels in an uproar. When or *if* they get back to us with another offer, we'll discuss it further. Only then will we know whether they're serious. In the meantime, I suggest its business as usual."

EPILOGUE

"Who would have thought it?" Jenny sat down at her desk and looked around the office. "When we first decided to start this agency, none of us ever thought it would really take off the way it did."

"No," said Sadie thoughtfully. She hadn't said much since they had arrived. In a way she was sad they were leaving the office. They'd had some good times here and now they were stuffing those wonderful memories into a box and shutting the lid. But, on the bright side, she now had a fantastic man in her life and a healthy bank balance. And, with Michael firmly installed as head of the accounts department at Andrew's firm, what more could a girl want?

The news of the sale of Divorcees.biz had been big news in the business rags for the last few days. Alex would be having a fit right now. Stuff Alex, though. Why was she even thinking about him? She should be making a to-do list. The first thing on her 'to-do' list, was to have a really fantastic holiday somewhere in the Bahamas. She had always dreamed of sitting on a white sandy beach, sipping some wonderful concoction served in a tall glass with a little parasol perched on the top. Yet she could have done that without selling the business. Their bank balance had been good. They could each have drawn out enough money for a holiday or whatever else they wanted to do. She heaved a sigh and gazed around their old office.

"You're very quiet. Are you okay?" asked Jenny. "It's so not like you to be this quiet."

"Yes, I'm fine." Sadie turned her attention back to the box she was filling. "It's just, I don't like this part."

"Hmm," Jenny nodded. "I know what you mean."

They heard a tread on the stairs. Then the door swung open and Connie and Lucy strode in.

"What are you looking so gloomy about?" asked Lucy. "Surely you should be feeling very happy today, since all that lovely money was deposited in our accounts this morning." She hesitated and glanced at Jenny. "Or is that it? Hasn't our money arrived?"

"Oh no. The money's there alright," said Jenny hastily. "I checked online before I came here. Everything's in order. No, we're just reminiscing about our time here."

"And it's not over yet." Reaching into her bag, Connie pulled out a bottle of champagne and held it aloft. "Ta-da!" she cried. "I thought we should go out the way we came in – so to speak. On a high."

"Shit! Of course, you're right," said Sadie. She leapt to her feet and went across to the cupboard to retrieve the glasses. "It's no good sitting here maudling about the past. We had a good time, with lots of laughs. We achieved what we set out to do, which was to find ourselves some lovely new men and we made a lot of money in the process. Now it's time to move on."

"It is?" asked Jenny. "So you're over the 'looking back stage'?" She made quotation marks in the air with her fingers.

"Hell, no." Sadie plonked the glasses down in front of Connie. "But even I know we can't ever go back. So let's have a drink, clear up, and get the hell out of here before I start wailing my eyeballs out."

****

After they all had a farewell glance around the office, Connie locked the door for the last time and slipped the key into her handbag. "That's it, girls. We're off. Let our new lives begin."

"What new lives?" Sadie asked. She looked at the others, but they seemed as surprised as she was.

"Who knows?" said Connie, stomping down the stairs. "We could sit back and do nothing or we could book tickets for the first commercial trip to the moon. Or…" she grinned, "we might even start another business. We seem to be getting good at it."

"Another business? What other business?" Sadie frowned.

"I have no idea – yet," replied Connie. "But I'm sure we could think of something if we put our heads together."

Outside on Park Lane the four women stared in amazement, when one of London's famous red, double-decker buses rolled past. An enormous banner was pasted along the side: 'Divorcees.biz. The Online Dating Agency for Divorcees Only'. There was also a picture of a man and woman sipping cocktails.

"They didn't waste much time," said Lucy.

"They couldn't afford to, not for what we made them pay for the business," replied Jenny.

Connie nodded her head in agreement. She thought back over the last few weeks, when they had been negotiating with the company wanting to buy them out. It hadn't been easy. But with Andrew and Michael's advice, they had held on until they got the best possible price.

"Way to go!" said Sadie, blowing a kiss towards the bus.

"Way to go," the others chorused. After a final glance at the building behind them, they linked arms and headed off in the direction of Oxford Street.

ABOUT THE AUTHOR

Eileen Thornton lives with her husband Phil, in the pretty town of Kelso in the Scottish Borders. She has been writing on a freelance basis for twelve years and during that time her illustrated articles and short stories have appeared in several national magazines. She has also contributed short stories to anthologies.

A selection of Eileen's published work can be found on her Website.

www.eileenthornton.co.uk

Made in the USA
Charleston, SC
02 February 2013